The Bachelor's Plough

Stephen J Brookes

Book I of the Pestlewick Trilogy

Dedicated to Ruth, Harry and Amy -
My beautiful family, what make it all worthwhile.

And to Craig and Paul who, frankly, just seem to get it.
Sad bastards.

I saw a mouse –
Where?
There on the stair!
Where on the stair?
Right there! A little mouse with clogs on,
There, I declare,
Going clip-clippety-clop on the stair –
Right there.

\-   *Traditional mouse verse.*

Cheese, cheese, cheese, cheese,
Cheese, cheese, cheese, cheese,
Cheese, cheese, cheese, cheese,
Cheese, cheese, cheese, cheese,
Cheese.

\-   *Mouse National Anthem.*

Like all good stories, this one starts with an elderly lady stumbling across some rusted scrap metal in a river.

When Edna Larkin saw something bulky and metallic just beneath the surface of the River Thames, on the outskirts of Boomtown (a thriving town some miles west of London, known for its rats), her attention was roused. During her years as a pensioner – she was now in her late seventies and had been drawing the Queen's farthing for over two decades – Edna had enjoyed a few modest windfalls, as the result of other people losing something. Among her more profitable finds were a Rolex watch, a mobile phone, a snuff movie, and a passport that she sold to a middle eastern gentleman for sixty pounds and the promise of a camel. The camel never arrived but the sixty pounds was vital to the purchase of her fish supper that same Friday.

Probably her best find was a wallet stashed full of twenty-pound notes. Frail and innocent though she was, she pocketed just short of £600 without a thought that day, before throwing the wallet into the nearest public bin. Courtesy of this windfall, she treated herself to a see-through dome-shaped umbrella and a tartan pull-along shopping trolley, after which modest expenditure she still had money for chips on the way home. So she treated herself to another fish supper. Like any old age pensioner, Edna was more than partial to a fish supper.

When she saw the metallic object in the Thames, Edna's first thought was that it was a push-bike and she immediately started calculating how much she could get for it. Depending on the make, model and general condition, she reckoned on being able to get at least a fish-supper's-worth for it, were she to put it in the classifieds section of the local paper. If she made a decent amount, she would capitalise on her good luck and buy an extra line on the Bingo. The thought made her smile, her tired watery eyes shrinking into slits, her toothless gums sliding across each other like greased up lovers in a Siamese mud bath.

On closer inspection, Edna saw that the object was not a bike at all. She couldn't exactly make out what it was, but it was clearly something much larger.

Through the riverweed and slime in which it was coated, it looked to be something mechanical, a piece of farm machinery or a prototype trouser press of extreme proportions. What Edna was certain of was that it was made entirely of metal. She guessed it to be iron or steel. As one might expect from a frail widow in her seventies, with a pull-along tartan trolley and a transparent umbrella shaped into an enlarged dome, her thoughts turned immediately to the local junk yard and what a lump of metal of this size would be worth as scrap. She reasoned that it had to be worth £100 at least.

It was surely worth some effort.

*

It was a brisk day, with a dark-grey sky and a chill bite in the air. Had it been warmer, Edna might have considered hitching up her skirts and petticoats and wading into the river to appraise the situation more closely.

The size of the object made it unlikely that she would be able to pull it out by herself, although she was aware of the untapped power of the human constitution. There are, for example, stories of weak, feeble, pathetic, pale, undernourished, unmotivated, slovenly, self-absorbed, frail, infirm, puny, ailing, emaciated and slightly-built mothers lifting cars from the ground to rescue their trapped baby. Admittedly, these stories never explain how the baby came to be under the car in the first place; or just how mangled they

6

are as the result of having a tonne of vehicle crushed down on them. But the tales remain, and they stand testament to the extraordinary potential of the human will.

It is a small leap of the imagination to envisage that an avaricious granny with an appreciation of scrap metal value would be able to hoist an item of heavy farm machinery from a cold river, by brute force alone, in order to convert the discarded material into hard cash. Especially if there was a fish supper and an extra line on the Bingo at the end of it.

But on this particular morning, it was just too cold for Edna to be wading into the icy waters of the Thames. As she reasoned with herself, in an internal dialogue: *Bugger that.*

Instead, she parked her tartan pull-along trolley on the riverbank (parking one of these things basically involves standing it upright, in order that its weight rests on the curved metal bar underneath. It is a simple mechanism, lending both balance and inertia to the vehicle) and creaked herself down on to all fours.

Her light-blue coat – made from that curious material used exclusively for old people's outer-garments, a mixture of nylon, crinoline and crepe paper – gave excellent protection from the dew-wet grass. In this position, looking very much like the central character in a porn film with an exceptionally low budget, she was able to crawl to the water's edge and assess the situation in more detail.

Peering over the edge of the bank, she saw her wrinkled gummy face staring back up at her and for a second, she thought it was a carp. The green waters of the Thames were murky and dark, but the dull glint of rusted metal rippled out from the depths. On closer inspection, the object looked like an old plough. It was covered in green weed and algae, and Edna wondered if its rusted state would reduce its value.

It didn't matter.

She leaned forward and dipped her hand into the cold water.

"'king hell," she said, in the same tone of voice she would have used to ask her grandson if he wanted some sponge cake.

The water was colder than she had anticipated. Her circulation was not great at the best of times and her fingers turned blue almost immediately. Muttering under her breath she drew reference to a brass monkey. She then made a more sophisticated analysis of the situation and concluded that it was cold enough to freeze the bollocks off a Sumo wrestler in a state of full retraction.

Hooking her fingers around the nearest part of the plough, she gave it a tug. The metal was slimy, but she managed to get some purchase.

The plough remained firm.

She thrust her hand further into the water and tried to find a better grip. Wrapping her fingers around the metal she pulled hard once more. The plough remained rooted, not giving an inch. She had no idea how long it had been here, but it had obviously been a considerable amount of time. It had sunk itself firmly into the riverbed. Already convinced that it would take more than an elderly lady's brute force to move the object, she gave it one more tug before rolling over on to her back, breathing hard with the exertion.

Laying there on her back, her chest rising and falling, she stared up at the grey sky and considered her options.

The obvious course of action was to concede defeat, crawl to her feet, retrieve her shopping trolley and make her way home where she could enjoy a nice cup of tea and a biscuit. She had given it a good try, at least.

The problem was Edna knew that she was in spitting distance of at least £100. It was there for the taking. If she were to go home now and leave the plough behind, it would play on her mind for the rest of the week.

The second option was to find an accomplice - a helpful man with some muscle, in need of a few quid - and

8

recruit his assistance. It was a reasonable idea, but she baulked at the thought of sharing the money. This was *her* find. This was *her* plough. Just because she lacked brawn, it seemed unfair that anyone else should share the fruits of her well-tuned commercialism.

It left her with one option.

The towpath ran parallel to a quiet road. As soon as she had regained her breath, she picked herself up and made her way out onto the road, pulling her shopping trolley behind her. To her delight she saw that a layby just a few hundred yards away contained the very hardware she was looking for.

An old, blue, battered Transit van was parked there, its owner nowhere to be seen. Crucially, the van had a towing hitch that, while admittedly worn, seemed sturdy and fully operational. Edna smiled on seeing the van and immediately hobbled over to it with her trolley. She couldn't have wished for more.

It was a minor inconvenience to find that the doors were locked but Edna was a woman of great resource. She put the driver-side window out with a rock and let herself into the van. She had seen enough films from the nineteen-seventies to know how to hotwire a car and with the use of a crowbar that she found under the driver seat, she made short work of the van's central steering column. Exposing the ignition unit, she found a couple of stray wires and touched them together.

The van rumbled into life.

Edna was in business.

Once the father of the gods in Ancient Greece, feared and revered by an entire people, Zeus had come down a bit in terms of his social status.

These days, far from deciding the fates of nations and the destinies of peoples, the ancient god now drove a lorry for *Bristow's Haulage*, at an hourly rate that was just above the national minimum wage. In classical times, Zeus had worn sandals spun from gold. These days, he had to make sure his steel toe-capped boots lasted him a year at a time because he couldn't afford to replace them.

It was a sacrifice in status but, as the father of the gods would often assert, "needs must".

It is a common story with gods, just as with any metaphysical personification challenged by mankind's evolving enlightenment. As belief in Zeus and the ancient gods diminished, their hold on power had shrunk almost to nothing. Their immortality remained, however, and so to avoid a life of eternal misery on the streets, living like common tramps (and not necessarily common tramps, either; it would be just as degrading for a god to live like any tramp, including the brightly coloured *tramp-warbler* or the ever elusive *lesser-spotted tramp*), they had to eke out a living like any other worldly inhabitant.

It was only in the deterioration of their divine status that it became clear how unsophisticated the Greek gods were in their grasp of existential metaphysics.

Most gods will inhabit a heavenly plateau, unreachable by man and known only to souls graced by a higher level of awareness. The ancient Greek gods on the other hand built their sacred dwelling at the top of Mount Olympus, which, in reality, can be reached by any bearded hiker with a rucksack, a pair of long shorts and packet of Digestive biscuits.

As gods go, they were extremely worldly and while this may be applauded for its sense of democracy, in the final analysis it did somewhat bite them on the arse when mortal reverence for them began to dwindle. They were some of the first gods to fall victim to man's growing cynicism.

These days, Zeus had to be content with his lot as a lorry driver but in moments of quiet self-reflection, he did look back to that golden age, when he was a mover and a shaker in the ways of gods and men. At such times he yearned for a more glamorous profession, one through which he could recapture the power and prestige that he believed was his birth right.

But things had changed and it was not to be. A god though he was, Zeus drove a lorry by day and he frequented his local pub, *The Bird in Hand*, most evenings.

The Bird in Hand was a great social outlet and thanks to his natural flair for playing darts, Zeus got some of the adulation he was so desperate for. With a long history of hurling well-aimed thunder bolts at localised targets, he had something of a metaphysical advantage, but as far as the pub darts team was concerned, he was just a gifted player; a natural. *The Bird in Hand* had display cabinets full of trophies. Since Zeus had been on the team, they had never lost a tournament.

Understandably, Zeus was a hero in his local pub. Here, at least, he *was* somebody.

As anyone lacking in divine status will tell you, the problem with *not* having divine status is one's subservience to material limitations. As a lorry driver, Zeus had a crippling lack of money. That was his first problem. The second, was that he was rubbish at reading maps. These two factors combined, led to issues in his private life that he could have happily done without.

*

The need for a satellite navigation system in his wagon was not new. Zeus was probably the last lorry driver on the road to be using physical maps.

He had finally given into the necessity for satellite navigation some months ago, after driving his articulated lorry into a multi-storey car park. The mistake was fully his and he admitted that. He simply couldn't read maps and had been aiming for the deliveries entrance to an industrial estate some two miles away. It wasn't his first dire error behind the wheel of his truck, but it was certainly his most spectacular.

What was most impressive, according to the salvage company who retrieved the wagon and its trailer, with the help of a crane and an angle grinder, was the fact Zeus had managed to get the lorry on to the third level of the car park before he noticed his mistake. By this time, the rig was well and truly wedged in and it became less an independent vehicle within the multi-storey edifice, and more of a supporting structure.

After this embarrassing incident, Zeus decided to stop putting his navigation in the hands of fate and resolved to take control of exactly where he was going.

To this end, he invested £99 in a satnav. The problem was, as desperate as he was to improve his navigation, he didn't really have the money for this new technology. After rent, bills, food and a few pints down *The Bird in Hand* of an evening, he hardly had a spare penny at the end of each month. So it was, against his thrifty nature, he borrowed the money from an acquaintance.

And this was where the trouble started.

The acquaintance was something of a festive personification who, while having his official residence in Lapland and operating his annual delivery schedule from his grotto there, lived for the most part in England. In contrast to the generous charity and moral flavour of his festive role, he operated in the Boomtown area as a professional criminal and was well known – and feared – for his ruthless brutality.

The undisputed boss of a violent and murderous gang, Father Christmas had deep involvement with the region's criminal underworld, with interests in extortion, prostitution, drugs, theft and robbery.

Zeus's acquaintance with Christmas came on the back of the fact the gangland boss extorted protection money from the landlord of *The Bird in Hand* and was seen in the pub at least once a fortnight. Zeus got used to seeing this charismatic gangster in the pub and he knew that, where banks would decline his application for a loan (Zeus had a bad credit history, after he had defaulted on repaying the loan he took out to buy his second-hand Austin Allegro), this great underworld figure would not be so reluctant.

The ancient god did appreciate that involving himself financially with this gangster – even for a sum as paltry as £99 – was a treacherous path to take. However, the need for a satnav was pressing; and Zeus felt certain he would be able to pay Santa Claus back, come pay day.

Had Santa's rates of interest been more reasonable, Zeus would indeed have been able to pay him back his money.

However, by the time pay day came around, just three weeks later, the calculated repayment figure had risen to £300, representing an interest rate of 200%. Zeus simply did not have the money to pay this off. Consequently, administration fees were incurred. The debt increased further.

Zeus tried to get to grips with his mounting debt but while he was able to pay off a hundred pounds a month (if he ate beans on toast for five days a week), the interest that he was accruing continued to spin out of control. His monthly contributions did not even make a dent in the sum he now owed.

It was four months since Zeus had borrowed the money and according to Santa Claus's accountant (an ex-boxer with a record for armed robbery, arson with intent to kill and GBH) Zeus was now in debt to the firm for £12,650. As Zeus tried to argue – though to little effect – it did seem a little excessive.

His situation was brought into stark relief on a dreary Friday night, as he walked home after a pleasant evening at *The Bird in Hand.*

*

Zeus lived in a small flat just above a fish and chip shop on Pearbury Hill. It was a five-minute walk from the pub and he was hoping that the rain would hold off until he got home. The night was dark and windy. Rain seemed imminent. Cold streetlamps cast an orange glow over the urban world and in the dreary light, everything seemed lifeless.

As he walked along the quiet road, his dustman's jacket pulled tightly around him, he didn't notice the car pull alongside the kerb next to him, until it was too late.

Had he been more aware, he might have made a run for it. That said, he was not the swiftest of foot and such exertion would have probably been in vain. As it was, he didn't even get to put it to the test. The car sped to a halt alongside him and three men sprung from the car, immediately surrounding the ancient god on the pavement.

Stopped in his tracks, Zeus pulled himself from his internal reverie and appraised his situation.

Father Christmas stood before him, his cheeks ruddy, his eyes dark and menacing. He was wearing a pin-striped suit, spats and a Fedora hat. He had loosened his tie and it looked casual against his white, silk shirt.

Flanking Father Christmas, and looking equally as menacing, were two well-built men. Zeus recognised one of them immediately. Vinnie "The Saw" Hopkins sometimes visited *The Bird in Hand* to collect Claus's money.

The other man was unfamiliar to Zeus but he wondered if it was Richie "Thumbscrews" Hooper. Hooper and Claus were known to be great friends and Hooper was possibly the most loyal and devoted member of Father Christmas's firm. Hooper was violent, brutal and merciless. His reputation was as terrifying as Father Christmas himself and if it truly was Thumbscrews Hooper that stood before him now, Zeus knew that he was in trouble.

Father Christmas took a step towards Zeus. He was taller and heavier than the ancient god and he had a life force that could crush rock.

"Where's my money?" He asked.

His voice was quiet.

"I gave you..." Zeus began. Claus didn't let him finish.

"You gave me a hundred quid. But you owe me more than twelve grand. I've been patient with you, Zeus – but my patience is wearing thin. It's time you paid up."

"But I don't have the money. I borrowed a hundred pounds from you because I was hard up. Where am I supposed to get twelve thousand pounds from?"

Father Christmas looked at his two companions.

"I really don't think he's getting it," he said. He gestured with a slight nod of his head. The two men stepped forward and took hold of the ancient god. Held fast, Zeus tried to shift but their grip was unyielding.

Claus glared at him. His face was thunderous and menacing.

"You wouldn't like me to lose my temper," he said, calmly.

The Greek god stared back at him, nervously. He wished he still had his divinity. Claus would never have dared to talk to him in this way, four thousand years ago. But divinity

15

is like breast milk. If the demand for it runs out, then the milk dries up, leaving but a fallow boob.

Zeus *was* a fallow boob.

"I'll get you the money," Zeus stuttered.

Father Christmas nodded, his eyes not leaving Zeus for a second.

"Fifteen thousand pounds,"

"Fifteen...!" Zeus nearly choked. It was worse than shopping in Tesco. The price was going up every minute.

"Fifteen thousand pounds, in cash, by next Friday. You've got a week."

"But I don't know if I can get the money by..."

Claus stepped forward and placed his hand over Zeus's mouth. He looked him coolly in the eye.

"You've got a week," he repeated. "If you don't have the money for me by next Friday, we'll start damaging you. Do you understand?"

Zeus nodded.

Claus said those words – *we'll start damaging you* – as casually as he would have ordered a Super Hot Pepperoni Pizza, with a stuffed crust and a mild garlic dip, from Dominos, before giving his address and agreeing to the forty-five minute delivery window. Zeus didn't even want to contemplate what it might mean in physical terms. He sensed that it would involve a fair amount of pain, however. And if there was one thing Zeus was allergic to (apart from hand cream) it was pain. It tended to bring him out in blood and bruises.

With a nod from Santa Claus, the two men pushed Zeus roughly aside. He tumbled into a wall and sunk down onto the damp pavement. Little more than a deified bundle in the street, he watched the three brutes return to their car. The black Mercedes spilled its fumes all over the road and they slammed the doors before screeching away into the night.

16

There was a time when Zeus could utter a word and it would decide the fate of an entire population. Right now, the only words that sprang to mind concerned his own destiny.

"I'm doomed," he said.

Edna backed the van on to the towpath, just a few feet away from the riverbank. Leaving the engine running, she climbed out and walked to the back, to check that it was close enough to the target. The rear of the van was resting just a few feet away from the plough and she nodded her satisfaction.

Without further hesitation, she pulled the side door open, in the hope of finding a length of rope inside. The back was empty save for a few old tins of paint and some dustsheets. She leaned inside and pinched one of the dustsheets critically. She shrugged. In the absence of rope, she decided, this would have to do.

Like a caterpillar of the apocalypse, she hauled one of the dustsheets out of the van and flapped it out so that it lay on the ground like a blanket. She then began to roll it up until it was one long, rolled length. She grabbed the sheet at two points, tugged it hard and nodded her approval.

"This should do it," she muttered to herself.

She carried the makeshift rope to the riverbank. Creaking to her knees, she leaned over the bank and deftly attached one end of the sheet to the plough, knotting it tightly. She doubled up the knot and gave the sheet a few quick tugs. It was secured fast. She tied the other end to the van's towing-hitch, again double-knotting it and tugging it hard to make sure it could take the strain. Finally, she got shakily to her feet, frail as she was, and clapped her aged hands together.

"Right," she said. "Let's have this bastard out."

She climbed back behind the wheel of the van and put it in gear. Letting out the clutch, she let the van creep forward a few feet. It was important to take up the slack in the dustsheet to lessen the danger of snapping it. As soon as she felt the tension she eased off on the gas. She couldn't see the dustsheet in the wing mirrors, but really, she didn't need to. She knew it was taut.

"Okay, sunshine," she said, licking her lips with concentration. "Let's have you."

She gunned the engine and the van spewed out black smoke, straining against the plough's inertia. She pushed down further on the gas. The van roared as it took the strain. Still the plough wouldn't budge.

"*Come on you bastard,*" she hollered, over the sound of the engine. She eased her foot down a little more on the accelerator and the van began to wheel-spin in the damp mud of the riverbank.

"*Come on you BASTARD!*"

She thought she felt the plough shift a little and acknowledging the advantage, she maintained the throttle, concentrating on steering the van, were it to suddenly lurch forward.

Behind her she could feel the plough beginning to shift in the deep mud of the riverbed. It still needed some persuasion and she let instinct take over. It wasn't too dissimilar to pulling out a tooth, she reasoned. It needed to be wobbled; pulled; goaded. She eased off on the gas and felt the van settle back, as the plough returned to its original position. Immediately, she gunned the engine once more. The van moved forward a few inches, while the plough freed itself further from the mud. She repeated this again and again.

Each time, she felt the plough become looser in its mooring.

It took nearly ten minutes before the plough finally came loose. The van screamed, kicking mud up all around it, as the plough gave up the fight and was dragged clumsily on to the bank. Edna smiled triumphantly and jumped out of the van to check that the plough was still well-secured. It was. The dustsheet held fast.

"You *beauty!*" She exclaimed, grimacing like a duck with a chainsaw.

All she had to do now was get the plough to the *Minotaur Scrap Yard.*

The only practical way to do this was to drag the plough through the streets, behind the van. It was dangerous and highly illegal – and drawing attention to herself would also draw attention to the fact she was in a stolen van – but the scrap yard was only a mile or so away. Edna was no stranger to risks. Once she had eaten some spam that was nearly a week out of date. As far as dragging a knackered old plough through busy streets behind a stolen van was concerned, she was pretty sure she'd get away with it.

She felt sure that come Friday, she'd be enjoying a well-earned fish supper.

Dun Roamin was a broken, ramshackle, badly maintained bungalow, hidden behind a sprawling mess of weeds, trees and bushes near the lower end of Totter's Lane.

To anyone that managed to get through the sprawling undergrowth to reach the bungalow, the grim nature of the place became immediately apparent. It was a decrepit old building, with bulging walls, damp doors and rotten window frames. The roof was sinking in, moss and lichen had taken root all over the edifice and several smashed windows gave the impression that the place was uninhabited.

But it *was* inhabited.

Horribly so.

Dun Roamin was home to three witches, known in equal parts for their great wisdom, their shared eye and their cannibalistic leanings. In ancient times they were known as the Stygian witches and were feared across the classical landscape of Ancient Greece. Now, after the erosion of human belief in ancient mythology, like so many washed up myths, they lived in relative obscurity in Pestlewick.

It was they who, believing it to be the height of suburban sophistication, had called the bungalow *Dun Roamin* and proudly displayed this legend on a rotted wooden sign at the end of the drive. The witches weren't usually given to such homely sensibilities, but it was a decision they had never regretted. At one stage they did consider calling the bungalow *Seaview,* but in light of the fact the nearest coast was nearly seventy miles away, they rejected this name on the grounds of common sense.

On this particular dreary afternoon, the three of them were within the bungalow's rotten shell. Among the peeling walls and smell of damp, they huddled in the front room like withered old hags from the pages of a nightmare. They stood

21

bent around a large cauldron, which bubbled and slurped, spilling its foul-smelling potion on to the already damp and mouldy carpet.

Like fiends of yore, the witches chattered and groaned.

"Who has got the eye?" Said one.

"I have it," said another.

"Give it to me," said the first.

The eye was passed from one witch to the other. It was a ball of crystal, about the size of a cricket ball (the sports version, as opposed to an insect's testicle). The witches were completely blind, their eye-sockets empty and horrific. By holding up the eye to her face, however, each was able to see. It didn't give them perfect sight. They figured that while this might be rectified with a monocle, to do so would look ridiculous. No one puts a monocle on a sight-giving crystal orb. They did explore the more discreet option of a contact lens, but discovered that no self-respecting optician would treat a disembodied crystal ball. Thus it was, they settled for having blurred vision. It was better than a poke in the magically-enhanced crystal orb with a blunt stick.

The witch now holding the eye held it up to a red and cavernous eye socket.

"There's menace in the air," she said.

"No, that's the new automatic air freshener," said the third witch. "It puffs out a whiff of perfume, every time you walk past it."

"It reeks of the burning pits in Hades," said the first witch, ominously.

"It is supposed to be forest glade," said the other.

They each fell silent, listening to the gurgling bubble of the cauldron. The witch with the eye looked down into the cauldron and sighed.

"I wish we had some meat to go in the pot," she croaked.

"A man!"

"A *young* man!"

"A *plump* young man!"

The witches champed their lips horribly, eliciting a ribbon of hungry groans and chuckles. As designates of ocular fashion, they left much to be desired. As voracious cannibals, they were untouchable.

A plump young man.

They could never have known that what would arrive was actually a weathered old man with a grizzled beard and a rough age of about four millennia.

Well, they *could* have known. They were, after all, very wise.

But they didn't.

It probably just didn't occur to them.

*

The orange Austin Allegro came to a squeaking halt outside *Dun Roamin.* The arse-end of the car was about an inch from the ground and from his skyward angle behind the steering wheel, Zeus knew full-well that the suspension was about to go. It was another expense he was unable to meet.

In the days when he used to ride in a burning chariot drawn by heavenly steeds, his suspension never gave him an issue.

The bungalow had its own driveway, but it was so chaotically overgrown that Zeus feared for the survival of his car if he were to chance it. It did also occur to him that there was every possibility he would want to make a quick get-away. The witches were known, after all, for their cannibalistic appetites. To have the car parked out on the road, ready to go, seemed a prudent course of action.

With the creeping stealth of an introverted badger on a midnight stroll, the ancient god made his way up the drive, fighting his way through the weeds and sprawling undergrowth.

He didn't relish the thought of putting himself in close proximity to the three wise witches. Apart from the fact they might eat him, he feared that their personal hygiene was likely to play havoc with his OCD.

He had met the three old crones millennia ago, back in classical times, when they lived in the wilderness near Tartarus. He had gone to visit them in their dark and filthy cave, to pick their brains about something concerning Jason the Argonaut and a loofah. He couldn't remember what, exactly. It was a long time ago. But what he did remember was how vile they were. The cave itself had a damp, cloying atmosphere, as if one were squelching around in the bloody stump of a pig's dismembered leg. The floor was scattered with old bones – some of them human – and the place reeked of stale urine. The walls were grimy, and they oozed a glistening secretion. It was all quite reminiscent of a multi-storey car park stairwell.

But it was the witches themselves...

Zeus shuddered at the memory. They had stood like ragged beetles around a bubbling cauldron, in the middle of the cave. Their clothes were tatty rags, their faces wrinkled and leering. Their skin was caked in dirt and muck and Zeus had seen the congealed fat on their hairy chins. They stunk of old blood and body odour. Beyond this, Zeus noticed that they had dirt under their claw-like fingernails. This was where he drew the line. Dirty fingernails were a cardinal sin in accordance with Zeus's personal law of hygiene (or would have been, had there been cardinals around at the time. Religion being what it was back then, it was, if anything, more of a pagan shaman's sin).

He understood too, that the witches shared a single eye, without which they were blind; he had also heard that they shared a single tooth, without which they could not eat. The whole sharing of the tooth thing gave him sleepless nights.

The front door to *Dun Roamin* was warped and rotten, with peeling paint. It didn't have a door knocker but there was one of those spring letterboxes that, while not designed as a doorknocker, if pushed in and then released quickly, can alert the occupants of the house to your presence.

Zeus pushed the letterbox in and released it quickly.

Inside the witches stopped their chattering.

"There's someone at the door," said one.

"They don't call you wise for nothing," said another.

"Someone's come for dinner!" Said the third. They all chuckled hungrily.

As one, they chorused.

"Come on in, it's open!"

Zeus pushed open the door with a creak and a groan. The door was fine, as the hinges were well lubricated with slimy mould. It was Zeus that creaked and groaned. He stepped through, into the dingy old shack.

The atmosphere hit him several seconds before the smell.

It was cold and damp; moist like foot fungus. The smell that came hot on its tails was of old cabbage, spilled blood and sour body odour. The front door opened directly into the front room and Zeus was immediately confronted by the witches, huddled around their cauldron, staring out at him with red empty eye sockets. They were all smiling, and he noticed that only one of them had a tooth. It looked detachable and its peripatetic quality made him feel queasy.

One of the witches had the eye and, balls of crystal being what they are in terms of light refraction, he wondered if she was seeing him upside down. If so, he wondered if his beard was hanging over his face and if his face was red with blood-rush.

He recognised each of the witches, but he couldn't remember which was which. Or which was witch. Or which witch was which. Or which witch was which witch. One of them was called Dread; one was called Alarm; and the last was called Horror. That much he could remember. But really, they all looked the same to him. One had straggly hair. One had greasy hair. And one had lank hair. That was as much as you could differentiate them.

It was the one with straggly hair who was currently holding the eye. She looked at Zeus with disbelief.

"It isn't...!" She creaked.

"Who is it? Who do you see?" Asked the second, her lank hair falling over her face.

"Is it that pervy German fellow?" Asked the third, smacking her lips. "The one from the news, who wants someone to eat him, by way of achieving the ultimate paradox in sexual satisfaction?"

"Ooo! *Is* it him?" The second witch thumped her fists together excitedly.

The witch with the eye spoke with something close to bewilderment.

"No, it isn't him. You won't believe who it is."

"Who? *Who?*"

"It's *Zeus!*"

"Zeus?" The second witch leaned forward, over the cauldron, as if it would enable her to see him better. "As in..."

"Yes! As in the god himself!"

"And that whole affair with Jason the Argonaut..." said the second witch.

"And the loofah," chimed in the third.

The witches fell silent, save for the liquid chomping of their hungry mouths.

Zeus wished to buggery that he could remember what had happened with that bloody loofah. Something deep inside told him that he ought to be ashamed - but he couldn't be sure. He felt it was prudent to play safe and steer the conversation away from unknown waters.

26

"So, what brings you to these shores?" Asked the witch with the eye, watching him carefully. It was times like this that she wished they'd managed to get that contact lens. She could see who he was, but she couldn't make out any facial expressions.

"I live on these shores."

The witches scrabbled to lean closer to him, over the cauldron.

"Really? Where abouts?"

"Nearby," said Zeus. He felt it would compromise his godly authority if he told them he lived in a small flat above a fish and chip shop.

"You live around here?" Asked the second. "In Pestlewick?"

"Yes. I've lived here for years. I thought you lot were wise. I thought you'd have known that."

"We see much..."

"But we're not bloody psychic."

Zeus shrugged.

"It's funny how so many of us from the old days live in Pestlewick now!" Mused the third

Zeus nodded. He may have lost the bulk of his divinity, but he was still a god. He kept abreast of developments in his own world. And it was true enough that many of his old contemporaries from ancient times had relocated to the Pestlewick area. It wasn't just myths and legends from classical times either. Pestlewick was awash with archetypes and personifications, from all cultures and religions. One is tempted to put it down to the house prices, or the quality of the region's social amenities. The problem with this is that Pestlewick's house prices are fairly astronomical; and the social amenities leave much to be desired. We can only conclude then that what attracts metaphysical embodiments and archetypal personifications to settle in Pestlewick is the bus service, which is very good.

"I saw Pegasus the other day," creaked the one with the eye. "It was quite sad, really."

"Pegasus, the winged horse?" The third witch cackled wistfully at the thought of this fine creature. "What a wondrous beast. Why was it sad?"

"He got hit by a bus," replied the witch with the eye. "He was flying across a main road and he misjudged it. A bit like when pigeons fly in front of a car. He totally miscalculated the speed of the bus and...BAM!"

Zeus listened with sadness. Pegasus was a glorious symbol of his age.

"Did he survive?" Asked the third.

The first witch shrugged.

"Not really. He was pretty badly mangled. One of his wings was torn off at the stump and by the way he was laying, I'd say he had broken his back. He was making a terrible noise, whinnying on the pavement, kicking supernatural glitter feebly from his hooves. He couldn't get up. He could hardly move."

"You should have brought that wing home," slurped the second witch. "That would have gone nice in a stew."

Zeus felt that the agenda was slipping away from him and he coughed politely.

The witches snapped their heads up, pointing their faces directly at him.

"Speak then. Why do you come here?" Asked the one with the eye.

"Well," Zeus cleared his throat. "I need your wisdom. I need some advice on how to get some money..."

In perfect synchronicity, the witches began to smile. They remembered the last time a man had come to them to ask their advice on getting money. That man was, simply, avaricious. And with avarice came stupidity. The witches had told him to *come closer. The secret to great wealth can be seen in the deep waters of the cauldron.* They had beckoned

28

him over, told him to *lean over the cauldron*, to *look into its depths*, to *look upon the answer for which he was searching...*

They all agreed, after that night's meal, that the man had tasted of chicken,

Seeing the witches smile so spontaneously unnerved Zeus to the bone.

"Come closer to us," sang one of the leering crones.

"The answer to your needs is here, *in the cauldron*," beckoned another.

"All you need to do is stare into its depths and you will see the answer you seek," said the one with the eye.

Zeus had been around a long time.

"Get off with you," he said, flatly. "I am a god – *Father of the gods of Olympus.* I know when I'm being taken for a saddle bag. If I go anywhere near that pot of yours, you'll have me in there as fast as you can say *pass the seasoning* and I'll spend the rest of the afternoon slowly braising on regulo five. I'm not stupid."

The shared look of disappointment on three craggy faces was stark.

"I need fifteen thousand pounds," said Zeus firmly. "And I need it by next week. Now how in the name of a gardener's compost heap am I going to manage that?"

The witches became quiet, ruminating over the problem.

"It's a difficult one," said the one in the middle.

"And maybe there isn't an answer," said the second.

"It's a lot of wonga," said the third.

They stopped, as one. Then they swung their ugly faces towards Zeus.

They were smiling hideously.

He was conscious of the one with the eye, slowly moving around the cauldron towards him.

Zeus was wily. He knew how the witches worked.

They would answer his question but in doing so, would try to distract him in order to bag him as the day's culinary speciality. He kept a wary eye on the approaching witch.

"There *may* be a way," said one of them in a sly voice.

The one with eye began to croon, manoeuvring herself cunningly towards him.

"The road to wealth is like a cow," she said.

"To find your gold..." said the third.

"*You need a plough!*" They all joined in, delightedly.

Zeus looked at each pf them, from one to the other. All of a sudden, he found himself doubting the depth of their wisdom.

"What the bloody hell is that supposed to mean?" he asked.

The witches cackled and Zeus was aware now of the other two as they slid around the cauldron, making their way towards him, their bony fingers feeling their way slowly across the room. Their eyeless faces were all fixed on him. It looked for all the world as if they could see.

"You've had your answer!" Said the one at the back.

"And now it's time to pay us for our troubles," said the second one.

In a sudden move the one holding the eye lashed out with her clawed hand, eager to lay a hold on Zeus's godly frame.

Zeus was ready for it. He stepped back, skilfully avoiding the reaching claw, and took a side-step. Then, in one simple move, he reached forward and plucked the crystal orb from her hand. He then moved out of reach, the eye held tightly in his hand. As a classical tableau from ancient times, one might have read it as the god Zeus holding a very round thunderbolt.

The witches fell silent, confused.

"He's got the eye!" Screamed the one who had been ambushed.

They let out a curdling scream.

"Give us the eye! Give us back the eye!" They chorused.

Zeus juggled it casually in one hand, surveying the witches in their foul and filthy lair. It had been surprisingly easy.

"Not until you give me some answers," he said.

The witches sighed with dark resignation. It wasn't the first time they'd been had in this way. Whenever they had a cannier visitor, he would end up swiping the eye from them and as a result, they would find themselves over a barrel. It was a real pain. And still they were never prepared for it each time it happened. It was an Achilles heel, that eye.

"Ok," said the one in the middle with an irritated sigh. "What do you want to know?"

Five miles away, an officious clerk with an officious outlook was trying to process an application for Universal Credit, at the Unemployment Bureau in Boomtown.

"Sorry," she said, leaning forward across the desk to make sure she was hearing properly. "Just run your name past me one more time."

"Thorax," said the man sitting opposite. "Thorax T Barbarian."

"And the T stands for..."

"The. Thorax the Barbarian."

The clerk stared at the applicant.

He was an unusually large character and when he had walked into the Unemployment Bureau everyone had turned to look. It happened wherever he went. You couldn't help yourself. So vast he was, that he almost seemed to possess his own gravitational pull. Were a spherical lump of rock with extra-gravitational properties to float within his sphere of influence it would be rendered, undoubtedly, a moon to his perambulatory mass.

In the absence of floating rock, he did attract a lot of fluff and this could often be seen clinging to his clothes and occupying his bodily nooks and crannies. Not least his belly button.

Thorax had dressed in his best suit for this occasion, feeling this was essential to impress the staff at the Unemployment Bureau. This whole outing was a first for him. The idea of turning to the state for financial succour was new to him and in his mind, it had taken on the quality of a serious job interview. If he was going to be approved for state support, then he was going to have to impress the panel.

His only suit, sadly, was the Sunday suit he had worn regularly as a teenager. It was a black two-piece affair and, in its heyday, had looked very smart. However, even in his teens Thorax had taken it through its heyday and all the way out the other side. By the time he reached sixteen it was frayed around the cuffs and was so shiny that on sunny days it gave off a painful glare. Even then it was growing too small for him.

At thirty-two years of age – and on his first visit to the Unemployment Bureau – it looked ridiculous. The trouser legs came down to just above his knees, the cuffs rode above his elbows and, overall, he looked like an over-grown seventeenth century pratt. This was another reason everybody had turned to look when he walked in.

"What is your national insurance number?" The clerk's fingers were poised over her keyboard.

"It's the personal identification number given to all UK citizens to facilitate payment into nationally-run social insurance scheme," replied Thorax. He had prepared assiduously for the interview.

She stared at him, trying to work out if he was trying to make a joke. His face was deadly earnest. More than that, he wore an expression that was eager to please. *Eager to get it right.*

"What is *your* national insurance number?" She asked, patiently.

"I don't know."

The clerk shrugged and asked Thorax for his address. She typed it into the computer and waited for some details to come up. The computer drew a blank and she asked Thorax for his previous address. Again the computer drew a blank. This she repeated a number of times until they had gone back ten years, to the limit of the database's scope. Still, there was nothing.

She looked up at Thorax, puzzled.

"There doesn't seem to be any record of you on the national database," she said.

Thorax looked appropriately concerned, though in truth he had no idea what this actually meant.

She frowned and hovered her fingers over the computer keyboard once more.

"Where were you born?" She asked.

"I wasn't born, I was delivered." Thorax said, matter-of-factly.

"And where did the delivery take place?" The clerk was used to dealing with all kinds of people. Pedantry wasn't new to her. She was patience itself.

"At my mum's house."

"A home birth?"

"No, a stork."

She shot him a look of cold contempt.

"Mr Barbarian, really I haven't got time for flippancy."

Thorax blinked. The conversation was beginning to confuse him.

"Were you born at home?" She asked again, sternly.

"The stork delivered me to my mum, at home," Thorax insisted, trying to frame his answer in a way that this woman would accept.

The clerk sighed.

"Alright. What was the address?"

Thorax recited the address, down to the postcode. She typed it in, along with his date of birth. For a few seconds they sat in silence. The clerk's own silence was laced with authority. Thorax's oozed discomfort. Finally she folded her hands on the desk and stared across at the applicant, who was wringing his hands anxiously. They were huge, like choice hams.

"Mr Barbarian, I am afraid we don't have any record of you."

"Is that good or bad?"

"Well, if you have been telling me the truth, it's bad. It means you don't exist. Not as a national, anyway."

Thorax attempted a look of concern, to reflect the clerk's tone. He wasn't quite sure what she was trying to tell him, or if it had any bearing on his application. He waited for what seemed an appropriate amount of time.

"So where do I pick up my money?" He asked, with a weak smile.

"Mr Barbarian, I am afraid you don't qualify for any social security. Furthermore, I am obliged to report you to immigration control who will inform the local police. You will then be held in custody while an investigation takes place to ascertain your identity."

"But I've told you who I am. I'm Th..."

"Please would you take a seat over there?" The clerk indicated a row of chairs in the middle of the office. Most of the chairs were occupied by existing claimants and new applicants. None of the occupants had taken nearly as much care over their appearance as Thorax and consequently, they all looked much smarter.

Thorax rested his huge hands on the desk. He leaned forward, his vast bulk casting a shadow over the clerk. She stared at him, expectantly. It occurred to her that his hair-style was several decades out of date and he had the curious appearance of an over-sized Tony Blackburn from 1972.

"So I can't get any money out?"

"I'm afraid it doesn't work like that, even if you did qualify for support. However, I'm afraid it is very much more serious than that now. I have reason to suspect that you may be an illegal immigrant. Would you please go and sit over there."

Thorax absorbed her stern tone with the same indifference as a rock absorbs heat.

He still had no idea what she was talking about. All he wanted was some money, but it didn't look as if he was going to get any – that much he did understand. He smiled politely and stood up.

"No, I won't stay," he bowed as inoffensively as he could. "Thank you for the offer. But I may as well get going."

He turned to leave.

"You *can't* go," she said, firmly. "And if you attempt to do so I will be forced to call security."

Thorax frowned. He was beginning to think that this woman was mad. She had told him that he couldn't have any money and yet now she was adamant that he stayed. It seemed fruitless. Everything seemed fruitless. Except for her. She was bursting with fruit. She was a veritable fruitcake.

"Thank you," he said, politely. "But I'll go, if it is all the same to you."

The clerk could not have known that Thorax was a natural force, as unstoppable as a tornado, as uncontrollable as the wind and as prone to saturating you by stealth as those fine, drizzly showers of rain you sometimes get. It wasn't that he was wilful, or obnoxious. He was, simply, a force of nature. When the clerk pressed the buzzer to call security, it was a like trying to contain Hurricane Hilda with a panel fence from your local hardware store.

Thorax got as far as the front door before two burly security guards stepped in front of him to bar his way. They looked thuggish and keen to inflict pain. Thorax stopped politely, waiting for them to move.

"Sorry mate, you're not going anywhere," said one of them, laying his hand on Thorax's arm.

Thorax gave them both a friendly smile.

"I really need to get on," he said, politely. "So if you'd just move out of the way..."

The other guard laid hold of Thorax's other arm.

"Like we've just told you, you're not going anywhere."

The sense of hostility in the guard's tone was unmistakeable. Thorax felt his patience draining with a rapidity that would have been alarming to the guards had they been aware of its potential consequence. He had tried to be friendly, but this was wearing thin.

"Am I right in thinking you intend to stop me from leaving?" He asked, just to get it straight in his head.

The guards simultaneously tightened their grip on the hulking figure. They were both aware of just how hard and unyielding his arms were. It was like taking hold of solid brick. They still fancied their chances against this (admittedly large) man, however. Large tended to mean docile, in their shared experience.

"Correct."

What happened next happened so fast that no one in the Unemployment Bureau was able to describe it afterwards, with any level of certainty. It was none the less spectacular.

Holding on to Thorax's arms as they were, the two security guards felt themselves being lifted off the ground and, just a split second later, were smashed together with force of two Reliant Robins hitting a tree. The wind was knocked out of them and they slid to the floor in a heap.

As they tried to get up, disorientated but determined to subdue their quarry, Thorax reached out to each side and grabbed two desks, one in each hand. He lifted them into the air and brought them down with force and accuracy upon the heads of the two guards. The sound of cracking skull resonated throughout the Unemployment Bureau like a salt and vinegar crisp undergoing the spontaneous splitting of one of its atoms. Thorax pressed down on the desks and began crushing the two men underneath. They gurgled helplessly from underneath.

When the barbarian turned around, it was to see a sea of shocked faces staring back at him.

Believing them to be in sympathy with his plight, he shrugged and shook his head in quiet disbelief.

"This place is a madhouse," he said.

Still shaking his head incredulously, he walked through the doors and out on to the street.

"A hundred quid, and I won't go any lower," said Edna. Her eyes were like steel, as they bored into the proprietor of the Minotaur Scrap Yard.

The proprietor looked back at her, his eyes scrutinising.

He was used to hard dealing, but this old dear was not so much a sweet old granny, as a hard-nosed Wall Street trader. He huffed in deliberation and his wide nostrils flared, spewing thick steam into the cold autumn air.

The problem was he had a weakness for ploughs. He always had done.

Edna waited. Just because the owner of the Minotaur Scrap Yard had the well-built body of a man and the large, broad head of a bull, this did not make her feel sorry for him. She felt certain that he was playing on his disability to try to bring her down in price. She knew in her heart that the plough was worth well over a hundred pounds as scrap metal and she was determined not to let her revenue slip below that figure.

She stared back at him. His large black eyes, framed by his black furry head and crowned with a set of magnificent, curved horns, stared back at her. He blinked once. And she knew she had him.

"What's your name, dear?" She asked, in a tone that suggested she was about to offer him a nice cup of sweet tea and a bun.

"Roger," said the Minotaur.

"Roger!" She smiled. "What a lovely name. It suits you! Come on, Roger. We're being silly. Let's agree on a price and wrap this up, shall we?"

"I really can't offer you more than eighty pounds for it," said the Minotaur. "It's covered in rust and slime. I'll be lucky to get anything for it myself. I'm just helping you really, taking it off your hands."

He cocked his head to one side, an action reminiscent of a caring social worker.

Edna chomped her wet gums together thoughtfully. Behind the Minotaur, a maze of old metal was piled high. She gazed beyond him, seeing the rusted vista of old cars and random parts. There was a double-decker bus, its windows smashed, its tyres flat. There were a couple of old vans, their doors removed and their panels bent.

A thought occurred to her.

"What would you give me for the van?" She asked.

The Minotaur's eyes widened. He straightened up. This, he hadn't expected. He looked over at the van.

"Well...it looks quite battered. I'm not sure what I'd get for it," he said, slowly. "It's pretty old. Rusty, by the looks of things. I suppose I could sell it on as a working van – but I'd probably say it just needs to be scrapped."

"So what's it worth to me?"

"Sixty quid," said the Minotaur.

Edna tilted her head, pinning the Minotaur in place with a knowing smile.

"*Roger...*" She could have been chastising a naughty boy.

"Eighty quid. And that's my final offer."

Edna gave a satisfied nod.

"So. Eighty pounds for the plough. Eighty pounds for the van. That's a hundred and sixty pounds. Now. In cash."

"Done."

Edna spat on the palm of her hand and held it out. The Minotaur did the same and they shook on the deal.

*

As Roger wandered over to the yard's portacabin to get Edna her money, he found himself reflecting on the old days. How tremendously feared and respected he was back then!

It wasn't a bad living, owning a scrap yard. But compared to what he once had...what he had once *been*...

It was like the lead singer of Hot Chocolate, Errol Brown, ending his days as a shelf stacker in his local supermarket.

Hardly a day went by when Roger did not think wistfully of his labyrinth at Crete. Today he could almost smell the hot stone walls, feel the marble floors beneath his feet, hear the echo of the bare and empty corridors. He missed those times so badly, it hurt.

He had no idea why but when the time came for him to hand over a hundred and sixty pounds in cash to Edna, he had the tune to Hot Chocolate's "It Started With A Kiss" playing in the back of his head.

Bobbies on the beat are not a standard feature of community policing these days, but the village of Pestlewick is one of the few places still privileged to have such a thing.

PC Terence Standing was Pestlewick's community police constable. He had been in the role for five years and as far as journey metaphors go, it had been a cheaply made rollercoaster.

When he began in the role, it represented a whole new start for him, and he was looking forward to an existence of relative ease. It was generally agreed among police officers of a non-ambitious bent (and Terence Standing was *most certainly* one of these), that a village constable was a nice thing to be. Community policing is one of the more predictable areas of police work and community police officers enjoy, on the whole, a fairly easy work schedule and the benefits of being accepted and respected by the citizens over whom they have jurisdiction. Because of this, it is a relationship of partnership that is more likely to blossom, than one of open hostility.

When he took on the role of community police constable, Terence Standing felt that he would be investigating nothing more than the occasional domestic burglary and that his life would be more about giving talks to school-children on the dangers of crossing the road, than it would about apprehending criminals.

Had he been given any other beat than the village of Pestlewick, this may well have been the case.

But Pestlewick was not a typical community.

Standing had regretted the decision on more than one occasion. He yearned for the days when he was on the Metropolitan force, where the most difficult thing he had to deal with was gangs of armed criminals, drug wars, serial killers, kidnap, extortion, street violence, domestic violence, laundrette violence, pet shop violence, riots and the plague. Things were simpler then. When Standing had taken on the job in Pestlewick, five years ago, he was thirty-two years of age. He was now approaching sixty.

The problem was that Pestlewick was peppered with metaphysics. None of Standing's intensive training – or his hard-won experience on the streets of London – had anywhere near prepared him for life on this unusual beat.

Only last weekend he had been called out to *The Anvil*, a sleepy pub on the Wessex Road, to deal with a belligerent and threatening customer. The customer had been drinking since lunch time and as the day wore on, he had become increasingly rude and threatening in his behaviour.

An altercation over television channels had led the customer to threaten other punters with a scythe and when he had been asked to leave, he had caused a foul and unearthly wind to howl through the pub, followed by a host of screaming souls.

Drunk and disorderly. Threatening behaviour. Breach of the peace. Take your pick.

When Standing had reached the pub, he was discomforted to find that the abusive customer was none other than Death himself. The Grim Reaper; harvester of souls.

Walking through the main door he had found the Reaper standing on the bar, swinging his scythe around in a threatening manner. He was leaning forward, shouting obscenities at the six-or-so customers, who were nursing their pints, staring back at him with obvious unease. The Reaper was clearly over the limit. As he swayed unsteadily from side to side, his dark hood sat wrinkled and lop-sided on his head. His black robes were twisted around his ankles. He was shouting like a tramp on a bus and most of what he said was unintelligible.

Tucking his natural apprehension under his belt, Standing had approached the bar.

"Would you come down from the bar, please." He said, calmly.

The Reaper's black, empty hood, filled with the void of eternity, turned to face him.

"Ahhh...*shish*!" He growled, flicking the scythe around randomly. "The *blaady law*...th'ole bill..."

His voice was like marble. His scythe cut the air to ribbons.

"Would you please come down from the bar," Standing asked, once again.

"Sod off, FILTH..."

A wide swipe with the scythe.

"I'll ask you one more time," PC Standing eyed the Grim Reaper calmly. "Will you please come down from the bar."

The Grim Reaper staggered around on the spot, preaching from his vantage point.

"*Yaaaaa*...you can't tell me what to DO, you *lanky streak of*..."

For a professional like PC Standing, there is little that can't be achieved with a truncheon and some pepper spray. Ten seconds later, the Grim Reaper was writhing around on the floor, a pair of skeletal hands thrust into his hooded void. The scythe had clattered to a halt, just a few feet away.

"ARGHHHH...CAN'T SEE...WHATCHA DONE TO ME...I'M BLIND...CAN'T BREATHE..."

As Standing handcuffed the drunken personification of nature's most undeniable force, he whispered gently into the hood.

"Don't worry, it'll soon wear off. It's just pepper spray."

He then read the Grim Reaper his rights and led him coolly outside to his Fiat Panda, much to the gratitude of *The Anvil*'s bemused patrons.

By the time Standing got the Reaper locked in a cell, back at his tiny community police station, the Reaper's attitude had changed. The aggression had burned itself out and Standing found himself listening to the Reaper as he enthusiastically wailed a deathly reproduction of The Village People's greatest hits from his confinement. Where – or why – the Grim Reaper had ever faithfully learned the lyrics to *In the Navy* and *YMCA*, Standing was at a loss to know. But as he sat at his desk, drinking a hot cup of coffee, he found himself smiling, cheered up by the Reaper's drunken renditions.

When he had booked the Grim Reaper in, bagging and locking up his small number of belongings in a safe box (apart from the scythe, these consisted of a bag of gold coins, a large iron key and a Fruit Gum), he had been surprised to discover that the Reaper's first name was Cyril.

*

His arrest of the Grim Reaper was nothing out of the ordinary for Terence Standing. The weekend before, he had been called to a domestic dispute between Mother Nature and Father Time, who shared a house on a road otherwise invested with suburban normality.

While their relationship was generally well-balanced, when the couple did have a set-to, it tended to be cataclysmic in its manifestation. This particular argument had been over the fact Father Time had spilled some tomato ketchup on the sofa, while eating his dinner in front of the TV. Mother Nature, house-proud as she is, had gone ballistic. In retaliation, Father Time had said that if she hadn't scrimped on the shopping – and had gone with Heinz as opposed to own-brand – then the ketchup wouldn't have been so runny and the spillage would never have happened.

The disagreement snowballed from there.

By the time PC Standing arrived at the house, he had to deal not only with a domestic incident, but with the full consequence of Mother Nature's wrath.

With nothing but his Fiat Panda and a battered old megaphone, he found himself overseeing an emergency crowd control situation as the local population tried to flee the sudden emergence of an active volcano, an apocalyptic earthquake and a thunderstorm so primaeval that a number of non-evolved amoeba in the vicinity had flashbacks to the beginning of time and needed to be treated for post-traumatic stress.

Fortunately for Standing, he was able to act quickly, achieving much more than would normally have been allowed by routine physics. This was due to the fact Father Time, in awe of Nature's fury, had slowed relative time down to a crawl in order that he could put a few miles between himself and the epicentre of her wrath.

It was all part and parcel of life on the beat for a community officer in Pestlewick.

A few weeks ago, Standing had been called to a house in a respectable part of the village, to investigate a burglary. When he arrived at the house, the next-door neighbour was in her front garden, trimming her begonias. He was making his way up the garden path to call on the victim, when the neighbour popped up from over the fence, begonia in hand. She was a homely looking lady, probably in her early sixties, wearing a floral apron and gardening gloves.

"Hello, officer," she had said, airily.

"Ma'am."

He would have thought no more of it, had she not waggled the begonia at him with a smile.

"Are you here to investigate the burglary?" She asked.

"Yes," He stopped and turned to face her. "Did you see anything?"

"No, I'm afraid I didn't. It's a terrible thing, having your house broken into. It's so *intrusive*."

"Yes."

"Now. Before you go in, you do *know* about Mrs Crickshaw, don't you?"

Mrs Crickshaw was the victim of the burglary. PC Standing was a few paces from the front door.

"Know about her?"

"Yes. What she *is*."

Standing wondered if this was going to be some kind of racist comment. Or a homophobic one. He had heard this kind of preamble before.

"And what *is* she, Mrs..."

"Kemp. Mrs Kemp." The woman smiled, glanced down and clipped another begonia before meeting Standing's gaze once more. "She's a banshee."

"Oh."

"Yes. You don't want to hear her scream, or it'll herald your death."

"Oh." He didn't disbelieve her for a second. He had worked the beat for long enough.

"Yes. I have to make sure I keep the telly up loud all the time. I can hear her through the walls sometimes, singing, and washing up, and hoovering and such like. The last thing I want to hear is her screaming!" Mrs Kemp made a comic action of having a noose pulled around her neck.

"Oh. Right. Is she likely to scream, then? Like, at any time?" Standing was a few paces away from the front door. He glanced at it, nervously.

"Well, I don't know. I was chatting to her about that the other day. She's very open about it, you know. She said she doesn't usually scream unless she's up a tree, staring down at you with eyes wide, hideous and tormented. But apparently, when she is upset, the odd fatal scream will kind of...creep out."

47

"Oh," Standing found himself twiddling his fingers distractedly. "Do you think she's been upset by this whole burglary thing?"

"Oh dreadfully. That's why I've got my telly up full volume."

Standing realised that throughout their conversation, he had been able to hear Mrs Kemp's TV blaring out from inside the house, despite the fact her doors and windows were all closed.

He nodded.

"Ok, good. Well thank you Mrs Kemp. That's all...very good to know. Do let me know if anything occurs to you about the burglary.

A lesser man would have made his way back to his car, never to return. PC Standing was made of sterner stuff. He drew himself up to his full height and approached the front door purposefully. Before ringing the doorbell, however, he ensured that his canister of pepper spray was fully locked down. The first thing you do when you are blasted in the face by CS gas is scream like buggery. Standing didn't want it going off, inadvertently, during this particular house visit.

And so you have it. This was the kind of day PC Standing was used to. It came as no surprise to him then, when he took the call one quiet, autumnal afternoon.

"Standing? It's Drummer."

Inspector Drummer was based at Boomtown's main police station. If PC Standing could be said to have a boss, then that would be Drummer.

"Hello, Sir. Your highness."

"I've told you, Standing. There is no need to call me that."

"My apologies, your majesty."

"Just *Sir* will do. Now, Standing, I just wanted to let you that there was an incident this morning in the town centre, at the Unemployment Bureau."

"Oh?"

"Yes. Rather unusual, actually. A suspected illegal immigrant trying to sign up for benefits. And when they tried to stop him, he put two security guards in hospital."

"Oh right. And where do I fit into this, Sir?"

"Well, a few witnesses said he took the number seventeen, straight afterwards. That goes to Pestlewick, doesn't it?"

The Number 17 bus travels between Boomtown town centre and the heart of Pestlewick.

"Yes, it does."

"Very good. I'll just ask you to keep an eye out then."

"Of course. No problem. What does he look like?"

"Well, I'll e-mail you through his full details. But he sounds like a big sort. I don't think you can miss him. Looms like a tower block. As wide as a skip. And a hairstyle like Tony Blackburn."

"Which year?"

"Nineteen seventy-two."

"Okay. And...do we know his name?"

"Well yes. Sort of. I'm not sure how far it will get you, though. He called himself Thorax. Thorax the Barbarian."

Standing froze for a few moments. *Thorax the Barbarian.* Suddenly he was back on *terra familiar.*

"That sounds about right," he sighed.

"You know him?"

"No. But I'm sure he fits in perfectly around here."

"Okay. Well let me know if you find him."

"Will do."

Standing wandered over to the doorway of his little police station and leaned against the door. He gazed out, wistfully. Dusk was falling and the world was cast in twilight. It was a mad job, but someone had to do it. With a small sigh, he gazed up at the tin grey sky. The silhouette of a lone dragon was flying overhead, beating its wings steadily. Small

49

bursts of fire glanced from its nostrils and in the dim light, it looked quite magical.

So now he had an outlaw barbarian to deal with as well.

He shook his head and sighed again.

Not for the first time, he wished he was back in London, being shot at by a drugs baron.

Zeus inspected the eye, thoughtfully.

The witches were gathered around the cauldron, each with a steadying hand on its rim. They stared out of empty eye sockets; their crooked faces were lined with foulness.

"What do you want to know?" Asked the first.

"I've already told you," replied Zeus. "How am I going to get hold of fifteen thousand pounds by next Friday?"

"It can't be done," said the first witch.

"There isn't a way," confirmed her sister.

Zeus shook his head. It didn't seem like an impossible ask.

"You said something about a plough..."

The witches all cackled, their faces creasing into a hundred twisted lines.

"There *is* the plough," one of them one crooned.

"And yet," said another. "The plough would not send forth its fruit in time."

"That is true," said the third. "A season must pass before the plough gives up its riches."

Zeus tightened his grip on the eye. Apart from the fact these women (for want of a better word) stank, shared a tooth and lived in squalor, they were absolutely infuriating.

"Well what is it? Tell me about the plough. Let me be the judge of whether or not it can help me."

"You don't know?" Squeaked one of the witches, sounding for all the world like a rusty door.

"No. Tell me."

"He doesn't know!" Said one.

"He doesn't know!" Said another.

"He doesn't know!" Said the third.

They all stared at Zeus with sightless eyes, their red, empty sockets boring into him.

"*The bachelor's plough,*" they chorused, as one.

"The...what?"

The witch nearest to him raised a crooked finger and sniffed the air. Her grey, straggly hair crawled with lice.

"The bachelor's plough, though hard and cold, does warm the heart..."

"*When it makes gold!*" The other witches chorused.

"Nope. I'm not getting it." Zeus eyed them carefully. There was something big here; he could feel it in his beard.

The witch furthest away from him leaned over the cauldron, thrusting her hideous face towards him.

"There is a plough," she said. "Once forged by Thor himself. It was long ago, way back in the *dark times*. Thor made the plough for a farmhand who was to marry his daughter..."

"Yes, they're like that, country folk." Zeus expressed some moral indignity, with a lazy tut.

"No - the farmhand was to marry *Thor's* daughter. And so, Thor made him the plough."

"A unique kind of gift," mused Zeus. "But no doubt useful to a farmhand in need of a plough."

"Ahhh. But this was no ordinary plough. When wielded by a bachelor, it has the power to make gold."

Zeus found himself stepping forward.

"Oh?"

"Yes. If a bachelor uses the plough to sow his crop, when the crop ripens, it will turn to gold."

"Bloody hell. Really?"

The witches were all nodding.

"And what - this works with any crop?"

"It has been tried with wheat," creaked the nearest witch.

"It has been tried with corn," whispered the second.

"It has been tried with sprouts," said the third.

"Blimey. And they all turned to gold when they ripened?"

The witches were nodding still.

The one at the back stood up as straight as her crooked frame would allow. Zeus saw sawdust fall from her clothes. Or it might have been dandruff. Or lice. She was shaking her head.

"But the plough is no good for you," she barked. "You need your money by next Friday. The bachelor's plough would not yield a crop of gold for many months."

Zeus stared at the witch, thoughtfully.

"It may not be good for next Friday," he was thinking aloud. "But...if I had the plough...I could be wealthy. I could be *extremely* wealthy. I could have as much gold as I wanted. And if I had as much gold as I wanted..."

The witches huddled together, to finish his sentence off for him.

"You could be *a god,* once more."

He stared at them, his heart beating quickly in his leg (he was way too distracted to wonder how the hell it had got down there. But that was where it was. He felt the dim pounding against his shin, through a mist of wonder).

"Yes."

A dingy silence fell over the room. The only noise was the bubbling of the cauldron.

"So, this plough," Zeus was chewing his lip. "Is it easy to find? Does it still exist?"

The witches giggled in low, hideous tones.

"It's funny you should ask that," said the one in the middle. She was gurning horribly. Had she been wearing a toilet seat around her neck, it wouldn't have looked quite so terrifying.

"*Because it has just been found again,*" they all said, as one.

In the skies above Boomtown, a gap opened between two clouds.

It was like the careful twitching of a pair of curtains, edged apart just enough for the occupant of the house to peer out on to the street.

From high up in the sky, a glorious telescope was trained on the rooftops of the village of Pestlewick. It slid over the houses, gardens, streets and parks until it came to the ramshackle old bungalow on Totter's Lane. *Dun Roamin.*

The base end of the glorious telescope - nearest the omniscient eye that peered through it - was twisted carefully, until *Dun Roamin* came sharply into focus.

With the telescope trained on the witches' abode, a wondrous ear-trumpet appeared next to it, positioned with its open end towards the same. It was a golden ear-trumpet, reminiscent in its gleaming beauty, of the trumpets that brought down the walls of Jericho. Only they were wind-based instruments of war; and this was an archaic listening device.

With some carefully-sought angle of dangle, the telescope hinted at the scene unfolding inside the old building. The three Stygian witches were gathered around a bubbling cauldron. And Zeus, one-time father of the gods tapped them for information.

One had to concentrate to hear the desired conversation through the ear-trumpet. The ear-trumpet heard everything within a fifteen-mile radius and so one had to discriminate carefully. However, the omniscient Ear cut through the superfluous noise, diligently - private conversations, public speeches, radio broadcasts, chattering television sets - until It heard the conversation It desired to hear.

...this plough. Is it easy to find? Does it still exist?

...funny you should ask that...it has just been found again...

*

In the skies high above *Dun Roamin,* there was a low rumble of thunder.

Not a barometer in the land had seen that one coming. Those of a Swiss lineage, famed for their accuracy and overall sensitivity to changes in atmospheric pressure, even raised their barometorial eyebrows in surprise, unanimously.

John Thomas hated his name.

Some people have a name that is rich with social potential. Great Scott and The Fonz are just two examples.

Others, sadly, have a name that hangs around their neck like a millstone. Russell Sprout. Wayne Kerr. Richard Head. Jack The Ripper. All of these are prime examples of evil parents getting away with nominal sadism. But for John Thomas it was worse. His name hung around his neck, quite literally, like a big willy with an absent testicular sack.

He had heard Johnny Cash sing, once, about a boy named Sue. In this song, a father names his son Sue, in order that the son will be bullied throughout his formative years, thus learning to defend himself and fight like a man. It is a shrewd policy. By the time he reaches adulthood, Sue is a vicious hard nut with a penchant for violence. It isn't that he ever comes to appreciate his nominal femininity; instead, he benefits from it (although one is led to question if the post-script to the song sees Sue in prison – or even on Death Row – as a result of his dysfunctional upbringing and if this is the case, then the song might be said to lose its light-hearted sense of frivolity).

John Thomas would have loved to have been called Sue. A girl's name it may have been, but at least it wasn't a euphemism for a penis.

Unlike Sue, John Thomas never learned to defend himself against the mockery caused by his penile labelling. John Thomas was just not one of life's fighters.

It would have been satisfying had he been able to say that he was a lover, not a fighter. But in truth, he couldn't even lay claim to that qualification. He took his technique for love-making from the bawdy British *Carry On* franchise, from the 1960s and 1970s. John Thomas thought Bernard Bresslaw to be the apex of seductive sophistication and his love-making would have been Bresslawian in its technique, had he ever actually managed to exploit his own John Thomas for its true procreative purposes. As it was, his sexual adventures went no further than a box of tissues and the Ladies Underwear page, in his mum's latest copy of the *Freeman's* Catalogue.

Thomas lived with his mum, Mrs Thomas, on Morewood Hill. At thirty-six years of age, he hoped to get his own place as soon as the time was right. For now, he was happy to live in a house where his ironing was done for him, his meals were cooked and he had his own bedroom. There was much to be said for such a situation, especially in light of the fact a new *Freeman's* catalogue came through the door four times a year.

Thomas's domestic situation also fitted in well with his job.

As a bus driver, Thomas worked shifts and was in and out at all hours of the day. It was nice to have someone at home keeping the house clean and tidy. When he hit that winged horse last week (it had flown out in front of his bus like an over-sized pigeon) he had been glad of the company when he got home. His mum made him some chicken soup, always his favourite since he was a boy, and had given him a hot water bottle to help steady his nerves. He had not been able to get the horse's agonised whinnying out of his head for days. It wasn't his fault. He couldn't have avoided the winged beast. But he felt guilty all the same.

And then there was John Thomas's other role. To this day, he didn't know how he'd become encumbered with it. He wasn't paid for it. He wasn't qualified for it. He certainly didn't want it. But the choice had never been his to make. He had just been kind of... *chosen*. It was a calling.

John Thomas was God's fixer on earth.

It was a broad job description but basically, if God needed a human instrument to enact His will on Earth, it was down to John Thomas to play that part. He was, in a way, like God's straight man.

It was agreed that the role would never interfere with John Thomas's job as bus-driver and that all duties were to be undertaken outside of work hours. But beyond this, Thomas's contractual rights were few and far between. The way God saw it, Thomas was lucky to have been given such a spiritually responsible role. You never heard the Pope complain.[1]

The Good Lord had even ordered him a badge to go with the role. It read:
John Thomas. Fixer.

---

[1] Unless he stubbed his toe. God had heard some pretty racy language coming from the Pope's chambers in the Vatican, on account of him stubbing his toe. All Popes stubbed a toe from time to time. It was an occupational hazard. But the current incumbent was a clumsy oaf of the highest order, albeit of papal standing, and he would paint the air blue at least once a week as a consequence of a full-on meaty toe stub.

The Austin Allegro pulled into the Minotaur Scrap Yard, squeaking as it trundled over the stony ground before finally coming to a stop. The arse-end of the car was perilously close to the ground and as he pulled the handbrake on, Zeus noticed not for the first time, that the windscreen was pointing up at the sky like a speedboat on full throttle.

"I'm going to have to get it seen to," he muttered to himself as he climbed out of the car. And then another thought occurred to him.

No I'm not! By this time next year, I will have a fleet of Bentleys! Or should that be Bentlies?

The meeting with the witches had been a revelation. Zeus had gone there to find an answer to an immediate problem. How was he going to get hold of £15,000 to avoid ritual dismemberment at the hands of Father Christmas? But what he had been given was an answer to *everything.*

Zeus had no money, no status, nothing. The only thing he had left, to identify him as a god, was his immortality. And that was more of a curse than a blessing, given that he now seemed destined to spend the rest of eternity working. It was not a rosy outlook for a god of his one-time status.

But the plough.

The bachelor's plough.

If what the witches were saying was true, then Zeus had the means to amass a personal fortune beyond his wildest dreams. And all he had to do, was plough a field and grow some crops. It was magnificent. This was where his renaissance would begin. With wealth would come status. With status would come respect. With respect would come worship. And within a generation or so, he would be a god, once more.

He would be a god.

All he had to do was get the plough.

He had never been to a scrap yard before but it was pretty much how he imagined it. Cars and vans, wheels and axles, metal and old parts were piled high. There was a double-decker bus. Dense puddles of oil sat in pockets on the ground. There was even a crane with a large magnetic disk at the end, for manoeuvring whole cars about. It was a large, untidy, junk-filled maze.

There didn't seem to be anyone around until a broad, hefty figure suddenly emerged from the portacabin at the back of the yard.

Zeus gazed in admiration. He'd heard of the Minotaur, of course he had, but he'd never met the fellow up close.

The beast cut an impressive figure.

With the well-toned body of a man and the large, broad head of a bull, it looked formidable, stripped to the waist as it was. Its head was black and massive, with flared nostrils and large mad eyes that seemed poised on the brink of insanity. A pair of huge horns curved out from its crown, each ending in a lethal looking spike. It was not the sort of character you would want to meet in a Cretan maze on dark night.

The Minotaur strode across the yard, huffing like a steam engine on steroids through its broad nostrils. He stopped a few paces away from Zeus, eyeing the bright orange Austin Allegro critically. For a few moments he said nothing. His heavy breathing filled the air.

"I suppose you want me to take that thing off your hands, do you?" He grunted, finally, indicating the Allegro with a nod of his head.

Zeus felt both alarmed and offended, in a single blow.

"No," he said, quickly. "Actually...I'm wondering where you keep your ploughs."

The Minotaur drew himself up. It was a defensive manoeuvre. His eyes began to roll and he glared at Zeus with suspicion.

"My ploughs?"

"Yes. I'm after a plough."

"I don't do ploughs."

"Oh. The thing is, I understood that..."

"My ploughs are not for sale."

"I thought you said you didn't..."

"I can do you a nice double-decker bus. Spares or repair."

"Well, that's very kind. But I'm in the market for a plough."

The Minotaur was breathing fast and very deep. He loved ploughs. It was a curious sort of passion; but it was a passion all the same. When, on those very rare occasions, a plough came into the scrap yard, he put it to the back of the yard with his other ploughs. He liked to look at them sometimes. Nothing more.

He had six of them now, after that old woman had brought him the one that she had dredged from the Thames. The latest one was old and rusty and covered in river slime. But it was a beauty, underneath. As soon as he got a few spare hours, he was going to clean it up and bring out its natural ploughiness.

Zeus scanned the scrap yard, for anything resembling a plough.

"Do you mind if I look around?" He asked. He took a step forward, but the Minotaur blocked his way.

"I'd rather you didn't," it growled, defensively. A proud budgie breeder, cognisant of an airborne hawk eyeing his prize budgies with hungry calculation, would not have felt more anxiety at this moment.

"Look, I just want a plough. You must have one somewhere. I heard that one came in this morning."

A broad, black, hairy mass of fuming bull's head was thrust in his face.

"*Where* did you hear that?"

"Oh...just word on the street."

The Minotaur's anxiety leapt up a few notches, the needle sliding uncomfortably into the red area of his internal angstometer. So his new plough was out there, being discussed. *It was common knowledge.* A man in love, however aesthetically challenged the object of his adoration might be, thinks that the whole world wants to make love to her. It was this lack of perspective that now tugged at the Minotaur's soul. Jealousy washed over him like a rug. A wet rug.

"The street is *wrong*," he said.

"Can I just..."

The Minotaur's face was now millimetres from the ancient god's. Zeus felt the hot breath of the hybrid monster blasting his face.

"Do you want the bus?" Hissed the Minotaur, clearly in no mood to negotiate further. "Spares or repair."

"No, I don't want the bus," Zeus conceded.

"Then please leave my yard." Zeus was nudged back as the Minotaur's nose pressed against his own. "*Now.*"

The ancient god sighed. He glared at the Minotaur for a few moments and saw that the beast's will was as pliable as rock. Reluctantly, he got back into his Austin Allegro and drove out of the scrap yard, leaving the key to wealth, power and divinity behind.

John Thomas was watching *The Weakest Link* with his mum, when the telephone rang in the hall. Mrs Thomas pulled herself off the sofa and went to answer it. A few moments later she returned to the living room.

"It's for you," she said, returning to her place on the sofa.

John's heart sunk. There was only one Person who ever phoned him at home. He stood up, unenthusiastically, and made his way out into the hall, closing the living room door quietly behind him. He picked up the phone and took a deep breath.

"Hello?" he said.

"John," The voice was unmistakeable. "It's God."

John Thomas did a curious bobbing manoeuvre, somewhere between a bow and a curtsey, and nodded respectfully down the phone.

"What an unexpected pleasure. How can I help You, O Lord?"

He awaited his instructions with quiet resignation. He had been God's Fixer for a few years now and the work rarely involved anything too strenuous. It was always just clearing up after the Good Lord's various activities, really.

A few weeks ago, for example, God had called him because on a visit to one of His many houses on Earth, He had absent-mindedly left his mug – still half-full of tea – on a shelf next to the altar. Had the mug been discovered, there would have been a theological crisis, which would have torn through the global church like a pair of old pants.

John Thomas had rushed down to St Mary Magdalene's (on the Wessex Road) to retrieve the mug and when he found it, it was unmistakeable as the Lord's chalice. It was a ceramic mug, white, with the legend GOD emblazoned on the side in bold red letters. Thomas had poured the remaining tea on to some flowers at the front of the church and slipped the mug quietly into his pocket. It was a crisis averted.

On another occasion God had discovered that an unwitting member of the public had captured both He and the Arch Angel Gabriel on film as they played volleyball down on the beach at West Wittering. The member of the public had been taking pictures of her family and had inadvertently caught the two holy beings in the background. You wouldn't have noticed unless you looked closely but when you saw their glowing haloes (wonky on account of their physical exertion) and their ethereally-glowing robes stacked in two neat piles on the sand, it was irrefutable. While they both wore swimwear to conceal their heavenly modesty, it was acrylic swimwear from the 1980s. As a result, the density of their divine packages was not left to the imagination.

It had been down to John Thomas to retrieve the incriminating photographs and destroy them, along with any negatives. It had been a challenge, this particular job – but with a bit of divine assistance (God got hold of an official Gas Company uniform, giving John Thomas the means to access the woman's house, through cunning deception), Thomas had seen it through. Once again, he proved himself an invaluable instrument of God's will.

There were other things. Like the time God wanted to play a practical joke on Richard Dawkins. It had been childish to keep sending pizzas to his house but it was an easy thing for John Thomas to do – he didn't even have to leave his house for that one – and it had proved massively cathartic for the benign Father of all creation.

Then there was the time God had become angry with a serial blasphemer.

He didn't mind blasphemers as a rule. Usually He could ignore them and He was happy to wait until they shed

64

their mortal coil before exacting His just revenge. But this particular blasphemer kept praying, to express his blasphemy in person to the Divine Being that he despised so vehemently. God found Himself astrally bombarded at all hours of the day and night with aggressively-fired prayers, and it quickly became tedious.

He finally decided to visit An Act Of Himself on the irritating little man (who, while claiming not to believe in God, spent countless hours telling people this and criticising the source of his disbelief), by way of making a large tree fall on his house. Unfortunately, God misjudged the angle and the tree fell on the house next door, taking out two of the upstairs bedrooms and putting an elderly Mrs Hempshaw in traction for two months, with a fractured spine. It was John Thomas's job to take Mrs Hempshaw a bunch of grapes and a puzzle magazine twice a week while she was in hospital.

*

Now, standing in his hallway with the phone to his ear, Thomas awaited some equally mundane instruction from the universal Supreme Being.

"We've got a problem," said God. He sounded genuinely troubled.

"Go on, O Lord."

"I don't know if you are aware, but Zeus, the ancient god of the Greeks, lives pretty near to you." Thomas thought he could hear God chewing His lip.

"No, I wasn't aware of that."

"Well, he does."

"Where abouts?"

"On Pearbury Hill. Just above the chip shop."

"Ah yes, I know where You mean. Zeus, eh? That's a turn up for the books!"

"Yes. Quite. Anyway, he's never really given Me cause for concern. He keeps himself to himself. He's got a steady job. He pretty much lost his divinity aeons ago, with the decline in belief and all that. He seems to have come to terms with it, pretty well. So all in all, in My eminence, I've not seen him as..."

God tailed off.

"As what, Lord?"

"As a *threat.*"

When Thomas spoke, it was in a silky voice, warm with unction.

"No one could pose a threat to You, O Worthy One of The Heavens."

"Well, you'd think so, wouldn't you? But you can never be too sure. There are circumstances..." God broke off, trying to find the right words. "Certain things could undermine My authority."

"Your Omnipotence! Don't say such things! You must be wrong..."

Thomas regretted the words as soon as they were out.

"*What was that?*" Snapped God. The Lord's voice was as harsh as sandpaper.

"Well, not...*wrong*...just...overly generous to the competition. You are, after all, benevolent to a fault."

"Well, that's true. But no. I'm right on this one. I have divine concerns. Divine concerns."

"Are you saying Zeus might pose a threat to you, O Lord and Father? Surely he is completely irrelevant, these days?"

God paused. Thomas could hear the sound of sacred breathing down the phone. In the background he thought he heard the voice of an angel, asking if anyone had seen his coat as he fancied going out for a fly and it was brass monkeys outside. He heard some muted, jerking noises from The Lord and he assumed that God was probably indicating to the angel to be quiet.

"He is. But I think that might be set to change."

Slowly, in laboured words that told Thomas the Good Lord was probably twiddling His beard around his fingers, God explained the recent appearance of the bachelor's plough and the interest Zeus was taking in it.

"If he gets hold of the plough, he'll be the wealthiest being on the planet," explained The Lord. "And when that happens, he will be worshipped, once more. And with worship, comes divinity. The thing is, I don't want to suddenly find one day that he has smat someone. As soon as that happens, and he gets a taste for it, he'll remember how to rule through fear. And then there will be no stopping him."

"Sorry – smat someone?"

"Yes. You know. Smat them."

"How do You smat someone?"

"You don't. You *smite* somebody. And once they've been smited, they're smat."

"I think You mean smitted, O Father..."

For the second time in as many minutes, Thomas regretted opening his mouth.

There was a long, sacred pause.

"Is...*that*...what I mean?" Asked God with threatening deliberation. His voice was tipped with brimstone.

"Ah. No. Come to think of it, I think You're right. It *is* smat."

"I thought so. And so, John Thomas, I am giving you an assignment of the utmost importance. Through this assignment, you alone will decide the fate of human spirituality. And you – *you* – will hold *My very preservation, in all its glory,* in your hands. John Thomas – you must stop Zeus from obtaining the bachelor's plough."

Thomas felt the dark, heavy curtain of despair begin to descend over his soul. This was a bit different to retrieving a mug from the local church. Or sending pizzas to Richard Dawkins' house. This sounded big. It sounded way out of his league.

"But, O Lord, I am not sure that..."

"Self-doubt is humility, my child. And humility is a godly thing. I should know. I'm practically brimming with the stuff. But doubt not thyself, O wandering lamb. Go forth and meet thy destiny."

"Okay."

"Good. Right. Bye then."

"Bye."

"...bye."

".......bye."

"...........bye."

They both said a few more cautious farewells, each concerned about putting the phone down without returning an equal number of goodbyes to match those received. For to do so would seem rude to the person still on the line, especially if there was an emergent goodbye halfway out of the remaining participant's mouth.

In the small flat above the chip shop on Pearbury Hill, Zeus flopped on to his bed, face down.

The plough was within reach. *The answer to everything* was in reach.

He was so near and yet...

He had almost forgotten about the money he owed Father Christmas. £15,000 had paled into insignificance next to the infinite riches contained within the iron body of the bachelor's plough. All he had to do was find a way to get the Minotaur to loosen his grip on the thing.

It was incomprehensible to Zeus why the Minotaur was being so possessive over it. He obviously didn't know about the vast power it contained or the scrap yard would have been closed and the Minotaur out sowing crops. It was baffling. The Minotaur was in the business of trading in scrap metal – and yet, despite a clear opportunity to liquify some stock, he denied the very existence of a simple plough. His random offer of the double-decker bus merely infuriated Zeus the more.

"Stubbornness," Zeus muttered to himself, into the pillow. "Pure, Minotaurian stubbornness."

If he could just find a way to persuade the great beast.

A thought occurred to him.

He pulled himself up off the bed and ambled over to the rickety old wardrobe in the corner of the room.

There was a suitcase on top of the wardrobe.

He pulled it down and laid it on the bed. Flipping it open, he began to rummage through the various items within. It was full of old clothes that he had never got around to unpacking. There were various sundry items too. A glass paperweight. A travel map of London. An old tin, full of buttons. A toy cheeseburger.

He delved down into the midst of the case and pulled out an old grey sock. Carefully, he unwrapped the sock's hidden secret. A dull, grey bolt of lightning, some two feet in length, fell on to the bed. He picked it up and closed his fist around its base, tightly. It felt great. So comfortable. So *right.*

There had been a time when he had cupboards full of these things. Back then he would hurl them at the earth from his vantage point atop Mount Olympus. A single bolt would have the power to destroy an entire city and yet at the same time, if he wanted to exploit his pinpoint accuracy, he could use them to take out individual people, or even single limbs thereof. It was said that Zeus could get a lightning bolt down a small chimney opening, successfully hitting a target located before the hearth, from several miles away. It is fair to say that Zeus was the forerunner of the modern-day cruise missile.

As his divinity had waned, so the lightning lost its potency. The bolt he now held in his hand was his last one. These days it was a dull grey in colour. In its prime it had shone silver-yellow, like the sun. It had sparked and vibrated with a crackling, bursting energy. Back then, it could easily have been used to persuade the Minotaur to give up the plough. Had the Minotaur refused, the consequences would have been dire. His smoking ashes would undoubtedly have smelled of ozone, with a hint of roast beef.

Now, Zeus would be lucky if the Minotaur would take the bolt as scrap.

He had hoped to find the lightning bolt with some of its original potency returning. With the prospect of infinite wealth, he assumed that his destiny was tipping – and as such, had hoped that divinity might already be starting to return. The dull, lifeless bolt of lightning told him that he was being over-optimistic on this score.

He was also a little irritated to find that the pointy end of the lightning had caused a sizeable hole to appear in the toe of his sock. A sock had seemed an obvious thing to house the lightning in, at the time. Now he wished he'd wrapped it up in a towel.

"There's a dragon *in my back garden*," said the woman, close to hysteria. "A fire. Breathing. Dragon. Will you stop telling me to *calm down*."

Poised on the woman's doorstep, PC Standing thought she looked dangerously pale. She was shaking uncontrollably. Her eyes were wide and stared out at Standing with horror. All he was trying to do was reassure her, but it wasn't going very well.

"Listen, madam, if you'll just take a few deep breaths..."

"FORGODSSAKEDOSOMETHINGABOUTTHATCREATURE!" She thrust her head forwards, sticking it in Standing's face.

Resigned to the circumstances, Standing took a deep breath.

Dragons were a pain in the posterial lobes but (and he never thought, five years ago, that he would ever hear himself say this) he'd dealt with them before.

He had been called to the house, close to the Primary school on Widow's Lane, because the woman had become hysterical at him down the phone, claiming that a dragon had just eaten her Koi Carp. On leaving the community police station to deal with the situation he grabbed his truncheon and some pepper spray, though he well knew that on this occasion, it wouldn't do him much good.

"Okay, madam, perhaps you could take me through to the garden."

"I'm not going out there!" She screamed.

"Well, then if you'll allow me to go and have a look..."

He pushed past her and made his way to the back of the house. There were French doors in the living room and through these, he saw the problem. It was probably the same dragon he had seen flying overhead the previous evening, he thought. It was a big bugger and no mistake and he guessed it must have weighed a good tonne or two. It was nothing out of the ordinary, for a dragon. In fact, it was a rather attractive specimen, with its green scales, its long swishing, barbed tail, its large yellow eyes and its beautiful shimmering wings. A person with challenged eyesight might have mistaken it for a big budgie. Or a parrot.

The beast was at the rear of the garden, slowly undulating its long neck as it gazed around the unfamiliar environment. It was sitting on its haunches next to a large garden pond. Netting had been stretched over the top of the pond, to prevent herons from attacking the stock. This was no heron though. The netting had been incinerated. It occurred to Standing that it had incinerated the protective netting, the dragon had probably boiled the water too and, as a result, had been treated to a well-cooked meal.

The woman peeped around the living room door.

"Is it still there?" She asked.

Standing turned to face her. He smiled and rolled his eyes. *Dragons, eh!*

"Yes, it's still there. But don't worry; they're not difficult to get rid of. Have you got any biscuits?"

"Yes, but..."

"We'll need biscuits and some music. It needs to be classical ideally. Have you got any Beethoven?"

"I've got an old Burt Bacharach record. Will that do?"

PC Standing looked undecided for a moment.

"Yes. Let's try Burt Bacharach," he said, in a business-like tone.

Bacharach, don't fail me now, he thought sternly.

The woman dug out the vinyl record and handed it to PC Standing. While he worked out how to use her old record player, preparing to unleash the voice of humanity's most prolific gift to easy listening music on the reptilian intruder, she rushed out to the kitchen.

She shouted through.

"We've got chocolate digestives, oatmeal crunch and custard creams."

"Chocolate digestives," he shouted back, his face serious and focused as he fiddled with the record player. She came back in brandishing the whole packet.

Terence Standing stood to face her.

"Right." He took the packet of chocolate digestives from her. "We're just about ready. If I can just ask you to stand out of the way, remain quiet – and leave the rest to me."

The woman nodded nervously and watched in fascination as the policeman got to work.

Moving with the cautious deliberation one tends to associate with bomb disposal experts – or check-out assistants at a busy high street chemist – PC Standing made his way over to the French doors. He unlatched them carefully then eased them wide apart. The damp afternoon air drifted into the living room.

He paused for a few moments, making sure the dragon hadn't detected his movements.

Slowly, carefully, he crept back across the room to the record player. He levered the needle over to the record and put it down gently. For a few seconds it crackled lazily. Then, like a rainbow from a faucet, the voice of the world's favourite uncle began to emerge. *The Look of Love* began to fill the air.

With calculated slowness, Terence Standing increased the volume. The song flowered into bloom. It started as a localised ball of sound around the record player. Then it grew to fill the entire room. Then, finally, it crept out into the garden.

Burt Bacharach was loose.

Standing glanced over at the owner of the house and gave her a reassuring nod. So far, so good.

Slowly and deliberately, with flowing movements, he found the release tab on the packet of biscuits and peeled them open. For a few minutes, biscuits poised, he studied the dragon to check that Burt Bacharach was having the desired effect. He was. The dragon looked more relaxed than it had previously done. Its neck was no longer undulating, the yellow eyes no longer watchful and alert.

Its tail flicked lazily.

Treading carefully, his eyes fixed on the huge scaly beast, Standing crept towards the door. He could smell the recent rain, could feel the damp air against his face.

He stepped out into the garden.

For a brief second, the dragon seemed to pause. PC Standing became completely still.

A few moments passed.

His eyes still locked on the dragon, he pulled a biscuit from the packet and with a single, elegant move, threw it on to the grass next to the dragon.

A small burst of flame erupted from the dragon's flaring nostrils. Then, inquisitively, it curved its neck, bending its great scaly head to the ground. It snuffled loudly, tasting the air around the Digestive. Terence Standing watched, tense and alert.

The dragon ate the biscuit. It chomped loudly, greedily, on something that was tantamount to a crumb in comparison to its vast size.

Standing threw a second biscuit. Then a third. The dragon snaffled them all up, chomping with surprised delight at this sudden windfall of biscuit heaven. Quite deliberately, the next couple of biscuits that Standing threw landed just out of reach of the dragon. It stood up and moved across the garden to retrieve the Digestive booty.

And now it was standing up.

PC Standing smiled to himself, as the soothing voice of Burt Bacharach washed out over the entire garden. He reached his arm out carefully, towards the dragon, waving the packet of biscuits from side to side, ensuring the savoury chocolate aroma played about the dragon's nostrils. The dragon was mesmerised, its head moving from side to side in time with the waving of the biscuits. Standing waved the biscuits up. And then down. To the side. And then across. The dragon followed slavishly.

Now was the time.

PC Standing heaved the packet of biscuits into the air, far over the head of the dragon.

In an instant, the dragon's wings flapped and it launched itself from the ground with its powerful hind legs. It flew up into the air and caught the biscuits, mid-flight. Then, as Standing had anticipated, it kicked its legs, changed direction and flew off into the distance.

Unstoppable, Burt Bacharach sang on, stoically.

"All done," said PC Standing, strolling back into the house. "He won't come back."

"But he's still here."

"Not Burt Bacharach. The dragon. He won't come back."

The woman thanked him and sent him on his way, giving him a pork pie from the fridge, for his journey. She didn't really like pork pies, she explained, but it had been given to her as a free sample by a door-to-door pie merchant.

As Standing left the house he couldn't shake the feeling that something big was unfolding around him.

Even as he munched on his pork pie, he felt it. A tension – a kind of dull electricity – was building in the air around Pestlewick.

It made the dragon seem like a minor distraction in comparison.

It is unusual for anyone to pay a second visit to *Dun Roamin*. Generally, they don't get the opportunity, on account of being boiled and eaten.

But Zeus was no ordinary man. He wasn't a man at all – despite his human frame, his classic white beard and his tendency to develop piles when sitting on wet concrete.

Zeus needed answers. The witches had only given him half the story. He now knew what the plough could do for him. And he knew where the plough was. But extracting it from its possessive owner was something else entirely.

He pushed the spring-loaded letterbox in and released it quickly. The small muffled thump was a pathetic attempt at notifying the occupants of his presence on their doorstep. But the witches were wise. They would know he was there.

After a few minutes of shuffling around awkwardly on the doorstep, Zeus wondered if perhaps they didn't know he was there after all. He knocked again.

Inside, the three witches looked up from their respective places around the cauldron.

"Was that the door?" Asked the first.

"I thought I heard it a minute ago," said the second. "I didn't say anything because I thought I might just be hearing things. You two didn't say anything."

"I thought it was a badger."

"Why would it have been a badger?"

The third witch had the eye. She cocked her head fiendishly. There was an awkward shuffling outside. She bid her companions be quiet, with a quick "ssshhhhh".

"Come in, it's open!" She cooed.

Zeus walked in.

As soon as she saw him, the witch with the eye groaned.

"Oh no, it's you,"

"Who? Who is it?" Asked the other two in unison.

"It's Zeus, isn't it," she said, unhappily. They too, groaned.

"What does *he* want?"

"I just need to pick your brains a bit more," said Zeus, cheerily. It seemed sensible to keep on the best side of them. There was infinite wealth riding on it.

"We've told you all," said the first witch.

"There's no more to tell," added the second.

"Yes, I know. And I'm really grateful. You've been a very helpful bunch of...old crones. But I need to know how I can *actually get hold* of the bachelor's plough. You told me it was with the Minotaur, in his junkyard. But you didn't tell me how completely unprepared he was to give it up."

The witches were smirking, conspiratorially.

"You didn't ask," came a sly croak.

"Well, I'm asking now. What do I need to do?"

"The answer you seek is *here*," said the second witch, gesturing to the cauldron.

"Come closer, peer into its depths..."

"And see the wisdom it contains."

Zeus kept his exasperation well-hidden. *Not this again.*

"Look into the cauldron," they continued.

"Deep inside..."

"All the way to the bottom..."

"All I need," said Zeus. "Is for you to..."

"Come look..."

"*Look now...*"

"The answer is in there, even now, swimming around, like a..."

"...a..."

".......a..."

"Fish."

"I told you before," Zeus felt his patience draining away. "I'm not going anywhere near that...oh this is ridiculous."

Without further ceremony, he stepped forward and grabbed the mystic eye, yanking it from the holder's withered claw. He stepped back, wholly unimpressed by the need for this pointless charade.

The ambushed witch muttered in a resigned monotone.

"He's got the eye."

"You're dicking me," said the second.

"You're pissing me," Said the third.

Zeus sighed impatiently.

"You can have the eye back when you tell me how to get the plough. Come on, you ancient hags. It's no big thing. Just give me the answer."

"Give us back the eye."

"Give it to us."

"Return the eye and we'll tell you all you want to know."

"Look, can we just forego all of this," Zeus groaned. "You are wise. You know I'm not going to give you back the eye until I have the answer I need. So you may as well get on with it."

"And then what?" Spat one of the witches. "You'll throw the eye in the garden undergrowth, like last time?"

"It took us ages to find it when you did that. I got all tangled up in the herbaceous border."

Zeus started whistling, to demonstrate his disinterest. It was a childish and highly irritating thing to do. But it did the trick. The witches leaned forward, their craggy faces serious and intense.

"And in this quest..."

"For gold, from seed...

In traditional form, they all spoke the last line.

"*A* barbarian *is what you need.*"

Zeus nodded slowly.

"So what? If I can find a barbarian, *he* will be able to get the plough? He'll batter the Minotaur into submission, I suppose?"

"He'll follow his *destiny*," said one of the witches, sagely.

"The quest will unravel for him," said the second.

"Only a barbarian can lay hands on the bachelor's plough for you," finished the third one.

"Now give us the eye," they chorused.

Zeus continued to nod his head thoughtfully. He knew of a barbarian, in the village. In his mind's eye he could see the bachelor's plough returning unto his godly bosom. He gazed at the three witches, who stared out at nothingness, chattering in hideous tones.

They were right. It had been a cruel trick to play, throwing the eye into the garden last time.

Carefully, he crept over to an old bookshelf in the corner of the room. It was empty of books and reached up nearly as high as the ceiling. It was warped and full of woodworm. Quietly, Zeus reached up and placed the eye on top of the bookshelf.

He made his way to the front door.

"I've left the eye on the floor for you," he said casually, as he left.

John Thomas sat at the computer in the study, trying to get a handle on his latest mission from God.

Mrs Thomas and her son called it "the study", but really it was more of a box room, situated upstairs next to the bathroom, and used for miscellaneous purposes. John Thomas sat at the tiny desk, hunched over the keyboard of his archaic PC, surrounded by drying clothes, several empty suitcases and multiple packets of super-quilted toilet roll. Mrs Thomas believed in being well-stocked up when it came to toilet roll. You never knew when you might need it.

Thomas always began his Divine Missions in this way. He believed that careful research was essential if the job was to be done well. It was important to know what you were dealing with, in order that you could understand it from every angle.

This was the theory.

In practise, his research was about as sophisticated as a Mills & Boon novel. Carrying out what he thought of as "research" made him feel intelligent and dynamic, like a professional investigator. During those periods when he was on a mission from God, he imagined himself portrayed through quick-changing, shaky, handheld camera shots, with lots of artistic angles of him in thoughtful, intense poses, as he researched the subject diligently.

But he flattered himself.

When God had asked him to retrieve the mug from Mary Magdalene's Church, that time, Thomas had conscientiously booted up the computer so that he could do his preparatory "research". The research consisted of typing "mug" into Google. Here he was directed to Wikipedia, where he learned: *A mug is a sturdily built type of cup often used for drinking hot beverages, such as coffee, tea, or hot chocolate.*

Mugs, by definition, have handles and often hold a larger amount of fluid than other types of cup.

This explanation of a mug caused him to nod, intelligently, as though a deep level of understanding was being revealed to him. He then used Google Images to bring up a variety of mug pictures. Again, he nodded wisely as he absorbed the visual characteristics of his latest objective. At this point he felt he was ready to carry forward the mission and retrieve the mug from the church.

This latest mission was much more complex, however, and the research would need to be multi-faceted.

God had spoken of the incredible power of the plough and had told John Thomas where it was. John Thomas was aware of the scrap yard, which was at the back of an industrial estate on the Wessex Road. He had noticed it on occasion, when driving the bus along the route.

God had also told him how Zeus had gained information by outwitting the Stygian witches and stealing their eye, and of the dire consequences to be expected, were Zeus to take ownership of the plough. Apart from the fact God's very status as a deity would be compromised once Zeus got into the swing of being a divine entity once again, it sounded like Zeus would be a trigger happy sort of god, and would end up smatting people left, right and centre. Thomas had to stop this from happening. *It was a race to the plough.*

If John Thomas was playing a game of chess, the plough was King. Only his opponent was also going for the same King. So the rules of chess would need to be modified to reflect this.

Thomas rolled up his sleeves, licked his lips and got to work on the complexity of his mission.

He typed "plough" into Google images.

From downstairs his mum called up and asked if he would like a cup of tea.

In a voice that reflected the seriousness of his current distraction, he told her that he'd love one. He was gasping.

The articulated lorry came to a halt, declaring its arrival with a pneumatic hiss of air-brakes. The old Scania cab had faded paintwork. Emblazoned on the trailer was the name of the company: *Bristow's Haulage.*

Zeus switched off the engine and the motor coughed once before rumbling into silence.

Zeus was a realist and while infinite wealth was hopefully just around the corner, he still had to earn his crust. Until he had the plough fully in his grasp, he would need to keep on trucking. Today he had been down to Portsmouth to deliver a consignment of batteries and pick up a trailer-load of nappies. When he reached Pestlewick, with the nappies still onboard, he headed for Horseshoe Lane, where he knew the village's resident barbarian lived.

He had seen the barbarian around on various occasions and was aware of the various stories circulating about his deeds of violence and valour.

Amazingly enough, no one ever seemed to put two and two together. Apart from Zeus, it didn't occur to anyone that this gigantic man, with muscles like anvils and a hair-do like Tony Blackburn's – this mountain of a character, with a trail of outrageous tales and conquests left scattered in his wake – was anything other than a psychotic idiot, fuelled by steroids. Even the subject himself didn't seem to realise what he was. But Zeus had been around for a long, long time. He knew a barbarian when he saw one.

As he climbed out of the cab, he saw that Coincidence had bounded on to the stage like an over-enthusiastic understudy. The barbarian was leaning out of his front door, putting some empty milk bottles out. He was looking over, casually interested in the lorry that had just parked at the end of his small garden and he looked surprised when the driver of the lorry climbed out and headed towards him.

As their eyes met, the barbarian raised his eyebrows in polite enquiry. Zeus saw that he was wearing a flimsy apron. It was light blue.

"Hullo," said Zeus, smiling broadly.

The barbarian smiled, uncertainly. On the doorstep, soapy bubbles ran down the empty milk bottles. Thorax the Barbarian believed in washing milk bottles in warm soapy water before leaving them out for the milkman.

"Hello. Can I help you?"

Zeus stopped just short of the doorstep.

"Well actually – yes. You can. I wonder if you've got ten minutes for a little chat."

"I'm a bit busy," said the barbarian. He looked a trifle panicked.

Zeus understood.

"I'm not a salesman," he said, calmly. He stared firmly at the barbarian. "And I really do need to talk to you."

"Aw, I don't know..."

"Maybe you could put the kettle on. What I am going to tell you may be quite a bit to take in."

The barbarian sensed that there was more to this than met the eye. He also conceded that anyone who went straight to the kettle when there was serious business to discuss was the sort of person he could do business with.

"Come on in," he said. "I hope you don't mind taking your shoes off as you come through?"

The trouble with Thorax the Barbarian was that he didn't *know* he was a barbarian.

Until just a few days ago, he had worked as a sales assistant in a greetings card shop, at the Barrelway Shopping Precinct – a job he thoroughly enjoyed. It was the most recent in a long line of non-barbaric roles that defined his daily life.

He had worked in Lawson's Cards for a couple of years and it was only because of a decline in business that the owners had, regretfully, to let him go.

Thorax had been a model employee with a flair for customer service that perfectly suited their ethos. He had never been late, had always done over-time without complaint, never took a day off sick and was brilliant with customers and suppliers alike. There had been a time when the owners had fully expected Thorax to take over management of the store – they were fully confident he would excel in the role – but when the growth of the online greetings card industry hit them hard, they saw the opportunity slipping away from Thorax like a lubricated rubber glove sliding down the cliff-side of hopelessness. It was a sad realisation.

Prior to his time at Lawson's Cards, Thorax had been many things, with a definite leaning towards retail and customer services.

He had worked in a shoe shop. He had been a shelf-stacker. He had taken on various warehouse jobs. He had swept streets for the council. He had been a milkman's mate. He had been a removals man. He had worked in a Pet Shop. He had worked on the customer services telephone desk for an insurance company. He had done shifts on a factory line. He had worked in dry cleaning. He had even helped (briefly) with a franchise selling crepes from a handcart on Boomtown's Broad Street.

And things were no more remarkable before this.

Prior to his life in the world of work, he had gone to school, just like anyone else. He never stood out academically, though he did do quite well in Geography lessons and he once got five house-points for baking an outstanding sponge cake in Home Economics. He proved himself to be mildly competent at Technology, with a decent talent for metalwork. And while he was never great at team sports, he did win his school a number of trophies for his excellence in some athletic disciplines, most notably the shot-put, javelin and discus.[2]

Thorax did not know that he was a barbarian. He certainly didn't act like one. But, as sure as a baker likes muffins, he *was* one. The trappings and natural situations of a barbarian's life gravitated towards him like an old tin hat from the First World War gravitating towards a large magnet.

*

It started when he was delivered to his mother by a stork (he hadn't been lying when he told the woman at the Job Centre this) something that his mother always kept as a dark family secret, for fear of the gossip and innuendo it would provoke.

You see her? That boy, well, he ain't hers. He was delivered by a stork. What does that tell you about her? She can't be normal, can she? I bet she eats soup.

---

[2] Had there been an inter-school wellie wanging league, he would no doubt have done very well at that too. Thorax did wang a Wellie once, just for the fun of it, and it went for miles. In fact, he nearly caused an incident. The Wellie hit a train and very nearly de-railed it. Fortunately, the train driver was an ex-stuntman and had been adept at driving cars along on two wheels. He discovered that the principle wasn't too much different with a train and that careful control of speed, steering and weight distribution ensured that he was able to land the lifted side of the train back down on the tracks after just a few hundred yards. It was a tragedy avoided.

He did come to realise that being delivered by a stork, as opposed to being born of a woman's womb, was not the norm. But he never fully appreciated quite how abnormal it was.

Beyond this he was, throughout his life, regularly beset by barbarically-infused problems. Trolls beneath the floorboards and in the wall cavities at home. Princesses begging for him to rescue them from the rank clutches of evil captors. Dark knights wanting to do battle with him, to prove their honour and vanquish his barbarity. Dragons needing to be slayed. Dwarves wanting to do shady deals, in the dim candlelight of low-beamed taverns. Magicians. Elves. Goblins. Evil rulers. Magic rings. Supernatural forests. The constant piling up of odd socks every time he did a machine wash.

The list went on. And Thorax, seeing nothing out of the ordinary, reacted to each situation with the same straightforward practicality he would apply to a dripping tap or a squeaky door. As soon as he dealt with a problem, he put it out of his mind and continued with his otherwise normal life.

He was the antithesis of barbarity too, in so many ways.

Contrary to what one might expect from a standard out-of-the-box barbarian, Thorax loved his home and his home comforts. His small home on Horseshoe Lane was his pride and joy. He kept it immaculately tidy inside and took uncommon pride in the spotless carpets and glistening kitchen floor. The house smelled of *pot-pourri* and there was always the lingering odour of baking bread when one went inside.

Thorax loved to bake his own bread.

He leaned towards chintz in his domestic tastes and his curtains, furniture and bedclothes too, all reflected this. His garden was no less attended to and though he was probably misled by his own bias, Thorax liked to think he had the brightest, most vivacious flower beds in the whole of the street. Not that he was competitive about it.

When Zeus followed Thorax into his house, he was aware of all of this. He knew that the barbarian was ignorant of his true destiny.

But Zeus had to make the barbarian understand who he was. *What* he was.

Only then could he offer him his latest barbaric quest.

The quest for the bachelor's plough.

"I've found it," said one of the witches, with a relieved grunt. "It was on top of the bookshelf."

The other witches chattered hideously, uttering foul and incomprehensible noises of relief. They were at random points around the room, on their hands and knees, searching for the eye. They had been at it for hours.

"Why did he put it up there?" Asked the second witch, groaning morbidly as she cracked herself up off the floor.

"It's ridiculous, this whole business with the eye," said the third. She clawed at the mouldy wall, pulling herself to her feet.

Slowly, they all shuffled across the room, their ragged arms outstretched, seeking the comfort of the cauldron. They reached it, finally, and each grasped the rim eagerly.

"We've got to do something about it," they agreed. "We know how it should work. Needy traveller comes to us for help. We give an answer."

"And then we eat him."

"Exactly. Which is fine is the traveller is a bit slow. But if they have a bit of insight...as soon as they realise how dependant we are on the eye, we're buggered. They just take it off us. And then we're completely at their mercy."

They all nodded. Their faces were etched with hate and bitterness.

"We need to decide on a strategy," the first witch continued. "I don't care what it is. But we have to compensate for this weak spot."

They chattered and cawed like crows and the room bubbled menacingly with dark noise.

After a few minutes, one of them piped up. She had both of her withered hands on the rim of the cauldron as she spoke.

"Well, I say we play tactically. We decide on a formation and lock ourselves down."

The other two nodded, seriously. There are a number of well-tried formations known to witches dependent on a shared optical faculty, that can be used tactically in such situations. It isn't too much different to playing chess, insomuch as different moves elicit different counter moves; and the choosing of a move can influence the entire direction of the game.

"So, what formation should we favour?" Asked the witch with the eye.

There was a short pause.

"It has to be the Heimlich Formation," suggested the second witch.

"Yes, that works for me," said the first witch. "It is simple and effective. It will work well in the confines of the room."

"Then the Heimlich Formation it is," resolved the witch with the eye.

The cauldron plopped and bubbled lazily.

"Woe betide our next visitor, however keen his insight!" Cooed the second witch.

"Oh come on, sister," said the first. "We' must make him feel welcome. After all..."

"He'll be stopping for dinner!" Finished the one with the eye.

They all cackled horribly as evening's dark fingers began to press against the cracked and grimy windowpane.

They sat drinking tea from china cups decorated with floral patterns.

Thorax the Barbarian had left Zeus sitting on the floral sofa in the living room, while he went to make up a pot. He returned bearing a tray on which was a teapot, cups, saucers, a small sugar pot, a small milk jug and a plate of Rich Tea biscuits. He put the tray down on a little table that he placed in the middle of the room.

Zeus watched incredulously as the barbarian poured the tea with regal care, before handing a cup to Zeus.

He continued to watch as the barbarian added milk to his tea, with polite concentration, which he followed by two lumps of sugar. He stirred it well and clinked the teaspoon against the rim of the cup before resting it in the saucer.

He then sat back with his cup and saucer poised, to hear what his visitor had to say.

Drawn into the whole mood of the thing, Zeus added a good amount of milk to his tea, followed by one lump of sugar. He took the charade a step further by selecting a biscuit from the plate (even though they were identical, he ran his finger over them all, back and forth, as if making a considered choice). He sat back, facing the barbarian, his biscuit held just above his cup.

"Now," he said, choosing his words cautiously. "You're obviously wondering why I am here. Perhaps we can start with some introductions. I am Zeus."

The barbarian raised his eyebrows and sipped his tea.

"As in...?"

"Yes. As in the god. Zeus. I am he."

"You're the god?"

"Yes."

"Well I never."

"Yes."

"Honestly?"

"Yes."

"The ancient god of the Greeks?"

"Yes."

"Crikey."

Zeus smiled modestly. It was good to be recognised for who he was. And it was good that the barbarian had heard of him. It would make things a lot easier.

"And perhaps I could have your name...?" Zeus raised an enquiring eyebrow and finally dunked his biscuit. He had to swoop his face down in a single movement to catch the soggy part in his mouth, as it detached itself away from the whole.

"My name is Thorax," said the barbarian. "Thorax the Barbarian."

Zeus stared blankly.

"That's your *name*?"

"Yes."

"Your first name is Thorax. Your middle name is The. And..."

"My last name is Barbarian. Yes. Why?"

Thorax seemed nonplussed by the descriptive nature of his name.

"So - would you say it reflects...you know...who you are? Your name..."

Thorax thought for a few moments.

"I'm not sure," he said, finally. He sipped his tea. "I've never really thought about it."

"Has it ever occurred to you that it might be...you know...more than a name? That it might be a...I don't know...a...*description*?"

Thorax looked surprised.

"No, not really."

"Well...did you ever ask your mum and dad why they called you that?"

"They didn't. I was already called that when I was delivered."

"When you were...?"

"Delivered. Yes. By the stork."

"You were delivered by a stork?"

"Yes." Thorax looked embarrassed by this intense focus. He couldn't see what Zeus was driving at.

"So you were delivered by a stork. And you're called Thorax the Barbarian. Does that strike you as...I don't know...slightly *strange*?"

Thorax shrugged. He leaned forward, grabbed a biscuit and dunked it in his tea.

"You work in a shop, don't you?" Zeus, like most people in Pestlewick, knew little bits of information about the barbarian. He was a good topic for gossip.

"I did, yes. I was laid off a few days ago."

"I'm sorry to hear that. What was it? Were you too aggressive with the customers?"

Thorax frowned. It seemed like a funny supposition to make.

"No. A decline in business just meant they had to let me go."

"Oh. And what will you do now?"

"Oh, I'll look for something else. I quite fancy getting back into the crepes business. It got a bit competitive last time, but I reckon things will have calmed down a bit now."

"Crepes."

"Yes."

"Thorax, I hope you don't mind me saying – but I think you're..."

"Yes?"

"Well, I think you're...kind of....missing the point."

"In what way?"

"Well. I think you've missed your vocation, somehow."

"What vocation?"

"Barbarity."

"Sorry?" Thorax drained his tea and reached for the teapot, to pour himself another.

"I think your vocation was...I think you should have been...I think you *are*...a barbarian."

Thorax stared at him, blankly.

"Would you like a refill?" He offered.

Zeus shook his head but did treat himself to another biscuit.

"I've heard things about you," Zeus said, climbing over his words as if they were large, craggy rocks. "Things that tell me you're not an ordinary man. Things that tell me you are a barbarian. In your heart. *In your very blood.* And this is before I knew that you were delivered by a stork and that your name is Thorax the Barbarian."

"What things? What do you mean?"

"Well. For example. When you were at school."

"What about it?"

"Some of the kids had pen-knives. But not you. You had an iron broadsword."

"That's right. I had to keep it nested down the leg of my shorts, because it wouldn't fit in my pocket."

"No schoolboy has a broadsword."

"I did."

"Where did you get it from?"

"It was given to me. By some woman. Well, a woman's arm, anyway. It came out of the old duck pond, when I was at the park. And it was holding the sword aloft, and it just kind of...gave it to me."

"And you thought that was normal?"

Thorax took another sip of his tea.

"I never really thought about it."

"And what about when you go out for a drink?"

"Well. What about it? Sometimes I pop down the old tavern for..."

"That's it. That's my point. Who the hell drinks in a tavern these days? Pubs. Bars. Clubs. But a tavern! You managed to find the only tavern in Pestlewick and you have made it your local."

"That's hardly..."

"And you have your own tankard there, that they keep behind the bar. Not a pint glass, mind. A tankard."

"So what?"

"It's the barbarian's choice of drinking receptacle. A tankard." Zeus took an impassioned bite of his biscuit. "Oh. And that's another thing – the company you keep."

"There's nothing wrong with Billy the Dwarf."

"No, there's nothing *wrong* with him. Except for the fact he is a *real* dwarf, who lives most of his life underground mining for gold."

"You can't hold that against him."

"No, I don't. Though let's not forget that he likes to fight with a hatchet, too and has a reputation for braining his enemies. Anyway, it isn't Billy the Dwarf I have a problem with. It is the fact you fraternise with him so naturally. It just shows *who you are.*"

"Aw, I don't know."

"Well, ok. What about *that.*" Zeus pointed to the large boar's head, mounted on the living room wall, between a framed reproduction of *The Laughing Cavalier* and sunny picture of a meadow.

Thorax looked from the boar's head to Zeus, defensively.

"It was in my garden. It was digging up my daffs."

"And so you..."

"So I took to it with an axe. I took its head off in a single blow."

96

"Let's just look at that, shall we? You discover a wild boar in your back garden, which just happens to be in the middle of a suburban street. Oh. And not just any wild boar – but a *huge* wild boar with tusks like pikestaffs. And your natural reaction is to lop its head off with an axe."

"Well...yes. What would you have done? It was ruining..."

"Your daffs. Yes. I know. You said as much. And then you mount it on the wall. Thorax – you must see that this is not normal behaviour for anyone of a non-barbaric disposition. Underneath all *this*," Zeus gestured around the living room. "You are *a barbarian.*"

"I'm not," Thorax sulked.

"What about the ninja warriors, then?"

Thorax shrugged, sulkily.

"What about them?"

"It's been the talk of the village for the past month."

The episode with the ninja warriors had occurred a few Fridays ago, down at Thorax's local tavern. Thorax had been enjoying a quiet drink with Billy the Dwarf, as he was wont to do most Friday evenings.

Always shy of conflict unless it made a point of coming to him, Thorax had spent the evening politely ignoring the increasingly rowdy party of ninjas that had decided to patronise The Boar's Head for the evening. Rumour was that the ninjas were in Boomtown for an international ninja convention being held at the Broken Mermaid Leisure Centre. Six of them had found accommodation in Pestlewick to suit their budgets and being in the area, they had gravitated towards the tavern.

Thorax successfully ignored them as the evening wore on, despite the noise they were making and the splintering of tavern furniture as they wilfully broke it. It was only when a couple of them pushed against Billy the Dwarf, while he was getting a round in at the bar that things took a turn for the worse.

Billy the Dwarf dared to reprimand the ninjas - albeit gently - for spilling a portion of his drink. *Try to be a bit more careful*, he had said, irritated at having lost some of his mead.

As soon as he had uttered the words, the ninja wrath was unleashed and within a mere second, six ninja warriors were in tight formation before him, crouched and ready to deal death.

Billy the Dwarf had looked at them, their skin-tight black costumes, and the black, silk masks over their faces. He had glanced at their gently curved swords, held parallel, at exactly the same angle. He had seen their eyes, hard, dark and staring. And he had realised that this was a tavern scuffle that was likely to have a fatal outcome. A dwarf to his bones, he had transferred both the drinks he was carrying into one hand and had reached down slowly, letting his hand rest on the handle of his hatchet. If the ninjas were waiting for an apology, they would have a long wait. Billy the Dwarf was not in the habit of apologising to anyone.

A strange kind of tension had descended over the tavern. The barman had stopped dead in his tracks, a tea towel stuffed inside a pint glass, mid-polish.

Across various well-used tables, the tavern's drinking community had turned, in silence, to see the drama unfolding under the rackety old roof.

Even the clock on the wall had stopped.

A large rat, helping itself to the salted peanuts kept under the bar, left its foraging to peer around the bar, watching in squeakless awe.

And in the middle of all this silence, the deadly tableau. Six ninjas. One dwarf. Face to face like a portrayal of unevenly matched nemeses.

The silence was broken by Thorax, whose chair scraped noisily as he got up from his table and sauntered over to his friend.

"Everything okay, Billy?" He had asked. He wasn't sure, but he thought he detected some hostility in the air.

"I think there may be some trouble," Billy had murmured, his eyes half closed in careful appraisal, as he surveyed the poised ninjas.

Thorax turned to face the crouching ninjas. He smiled, warmly.

"You don't want any trouble, do you gentlemen?"

As one, the ninjas shouted out one harsh syllable and took a threatening step forward. Six curved swords rose up into the air, ready to slice on the downward stroke.

Billy the Dwarf had been shoulder-to-shoulder with Thorax in scuffles before. Together they had fought a variety of monsters and trolls and weird creeping things. Once they had done battle with Donald Trump's hair piece, which was perhaps their toughest fight to date. What Billy had learned over time, was that due to their respective sizes and fighting prowess, an unequal division of labour was necessary to ensure a successful outcome.

"I'll take the one on the end," he had said. "You take the other five."

And that was it.

Billy the Dwarf went at his chosen ninja with his hatchet, while Thorax used a variety of improvised weapons, including chairs, tables, glasses, bottles and the barman's tea-towel, to disarm and vanquish the remaining five.

By the time the fight was over, three or four minutes later, Thorax had piled all five bodies on top of each other, directly in front of the bar. The injuries sustained by the warriors at the hands of the barbarian would have filled a ledger. Thorax would have added the sixth ninja to the pile, but Billy the Dwarf had been so enthusiastic with his hatchet, that it would have taken too long to gather the parts up from around the tavern. As a token gesture, Thorax rested the sixth warrior's arm at the top.

It was a notable postscript to the incident that Billy the Dwarf didn't spill a single drop of the two tankards he was holding in one hand throughout the entire scuffle.

*

"And so you felled six ninjas," said Zeus.

"Five."

"Okay. Five ninjas. It hardly matters. You took on the ultimate disciplined fighting force and you crushed it, without a second thought."

"Well. They were rude."

Zeus shook his head in disbelief. He spilled out countless other examples of Thorax's undeniable barbarianness. His penchant for rescuing princesses from malign captivity. His uncanny knack of running into dark knights keen to do battle. His dealings with wizards and warlocks and goblins and elves. Dragons that he had slain. Trolls that he had fought.

"You must see that you live an extraordinary life," Zeus asserted. "You are not *the norm.*"

When it was put with the persistence and clarity that Zeus was now employing, Thorax had to admit that the evidence did stack up a bit.

The thought of it made his head feel numb. He had always seen himself as civil. Urbane. He was the model of courtesy. He believed in good manners and high morals. On top of all this, he had a sensitive streak the size of an eight-lane highway. Sometimes it had traffic cones on it.

He poured himself a third cup of tea and was pleased, through the haze of his emerging shock, to see that it was now extremely well brewed.

Without even asking, he poured Zeus another cup. He could see that Zeus's cup was empty and Thorax was nothing if not hospitable.

"So...you really think that I might be a barbarian, then?" He asked, in simple wonder.

Zeus nodded, dunking a third biscuit into his stewed cup of tea.

"Yes, you are. I am convinced of it."

Thorax sipped his tea. His eyes rested on his godly visitor.

"Well I never!" he said.

In the skies above Pestlewick a glorious telescope and a wondrous ear trumpet were retracted into the heavens, leaving a couple of clouds to swing back together like a pair of curtains.

God got straight on the phone.

"Ah yes, hello Mrs Thomas. Is John at home?"

"Yes, he's just watching The Weakest Link. I'll go and get him. One moment."

God waited while Mrs Thomas went to fetch her son. He heard her in the background.

It's for you. Who's winning? Oh - I know that one - Leo Sayer. *No. No.* Brian May! *I always get confused with those two, because of the hair...*

"Hello?" Came John Thomas's voice on the phone.

"John, it's God."

"Hello, God."

"How come you're watching The Weakest Link?"

"I always watch The Weakest Link."

"John, I'm not being funny, but the course of human salvation is in peril. I need you on the case. The Weakest Link can wait for now."

"Sorry, God. I just felt that I needed a break. I've been on it non-stop since we spoke yesterday."

"Things are moving faster than I had feared, John. Zeus is buttering up a barbarian, to get him onside."

"Is that bad?"

"Really bad. If he turns this into a quest, as he is clearly doing, having a barbarian on his side will give him a massive advantage. The barbarian will go at the plough like a bird at a worm. We've got to move quickly. I want you to get to the scrap yard, first thing, and get that plough."

"How do I do that?"

"Just use your initiative. Buy it, if you can. We have *got* to get that plough. I'll be at hand with all the Divine assistance you need. Just send up a prayer if you need anything. I'll keep a line free for you."

"I'll do my best."

In the background, God heard Mrs Thomas call out.

That woman is callous. Callous! Who, anywhere, *knows that the capital of Papua New Guinea is Port Moresby?*

"I do," said God, casually.

John Thomas took a deep breath.

"God, I wonder if I can ask You something?"

"Fire away."

"Well – this plough. I've been thinking. *I'm* a bachelor. If I get the plough...can I keep it? I could do with a bit of wealth."

"No. The plough needs to be cast back into the river, from whence it came. No man ought to have the power of the plough for his own ends."

"What if I keep it anyway?"

"Then you'll be rendered well and truly smat."

"Oh." John paused. "God. Can I ask You something else?"

"I'm starting to feel like *I'm* on The Weakest Link," said God with a chuckle.

"Well – people talk about the Holy Ghost. I was wondering. What *is* the Holy Ghost? I understand You. And I understand Jesus. But I can't quite figure out where the Holy Ghost fits into everything. What is it?"

God paused to think. He looked over at a framed picture of Himself, His son and the Holy Ghost that was hanging on His heavenly wall.

"The Holy Ghost. Well. The Holy Ghost is...sort of...sort of...a *triangle*," He said, finally. There was no other way to describe it. He could have said a *fuzzy* triangle but He

103

felt that would be complicating things too much. "Now get Me that plough."

"Okay, God. I'll see what I can do."

"Good. Good. Right. Cheerio, then."

"Bye."

"...Bye."

"......Bye."

God placed the phone back on its cradle and took a deep breath. He puffed out His cheeks and stared bleakly ahead of Him.

It had been a few years since He had felt this unsettled about anything.

John Thomas finished his shift in the early afternoon and as soon as he had handed the bus over to its next driver, he made his way to the industrial estate on the Wessex Road. He had no idea how he was going to approach the proprietor of the scrap yard but felt it couldn't be too difficult. The scrap yard was in the business of selling scrap for money. All Thomas had to do was offer the right price for the plough – and the Lord's work was done.

As he came within sight of the scrap yard, he began to feel a little unprepared. It occurred to him that he would look a bit suspicious, walking into the scrap yard with nothing but the clothes on his back. He needed a reason to be there. He stopped to think. Glancing up at the sky, he decided that a prayer could not do any harm. He sunk to his knees on the cold pavement, clasped his hands together and stretched his face up to the sky.

"O God, hear my prayer," he began. He was used to talking to God on the telephone. This method seemed a bit hit and miss. "Erm. It's me. John. John Thomas. I'm about to go and see if I can get the plough. But I could use some Divine assistance. Give me an excuse, O Lord, to venture into the yard. Use Thy holy wisdom to give me a pretence, under which I can ask for the plough. This I ask Thee, O Lord. Um. In Thy hallowed name. Who gavest me a loaf of bread. Thank You. Yours sincerely. John Thomas. Amen." He thought for a second, then added, "Bye...bye..."

In the sky above, a small hatch opened and an object was dropped through. It was so far up that it was invisible to the naked eye.

John rose to his feet and brushed his trouser legs down. He didn't move, and stood uncertainly, wondering if the Good Lord had heard him. He found it unlikely. He chewed his lip, unsure of what to do next. He would have to make a move sooner or later. He couldn't stand around all day waiting for inspiration to strike.

Ten minutes passed and inspiration didn't strike.

I'm just going to have to go for it, he told himself, finally. He was just about to make a bold path for the scrap yard when a police car pulled up alongside the kerb. It was a Fiat Panda. PC Terence Standing grabbed his hat from the passenger seat and climbed out of the car. Positioning his cap on his head, he walked over to John Thomas with an officious expression.

"I wonder if I might have a word, sir," he said.

"Of course, officer." John Thomas smiled. He was relieved to be thwarted from his mission, albeit momentarily.

"Do you mind telling me what you are doing here?" PC Standing looked John Thomas up and down, critically.

"Not at all. I was just about to pop into the scrap yard."

"Oh? What for?"

"Um. Just a browse, really."

"A browse?" Standing continued to look him up and down, unconvinced. "The thing is, I have had a report of a man - fitting your description - acting in a suspicious manner."

"Suspicious, officer?"

"On his knees. On the pavement. Praying." He glanced down at Thomas's trouser legs. "I see that your trouser legs are dirty."

Thomas shrugged. He decided the best course of action was to say as little as possible. If his mum found out he'd been questioned by a policeman she'd go mad.

Standing gazed at him for a few more moments. There wasn't much to go on. Praying in the street wasn't an offence as such. And the man seemed harmless enough. But these days, you had to be sure...

106

"Look," Standing took his hat of and twiddled it between his hands. "You're not one of them single cell fundamentalist terrorists I keep hearing about, are you?"

Thomas shook his head.

"No. I've thought about it. But no."

"Okay. Well, we'll leave it there..."

The car door hit the ground next to him with such force that for a split-second PC Standing thought a bomb had gone off in his face. For the briefest moment he thought the man that was standing before him had suicide bombed him. However, he quickly realised this was a ridiculous notion. A suicide bomber needed to pull a cord to detonate a bomb, something akin to a parachute cord or the activation string at the rear of a talking Action Man. Everyone knew that.

The man had been standing with his arms by his side for the duration of the event.

Besides, there was now a car door spinning on the pavement, which had just appeared out of nowhere. It looked like it belonged to an old Austin Maxi.[3] It was clearly this that had made the noise but where it had come from, Terence Standing was at a loss to know. It seemed to have just fallen from the sky.

"Bloody hell!" Standing exclaimed, catching his breath. "Where the hell did that come from?"

John Thomas shook his head, affecting alarm and confusion, though when the police officer wasn't looking, he winked conspiratorially up at the sky. *Thanks God.*

"I don't know," he said. "But I'll tell you what. We don't want it littering up the pavement. I'm going to the scrap yard – I'll take it with me."

---

[3] God did once do a tour of his worldly parish, back in the seventies. He used an Austin Maxi to do this as the Maxi had a fitted bed facility in the back and was designed for travelling. It was very much marketed on this basis, though not many people realise this today.

He scraped the car door up off the ground and carried it towards the scrap yard, leaving PC Standing alone on the pavement, fighting to catch his breath.

*

God's Fixer walked confidently through the open gates of the Minotaur Scrap Yard, holding the car door to his chest.

He looked around the untidy yard.

It was a maze of broken cars and vehicles. The ground was nothing more than compacted dirt, still hard from the frosty conditions of the morning. Cars were piled high, in ungainly stacks, obviously having been put there by the large magnetic crane in the middle of the yard. A broken old double-decker bus, smashed and punctured, loomed out from behind a stack of mangled vehicles. It saddened John Thomas to see it. Broken buses always saddened him.

He stood holding the door, wondering where he needed to go to make his presence known.

Just as he was wondering this, a family ambled into view from behind a pile of rusting metal. They were all holding hands, talking contentedly as they walked, happy and care-free. A man, a woman and two children, probably of around six and seven in age.

They strolled towards John Thomas, heading back towards the yard entrance.

A friendly shout came from the rear of the yard and Thomas saw a large figure emerge from the portacabin there. He gasped. He'd never seen anything like it. It had the well-toned body of a man and the head of a bull. Its head was huge and black, vicious looking, with two aggressive horns that curved out threateningly. The creature began to jog towards the family.

"*What the hell is that?*" Thomas heard himself say, the to the family: "Look out!"

The family glanced over at him, with mild interest.

"Behind you!" He almost screamed. "Run! For god's sake, *run*!"

The family looked around and saw the Minotaur jogging towards them. They stopped walking and waited for the creature to reach them. John Thomas watched in horror, dreading what was to come.

The Minotaur slowed to a walking pace and ambled his last few paces. It stopped in front of the family.

"See anything you liked?" It asked, its voice low and friendly.

"Oh, lots that we *liked*!" The father smiled broadly. "But nothing we really want, today."

"You've got some nice bumpers in," the mother chipped in.

The Minotaur nodded. As much as a bull can be said to smile, it smiled.

"We wanted a windscreen wiper!" Said the little girl.

"And a hubcap!" Said the boy.

Unable to resist the beautiful innocence of young children, the Minotaur told them all to wait there. It wandered off into the midst of the yard and came back a couple of minutes later, with its arms behind his back. When it reached the family it brought its arms out, to reveal its hidden treasure. It handed a windscreen wiper to the little girl and a hubcap to the boy, then patted them both on the head.

"Have those on me," it said, warmly.

The mother and the father looked at each other and beamed at the Minotaur.

"What do you say?" The father prompted his offspring.

"Thank you," the children chimed.

"We'll probably be back in a week or two," the father smiled warmly at the Minotaur. The Minotaur held up its hands.

"Any time. You know you're always welcome to have a look around."

They wandered off and as they passed John Thomas the father winked at him.

"Nice door," he said. "Looks like a Maxi." Without a further word, the family walked out through the yard entrance.

John Thomas was face to face with the Minotaur.

The Minotaur looked at him, its bullish face impassive. Its previous warmth had dissipated.

"Can I help you, sir?" It asked.

God's Fixer on Earth smiled.

"I've...got a car door for you," he said.

The Minotaur looked at it, largely uninterested.

"Looks like an old Maxi," it said. Thomas nodded. In truth, he had no idea. He wondered why God would have spare parts for an Austin Maxi.

"Do you want it?" Thomas asked.

"I can take it off your hands," the Minotaur offered. "I can't pay you for it though. It's not worth anything."

"That's fine. Thanks." John Thomas handed the car door over to the Minotaur. The Minotaur looked suspicious.

They stood for a few moments, gazing at each other. The Minotaur was watchful. John Thomas was smiling.

"Got any ploughs?" He asked.

The Minotaur threw the car door aside and it landed with a heavy thud. It took an aggressive stride towards Thomas and thrust its huge head forward so that it was bare inches away from Thomas's face. Its nostrils flared as it breathed and snorted, like a bull in an arena. Thomas saw that the Minotaur's eyes were bloodshot, as they rolled around its head. It began to swing its vast horns from side to side.

"Why do you want to know?" It growled in a voice like Grecian thunder. Its arms were outstretched, ready to pummel on a whim.

John Thomas stepped back, nervously.

"I...I'm just in the market for a plough, that's all."

"I haven't got any ploughs," the Minotaur pushed its huge face forwards. John Thomas felt hot breath on his cheek. "So you can just turn around and get the hell out of my yard."

"I'll pay handsomely?" Thomas suggested, his voice now something of a squeak.

The Minotaur roared. It was a roar of primaeval territory. A roar of jealousy. It shook the very ground and filled the skies above.

John Thomas backed away from the swaying beast. He could see madness in the creature's eyes. He thanked his Unofficial Employer that he hadn't worn his red cardigan.

"That's a no, then...?" He squeaked.

The Minotaur took great strides towards him. It roared again.

It towered over John Thomas like a bad dream, bearing down on him with all the fury of a maddened bull.

"You've got *three seconds* to *get out of my yard*," it threatened, its voice like jagged metal. "And if I see you here again, *I am going to tear you limb from limb*."

It began to count. By the time it got to "two", John Thomas was out of the yard and halfway up the road.

Sitting high in the cab of the Scania truck, Thorax the Barbarian rode shotgun with the god Zeus. They were headed for the Minotaur Scrap Yard.

Once Thorax had admitted - reluctantly at first - that he *may* have some barbaric qualities about him, it had been easy for Zeus to talk him into accepting his first quest. Using words like "destiny", "fate" and "glory" (and carefully avoiding words like "Tony" and "Blackburn", which were inexplicably at the front of his mind), Zeus had captured the barbarian's imagination and convinced him that he needed something purposeful to get his barbarianly teeth into.

He had outlined the story behind the bachelor's plough and explained to Thorax how important it was to gain ownership of the plough. He also told Thorax that as a barbarian, he would not be expected to accept the quest for nothing. As soon as Zeus had cultivated his first crop of gold, he would pay Thorax handsomely.

Thorax saw in this, the opportunity to make a real *go* of a new portable crepe retail outlet. This could set him up in business for a long time to come.

Zeus parked the lorry away from the scrapyard, out of sight. Thorax was sitting apprehensively on the passenger side, looking distinctly unbarbaric in his brown corduroy trousers and green cardigan.

"So just get in there and tell him you want a plough," said Zeus.

"And then what?"

"Well, hopefully he'll show you what he's got. I can't imagine he has got too many ploughs."

"How will I know which is the right plough?"

"The plough you are after was, in its day, a fiery red colour. Woven into its fabric were the very embers of Thor's furnace. But if this isn't obvious, just look for the most rusty, unkempt plough. Don't forget it has been in the Thames for a long, long time."

"And what if he doesn't show me any ploughs at all?"

"Just do what comes naturally to you. You are a barbarian. I don't think he'll be able to threaten you like he did me. I am sure you can be very persuasive, given the right motivation."

Thorax looked unsure. He took a few deep breaths.

"I'm really out of my comfort zone with this," he said, weakly. He wanted Zeus to let him off the hook.

"It's in your blood, Thorax. *It's in your blood.* Think of your crepes."

Thorax nodded, swung open the door and jumped down. He made his way towards the scrap yard like a man going to the gallows.

The Minotaur was near the front of the yard sorting through some old bits of exhaust pipe when Thorax slinked through the gates. He looked over at the barbarian and stood up to face him. Thorax smiled, bobbed his head and gave a little wave of his hand.

"Can I help you?" The Minotaur breathed, heavily. Old exhausts lay on the ground all around him.

"Yes, I hope so." Thorax scratched his chin. "I'm looking for something quite specific actually."

"Fire away. I'll probably have it here somewhere. Or something like it, anyway."

Thorax couldn't stop thinking about how the Minotaur had reacted when Zeus asked for a plough. The thought of conflict was tying him up in knots. He looked around the scrap yard, uneasily. The double-decker bus loomed out of the junk like an icon of joy.

"Well...um...have you got any...er...double-decker buses?" Thorax asked, weakly.

The Minotaur raised his bullish eyebrows, causing his horns to move back a little. He pointed over at the old bus, his broad face now helpful and open.

"There's that old bus over there. Needs a bit of TLC – but it's good for spares or repair. Why don't you go and have a look at it, see what you think?"

Thorax thanked the Minotaur and sauntered over to the bus, with false enthusiasm. Already, he was losing his grip on his purpose. It wasn't going to help that he didn't really know the first thing about buses.

On reaching the bus, he made a show of appraising it critically. He knew that the Minotaur was watching him and he knew that his acting skills were now essential if he was to drive his campaign forward.

He stroked his chin and wandered up and down the bus's broad flank, nodding to himself. He rapped his knuckles at various points along the bus, angling his head as though listening carefully to the tone and resonance. Affecting satisfaction, he then yanked the front door open (the hydraulics were not operational and he had to do this manually) and boarded the bus. He made a show of leaning over into the driver's cab and trying out the steering wheel. He then rapped the ceiling a few times and tested the device that wound the destination sign round. He cocked his head to one side and then jumped down, making his way back to the Minotaur with a couple of thoughtful backward glances.

As performances go, it was Oscar-winning.

"Well, what do you think?" Asked the Minotaur.

Thorax made a face like a plumber about to give an estimate.

"It's hard to say," he laboured. He shot the Minotaur a direct look. "It's not quite what I'm looking for. It's a nice bus, don't get me wrong. Were I a younger man, I'd snap it up. But...I don't know."

The Minotaur nodded.

114

"It's just not got that X Factor, has it?" He concurred. "I've been trying to knock it out for months but no one quite wants it. I'll probably end up scrapping it but...I don't know. It always feels sacrilegious, scrapping a bus."

"I know what you mean," Thorax nodded.

"Is there anything else you might be interested in?" The Minotaur asked.

Right into my hands! The barbarian's inner voice squeaked out triumphantly.

"No, I don't...*hang on though.*" Thorax pretended to be thinking. He looked at the Minotaur as though the thought had just occurred to him. "You don't happen to have any *ploughs*, do you?"

The air seemed to turn cold. The Minotaur froze. His eyes grew wide and his breathing quickened. Thorax saw the rage, a spark of fire in the Minotaur's eye.

"Why would I have ploughs?" He snarled.

"Well...a scrap yard...I just thought..."

"Does this look like a plough emporium to you?"

"No, but..."

The Minotaur exploded, spitting and growling at Thorax, as it moved towards him, with menace in its stride.

"*What do you know? Who sent you?*"

Thorax plumbed deep of the well that was his customer services experience, utilising his broad artillery of customer care skills.

"I merely enquired," he said, reasonably. "I'm certainly not out to upset you." He extended a hand of conciliation, as the Minotaur huffed and snorted loudly before him.

Roger's eyes were rolling in his head.

"Now let's just try and get some perspective," Thorax suggested. "I'm honestly not here to cause trouble. I'm Thorax, by the way. And you are...?"

"Roger," the Minotaur growled, defensively.

115

Thorax smiled.

"Well, Roger. It was just a passing interest, this thing with the plough. No ulterior motive. Just an interest. I'd always imagined you'd get ploughs in a scrap yard, that's all."

"Well you don't." Roger snarled.

Thorax shrugged.

"Pity," he said. "I like ploughs."

"I like ploughs too," growled Roger, with a glimmer of sentiment. "But there aren't any here. Now I'll kindly ask you to leave."

Thorax stood his ground for a moment or two. He and the Minotaur were evenly matched in terms of their size and brawn. But when it came to barbarity - if Zeus was to be believed - then Thorax had the edge. Roger would have about as much chance against Thorax as a Victorian pugilist, playing by the Queensbury Rules, would have against a terrorist with an Uzi.

And yet...

Thorax gazed at Roger carefully and saw anguish in his eyes. He looked thoughtful for a few moments, before nodding decisively.

With nothing further to say, he turned on his barbaric heel and walked away.

*

"I don't know," whined Thorax as they rumbled along in Zeus's Scania. "He seemed like a nice guy. I liked him."

Zeus made an exaggerated check of his mirrors, emphasising his disbelief through the expressive medium of driving.

"He's a *Minotaur!*"

"That doesn't make him any less human!" Thorax paused. "Well. Okay. It does. But it seemed wrong, taking it from him by force."

"You're a barbarian. You want something. He's got it. Nothing should stand in your way."

"He let me look around his bus," argued Thorax.

Zeus made a clicking sound. Words failed him.

"It seemed wrong, that's all I'm saying. He didn't want me there. I'm not even sure he *has* the plough."

"Oh, he has the plough." Zeus sighed, falling silent as he negotiated a roundabout.

"I just couldn't get violent with him, Zeus. I just couldn't."

Zeus shook his head, hopelessly.

He leaned forward and switched on the radio. Pop star Alesha Dixon was singing something about the washing up and Zeus found himself wondering what had possessed her to alight on a subject so mundane to sing about.

God was pleasantly surprised that for once John Thomas picked the phone up himself.

"Did you get the car door?" He asked, eagerly.

"Yes, thanks. What was it? An old Maxi?"

"Yes."

"How come You had spares from an old Maxi handy? Do You own one?"

"Some of one, yes. It's missing a door, now."

Thomas mused over the thought of the one, true, monotheistic, universal God in an Austin Maxi. Arguably a spacious car, it seemed to him that even a Maxi would have difficulties accommodating omnipresence.

"So how did you get on?" Asked God.

"Not brilliantly, I must admit." He heard God sigh impatiently down the phone. "I tried, God. I did try. But the owner of the scrap yard...well. He's pretty fearsome. And he gets pretty touchy when you ask him about ploughs."

"Well, did you show him your badge?" God dithered.

It was John Thomas's turn to sigh. God had it in His head that all you had to do to command authority in any situation, was to show your badge: **John Thomas, Fixer.** God had an unsophisticated, rather naive belief in the power of a badge.

"I was wearing it. It didn't make any difference."

"Did you offer him money?"

"Yes. He wasn't interested."

"And what about My name? Did you invoke My name?"

"Only as I was legging it out of the gate."

"You ran?"

"He chased me. God, You have to see this guy to believe him."

118

"Okay." The good Lord puffed out His cheeks. Thomas could hear Him do it. In the background he heard a choir of heavenly angels singing *Phantom of the Opera*. "You've got to get that plough, John Thomas. You've got to."

"I will, God. I've got a plan up my sleeve."

"Work fast, John Thomas. Work fast."

"Leave it with me, God. Rest assured, in Your omnipotence, that plough is as good as ours."

"Mine."

"Yes. Yours."

God was just about to say something else, when He burst into an angry shout, which was muffled by His hand covering the mouthpiece.

"*Raphael – for My sake, stop leaving underpants on top of the fridge!*"

When He came back on the line, He sounded harassed.

"Look, John, I have to go. I've just caught Raphael putting his pants on the fridge again. Get Me that plough, John Thomas. Just get Me that plough."

In the night sky above Pestlewick, a magical journey was underway. It was the stuff of childish fantasy.

A silver sleigh, pulled by six galloping reindeer flew through the chilly air, leaving a trail of glitter in its wake. The reindeer pulled and dived, steering the sleigh through the darkened void, beautifully framed by the countless stars above.

It was a picture of innocent dreams, of boundless hope, of childlike excitement. It spoke of goodwill and of giving, and of selfless charity. It was the symbol of man's warmest qualities.

The reality was much different.

Santa Claus sat confidently at the front of the sleigh, the reins held loosely in one hand. In his other hand he gripped a large Cuban cigar, which dispersed its odorous smoke into the empty air. He was wearing a bold suit, a throwback from the 1930s.

It was Claus's style.

The grey pin-striped suit would have cost several thousand pounds, had he paid for it. He wore white spats on his gleaming shoes and a cream fedora hat was perched elegantly on his head. His bright red silk tie was matched by his bright red silk socks. He was a picture of twentieth century decadence, and this was mirrored in his face which, despite his bushy white beard and fluffy eyebrows, was flushed with excessive living and as hard as granite.

Father Christmas wasn't new to crime. He had once led one of the most powerful underworld gangs in Prohibition Chicago, a gang that rivalled even Al Capone's organisation.

Since moving to Boomtown in the early 1990s, he had re-ignited his criminal interests and now boasted an empire of criminal activities that included drugs, prostitution, extortion, organised theft and arms dealing. Claus's gang dominated the underworld landscape of Boomtown and while he had an army of professional criminals on his firm, large bodies of the civil service were also on the firm's payroll. It was said that around half of the Thames Valley Police force was loyal to Santa Claus, while magistrates, judges and waste removal technicians had strong affiliations to the firm.

The Member of Parliament for Boomtown West practically ran the constituency on behalf of Claus.

Conversely, the Member of Parliament for Boomtown East, having refused the "Christmas shilling", lived in constant fear, having suffered numerous threats and accidents since.

Only a handful of very close associates knew that the white-haired bearded gangster, popularly referred to as "Santa Claus", actually *was* the festive personification himself. He was well-known as a criminal figurehead in the area and was accepted as a businessman in many circles. While his jolly, ruddy-faced appearance was unusual for a boss of the underworld, this did not detract from the fear he inspired in people. What was known was that he was a violent and ruthless man who would stop at nothing to achieve his ends. It was also known that if you needed anything doing, of a criminal nature, he was the man to talk to.

On the night that Zeus had approached Santa Claus for a loan of £100 for a cheap satellite navigation system, the festive personification had been at the pub collecting protection money. The pub landlord had been paying Claus for many years, for a service that essentially amounted to not having his pub burned to the ground.

The money due to Claus's firm was collected every two weeks, when a delegated member of the organisation would pay a visit to the *Bird in Hand*. Often, Claus would send one of his men. Vinnie "The Saw" Hopkins was a favourite for this sort of work, but occasionally Claus would drop by himself. He liked to keep the personal connection with all of his business interests.

Zeus was used to members of Claus's criminal organisation dropping into his local. All the regulars were. He knew only too well the nature of their business. Characterised by expensive suits, heavy jewellery and hard-set features, they would enter the pub as though they owned it, and would expect immediate attention at the bar. If they ordered a drink, they would never expect to pay. And when they saw Dave, the barman, a warm handshake was always accompanied by the discrete exchange of a brown envelope.

For all his historical godliness, even Zeus himself had no idea that the gangster in their midst was the real Santa Claus. It didn't really matter. With the need for a satnav bearing down on his shoulders, the gangster had been the only person Zeus could turn to for a loan.

God, did he regret it now.

*

The reindeer scooped the sleigh up with a final flourish, spreading glitter all over the sky, before making a fast and graceful descent. It was the early hours of the morning and streets of Pestlewick were empty, but for a couple of milk floats.

Claus guided the sleigh skilfully on to a frost-covered rooftop, coming to a graceful stop next to the chimney. He had calculated his landing quite deliberately. He was on Pearbury Hill, directly above the chip shop. Immediately below him, just a chimney-drop away, was the target apartment. And it was here that he intended to pay this nocturnal visit.

Zeus owed him £15,000. There was no ambiguity about it. He had lent the impoverished old lorry driver £100 and expected repayment with interest. Admittedly, an interest rate of fifteen thousand percent was excessive in comparison to some interest rates available on the market (Claus had seen

122

that Natwest was offering a 1.5% interest rate on short-term loans). But the reason Zeus had come to Claus in the first place was because his credit rating prevented mainstream organisations from lending to him. He thus represented a risk – and Claus reflected that risk in his rates of interest. Furthermore, the interest rate was exponential. Had Zeus paid back the loan within a day, the rate would only have been 100% and that would have been an end to it. Zeus's own lack of financial care and his fiscal procrastination had led to the punitive interest rate he was now facing. It was his own fault.

He had just a couple more days to find the money he owed.

Santa Claus as paying a quiet nocturnal visit to Zeus, to remind him how important it was that he repaid the loan. In his experience few things were quite as effective in concentrating the mind, as being woken up in your own bed, in the middle of the night, with the threat of dismemberment. Claus was seasoned in these matters.

Invigorated by the chill night air, he stepped out of the sleigh.

He reached into the back, into the sleigh's hold, and brought out a claw hammer. It was stained blood red from the last time he had used it. He tested the hammer against his palm a couple of times, to get a feel for its weight and balance. It was a trusty bit of kit and it felt friendly and warm in his hand. With a satisfied nod he slipped it into his belt and mooched over to the chimney.

Checking around quickly, to make sure no one was watching, he swung both legs over the chimney pot and dropped himself in.

It was a ludicrously thin chimney and it was only when Claus reached the base of it that he understood the predicament he was in.

At some point in the past, the fireplace had been bricked over.

There was no way out.

Santa was now pressed against the inside of a sooty chamber, contorted and crushed and unable to move. He pushed his bulk against the bricked-up fireplace, hoping that the brickwork was weak and that it would give beneath his weight. It didn't. It had the integrity of a Pharaoh's outhouse.

Behind the wall he could hear Zeus snoring loudly.

He tried to look up, but the chimney was so constrictive that he could only move his head a short way. His arms were down by his side, crushed against the tight sooty walls. His legs were twisted together and he could feel the claw-hammer pressing uncomfortably into his thigh. The only way was up. But he couldn't move. His eyes blazed in the pitch darkness as the reality of his situation dawned on him.

Father Christmas was in someone's chimney on an illegitimate pretext. And he was *stuck*.

Evening came early.

It was dark when John Thomas rang the doorbell of the little terraced house. The smell of coal smoke was in the air, something that always gave Thomas strong feelings of nostalgia. Why this was, he had no idea. He'd never had a coal fire in his life.

The bell chimed politely and Thomas waited for the lady to come to the door. As it happened, there wasn't actually a physical door there. It had been blown off by a doodlebug at the end of the Second World War and Edna Larkin had never seen fit to have a new one fitted. She was used to a world, after all, in which it was always safe to leave your front door open without the fear of being burgled.

When she appeared, Thomas saw her to be an elderly lady. She wore an expression of attentive enquiry and had grooves on her shoulders where her dome-shaped umbrella had left its mark. John Thomas gave her a warm, disarming smile. He was pretty good with old dears, even if he did say so himself. He got a lot of them on the bus and was proud of the repartee he had with them. What he did not know about colostomy bags and featureless biscuits wasn't worth knowing.

With her pale blue acrylic dress, her floral apron and her grey hair in a bun, she looked every bit the perfect old granny.

"Yes, dear?" She asked, sweetly.

John Thomas' smile became even wider.

"Ah, hello!" He bobbed his head inoffensively. "I'm sorry to trouble you – I just thought I might have a quick word."

The plan had come to John Thomas while he was running at speed away from the Minotaur Scrap Yard. If he could find the original owner of the plough then he might be able to use legal grounds to get the plough back from the Minotaur. Possession is nine-tenths of the law after all.[4]

With this notion, John Thomas had prayed to God to send him guidance in finding the original owner of the plough. Twenty minutes later a torn piece of paper fluttered out of nowhere and landed at his feet. It read: *I should'nt really give out confidenshal informashun, but...*

Edna Larkin's name was scrawled untidily on the scrap of paper, along with an address. Thomas was shocked by the Good Lord's spelling and His incorrect use of punctuation but he thought it best to keep it to himself. Bearing in mind God's omniscience, he hoped to buggery that He hadn't heard the thought.

The old woman looked uncertain.

"I don't want to be rude, dear," she said. "But I'm just in the middle of my fish supper. Well, I don't usually have one unless it is a Friday...but I just fancied it tonight."

"Oh, that's alright," said Thomas. "I don't want to take up any of your time. And I wouldn't want to stand between a lady and her fish supper!"

He smiled broadly and saw that his charm was taking effect. Edna was dribbling.

"Well, alright then, dear. What can I do for you?"

"Do you remember taking a plough to the scrap yard a few days ago?"

Edna nodded, pleasantly.

"Of course I do, duck. It's hard to forget. I think I put my back out!"

"Oh dear! Are you alright now?"

"Oh yes. Apart from the odd little mishap. I burst a varicose vein, you know. And I lost control of my bladder. Sometimes you wonder if it was all worth it!"

---

[4] Which pisses demons off no end. They see it as a discriminatory imbalance.

"I know what you mean! I was wondering how you came to find the plough."

Edna looked thoughtful.

"Ooo – now there's a question. My memory isn't what it used to be. Now let me think. It was in the river..."

"Did someone point you to it?"

"Yes. Our Gavin, he...no, wait a minute. I tell a lie. I just found it. That's right. I was walking along the river. I'd just got my pension, you see. And I saw it. Just beneath the surface it was. I thought it was a bike."

"And so you decided to dredge it up and take it to a scrap yard?"

"Yes, that's right, dear."

"It must have been quite difficult to get it out. Who helped you?"

"Oh, no one! I managed to find a van, you see. So I broke into the van, hotwired it, hooked the plough up to the towing hitch and dragged it out."

"By yourself?"

"Yes, dear. I had to give it some throttle, I can tell you! It was well wedged in. It reminded me of the time an unexploded doodlebug landed in our street, back in the war. It wedged itself in a crack in the middle of the road. Ooo, it were a beggar to move! I remember old Joe the butcher tried to pull it out with a winch. But it went off and blew his legs off."

She chuckled at the memory.

"So...you don't know who put it there? You don't know who it actually belongs to?"

"The plough? No. It looked as though it had been there for years. I don't imagine anyone owns it as such. Why? Are you after them for fly tipping?"[5]

---

[5] A variation on cow tipping. Cow tipping sees the perpetrators sneaking up on cows during the night, while they sleep, and pushing them on to their sides. Fly tipping is the same sort of thing, but on a smaller scale.

"No, no. I'm just interested to find out who owns it."

"Well, I don't know who *did* own it. But old Roger down at the scrap yard – he owns it now. And he's eighty quid the lighter for it."

John Thomas thanked Edna and told her to enjoy the rest of her evening.

As he walked back down the garden path, the smell of burning coal lingering in his nostrils, he knew that he had already hit a dead end with this hopeful line of enquiry. Getting his hands on the plough was going to need something more than proof of legal ownership.

He sighed as he reached the garden gate.

From behind him in the house, he could hear the clattering of stainless steel cutlery, accompanied by the squelching sound of a toothless old dear going hell for leather on her fish supper.

From his squashed position behind Zeus's sealed up fireplace, Santa Claus listened to the ancient god's morning routine.

The alarm clock went off and was banged into silence after about half a minute.

A five-minute silence followed.

The alarm clock went off again and, once more, was banged into silence. This happened two more times, before Claus finally heard Zeus grumble that the nights were getting shorter. He then yawned loudly, in an exaggerated fashion.

Claus stared blankly into nothingness as he heard Zeus stumbling around.

There was the sound of a kettle being filled. Cupboards were opened and there was the sliding of drawers. There were some scuffling sounds and then Zeus's voice, sounding annoyed.

He was talking to himself.

Why do I never have a complete pair of socks? How can they all be odd?

Further scrabbling.

This is ridiculous. I've never even owned pink fluffy ones. Where is my cardie? Why has it disappeared? Why can't anything stay where I put it?

A dull *flump*, like a pile of clothes falling on the floor.

Oh for...why have I never got any room?

A pause.

How the hell did my toy cheeseburger get in here?

Claus listened with dull impatience. It was impossible to tell but he estimated that he had been stuck in this position, squashed in this chimney, for at least six hours. As accustomed as he was to being down chimneys, the duration was never usually more than a few seconds. Even by the standards of a Victorian urchin, this was turning into a marathon.

He was uncomfortably aware of his reindeer up on the roof and of his sleigh glittering into view as daylight broke. There was nothing he could do. He hoped with every nerve in his personified body that no one walking the streets below would chance to look up.

Being stuck in a chimney was hard. Having to listen to the early-morning routine of an ancient god was nigh unbearable.

Zeus made a cup of tea and it obviously perked him up because a few minutes later, he was whistling tunelessly. Claus winced, unable to escape, unable to distract himself, as the whistling continued. It was beyond irritating. He felt sure that under the Geneva Convention his predicament would be outlawed on the grounds of torture.

By the time Zeus finally left the flat, slamming the door loudly behind him, the father of the Christmas season was banging his head violently and repeatedly against the flue.

The arse-end of Zeus's Allegro was now so close to the ground that when he went over a bump, the bounce caused contact to be made. In the rear-view mirror he saw sparks fly out from the back of the car. Now, as he drove along, he was not so much looking ahead of him as gazing up into the sky. There was no doubt that the car would soon be meeting its maker (up in that great British Leyland factory in the sky) and he hoped beyond hope that the plough would be his by then.

The car squeaked, bounced and scraped its way into Horseshoe Lane and Zeus was relieved when he reached Thorax's house. The car no longer gave him confidence that he would conclude a journey once he had embarked on it. It reminded him of a flaming chariot he once had, with a wonky wheel.

Thorax the Barbarian was inside cleaning his windows and he waved at Zeus with a yellow duster when he saw him arrive. Zeus winced at the fact his chosen barbarian was wearing an apron and had Johnny Mathis playing on full volume as he cleaned. He strode down the path, aware of the perennials that Thorax had sown into his flower bed. The barbarian came to the door and stood expectantly, a can of window cleaner in one hand, his yellow duster in the other.

"We've got to go and see the witches," Zeus said.

"Do we have to?" The barbarian was a gnat's flutter away from whining.

"Thorax. You really need to focus on this quest. I cannot overstate its importance. We have got to get the plough. Yesterday you failed."

"I wouldn't call it failure, just consideration for..."

"You *failed*." Zeus let the word drop like a stone. "Now. We need to find a way to overcome the Minotaur. And for that, we need the witches."

Thorax sighed. The duster hung limply in his hand.

"I suppose we could, if you think it's necessary."

"I do. Now put your cleaning condiments down. Take your apron off. And start behaving like the barbarian you are."

*

Thorax had to scrunch his entire body up to fit into the Allegro. Every time Zeus changed gear he brushed the barbarian's leg, a fact that neither of them alluded to but both were equally embarrassed about. For any casual pedestrian, the sight of the lurid orange car bouncing past, stuffed full of beard and barbarian, and sending showers of sparks all over the road behind it, would have been an arresting sight.

At one point along the journey they passed a blind man and his dog. Hearing the scraping, squeaking din as it passed him by, the man tensed up in horror, thinking that Armageddon had arrived. He then relaxed, realising that he had made a schoolboy error and that it was merely an Austin Allegro with knackered suspension.

They pulled up outside *Dun Roamin.*

Zeus left the engine running and waited for Thorax to get out.

Thorax looked at him, a slight look of panic on his face.

"We are going in together, aren't we?" He asked.

"I'd love to join you, I really would," said Zeus. "But I think I've used up all of my goodwill allowance with those ladies. Anyway, this is your quest. To be honest, I shouldn't really be getting involved in it as much as I am. I feel like your mum, dropping you off at school. You need to take ownership of your own quest, Thorax. It's how these things work."

"Well...what am I supposed to say?"

Zeus stared at him, blankly.

"Any normal barbarian would smash his way in and demand that they tell him how to get the plough. If they so much as hesitated, he would massacre them with his weapon of choice."

"That seems a bit harsh."

"Yes. You'll probably suit a different approach. Perhaps you should just ask them, nicely, how you can get hold of the bachelor's plough."

"What if they get angry?"

"What do you mean?"

"What if they don't want to tell me and they get...you know...angry?"

"Well, just get angry back at them. Remember who you are. Remember *what* you are. They're three frail old women. I'm sure you can persuade them."

Thorax looked doubtful as he unfolded himself from the car.

A barbarian disappearing into the jungle that was the front garden of *Dun Roamin* should have been an awesome sight. Thorax, though, merely wove the illusion of a large man walking into a garden centre. He took a path through the garden, treading carefully over the creeping undergrowth and picking his way through the hanging tendrils of sprawling ivy and drooping branches. The garden seemed to fall silent, interested by the appearance of the hulking brute in its midst.

The barbarian reached the door of the bungalow.

He was shocked by the ramshackle nature of the place and wondered how anyone could let their home fall into such disrepair. The roof was falling in and there were large gaping holes in it. Some of the windows were smashed but those that were intact were cracked and grimy. The sills were grubby and chipped with flaking paint. The smell of damp fungus oozed from the dwelling.

Thorax shuddered and thought gratefully of his own cosy dwelling.

He listened for any sounds coming from within and thought he heard a low bubbling sound and some quiet cackling.

Realising there was no doorbell, he pushed the letterbox in and let it go again. It made a muffled thump. There was a quick intake of breath from inside.

A few sharp, whispered words and then:

"Come in! It's open!"

Thorax pushed through the door and walked into the bungalow.

*

He gazed in horror at the three old hags crowded round the cauldron. They all stared out at him with eager malevolence, yet he saw that their eye sockets were empty, gaping voids. Their clothes were tattered rags, their faces pinched and hateful. He felt his skin crawl at the insects which lumbered through their greasy, matted hair. The room was humid and smelled of damp masonry and stale urine. The cauldron bubbled and he thought he saw a human hand float to the surface, to be pushed down promptly by one of the crooked hags.

One of the witches was holding a glass ball to her face and she seemed to be staring at him with more interest than the others.

"What do you see?" Asked one of them.

"Tell us what you see," barked the second.

The witch with the eye stared at Thorax for some time, her head jerking from side to side as she examined their visitor.

"It's a man," she said, with relish. "A big man. A *healthy* man."

The other two witches chomped their lips hungrily.

134

"Do you come to seek our guidance?" Asked one of the other witches. She was smiling, a contorted, eager grimace.

Thorax smiled, as pleasantly as he could in the circumstances.

"Actually, yes," he said. "I do need your help. If that's possible?"

The witches chuckled darkly.

"Oh yes," they said, slowly. "Of *course* that is possible. Why don't you come closer, so that we can all talk more easily?"

As he stepped closer to the cauldron, Thorax saw the witch with the eye shuffle so that she was behind her two friends. This was the Heimlich formation that the witches had decided on, to protect them from further eye-theft.

The basic principle of the Heimlich formation is that the witch with the eye stands at the back, peering over the right should of the witch in front. That witch stands behind the final witch, so that she is also peering over her right shoulder. The rear witch holds the eye close to the middle witch's head, directly above her shoulder.

The idea of the Heimlich formation is to keep the eye protected from attack, with several layers of defence in place to keep it safe. It is a text-book manoeuvre for witches with shared faculty of sight, to be used at times of ocular vulnerability.

Thorax approached the cauldron. He watched the witches suspiciously.

"I'm after a plough," he said, as he reached the edge of the cauldron. The thick liquid inside was sludge-brown and slick with grease. There was hair floating in it. There were roots and leaves. He saw a piece of rotten meat bob to the surface before sinking back down. A few maggots broke away and wriggled lethargically in the soup. It stank of rotten meat and vomit.

"A plough?" Said the witch at the front.

"The bachelor's plough," said the middle one, with certainty.

Thorax nodded eagerly.

"That's right. I need to get hold of the bachelor's plough. The thing is, I know where it is. It is in a scrap yard. But the guy that owns the scrap yard - he's a kind of cow, or something - he doesn't seem to want to let it go. He won't even let me see it. I was wondering if you might tell me how I can get it from him?"

The witches all fell into a dark rumination and they began to murmur incoherently.

Their mouths worked, their eyeless sockets stared out. They seemed to be thinking, while they groaned and chattered like pigeons in a roost.

"It can't be done," said the one with the eye, finally.

"But surely there must be a way?" Thorax was pleading.

All three of them were shaking their heads. The middle witch spoke.

"The owner of the scrap yard is..."

"*The Minotaur*," crowed the front witch, finishing the middle one's sentence.

"He loves ploughs," said the witch with the eye. "You'll never prise a plough away from him once he has it."

"Never."

"Never."

"But I've got to get it," Thorax argued weakly. "I have to find a way."

The witches became quiet once more, chattering and murmuring to themselves.

"Well maybe..."

"There *is* a way..."

They all began to cackle, conspiratorially.

Suddenly all three witches were glaring at him, intensely.

"If it's not too much trouble, I'd love to hear it." Thorax smiled.

The witches paused, staring at him excitedly. As one, they spoke.

"Medusa!" They said.

Their filthy old voices combined obscenely in the damp air.

"Come again?"

"Medusa!" The middle witch leaned forward, over the shoulder of the one in front. "Therein lies the only way to defeat the Minotaur. Therein lies a sure way to get the plough."

"The bachelor's plough!" Cried the one at the front, delightedly.

Her sightless eyes drilled into him and he found himself having to turn away from her grotesque grin.

"Medusa the Gorgon," whispered the witch with the eye. She was smiling horribly. "Any creature that looks into her eyes..."

"*Turns to stone!*" The witch at the front shouted out the words in a kind of ecstasy.

"Capture the Gorgon," grinned the old hag in the middle, clapping her hands. "And put her before the Minotaur. When he is stone, he will *never* be able to prevent you from taking the plough."

The witches broke into a cacophony of excited laughter.

"And where do I find this Gorgon? This Medusa?" Thorax was unconvinced by the whole thing. It sounded far-fetched.

The witches gave up Medusa's location with a shared cackle.

Thorax had expected her to live in a cave, or on the Stygian wastelands, or on the putrid banks of the River Styx. The address of 59 Beverley Road came as a surprise to him.

Thorax had known Beverley Road all his life and he never realised a Gorgon lived there.

When the witches described her, he wondered how he had not noticed a woman with venomous snakes sprouting from her head. But sometimes you just missed the obvious, he supposed.

"But beware!" The old hags leaned towards him. "If you look her in the eye, *you yourself* will become as stone."

"Blimey," he said.

The witch with the eye cocked her head to one side.

"Now, dear," she crooned. Her voice was like rusting metal. "Why don't you look into the cauldron, to see what you must do?"

"Ah yes!" Said the second. "Look inside, *deep* inside. For in its depths, you will see your destiny."

"*Your future!*"

Thorax raised his eyebrows.

"What – I just need to...?"

"Look into the cauldron, yes." The witches were salivating as Thorax moved towards the cauldron. "Lean close..."

"*Look deep within...*"

"See your answer swimming in its depths..."

"Like an old tyre," the witch at the front said, weakly. The other two paused visibly at the dubious simile. They chose to ignore it.

Thorax peered over the side of the cauldron and positioned himself lower so that his head was just inches from the stinking contents.

It bubbled and plopped before him.

He looked hard but he couldn't see anything that might resemble his destiny. A pig's trotter faded into view for a moment, its skin hanging ragged from the bone, but he assumed that wasn't the destiny they were talking about. He certainly hoped not. It seemed poorly lacking, as far as destinies went.

He was concentrating hard, trying to see into the murky depths, when the witches pounced. Like a pack of animals, they circled their prey with lightning speed. They each put their withered, clawed hands on the back of his head and pushed, hard.

They had done this before and the unexpectedness of their attack, twinned with the poor balance of the victim as he leaned forwards into the cauldron, usually sent him tumbling into its bubbling depths, to meet his grisly end.

Thorax, however, had the immovability of a mountain.

He continued to stare into the foul and putrid liquid, as the three hags pushed down forcefully on his head. It was like pushing down on a brick wall. They heaved and slammed and worked every move they knew to get their visitor into the cauldron. Thorax didn't even notice the attention. He stared into the belly of the cauldron, faithfully trying to locate his destiny. Eventually, the witches gave up, and staggered back, breathing hard with the exertion of it all.

Thorax stood up and shrugged.

"Be damned if I can see it," he said, simply. "Mind you, I can never see those magic eye things, either. You know, where you're supposed to see the Mona Lisa or something, in a random pattern. It's probably the same sort of thing. My mind just doesn't work that way."

The witches stared and said nothing.

He looked disappointed as he left but he thanked them for their help. They had told him how to get the plough and that was what he had come for.

Right now, he couldn't wait to get home for a nice hot shower. Being in that place made him feel dirty.

With Zeus gone, Father Christmas used the claw hammer to scrape at the mortar of the chimney. He wondered how long it would take him to get the soot out of his beard. He was caked in the stuff. However long it took, he mused, it would take twice as long to get Zeus' infernal whistling out of his head.

He had continued to bang his head violently against the flue long after Zeus had left that morning but finally he exorcised the cacophonous demons from his head and began to think about how to get out of his predicament.

The brick wall in the fireplace was sturdy, but it occurred to him that if he could manoeuvre the claw hammer enough to start scraping the cement away, then he might loosen the integrity of the wall and eventually smash through. It was the only way. There wasn't a burger's chance in Graceland that he would be able to manoeuvre himself back up the chimney. The only way was through.

It had taken a lot of concentration and considerable patience, but he eventually managed to ease the hammer out of his belt and into such a position that he was able to begin scraping.

He had been going at it for three or four hours when he finally felt a few bricks begin to loosen. Half an hour later he made the breakthrough he needed – and with a final solid push, the wall gave under his assault and crashed in, all over Zeus's threadbare carpet, in a cloud of soot. Father Christmas heaved himself out of the fireplace and stood up slowly. His back had seized up in the chimney and he winced with pain. He was black with soot and saw that Zeus's flat had not fared much better.

He glanced around.

It was more of a bedsit, really. The room clearly doubled up as a sitting room and a bedroom. The unmade bed was against the wall and puddles of underwear littered the floor around it. A small kitchen area was unseparated from the living and sleeping area. The bathroom was small and windowless, and its door was hanging off its hinges. There were a few sticks of furniture – a worn out old chair, a rickety chest of drawers and a wardrobe that leaned so dramatically, at a forty-five degree angle, that it looked set to tumble at any time. The place was a state. Even before Claus had come crashing through and brought half a tonne of rubble into the room, it had clearly been a total mess.

He scratched his beard and a shower of soot fell to the ground.

He wondered why there was a toy cheeseburger on top of the chest of drawers.

The sudden explosion of soot had coated the walls and much of the furniture. Had it been a more salubrious dwelling, Claus might have ransacked the place for any valuables. He doubted if there was anything of value here, however. The toy cheeseburger and the cheap yellow underpants on the floor summed it up, really. The wall around the fireplace was black and he saw a perfect canvas to leave a message. He scrawled a message into the soot, to be seen by Zeus when he returned:

Be clever. £15k by tomorrow. Or else. Merry Xmas.

When he stumbled out of the flat, blinking into the sunlight, he gazed up and saw his reindeer and sleigh perched on the roof. It was fortunate for Claus that Pearbury Hill never gave anyone a reason to look up. Pedestrians on Pearbury Hill always tended to watch the ground at their feet. Drivers watched the road ahead. On the roof, the sleigh glinted in the midday sun. A few cars idled past and the drivers looked over in amazement at the blackened figure standing in the street. His eyes blinked out, white within the soot, giving him the curious appearance of a vaguely festive Black and White Minstrel. His beard had lost its lustre. Even his spats were black.

He whistled up to his reindeer and they looked down obediently. A lesser animal might not have recognised its master but the reindeer were well-trained in the vagaries of chimney diving. They saw Claus and they understood his command.

With a perfectly synchronised prance they leapt up into the sky, scattering silver glitter into the air. After completing a quick airy circle they dived down gracefully, pulling the sleigh behind them. They stopped to let Claus board the sleigh and within seconds Father Christmas had taken hold of the reins and given them a quick flick. The reindeer didn't hesitate. Moments later they were airborne and the ground was far below.

Claus was so exhausted by his experience – and so angry by his failed mission – that he didn't even notice the police car screech to a halt to avoid him, as his somewhat unconventional vehicle took off into the sky.

"How did it go?" Asked Zeus, as soon as Thorax had scrunched tightly back into the passenger seat. He gave the car some throttle and they bounced away from the kerb. Sparks flew out behind them.

"Better than I expected," mused the barbarian. "They weren't so bad, really."

"Did they try to eat you?"

"No."

"Did you have to steal the eye?"

"No, they were very open with me. It wouldn't have been easy to get the eye, anyway. They were kind of standing behind each other, with the eye at the back."

"That'll be the Heimlich formation," Zeus smiled to himself. The witches were upping their game. "What happened, then?"

"Well, I told them I wanted the plough and asked them how I could get Roger to give it up."

"And?"

"Apparently there's some Gorgon or something, lives on Beverley Road."

"Medusa," Zeus nodded, thoughtfully. "Yes."

"From what the witches were saying, anyone that looks her in the eye turns to stone. All I have to do is get her to the scrap yard and put her in front of Roger. He'll turn to stone and Bob's your uncle. I take the plough."

Zeus glanced over at his passenger.

"Hang on a minute. You weren't willing to do some simple, rudimentary violence to him. But you're happy to have him turned to stone?"

"Yes. Well – it's not the same, is it?"

143

"If you say so. So we need to use Medusa. How do you intend to go about it? You need to be careful with Medusa, my friend. One look from her, and you're toast."

Thorax gazed out of the window.

"I need to think about it."

"You could chop her head off and take it to the scrap yard. It's only the head that you need, really. That's what Perseus did, when he defeated the kraken."

Thorax pondered the image that had suddenly appeared in his head, of a warrior holding a severed head up before a cream cracker. He was baffled by the idea – it seemed very much like using a sledgehammer to crack a nut – but he didn't pursue it.

"It seems a bit..."

"Harsh. Yes, I thought you might say that. Well, it's something to think about. Medusa won't go willingly with you. You mark my words. She's a difficult customer."

Thorax felt emboldened. He knew how to deal with difficult customers. Mr Biggins had come into the greetings card shop pretty much on a monthly basis and he was impossible. Nothing was ever right for him and he always haggled for a discount.

"I'll give it some thought," he said, quietly.

All of a sudden, Zeus looked in the rear-view mirror and cursed. A police car had pulled up behind, with its blue light on.

The ancient god gritted his teeth.

"I don't believe it. It's the old bill," he said, and pulled over with some trepidation.

*

PC Standing walked authoritatively up to the side of the knackered Allegro and motioned for Zeus to wind his window down.

144

Zeus smiled up at the law.

"Hello, officer."

"Is this your car, sir?" He was looking at the car, critically.

"Yes, I am proud to say that this is my means of local transportation, officer."

"Do you have any idea why I stopped you?"

Zeus shrugged and smiled nervously. Allegros have square steering wheels and Zeus ran his hand comfortingly around the perimeter.

"There's a maniac on the loose and you wanted to warn me?" Hazarded the god.

Standing stared at him, coldly.

"I've noticed that your rear suspension seems to be somewhat lower than regulation would dictate," he explained. "I'm not sure if you are aware, sir, but the arse end of your car is dragging along the ground. It is sending sparks flying across the road. It's a hazard."

Zeus affected surprise.

"I've never...is that right, officer? It must have just happened. It was fine this morning."

Standing asked to see Zeus's license and Zeus fished it out diligently. He handed it to the police officer, who read it with a frown.

"You've got an HGV license, I see. You must be aware of the intricacies of road safety. And you must be aware of the penalties for driving a vehicle in this condition."

"You make me sound pregnant," Zeus quipped.

Standing didn't laugh.

He squinted down at the license.

"Is this your name? Zeus Roberts?"

The god nodded. He had needed to construct a surname long ago, to comply with UK bureaucracy and social expectations. Roberts seemed solid and, in conjunction with the name Zeus, had a rolling timbre.

145

"Unusual name. It sounds foreign. You're not one of those single cell fundamentalist terrorists I keep hearing about, are you?"

The god shook his head vehemently.

"I've thought about it, but no. I'm not."

Terence Standing stood back, his face grave.

"Sir, I'm afraid I do need to ask you. Have you got any bombs in your car? Or improvised explosive devices?"

"No."

"Any hostages?"

"No."

"Guns or machetes?"

"No."

"Oppressed women?"

"No."

"Mountain-based hide-outs?"

"No."

"Bearded extremists?"

"No."

"Remote desert training camps?"

"No."

"Re-usable shopping bags?"

"Yes – there's one that I use for my Tesco run."

PC Standing nodded. He seemed satisfied. He glanced at the driving licence for a few more moments then peered over to examine the passenger. From his scrunched-up position, Thorax waggled his fingers in an embarrassed wave. Zeus fiddled nervously with the gearstick and Thorax thought that he was stroking his leg to comfort him.

"And can I ask you name, sir?"

"It's Thorax. Thorax the Barbarian."

Standing froze. There couldn't be too many people with that name – and the man in the passenger seat matched the description Standing had been given after the incident in the Unemployment Bureau. Absolutely massive with a hairstyle like Tony Blackburn. PC Standing took a deep breath. He had been told to look out for this character.

By sheer chance, he had stumbled on a dangerous outlaw.

"I wonder if I could ask you to step out of the car," he asked, calmly.

Thorax bobbed his head, nodded and smiled in a single movement of friendly deference. From his impossible position, he managed to find the door handle. The door sprung open and the huge barbarian squeezed himself out of the car, into the open air.

PC Standing was already there. Before he knew what was happening Thorax got a blast of pepper spray to the face. He crumpled to his knees, holding his hands to his face, rubbing his eyes in agony.

"Oh sweet Jesus!" He cried. "What the hell is that stuff?" His nose was running uncontrollably, and water ran from his eyes in rivulets. He tried to open them, but the discomfort was too much. Standing moved with practised speed. Bringing the barbarian's hands behind his back, he handcuffed him quickly.

"Thorax the Barbarian, you are under arrest," he said. "You do not have to say anything but anything you do say may be written down and used as evidence against you in a court of law. Do you understand?"

"Arghhh – I'm blind..."

Thorax fell forward on to his face, moaning at the sheer discomfort of it. Temporarily disabled and with a natural respect for the law, he allowed Standing to escort him to the police car where he was ushered gently into the back. He sat hunched on the back seat, leaning forward to rub his eyes on the headrest in front of him. It afforded him scant comfort.

Zeus watched as the questing adventurer was driven away in the back of the police car, and wondered what the hell he was going to do next.

The ancient god stood motionless and surveyed the state of his bedsit. This was turning into a very bad day.

It was a complete mess.

Thick soot was over everything and Zeus didn't even know where he would start in trying to get it clean. The untidy pile of bricks in front of the hearth suggested that there had been a structural mishap while he was out. His first thought was that the brickwork must have been shoddy and that it had just given way. But he saw the words, scrawled into the soot above the fireplace - **Be clever. £15k by tomorrow. Or else. Merry Xmas.** - and he knew that the truth was much more sinister.

Father Christmas had been here, in his flat. He had burst out of the chimney with no regard for Zeus's property or his privacy. *He's even seen my pants*, thought Zeus, bitterly. Had he chosen to, Father Christmas could have dropped by during the night while he was asleep. While he was vulnerable. Zeus felt sick at the thought of it.

He wandered over to the chest of drawers and absent-mindedly picked up the toy cheeseburger. With Thorax banged up in prison, he had no idea how he was ever going to get the bachelor's plough. He needed a barbarian, the witches had told him that. And as far as he knew, there weren't any other local barbarians to be had. Thorax, for all his delicate sensibilities, was it.

But right now, the bachelor's plough was not even the priority.

Father Christmas's break-in reminded Zeus in the starkest terms that he had to find a huge amount of money by tomorrow. If he didn't...

He had almost forgotten about the immediate threat hanging over him. He had been so focused on getting hold of the bachelor's plough that he didn't consider the possibility of his own physical manglement, prior to cultivating his golden crops. The plough was great as a long-term money spinner, but Father Christmas was not going to wait an entire season for a return on his investment.

Zeus had to come up with the cash, and fast.

He tossed the toy cheeseburger into the air a couple of times, thoughtfully.

A glance around the room told him that if he sold all his worldly goods, he could probably raise close to a hundred and fifty pounds. A hundred and sixty if he chucked in the Allegro.

It was nowhere near enough.

"I'm doomed," he muttered to himself.

The witches had been as good as useless. The only advice they had given him was to get hold of the plough and sow crops of gold. There was no short-term solution, according to those withered old crones.

He remembered them, standing there, horrible and grotesque, looking at him with the help of that ridiculous glass eye.

And in that moment the answer hit him, with all the force of a badger on a rollercoaster.

With the vast figure in the back, weighing it down, the police car did not handle well at all. Terence Standing had to slow down significantly on even the gentlest of bends, taking care to ease the car carefully through every curve. The front wheels hardly seemed to be touching the ground.

Thorax was moaning pitifully, banging his head against the back of PC Standing's head rest. Standing felt the shock of each impact.

"It should wear off in a few minutes," he said.

His aim was to get Thorax back to the community police station. There he would question him further, before deciding how to handle the situation.

The proper thing to do would be to inform Boomtown Central of the arrest, so that they could pick up the prisoner and deal with him themselves. The problem with this was that Standing resented their sense of superiority over him. Pestlewick was under his jurisdiction. *He* would decide who was and who was not a criminal, on his beat. As for this man being an illegal immigrant, Standing wasn't so sure. He had often seen him around the village and the man never seemed suspicious in any way (except for those times when he wore chainmail and garments made from leather straps – but Standing liked *The Village People* and he sympathised with such gestures of self-expression).

Fortunately, Standing knew how to root out an illegal immigrant. It was one of his specialities. He would question Thorax diligently. It wouldn't take him long to find the truth.

They were just a few minutes away from the community police station when the car's radio crackled into life. A police presence was required on Pearbury Hill, to deal with some threatening and aggressive behaviour. The perpetrator was dressed in a black hood and robe and seemed to be drunk. He was waving some kind of farm implement about, threatening motorists and causing a general nuisance.

. Standing agreed to go and check it out. From the description, he already knew what – and who – to expect.

Sure enough, when he got there he found the Grim Reaper, harvester of souls, standing on the kerb leaning out into the road. Cars were swerving to avoid him as they drove past. He was waving his scythe around in a haphazard fashion and to the keen eye, it could be seen that the very air was being sliced into ribbons. In his other hand he held a bottle of Scotch. It was almost empty.

"This guy's got a drink problem," Standing said to himself, as he climbed out of the car. He turned to Thorax, who was finally managing to keep his puffy eyes open. "Stay there," he ordered.

PC Standing edged cautiously towards the Grim Reaper. A torrent of abuse was falling from the Reaper's mouth as he swayed and staggered around on the pavement.

"Yyyyaaa bloody WASTERS!" He yelled, pointing his scythe at any car that went by. "Antcha got no JOBS to go to? Itsh the middle of the DAY. Why ent y'all at WORK? Scrounging off the state, entcha? Leavin it to the likes of me to pick up the pieces. Arghhhh. You're all SHHHHCUM!"

Standing moved as close as he dared, keeping clear of the scythe's fatal influence. He coughed to announce his presence.

"Cyril," he said, gently. "It's me. PC Standing. Remember me?"

The Grim Reaper swung round to face him. Standing could see nothing beneath the dark, eternal hood. But he could feel bleary, unfocused eyes gazing at him, as the Reaper swayed from side to side. The Reaper leaned forward coarsely.

"Agggghhhh PIG! 'Course I member you. You locked me aaap...y' BASHTID!" He spat out the final word with utter contempt.

"Oh come on, Cyril. We ended up getting on very well. Once you'd sobered up a bit."

"Y'shayin' I waszh...*jdrunk*?"

Standing gave him an admonishing look.

"Yes. You were drunk then. And you're drunk now. Look – you've nearly finished that bottle of whiskey."

"Nah...the bottle's always half empty to you coppers. It's half full to us...deathses."

"Look, Cyril..."

"*Itsh Death to you, PIG.*"

"Okay. Death. I'm going to level with you. I think you've got a problem. Look at the state of yourself. You're completely drunk, you're scaring innocent people and you're making a complete fool of yourself. And it's not even lunchtime yet."

"Arghhh....and you're *SHO* perfect..."

"No, I'm not saying I'm perfect, just..." Standing was cut off mid-sentence as the Reaper leaned out at a passing minibus, shaking his scythe at the occupants aggressively.

"WHATCHA LOOKING AT? EH? EH? DJA WANT SHUM, DO YA? *DO YA?*"

Standing looked at the Reaper, square on.

"Right Cyril – Death – one more stunt like that and I'm going to have to take you in. This behaviour is not acceptable. You're drunk and disorderly. You're using threatening behaviour. You're causing a breach of the peace. And you're a danger to motorists."

"Ah, pishhh off..."

"I'm warning you, Cyril..."

"KEEP YOUR EYESH ON THE ROAD YA DAFT OL' COW!" This to an elderly lady in a Ford Fiesta. "OR I'LL PUT YA WINDSHCREEN OUT, Y'OLE *TART!*"

"Cyril, I have warned you..."

"I've told ya. Itsh *DEATH* to you. *DEATH*. Ya useless blaady coppARGHHHHH!"

Having released the pepper spray, Standing stood back, to allow the Reaper to wallow in his agony.

The Reaper stumbled forward and sprawled, face first, on to the stony pavement. His hood had crumpled back as a result of the fall and it looked wonky and misshapen on his head. He writhed in agony on the ground, cursing as he put his bony hands inside his hood's gaping void. His scythe lay a few feet away, where it had dropped from his hands. The tarmac pavement was sliced to ribbons where it had fallen.

"Yashonofabitch..." Screamed the Grim Reaper. "What ish that shtuff you keep spraying in my face...?"

"It's just pepper spray, Cyril. It's for your own protection, as much as for mine. It will wear off in a few minutes."

While he was saying this, Standing was kneeling next to the Grim Reaper, pulling his hands behind his back for handcuffing. Once he had him handcuffed, he pulled him steadily to his feet. The Grim Reaper was groaning painfully.

"This behaviour really needs to stop," Standing said gently, as he walked the Reaper to the police car. "You're not doing yourself any favours, Cyril."

He helped Cyril into the back of the car, squeezing him in next to the handcuffed barbarian.

"Full house today!" He said, as he pulled away. The Grim Reaper was still groaning, shaking his head from side to side, trying to use the inside of his hood to soothe his eyes. PC Standing heard Thorax say a few comforting words, telling The Reaper that the pain would subside soon enough.

He was just wondering how he was going to move them both into a cell when he had to slam on the brakes, effecting an emergency stop.

The Panda screeched to a halt, throwing its rear occupants hard against the seats in front. The Grim Reaper gave a despairing cry.

"What the bloody hell...?"

PC Standing leaned forward over the steering wheel and looked up at the sky, through the windscreen.

Whatever it was, it was gone now.

It had been just a second or two, no more.

But he was sure - *he could have sworn* - that he saw six glittering reindeer fly out in front of his car and up into the sky. They were pulling an elegant silver sleigh and sitting at the helm, the reins held loosely in his hands, was a figure.

He looked like a pitch-black Santa Claus.

The witches moved with lightning speed, falling quickly into the Heimlich formation. Zeus meant business and had not stood on ceremony this time. He had flicked the letterbox and barged straight in without waiting for an answer, and now he stood before the witches, his face hard and determined.

The witch at the back of the formation, holding the eye, cussed.

"It's Zeus again," she said.

"Why don't you leave us be?" The witch at the front spat at him. "We have given you all you need, old man."

"No, you haven't." Zeus smiled, a cold, predatory smile.

"Yes we have," snapped the third witch. "And in exchange for our generosity, you hid the eye."

"It took us all afternoon to find the bugger," chimed in the first witch.

Zeus shrugged.

"You're supposed to be all-wise. How hard can it be to find a mystic eye?"

"Very hard, for your information," one of them said, with a scowl. "It's like going to pick your car up and needing to use the car you are picking up to get there."

Zeus gave a puzzled look.

"Go, old man. We have nothing more to tell you."

He smiled. There was something of the night in his stare.

"Nothing to *tell* me, no. But you have something to *give* me."

The witches huddled closer. Their eyeless faces stared out at him with foul malevolence. He could smell them from several feet away.

Anyone who knows anything about the tactics associated with shared-eye possession knows that the standard response to the Heimlich formation is the Kettering manoeuvre. Zeus was well acquainted with such rudimentary moves.

With the Heimlich formation, a blind side is created. Gazing over the right side of the witch in front, the witch with the eye was currently unable to see anything coming in from the left. Zeus saw their formation and smiled to himself. This would be like taking water from a pond!

Fully aware that the element of surprise was his greatest asset, he circled around the witches, to their left, and homed in on the old hag at the rear. He leaned over carefully and in one quick move, grabbed the eye and yanked it away from her leathery grip.

She didn't see it coming.

There was a gasp, a breathless curse. And then she spoke.

"He's got the eye." Her voice was emotionless.

"You're shitting me," said the second witch.

"He can't have!" Cried the third.

Zeus wandered to the front door, chuckling to himself. He tossed the eye into the air a couple of times.

"Oh yes he can!" He said, gleefully, without even looking back.

"Give us back the eye!"

"Give it us!"

"You've taken the eye!"

"Tell us what you want to know. We'll give you the wisdom you need..."

Zeus was beaming as he bounded out of *Dun Roamin*, through the door and into the open air.

"Give us the eye!" The witches sounded panicked.

"Where are you?"

"Where have you gone?"

"The eye..."

"*Give us the eye.*"

In the near distance they heard the sound of an Austin Allegro being started up. There was a bang, a squeak and then a rhythmic scraping sound as it bounced off down the road.

The witches fell silent. Never in their witchful career had they lost the eye completely. This was a first.

The significance of the situation dawned on them and when they finally spoke, they spoke as one.

"Oh bollocks," they said.

Their voice was like the growl of a wounded hyena, forced to wear a silly hat for the purposes of an advertising campaign with a supposedly funny anthropomorphic theme. It would probably be selling beer.

"Hello, Mrs Thomas," said God. "Is John there, please?"

Mrs Thomas told the Good Lord to hold on, and then went to fetch her son. John Thomas was in the middle of a bowl of soup when she told him that there was somebody on the phone. He knew it must be God and he cursed under his breath. By the time he got off the phone, his soup would be cold.

"Hello?"

"John. It's God."

"Hello, God."

"How is it going? Did anything come of the idea you had?"

Thomas clicked his tongue.

"No, sadly not. I went to see the old dear who found the plough. Edna. Thanks for giving me her details."

"That's okay."

"I was hoping that she would be able to shed some light on who actually owned the plough. Who its original owner was. I thought that if I could prove some kind of ownership, then the guy at the scrap yard would have to give it up."

"So, what – no joy?"

"Not a baked bean. She had no idea who owned it. She just found it in the Thames. As far as she is concerned, the scrap yard is now the rightful owner."

"Hmm. Well, no matter. I've been watching Zeus and that barbarian friend of his. They've been in and out of that witches' bungalow like a whore's draws."

John Thomas said the words before he even realised they had been formulated.

"That metaphor doesn't really work," he said.

158

"I beg your pardon?"

Thomas cringed. He berated himself in silence, wishing there was a way to retract the statement. But there wasn't. He'd have to plough on.

"Well, You usually say that something is *up and down* like a whore's drawers," he ventured. "To say that something goes *in and out* like a whore's drawers, doesn't really make any sense."

"Doesn't it." The Good Lord said it in such a way as it was not so much a question, as a threat.

"Um. No."

"Let Me ask you something, John Thomas." The Lord's voice was as thunder. "Who would you say is the larger, out of you and Me?"

Thomas felt himself diminish.

"Well. I'm five-foot-eight. And You're omnipresent. So probably You, O Exalted One."

"Indeed. And who would you say is the stronger, out of you and Me?"

"You, my Lord. You're omnipotent. Sometimes *I* can't even get the screw-cap off a jar of pickles."

"Quite. And what about in terms of overall knowledge? Who would you say is more knowledgeable, out of you and Me, John?"

"You, God. You're omniscient. I tend to rely on Google."

The Divine Being allowed a few uncomfortable moments of silence to pass, in order that John Thomas could think about his transgression.

"Can I suggest that instead of contradicting Me - Me, who art bigger than thee, more powerful than thee and more knowledgeable than thee - instead of contradicting Me, you take it as read that My word is Truth? If, in My divine omniscience, I tell you that a whore's drawers have the potential - *the potential, mind* - to go in and out, *then go in and out they can.* Do I make Myself clear?"

"Patently, O Lord. And actually, now I think about it, the metaphor does make sense. I am an unholy ignoramus of the lowest order."

"Don't beat yourself up about it. So anyway. I have been watching Zeus and the barbarian closely and they have been in and out of the witches' bungalow like a whore's drawers..." The Good Lord paused, ominously. "Which tells Me the witches have a pretty good grasp of the situation and are offering advice on how to get the plough. They're wise women, those witches."

John Thomas knew what was coming. He didn't like it one bit.

"So what I was thinking," continued the Lord. "Was that you ought to pay them a visit yourself. If they're giving advice to Zeus, then they'll give advice to you."

"A commendable idea," said the Fixer, without a trace of enthusiasm.

"Verily," agreed the Lord.

In the background, John Thomas could hear the theme tune to *Murder She Wrote*. God suddenly seemed keen to get off the phone. Thomas thought it strange that the Good Lord would enjoy watching crime drama, as He'd surely know who had done it from the start.

There was only one cell in the small police station and PC Standing had no compunction about putting both of his arrests into it.

It was true that the Grim Reaper was unpredictable and might turn aggressive at any moment, but Standing felt certain Thorax would be able to look after himself. Standing, like Zeus, fully understood that Thorax's name was actually a description, rather than the nominal product of eccentric parents.

Before moving to Pestlewick, Terence Standing would never have considered the possibility of encountering an archetypal barbarian during the course of his duties. He would never have believed either, that he would be dicing with Death, having nothing but his truncheon and some pepper spray to get the upper hand. Now he would believe just about anything (although when Barry Manilow phoned him up on his birthday to wish him many happy returns, he *didn't* believe it was the singing sensation himself and hung up the phone, thereby missing out on a special conversation with his greatest hero).

There was nothing he could do about Cyril until he sobered up.

Last time it happened, the Reaper was very contrite after sleeping off his inebriation. He was apologetic and sheepish and PC Standing had hoped that would be the end of it. If Cyril presented a similar attitude after sobering up this time, Standing would try to talk to him about some professional counselling. The cowled personification clearly had a problem and was trying to find the answer in the bottom of a bottle. Standing had procured some leaflets on the subject, which he would offer to the deadly Reaper when he was ready to listen.

But for now, he needed to deal with Thorax the Barbarian.

If he could prove to his own satisfaction that Thorax was not an illegal immigrant, he would let him go. He didn't care what Boomtown Central said. This was Terence Standing's jungle and he was the superior vine. He was the leafy kingpin in the arboreal canopy. He was the head monkey. The chief lion. The king zebra. The papal giraffe. The episcopal sloth.

PC Standing had developed sophisticated questioning skills during the course of his career and he would use these to their maximum effect, in getting to the truth. The barbarian didn't stand a chance. PC Standing *would* know the truth.

It was fortunate for the community police officer that Thorax the Barbarian had a natural respect for authority.

When he let the Thorax out of the cell, the barbarian came obediently and waited to be directed by the officer. His compliance was doubly useful, for as he was mooching out of the cell, the Reaper made a lunge for freedom, in an arcing, drunken swagger. By telling Thorax to hurry up, Standing was able to slam the door shut just as the Reaper got to it. The hard thud of bone against the padded door caused both Standing and the barbarian to wince simultaneously.

Cyril's groans didn't subside for some minutes afterwards.

*

Standing offered the barbarian a seat on the opposite side of the desk. He took his own seat casually. Suddenly, with a look of sudden focused agenda, he flicked on the desk lamp and pointed it directly in Thorax's face. It was the element of surprise necessary to disorientate his subject and knock him off guard.

162

Thorax moved his head, trying to move out of the light. With his hands still cuffed behind his back, he was unable to cover his face.

Standing came straight to the point.

"Are you an illegal immigrant?"

Thorax blinked, like a mole walking out of an illicit massage parlour into the sunlight. Moles are terrible for that. And they always want extras.

"No, I don't think so," Thorax offered, helpfully.

Standing was behind him, suddenly. He moved with lightning speed. The desk lamp shone into Thorax's eyes but he was gradually getting used to it. Standing leaned forward and whispered aggressively into Thorax's ear.

"You see, *we* think you are. *We* think you've come here under false pretences. *We* think you're taking us for *mugs*."

Standing pushed himself away from the back of the chair in that aggressive manoeuvre so reminiscent of angry cops from the 1970s. Thorax tried to turn around to see him, but he was unable to twist his body that far.

There was a sudden bang as Standing slammed his hand down on the desk.

He was standing directly in front of Thorax now.

"We don't like being taken for *mugs*," he said, leaning down, his spittle flying into the barbarian's face.

"Look officer," Thorax looked plaintive. A fan of Tony Blackburn would have melted. "I'm honestly not taking you for a mug. I'm not an illegal immigrant."

Standing was suddenly sitting down on his side of the desk, nodding sympathetically. The good cop, bad cop routine was well-tried. He swore by it. Admittedly, it was a little more difficult by yourself. But his staffing levels didn't give him much choice.

He twisted the lamp away from the barbarian's face. Calmly, he pulled out a packet of cigarettes from his shirt

163

pocket and offered one to Thorax. Thorax shook his head, gratefully. Standing then poured himself a cup of coffee from his flask and looked askance over at his prisoner. Thorax nodded, pleasantly surprised. This was more the constructive dialogue he liked to engage in.

Standing poured a second cup and slid it across the desk to the barbarian. With his hands bound behind his back, Thorax leaned over and sipped at the cup uncomfortably.

"I understand," Standing said with a warm smile. "I do. It's all been a bit of a shocker for you. Just half an hour ago you were happily driving along with your friend. Since then you've been pepper sprayed, handcuffed and now you're being interrogated down at the police station." He smiled. "We're just trying to get to the truth. You understand that, don't you?"

Thorax nodded, still bent over his coffee, sipping it carefully.

"So just let us know what you're doing here and – well – maybe then we can put all this behind us?"

Thorax shrugged. The officer sounded so reasonable all of a sudden. He was just about to reply when the desk lamp was thrust back in his face once more.

PC standing leapt to his feet and threw his coffee cup across the station.

"Let's stop this pussy-footing around, shall we?" He boomed. "What are we? Social workers?" He thrust his face forward angrily. "Who. Are. You? What. Are. You. Doing. Here? Who. Are. You. Working. For?"

"I...I..." Thorax stared at his interrogator in confusion.

"Come on! Cat got your tongue? You came in the back of a lorry, didn't you? Who did you have to pay to smuggle you in? Where are you living? What's your cover?"

"Officer, honestly, I..."

Standing walked over to the wall, facing away from Thorax, clutching at his hair. Thorax tried to move out of the bright light.

Suddenly Standing was behind him and his voice was in his ear, a threatening whisper.

"I don't know if you realise it sunshine – but we don't play by the rules in here. If we want answers, we get them. By whatever means. *Kapish?*"

Thorax was about to answer when the lamp was moved away once more. To his increasing bafflement, a pleasant, sympathetic Standing was sitting on the desk gazing down at him benevolently.

"Ah, we don't want to fall out with you!" He said. "You just want to tell us the truth, right?"

Thorax nodded.

"We've all got our jobs to do," Standing continued. "But underneath it all...well, we're all the same, aren't we? I mean – you and I would be good mates if we met each other down the pub, wouldn't we!"

The barbarian smiled.

"So come on, just between us. Between friends. Are you an illegal immigrant?"

Thorax shook his head and gazed at Standing with all the sincerity he could muster.

"No, officer. Seriously. I've always lived here."

Standing kicked the desk back. It topped over, spreading paperwork all over the floor.

"You see!" He screamed. "This is what happens when you try to befriend the little bastards. They're scum. Of course he's going to say he's not an illegal immigrant. He's not going to own up to it. All this good cop, bad cop stuff...it's bollocks. They just walk all over you."

Thorax watched in amazement as Standing changed position and glared back at the spot where had just been sitting.

His voice was calmer, more controlled now.

"No they don't. He's telling the truth, I reckon." He looked down at Thorax. "You're telling the truth, aren't you?"

Thorax nodded.

"See?" Standing said, quietly.

He leapt back into his former position and began to shout.

"Of course he'll say that! For Christ's sake! He's living a *lie*. That's what these people do!" Suddenly Standing was hollering into Thorax's ear. "You're scum, you lot. You lie and cheat and steal and...we're not all soft in here you know. Some of us believe in treating people as they deserve. And you deserve this..." He held his truncheon before Thorax's face, threateningly.

"I don't know what else to say," said the barbarian. "I've always lived here. I went to school here. This is my home."

Standing let out a strangled noise of disgust as he turned to face the wall. He stood motionless for some minutes, breathing hard. Thorax waited.

Finally Standing turned to face him. He looked calm and friendly. His normal self. His sophisticated and comprehensive interrogation was at an end, and he was convinced.

This man was innocent.

He stepped over with a smile and reached behind Thorax to undo the handcuffs. Thorax waggled his hands around, getting the blood to circulate again.

"Right, that's it," Standing said, airily. "You can go."

Thorax the Barbarian looked at him suspiciously, without moving. He waited for the change.

"Are you sure?" He asked.

"Yes, on your way."

The barbarian stood up, warily, and walked out of the station, into the open air. Like an under-cooked pancake, he sat uncomfortably upon the steed of his own bafflement.

PC Standing was left to clear up the mess resulting from his well-honed interview technique. There was paperwork all over the place and the most annoying thing was that he'd written an important telephone number down somewhere, only this morning, and now he didn't know where the hell it was. For a second he thought it was on an old witness statement that was on his desk but it turned out not to be.

The drunken rendition of Olivia Newton John's *Let's Get Physical*, droning out from the Grim Reaper's cell, should have cheered him up. But it didn't.

Had he lifted the peep-hole cover to glance in, he would have seen the eternal reaper of souls doing a 1980s aerobics routine as he sung. But even this wouldn't have cheered him up.

He had lost the most important telephone number he had ever had. It had been given to him by a friend of a friend who happened to work in the music industry. To Terence Standing, this number was more valuable than gold

It was the home telephone number for one Barry Alan Manilow.

The all-seeing crystal eye that Zeus had stolen from the witches was an awesome bit of technology.

Whatever your level of vision, the eye gave sight beyond that. The blind witches were able to see the physical world, but somebody with full sight, who could already see the physical world, would be given the ability to see the world *beyond* the physical.

Anyone who knows the first thing about metaphysics understands that the world beyond the physical *is the spirit realm itself.*

Using the all-seeing eye, a sighted person was able to see the dark, hidden world of the dead. Some people find this spooky. Some people find it utterly fascinating. The dead simply see it as intrusive and feel they have to keep the place tidy all the time in case of unexpected voyeurs.

Through a commercial lens, Zeus, reasoned that it made the eye quite desirable. People would pay good money to see the spirit world in real time and this gave the eye significant monetary worth. This was the motivation behind his theft. He fully intended to give it back to the witches, but for now he would pawn it. In so doing, he would be able to raise some ready cash and would use this to pay off his debt to Father Christmas. As soon as he yielded his first crop from the bachelor's plough, he would buy back the eye from the pawnbroker and return it to the witches. It was a godly plan.

He knew of a pawnbroker shop near the Barrelway Shopping Precinct.

He had always wondered why anyone would use such a place.

Now he knew.

A lot of people out there must have fallen into serious debt due to the need for satellite navigation.

*

A little bell rang above the door as he walked in.

He closed the door reverentially behind him and felt the musty silence of the place wrap itself around him like a damp cloak. It was a strange sort of shop, with all manner of objects on display. In the window he had seen a few old clocks, a gold cigarette case, a dead tarantula in a wooden frame, a World War II gas mask and a signed photograph of Elvis Presley. Inside the shop the objects became more random, with bags of golf clubs, a fishing rod, a flat screen television, a Fender guitar and a stuffed crocodile, all of which were scattered about untidily.

And that was just the tip of the iceberg. He reckoned that it would take weeks to catalogue everything in the shop and wondered how far back some of it went.

He had been in the shop for mere seconds when a man emerged from out the back. He was a tall man with a dark blue velvet coat, yellow trousers and a salmon cravat. Inexplicably, Zeus wondered if he liked pickled gherkins.

The man smiled, pleasantly.

"How can I help you?" He asked.

Zeus coughed. He moved about shiftily.

"I need to pawn something," he said. It felt like a guilty secret, doing business in a place like this.

"I'll certainly have a look at it. What have you got?"

Zeus pulled the eye out of the pocket of his cardigan and held it out for the man to see. The man looked at it with courteous interest. A glass orb, the size of a cricket ball.

"A paperweight, sir?"

Zeus shook his head, gravely.

"Much more than a paperweight," he said.

169

"Hmm. It is very nice, as an ornament...but I don't really think it has much intrinsic worth, sir. I could probably offer you a fiver for it."

Zeus looked down at the eye. Even now, as he held it in his hand, he could see the shadows of the dead moving all around them.

"I think you'll find it is worth very much more than that," Zeus gazed at the man with what he hoped was a significant expression.

"Not to me, sir." The man smiled, thinly.

Zeus held out the eye.

"Just take a look at it," he urged. The man reluctantly took the eye. He looked surprised at the weight of it.

"It is pure crystal," Zeus said. "And it has properties that would amaze you."

The man looked up at him.

"How so, sir?"

"This crystal ball," said the ancient god, drawing himself up to his full (if modest) height. "This *paperweight*, as you call it, was fashioned by the gods themselves back in ancient times. Hera...no, hang on...or was it Athena...?" He stuttered. "No, no, I tell a lie – I remember now. It was Beryl, Goddess of Charity and Domestic Order![6] Beryl created the ball for her old friends, the Stygian witches, who were blinded by their own hate and greed."

"It seems unlikely, sir."

"That it may. That it may. But it is the truth. Beryl made the crystal orb over the course of forty days and forty nights. For the whole of this time she didn't sleep. And when

---

[6] Goddess of charity and domestic order. Beryl is the lesser-known of the Olympian gods. She has been pretty much undocumented and it is only meticulous research by the likes of Clint Eastwood's Dirty Harry and Mike Myers' Austin Powers that has brought the thirteenth Olympian to light, in recent years. Beryl is represented by the Lesser Spotted Woodpecker, the humpback whale, the rice paddy and the bedroom slipper.

she had finished, a miracle she had created. *A miracle*. And a window into the forbidden. For by the use of the orb, or Beryl's eye, as it came to be called, the blind witches of Stygia could now see the world about them."

"I sympathise with your efforts to give some provenance to the thing, sir, but I'm not sure you are pitching it very well."

"I am only telling you the truth. But you can test it." Zeus looked at him eagerly. "The eye is a window into the next world. Look through it yourself. Do it now. And you will see the shadows of those that have passed over."

The man looked unconvinced but he brought the crystal up to his eye and squinted through it. Zeus saw his face change quickly from disinterest to amazement

"I say!" He said. And never a truer statement had he uttered.

He swung around, gazing through the eye at the shop around him. He seemed to have trouble comprehending it and he kept taking the eye away from his face to see the shop as it really was, before returning the eye so that he could look through it once more.

When he finally lowered the eye and looked back at Zeus, he was pale. His expression was one of shock.

"But...I saw..."

"Dead people?" Zeus offered.

"Hundreds of them. They're all around me. They're everywhere. And yet when I'm not looking through the orb..."

"They are nowhere to be seen. That is the nature of it. It's a neat bit of kit, isn't it!"

The man shook his head in wonder.

"I've never seen anything like it."

Zeus beamed.

"Okay, let's talk turkey," he said, rubbing his hands. "How much is something like that worth to you?"

The man looked down at the eye and then back over at Zeus.

"Well." He was very pale. "It certainly is a novelty. I'm sure it is something *some* people would be interested in."

Zeus nodded. A window into the world of Spirit. It was priceless!

"I reckon..." The man swayed his hips suggestively as he did some internal calculations. "A hundred pounds."

Zeus felt his body slump.

"What?" He was impressed by how high his voice had become. "A hundred pounds? That thing is a window into the spirit world. There's nothing like that anywhere in existence. Beryl, Goddess of Charity and Domestic Order, made it as a one-off for the Stygian witches. Thousands of years ago. Back in classical times. Forty days and forty nights she worked on that bugger. A hundred pounds? You're having a giraffe."

The man shrugged. The eye felt heavy in his hand.

"It's a niche area," he explained. "Who is going to want one of these things, out of the blue?"

"*One of these things?* It is the only one!"

"That it may be. But seriously, not many people will be that interested. To most people, all we have here is a paperweight."

"Yes, but if they look through it, they'll see..."

"Okay. I'll tell you what. My cash flow isn't what it used to be. But I'll stretch for you. I'll give you two hundred quid."

Zeus sighed. This was useless.

"I was looking for a lot more," he stated hopelessly.

The man shrugged again.

"I suppose I could barter with you, given how unique it is. I wouldn't usually, but..."

Zeus waited. He needed fifteen grand and he'd just been offered £200.

172

His debt to Santa Claus was turning into the IOU from Hell.

Whatever he did, he just couldn't get close to paying it off.

But if the man was able to offer him something in kind, some kind of unusual barter, it might give him something tangible to negotiate with, when Claus came to collect the cash.

Zeus was desperate.

It was this desperation that led him to walk away from the pawnbroker with two hundred pounds in cash and a worn out trombone with a dent in the horn.

The *Boar's Head Tavern* was a spit-and-sawdust establishment. It was the kind of place that most people didn't know existed, even those who passed it every day. An angular, tumbling, medieval pile, its windows were so grimy and caked in dirt, soot, smoke and sweat that even with Beryl's eye, a telescope and a powerful torch, you would never see further in than the fourth of fifth level of dirt. It was impenetrable to light.

Inside, it was a dark, dingy hole. On the flaking brick walls, flaming torches were held in iron brackets and threw out a dim flickering light. The flagstone floor was dipped and worn. It was sticky with years of spilled liquor. Here and there, ominous dark stains spoke of random violence that had been perpetrated over the years. Heavy wooden tables were positioned in no discernible order and wooden chairs and stools sat around them untidily, adding to the sense of casual disorder.

Part of a huge tree trunk lay across the middle of the tavern. One side had been chopped flat, to create a flat surface. This was the bar and small selection of drinks was always on tap. It wasn't a selection typical of a twenty-first century pub, but it suited the clientele of the *Boar's Head* very well. For loping thugs of a generally barbaric disposition, the choice of home-brewed ale, home-brewed mead, home-brewed cider and two litre bottles of Pepsi Cola from the cash and carry, was more than enough.

Above the bar, a matrix of dun-coloured hooks held a grimy array of glasses and tankards, all of which had never seen a drop of clean water in their lives.

This was the tavern that Thorax had made his local.

Thorax the Barbarian and Billy the Dwarf sat on either side of a wonky table, nursing their tankards. Froth spilled over the top of both, and each man took an occasional gulp of the dubious liquid that lurked beneath. Thorax had been telling Billy about the rollercoaster of the last few days, to which Billy listened with the rare sensitivity of a sympathetic dwarf. The only time he spoke was when Thorax relayed Zeus's adamance that he was a barbarian. To this, Billy took a swig of his mead, nodded and said, "makes sense".

Despite the fact he was wearing a brown cardigan and cream coloured trousers –
and had delicately crafted his impeccable Tony Blackburn hair-do – Thorax looked like a barbarian in crisis. He took a gulp of his ale and looked over at Billy the Dwarf with a tortured expression.

"And so they told me to go and see Medusa," he said, unhappily. "Medusa! A woman with snakes for hair and a glare that turns you to stone."

"What is it they expect you to do when you get there?" Billy asked.

Thorax shook his head and stared into his tankard.

"I don't know. They said I need to get her in front of the Minotaur and that when he looks at her, he will turn to stone. Then I can take the plough. But Zeus doesn't think she will come willingly. He thinks I should chop her head off and just take that."

"Seems a bit harsh," Billy's thick eyebrows lifted critically.

"That's what I said. I just don't know how I am going to get her there though. I mean, she might even come willingly. I don't know. But to be honest with you, I don't much fancy the idea of being immortalised in stone if I get on the wrong side of her."

Billy nodded.

"It's a tough one," he said.

They drank in silence for a few minutes, until Billy suddenly put down his tankard and leaned across the table towards the barbarian.

"I'll tell you what," he said, his beard rising and falling with dwarfly emphasis. "You need to approach this strategically."

"Go on." Thorax sipped his ale.

"Well, Zeus might be right. As a last resort, perhaps cutting her head off is going to be necessary. But there are steps to take before that. I mean, first of all you need to find out if she'll come willingly. You can't judge a Gorgon by her hair, I always say. She might be very amenable to the idea."

"And if she's not...?"

"Well, if she's not, then perhaps you can bung her in a cage or something and take her there by force. There must be some kind of contraption we can devise, to hold a Gorgon. You could bung her in it, get it to the scrap yard and then have some kind of viewing window that opens when you press a button. You press the button when Roger is there, he sees her through the viewing window...and Bob's your milkman."

Thorax was nodding thoughtfully. He was already forming a suitable contraption in his mind, involving the use of an electric milk float, some wooden pallets and a tin of peas.

Billy shrugged.

"And if that doesn't work, then..." He pulled his hatchet out from his belt and made a motion of holding someone's hair while chopping off their head at the neck. Had he been more proficient at expressing himself through mime, he might have embellished the tableau by enacting a struggle with two-dozen cranially located snakes. But he was very poor when it came to dramatic skills. In attempting such an ambitious display, he would be liable to hurt himself. At the very least, he might fall off his chair.

The barbarian took a long swig of ale and looked troubled.

"It's all very well," he said. "But you're forgetting one thing. If I look at her, I turn to stone. How am I going to approach her about the whole thing in the first place? No sooner will I have introduced myself than I'll be instantly petrified. I'll end up looking like some kind of over-grown garden gnome. At least if I chop her head off I can approach her from behind and get the upper hand."

Billy was smiling.

"If you look her directly in the eye, you turn to stone," he said. "But if you look at her *in a mirror...*"

"What – you think if I look at her through a mirror I won't turn to stone?"

Billy shrugged and nodded.

"It's got to be worth a shot, hasn't it? It makes sense."

Thorax was frowning, with all the uncertainty of an Alpine goat behind the wheel of a Maserati.

"Well, I don't want to go giving it a try if the theory is wrong," he ventured. "But I suppose if there was some way to test it out..."

Billy was smiling again. He took a slow, deliberate sup of his mead before placing his tankard down carefully on the table.

He resorted to mime, once more.

This time he used his hands to make bunny ears above his head and made a show of bouncing around on the spot, while hooking his upper teeth over his bottom lip. Quite unavoidably, he got a mouthful of beard.

Thorax, who had absolutely no idea what his friend was getting at, thought that he had gone stark raving mad.

It wasn't often that Zeus felt nervous while levelling his dart at the board. Tonight was an exception. His dart-throwing prowess would bring the pub to a standstill on most nights, with his pin-point accuracy and his blasé confidence in hurling the missiles. Tonight though, he had missed too many easy shots.

At one point his dart missed the dartboard altogether and sailed straight into the face of Her Majesty the Queen, who was hanging in a battered frame just a few feet to the right of the board. A speculative conversation ensued, as to whether Zeus's bad aim constituted high treason or not. The general consensus was that it probably did but since Zeus was known to everyone involved – and as it was a cold and windy night outside – it was decided that general complicity in the treason was probably the best course of action for the time being.

The terrible nerves from which Zeus was suffering had nothing to do with the darts match itself. Neither were they the result of harbouring treasonable intentions.

Zeus was nervous because it was Friday. And Santa Claus was expecting his money. All £15,000 of it.

The ancient god had only a fraction of that. He had with him £200 in cash and the battered trombone from the pawn shop. Deep down in his heart, he doubted that it would buy him any favours from the festive gangster. The whale of desperation, however, lives on the plankton of hope.

Feeling like a lamb to the slaughter, he had arrived at the *Bird in Hand* just after eight.

Since then, every time the door had opened Zeus had swung around anxiously, expecting to see the dark brooding figure of Santa Claus standing in the doorway. It was now past ten o'clock.

Zeus had not touched his drink all night. The glass of gin and slimline tonic sat, wet but unloved, on the table. He played a few darts matches throughout the evening in the hope of distracting himself and passing time, but all he succeeded in doing was staining his reputation as an impeccable player.

Next to the table where his beer was festering, his black dustman's jacket was folded up on the floor. Sitting ontop of it, was the battered trombone. The dull brass looked yellow in the insipid light.

Whenever his eyes fell upon the instrument it made him feel physically sick.

He couldn't believe his audacity, that he was actually going to try to use the trombone to make up a shortfall of £14,800. Even a salesman of Ted Bundy's calibre would have trouble pulling that one off. That he was going to attempt this with Boomtown's most notorious gangster, caused bowel movements inside of him that hinted at an imminent prolapse. He couldn't remember a time when he had been so fearful for his own welfare.

When the door flew open to admit not only Father Christmas but Vinnie "The Saw" Hopkins and Reggie Watts, "The Hat", Zeus's life flashed in front of him.

His was a long life and it took ages.

By the time it had finished playing out, the three men had been to the bar, got a drink, played a game of pool, told some crude jokes and indulged in a bit of friendly competition to see who could blow a rubber glove up the furthest before losing courage and letting the air back out. The thought of the rubber glove exploding in their face became too much for Hopkins and Watts; but Claus, with nerves of steel, continued to blow his glove up (a yellow Marigold) even after his friends had quit and he had won the competition.

When the glove exploded, sending a light powdery substance into Claus's face, the bang was so loud that several customers in the *Bird in Hand* thought there had been a

179

shooting. The three gangsters laughed hard at the effect and even Claus admitted that it had "shat me up".

Claus and his two men strode across the pub, the ancient god in their sights. They surrounded him, backing him up against the wall.

In their dark suits, they oozed menace. Claus stood face-to-face with his debtor. Uncomfortable at the intrusion into his personal space, Zeus had to lean back to avoid being touched by Claus's beard. He found it hard to meet Claus's eyes, but tried to gaze back respectfully.

"Take a seat," Claus said, quietly. His voice was tipped with menace as he gestured for Zeus to sit down at the table. Zeus obeyed.

Santa took the seat opposite. His two henchmen stood behind next to him, glaring at their bearded quarry.

The gangster sipped his drink, casually.

"You've got my money." He said. It was a statement, not a question. His dark eyes were flat and lifeless.

Zeus fought the inevitability of his rectal prolapse.

"Yes," he said. A satisfied smile spread across Claus's face and he nodded. He had expected no less. It made Zeus's postscript all the more difficult.

"*Some* of it," he added.

Claus's face fell.

His eyes widened, slightly and a dull light began to dance in his eyes.

"What did you say?"

Zeus saw that the festive personification was working hard to control his breathing.

"Well...I...*some* of it," Zeus repeated. Reggie Watts and Vinnie Hopkins stepped forward. With Claus in the middle they presented a solid wall of muscle to the trembling god.

Father Christmas allowed a few moments of silence to play between them. He glared at Zeus across the table.

"For a minute there – *just for a minute* – I thought you said *some of it.*"

Zeus said nothing. He stared back, fearfully.

"Is that what you said?" Claus asked. His face was grey. Zeus stared back, fearful, silent. "IS THAT WHAT YOU SAID?"

Claus banged his fist down, hard, on the table. His eyes were dark and unforgiving. His anger boomed out and the pub became immediately silent.

All eyes were on the unfolding scene.

Zeus squirmed in his seat.

"How much have you got?" Claus hunched forwards, leaning on the table.

Slowly, Zeus pulled an envelope from the inside pocket of his cardigan. He opened the envelope. With a shaking hand, he began to count the money on to the table. Note by note, he placed down two hundred pounds. He then leaned behind him, took hold of the trombone and laid that on top of the money.

Father Christmas stared at him.

"What the fuck is that?" He growled.

"It's a trombone," said Zeus.

"I can see it's a trom-fucking-bone. What's it doing on the table?"

Zeus toyed with his own fingers, uncomfortably.

"Well, I thought it might go some way towards making up the shortfall."

"Two hundred quid and a trombone." Claus looked from one of his friends to the other. There were times when this would be considered funny. At this moment, none of them were laughing.

"TWO HUNDRED NOTES, *AND A TROMBONE.*" Claus was shaking.

Zeus nodded, helpfully. He was starting to think he might just pull this off. Being able to read situations was not one of his strong points.

"You owe me fifteen grand. *What the fuck am I going to do with two hundred quid and a trombone?*"

"I thought..."

Claus reached over the table and grabbed the back of Zeus's head. With a sharp movement, he pulled Zeus's face down violently. The ancient god groaned as his face smashed against the hard surface. He felt something rupture inside his nose and when he was yanked upright once more, the warm blood streamed over his upper lip and into his mouth. Stars were exploding before his eyes. Through a haze he saw Father Christmas, his face contorted with rage.

Before he knew what was happening, Reggie Watts and Vinnie Hopkins were on either side of him, yanking him out of his chair. He felt their brute strength as they dragged him to his feet, holding him up so that his toes were just touching the floor.

Claus stood in front of him, his eyes hard and wild. They were the eyes of a mad man.

"Look, I'll sort it," he pleaded with them.

Claus was shaking his head. His eyes sparkled viciously.

"It's too late for that," he said. "I lent you the money in good faith. And this -" He lifted up the trombone and held it up before Zeus, contemptuously. " *This* is how you repay me."

"Please..."

"I can't let you get away with this," Father Christmas's voice was a sinister whisper. "If I let *you* get away with it, *everyone* would think they could get away with it."

"No, I'll pay you..."

Claus thrust his face forwards. The two men stood, beard to beard.

"I gave you the chance," breathed Santa. He looked at his two men. "Hold him," he said, softly.

Zeus felt their grip tighten and he saw Father Christmas weighing the trombone in his hand, thoughtfully.

And then it happened.

Without warning the instrument smashed into the side of his head. He cried out. There was another blow. And another. He felt them, brass instrumental blows raining down on his elderly frame. He cried out for mercy, begged Claus to stop. But Christmas was in a frenzy. He stopped aiming and just continued to lash out, beating Zeus's constrained body to a pulp. Zeus felt the blows to his body, his arms, his head, his legs. Each blow was accompanied by an explosion of pain that ripped through his entire body. He had never known pain like it.

He had never known a sense of helplessness like it.

For millennia, the ancient god had presumed that he was immortal. But now, with the elegantly dressed personification of the festive season raining down his anger on him, he wondered if he was about to make theological history.

PC Standing made his way slowly into the dark obscurity of the park. It was a wet, windy night and he could think of much better things to be doing late on a Friday night. But he was here on business of *the utmost importance* – or so Mrs Howlett would have him believe – and he had to be seen to be doing his job.

Mrs Howlett crept with him into the gloom, following just a few paces behind. As he swept the beam of his torch from side to side, he could feel her behind him, watchful and alert.

It had started with a phone call from the distressed woman just a couple of hours ago.

"There is a flasher in Hillrise Park," she had gushed, hysterically. "He has just exposed himself to my daughter."

Standing had been delighted to hear it. It was a relief to have something ordinary to deal with for a change.

Friday evenings were always unpredictable, and he had been haunted all afternoon by the intuition that he was going to have another drunken episode from the Grim Reaper to contend with. A routine flasher in the park was much easier. He would get a statement from the victim, reassure the mother that he would look into the issue and would then make some simple discrete enquiries. It meant a quiet Friday night for him.

Mrs Howlett had other ideas.

When he had arrived at the house in Taylor's Way, he had been ushered straight into the living room where the daughter was sitting, drinking cola. She didn't look so much shocked or distressed as completely embarrassed by the involvement of a policeman. At sixteen years of age, she was an independent sort of girl and it was only in passing that she had mentioned the incident to her mother. Her mother had immediately lost all sense of proportion.

Standing had tackled the issue sensitively, realising the dynamics that were at work in the family unit. With Mrs Howlett standing by throughout the whole interview he had to be seen to be taking it with the utmost seriousness.

"So can you just tell me what happened?" He asked the girl, softly.

She shrugged and described the incident.

She had been walking through Hillrise Park, on her way home from hanging out with some friends, when the man slid out in front of her. He had emerged from behind a tree and had turned to face her. He was wearing a long brown coat with a hood. She didn't see his face. The robe was tied together with just a length of white rope. The man stood silent and still. Eerily so. Before she realised what he was doing, his robe was opening to reveal the contents beneath.

Standing nodded, his notebook poised.

"And you didn't see his face?" He checked.

The girl shook her head. Because of the large, overhanging hood, his face was entirely in shadow.

"And you say that he slid out from behind the tree," Standing said. "What do you mean by that? Was he on a skateboard or something?"

She tried to explain how the man had seemed to drift, almost as if he were floating. She wondered if it signified that he was proficient in ballet or something.

Standing nodded at the canny observation.

"Now," PC Standing gave a nervous sideways glance at Mrs Howlett. "I don't want to upset you. But can you tell me – underneath the robe. When he flapped it open, for all to see. When he opened the portal to Armageddon...what was he wearing?"

The girl flushed pink. She looked down at her hands as she described the flasher's hidden contents.

Standing paused, his pencil poised above the notepad.

"So...he was wearing cream-coloured long johns and a hair shirt?" He grappled with the idea of a flasher in such thick undergarments.

The girl nodded.

"Did you see anything of...anatomical intimacy?"

She wasn't sure what he meant by that.

"His wayfarer's dongle," he explained.

Still, she wasn't getting him.

"His royal python."

She frowned.

"His Mr Bo-Jangles."

She was perplexed. He ploughed on.

"His partner in crime."

She shrugged, helplessly.

"His willial attachment."

She looked at her mother, desperate for a clue to help her understand Standing's purport.

"His dinky travis."

She tried desperately to understand.

"His Dorothy Perkins."

She blinked.

"His garden hose."

She coughed, embarrassed.

"His meat and two veg."

Sorry...

"His family jewels."

She so wanted to help him.

"His dangly love stick."

She shook her head. She didn't see anything, she said firmly, not even the man's penis. The long johns had reached down past the man's knees.

PC Standing looked at Mrs Howlett with careful sensitivity. This was turning into an awkward situation.

"I'm not sure that what this man did constitutes an official flash," he explained, gently. Mrs Howlett hit the roof.

"If course it does," she ranted. "He exposed himself to my daughter."

"Yes, but he didn't, exactly, he..."

"He slid out from behind a tree - he had been *lurking* behind a tree - and he flapped open his robe. *Flapped open his robe.* What is he, if he isn't a flasher?"

Standing wasn't sure where this man stood on the official flasher spectrum, but he was fairly certain that revealing some quantity of genital flesh was necessary to imbue him with legitimate flasher status.

"Mrs Howlett," he began to explain. "I think that for him to be considered a flasher he would need to have shown his..."

"His what?"

"Well, his...Sidney Jones."

"His *what?*"

"His swinging bishop."

"I'm sorry?"

"His pride and joy."

"Eh?"

"His intergalactic love weapon."

"I don't understand."

"His man's best friend."

"Come again?"

"His lady-killing sausage flambé.

"His...?"

"His John Thomas."

A few streets away, God's fixer on earth found that his ears were burning inexplicably. Mrs Howlett gave up on trying to guess what the police officer was on about.

"Look," she said. "I know you probably think that a man needs to expose his penis to be a flasher. What this man did was even worse."

"What do you mean it was worse?"

"Well, think about it. When a woman wears lingerie, she does so to tease a man. It is arguably more powerful to keep her most treasured assets hidden, than to reveal herself in her perfect nudity. It has a psychological element, you see."

Standing nodded. What she was saying was true.

She continued.

"So, in wearing his long johns, and thereby keeping his genitals hidden from my daughter, this man – this *fiend* – ensured that not only was he terrorising her by the physical act of flashing, but he was having a psychological impact as well. He was accentuating that which was hidden. This will scar her for a very long time to come. You mark my words. He is *worse* than a flasher."

PC Standing frowned.

"So you're saying that if he had *not* been wearing long johns – if he had just flapped his willy out – that it would have been less of an offence?"

Mrs Howlett nodded. Her logic was persuasive, he had to admit. And for the life of him he couldn't find a decent enough loophole to squirm through. It didn't occur to him that by Mrs Howlett's logic an Eskimo wearing eight layers of sealskin beneath a polar bear cloak and a Millets cagoule was the equivalent of top-shelf pornography.

Standing was a little bit bemused when Mrs Howlett left the room and came back moments later, wearing her coat. She insisted that they went to Hillrise Park to see if the flasher was still there. He explained that it was unlikely, given the fact it was raining hard and it was incredibly windy. But Mrs Howlett would not take no for an answer.

She would not be denied.

Thus it was, against his better instincts – and lamenting the loss of a quiet Friday night – Standing found himself venturing into Hillrise Park on the darkest of nights.

*

As they crept forward into darkness, the park seemed empty. Beyond the blustering wind and the swishing of the trees, there wasn't a sound to be heard. Standing was sure that whoever it was that had exposed his archaic undergarments to the girl would be long gone by now. There was no reason for him to be out.

Mrs Howlett was fairly certain, from her daughter's description, that she knew exactly where the incident had taken place. She urged PC Standing on, deeper into the park, until they came to a clump of trees. Here, Mrs Howlett hung back a little. She was clearly unnerved by the prospect of a second emergent flash.

"That's where he came from," she whispered. "That's where you'll find him."

PC Standing pointed his torch beam at the trees. He could see nothing but ghostly tree trunks and dark, impenetrable shadow. The rain was coming down hard and the wind was whipping itself up into a frenzy.

"You wait there,"nhe whispered to Mrs Howlett. He made his way slowly towards the trees.

For a little while he scanned the area with his torch, looking in amongst the trees, for the slightest clue as to the flasher's presence. He could see nothing. Mrs Howlett stood a few yards away, looking on anxiously. He was about to call it a night when she called out, hysterically.

"There he is! Behind you!"

Standing swung round, not sure what he was expecting to see.

To his amazement the dark, cowled figure of a monk slid out from behind a tree. It seemed to glide along and appeared not to be touching the ground. He shone his torch at the monk but the light was somehow absorbed by the figure. The monk had its own ethereal glow, a dim internal energy.

189

PC Standing saw that it was wearing a brown habit. A length of white rope tied it at the middle.

The figure stopped in its progress.

Slowly, it turned to face Standing, who was aware of the light from his torch being swallowed up into nothingness.

"Soooo ashamed..." The monk whispered, dolefully. Standing wasn't sure if the monk was addressing him. It seemed to be addressing no one in particular and its quiet words, full of pathos, melted into the air.

"Soooooo ashamed..." It repeated, sadly.

Standing stepped up to the breach.

"Good evening sir," he said, having to shout a little to be heard above the wind. "I wonder if I could have a quick word."

The monk swayed slightly from side to side. Standing felt himself staring into the black void of its hood.

"Soooooooooo ashamed..." It said.

"I guess by that, you are referring to the incident with the young girl earlier this evening," Standing asked, trying to sound simultaneously authoritative and sympathetic.

The monk stood quietly, staring back at him. There was something very eerie about this figure. Terence Standing suddenly found himself wondering why anyone would be dressed as a monk out here, in the park, on a night like this. It wasn't Halloween. And there hadn't been an abbey in Boomtown for centuries.

"Soooo ashamed," It repeated, almost to itself.

"Yes, you have intimated as much." Standing wondered how to take this conversation forward. "Perhaps you'd like to tell me why you are so ashamed?"

Mrs Howlett had been watching the scene unfold from her vantage point, a few yards back.

"*That's him, officer. Why don't you arrest him?*"

Standing spun around, irritated.

190

"We don't know that it *is* him," he snapped. "I'm just trying to find that out now."

"Of course it's him! *Look* at him! He's a nasty piece of work. I mean look at his eyes! *Way* too close together. You can't trust a man with eyes that close together."

Standing stared into the monk's hood.

"You can't see his eyes," he answered.

"Well!"

The monk remained silent throughout this exchange, swaying gently where it stood.

Keen to get some sense out of the monk, PC Standing stepped forward and tried to take hold of his arm. His hand went straight through the figure, as though it were thin air. The monk didn't seem to notice the intrusion, despite the fact Standing's hand was now effectively plunged into its intestines.

PC Standing leapt back in horror. Where his hand had been was icy cold. The monk was nothing more than a mass of freezing air.

He realised immediately that he was experiencing an encounter with a spectral monk.

"*Arrest him, officer!*" Mrs Howlett was practically screaming.

"It's not quite that easy," he said, weakly. The monk stood its ground, swaying gently, staring out at him from its cowled blackness.

"Sooooo ashamed," it almost whimpered. "Myne fastening loosened...the wind blew open myne habit...and myne undergarments, they didst knowest exposure."

"It was the wind?" Standing asked, carefully. He wasn't entirely sure how to address a spectral monk. This had never been covered in basic training. He wondered if he ought to call it Brother, or Your Holiness, or something.

"The wind didst blow myne habit asunder. And a young maid...a young maid...didst see myne hidden attire. Soooo ashamed...sooooo ashamed..."

The monk began to fade away until, just a few moments later, he was nothing but a memory, his final words blown away by the howling wind.

And then there was nothing but the dark, wet, windy night.

PC Standing turned to face Mrs Howlett who began to berate him for letting the suspect go.

"It was obviously him," she chided. "The man is a pervert. He wants locking up. How could you let him go?"

Wondering how Mrs Howlett had seemingly missed the supernatural nature of the monk's disappearance, Standing considered the best way to frame his answer.

It was at that moment his radio burst into life.

"PC Standing. Come in, PC Standing."

There was the hiss of static.

He put the radio to his face and lifted his eyebrows.

"Rubber Duck to Smokey Central," he said with relish. "I read you. Over."

There was a pause. Nobody in the force quite knew how to deal with PC Standing's idiosyncratic use of the radio system. He was the only policeman in the force with a bespoke "handle". His colloquial style embarrassed just about everybody, mainly because he genuinely seemed to think it made him sound streetwise.

"We've just had a report of a fight at the *Bird in Hand* pub in Pestlewick. Are you anywhere in the vicinity? Over."

"Rubber Duck to Smokey Central. That's a big ten-four, over. I'll run to the gun and make my way. Over."

"You'll what, sorry? Over."

"I'll get in the race and show my face. Over."

"Are you going to go there, over?"

"That's a big ten-four, Smokey Central. They're a-runnin' out of luck, 'cause here comes rubber duck. Over."

"Just get there."

Standing slid the radio back into its holster.

He looked back at Mrs Howlett, glad to have an excuse to get away from her and put this whole sorry episode behind him. No handcuffs in the world would hold an arrestee made from thin air. And he felt certain that pepper spray wouldn't have the slightest effect. Even if it did, the monk was clearly into self-chastisement, what with the hair shirt and everything. Such an individual would probably reach the giddy heights of spiritual ecstasy with a shot of CS Spray to the face. Standing did not want to encourage such a fetish.

*

When PC Standing got to the *Bird in Hand*, Santa Claus and his two henchmen were halfway through killing Zeus.

The ancient god was laid across the bar while they punched him repeatedly to the face. Father Christmas was also wielding the trombone and was using it to hit Zeus with frenzied violence across his entire body. The instrument was now bent completely out of shape.

The fracas had become increasingly bloody.

Claus had pulled Zeus roughly out of the corner and beat him without mercy, all over the pub. The regular customers had removed themselves from the arena of combat, to discrete corners of the pub. There they watched uncomfortably as Zeus was hurled from one place to another, enduring volleys of kicks and punches as he went.

There was no sport in it. Father Christmas and his men were seriously trying to hurt the ancient god. After a few minutes, Zeus stopped struggling. A few minutes more and he was no longer even whimpering. He was limp and helpless, a ragdoll; the plaything of underworld violence and bloodlust.

Dave the barman looked on uncomfortably, wiping a succession of glasses, as Zeus was hurled across tables, smashed into walls, kicked to the floor, pulled to his feet,

193

smacked around the face, punched across the head, kicked, pulled and beaten. He wanted for it to stop but like everyone, he dared not get involved. There was madness in the eyes of the white bearded gangster. His men looked mean and uncompromising. To get involved at this point would be suicide.

When PC Standing arrived, he was shocked at what he found.

The pub was in disarray, with over-turned tables and scattered chairs. But what shocked him was the way an old man was being beaten to a pulp across the bar, in clear sight of everyone present – and yet no one was lifting a finger to help him.

The old man's face was bloody, his beard matted and caked in blood.

His body looked racked and broken.

Standing realised almost immediately that it was the same man he had pulled over in the Austin Allegro with a descendent arse-end. It was the friend of the barbarian that he had so brilliantly interrogated on suspicion of illegal immigration.

Without a thought, he lunged across the pub and caught Reggie Watts' fist as it was about to deliver another crushing blow to Zeus's bloody face.

Watts spun around, his face enraged and hard like granite.

Standing didn't have time to register it as he lashed out with his other hand to stop the broken old trombone as it arced down through the air. He caught it and held it fast, preventing it from delivering another violent blow to the helpless victim. This time it was Claus's turn to stare at Standing with hateful contempt.

The festive gangster pulled back and motioned for his two men to do the same. The three of them moved away from the broken body on the bar and stood to face the source of the interruption. They stared at PC Standing, their faces etched with hatred, and he tried to remember if he'd ever encountered such unquenchable malice.

He didn't care. He had faced down harder men than these. He didn't know who the three men were, but they clearly had some sinister authority in these parts. People were scared of them. That much was obvious.

He stared back at them, impassively. The old man on the bar was unconscious and Standing thought it was a small mercy. Beaten to a pulp, he was hardly recognisable, just a mass of blood and gore. His only recognisable feature was the vague imprint of a trombone horn just below his ear.

"What is going on here?" Standing asked. He glared at the three men. They were trying to stare him into submission but he refused to look away.

They gave him no answer.

Standing turned to the pub at large.

"Can *anyone* tell me what is going on here?"

An empty silence settled over the place. To everyone's surprise - not least the barman who ponders it to this day - a ball of tumbleweed rolled across the floor, bouncing along in the slipstream of a lazy wind. It bounced into the gents' toilet and was never seen again.

Father Christmas held up his hands in a placating manner. His face, a countenance of pure fury just moments before, was warm and conciliatory.

"Just a small disagreement, officer," he said. A broad smile ruffled his beard. "It's nothing serious."

PC Standing looked over at the unconscious man on the bar.

"Nothing serious?" He spoke the words coldly. "This man is half dead."

Father Christmas looked from one to the other of his colleagues with a relaxed expression. He flashed Standing a broad smile.

"It just got a little out of hand," he said.

He looked down at Standing's badge.

"PC Standing," he said, thoughtfully. "I don't believe we've met before." He took a step towards Standing and reached inside his suit jacket. Slowly, deliberately, he pulled out a rolled-up wad of fifty pound notes and began to peel them off, one by one. The pub was silent as Santa Claus counted out two-thousand pounds in fifties.

"We've all been a bit...over excited," Claus continued. "We'll pay for any damage, of course. And for any...*inconvenience*. Here's a small offering. For a charity of your choice."

Claus looked Standing in the eye, significantly, as he offered him the money.

PC Standing did not take the money. He had seen *The Untouchables*. He knew what was going on here. He glared at Claus and his two henchmen.

"I would arrest you all now, if I thought it would do any good," he said. "But I get the impression no one in here is going to testify against you. I won't forget this. I won't forget any of you. Now get out."

Vinnie Hopkins and Reggie Watts did not move. They stared at PC Standing, their faces hard. Claus stood between them, examining the officer that had just obstructed his business. He nodded, slowly, his eyes not leaving the officer for a second. His smile had faded.

"You're a brave man," he said, finally. "Stupid. But brave. I think we'll meet again."

Terence Standing stood his ground.

The clock on the wall was ticking quietly.

"Come on boys," Claus said. And now he was smiling. The quintessential Father Christmas. The tension in the room dissolved in an instant.

Claus took a final hard look at the policeman then walked casually out of the *Bird in Hand*, Hopkins and Watts following close behind him. Hopkins flashed a final look back at the policeman at the bar.

"Until we meet again, PC Standing," Claus called back without a glance, as the door to the pub swung shut behind him.

Zeus, Father of the gods, awoke.

He lay in darkness, his heart beating fast. His entire body screamed out with pain. He ached all over. His face was tender and sore. His head throbbed and he could feel that his eyes were badly swollen. He looked out at the world through puffy slits.

He groaned.

*

After Terence Standing had seen off Claus and his men, he and a number of the regulars had moved Zeus on to a soft bench by the window. They laid him out and checked his responses. He had a pulse and he was breathing steadily, albeit with some considerable amount of wheezing. With what they all believed to be medical panache, they pulled open his eyelid and shone a light into his eye. His pupil contracted. None of them knew what it meant, but they were fairly certain it was a good thing.

They tried to bring him round, but to no avail.

They began by prodding him lightly, then dabbing some brandy on his lips. When that had no effect, they poured a shot straight down his throat. Still seeing no improvement, they poured a more generous shot down his throat before following it with six measures of Jack Daniels, some vodka and a flaming Sambuca.

Zeus groaned quietly, which they saw as affirmation of their restorative technique. They were going to move on to some Tequila Slammers but Dave the barman raised the issue of how they were going to fund this intensive first aid. Consequently, they tried the less elegant approach of throwing a bucket of cold water in Zeus's face. Despite some panicked coughing and heavy spluttering on Zeus's part, he still didn't wake up.

It was at this point that they decided to carry him home, believing a good night's sleep to be the best restorative.

When Standing, along with a couple of the pub regulars, carried Zeus into his flat, he was shocked by the state of the place. It was only a small bedsit and would have looked messy under any circumstances. But the entire flat was covered in soot and an untidy pile of dirty bricks lay haphazardly in the middle of the floor. Standing saw that the fireplace must have been bricked up and that it had caved out, causing the mess. Realising that he was on Pearbury Hill, he made some connections between the flat, the pitch black "Santa" that had flown out in front of his car, the beaten old man and the bearded gangster he had encountered tonight. In some inexplicable way, it all seemed connected.

They had left Zeus asleep on his bed. He was breathing heavily when they closed the door behind them.

*

Now, as he lay in the dark, a dull orange glow from the streetlamp outside filling the room with fluorescent light, Zeus tried to remember how he had got here.

He could remember being in the *Bird in Hand*, and waiting for Father Christmas to arrive.

At first that was all, but suddenly, in a rush of terrified emotion, everything came flooding back. He remembered Claus and his two heavies, walking into the pub. He remembered being cornered by the festive gangster. He remembered Claus's face when he realised that he wasn't going to get his money. And he remembered the trombone...

The trombone.

He rubbed his neck and felt the indent there, a painful scar caused by the impact of a violently aimed brass horn. His head throbbed and his whole body was a symphony of pain. It hurt when he breathed and he felt certain that some ribs were broken. He put his hand up to his face and felt the crusted blood that was dried into his beard. He groaned, and winced when he felt how dry and sore his lips were.

It wasn't over. He knew it wasn't over.

Somehow he had managed to get out of that pub alive. He had even managed to get home.

Father Christmas had given him a sound beating but that wouldn't be an end to it.

Zeus still owed him money.

He dreaded what else the festive personification might have in store for him.

His eyeballs were pulsing in his head, in time with the painful banging of his brain. It felt as though they were going to burst and he prayed this wouldn't happen. The last thing Zeus needed was eye-juice all over his carpet.

He tried not to move but it was agony to lay still. When he did move, it was worse. He'd never known pain like it. He seemed to be drifting in and out of sleep, ebbing gently into blissful unconsciousness, before sliding back into pained awareness. He waited for sleep to take him in its arms, to soothe him of his mental and physical anguish.

He lay in agony, waiting for sweet oblivion...

Then he remembered the fireplace.

Slowly, painfully, he looked over at it. In the dark it was a black gaping hole in the wall. It looked cold and threatening. The occasional small shower fell from the chimney.

Zeus felt his eyes throb harder.

He wasn't safe.

The gangster had already come in that way once, and that was when there had been a brick wall there. Now it was an open portal.

He wasn't safe.

Fearfully, like a child who knows there is a monster in the wardrobe, the ancient god stared at the gaping hole. If Claus dropped in now, intent on doing more violence, Zeus wouldn't stand a chance. He was vulnerable here. No one would hear his cries.

He had to get out.

Panic took hold of him and he wrenched himself up from the bed. Every nerve in his body screamed in pain. His head was spinning. Bright stars exploded in his head. He stumbled to his feet and lurched, disorientated, across the room. He found the front door and when he grabbed the handle, white hot pain ran shot through the gaping cuts on his hand. He groaned, mumbling incoherently, and stumbled through the door. Step by laboured step, he limped his way down the stairs and burst through the front door, out on to the street.

Pearbury Hill was quiet.

It was the early hours of the morning. The wind had died down and the road glistened, glowing wet beneath the early morning streetlamps. Zeus felt the cold air against his face and it soothed him. He murmured something – *not safe, not safe* – and staggered away from the door towards the road.

As he stepped off the kerb his body gave way and he fell forward on to the hard surface of the road.

He was there until a lone car had to steer around him, nearly an hour later.

The driver called an ambulance, directing it to the crumpled mess of old clothes and dirty matted hair that had once been the Father of the gods.

Despite a healthy range of well-engineered domestic cleaning products on the market, the removal of stubborn stains is often achievable only with the application of good old-fashioned elbow grease. Admittedly, the degradation of such a stain will be *aided* by a manufactured cleaning product, but localised physical effort is essential for eliminating the stain completely.

Thorax the Barbarian knew this better than most.

He often saw his spare time as the battlefield on which he waged his war against stubborn stains in the home. As house-proud as he was, it was inevitable that the occasional blemish would make itself known on his carpet, or his furniture. As soon as this happened, Thorax was on the case, usually on his hands and knees with a heavy-duty rag, a bowl of warm water and some concentrated solution.

The recent visits by Zeus had led to a few unsightly stains.

Most harrowing was the muddy footprint on the living room carpet.

This particular stain disturbed Thorax on two levels.

Firstly, a stain on the carpet offended him, whatever its nature, and one so blatantly visible as this, in the middle of his living room, gave him a creeping sense of anxiety. But more disturbing was the fact Thorax had requested Zeus to take off his shoes before coming into the house, a request Zeus had readily complied with. The stain on the carpet, despite its quality being consistent with residue from a muddy shoe, was actually a dark secret from the outer recesses of Zeus's sock. It was what stain experts refer to as "sock collateral".

That anyone could have this kind of dirt on their socks offended Thorax to the core.

He was on his hands and knees, attending to the stain, when there was a knock on the door. The barbarian glanced up, his face flushed with exertion, and dropped his rag into the bowl of warm soapy water.

"Come in, it's open," he called. The door opened and Thorax was surprised to see PC Standing, framed in the doorway. He stood up, brushing himself down, and ambled out to greet him.

Terence Standing looked at Thorax's apron with vague surprise.

"How can I help you, officer?" Thorax wondered if it was the good cop or the bad cop that he was addressing. He anxiously hoped that this wasn't the bad cop, returning for another round of intense conflict. He really needed to combat this stain.

PC Standing was wearing a concerned expression.

"I just wanted to let you know that the man you with the other day when I arrested you..."

"What about him?"

"He's in hospital. I'm afraid he was quite badly beaten up last night."

Thorax flung his hand to his mouth, his eyes wide.

"Oh my god," he said, quickly. "Is he alright? Why is he in hospital?"

"They don't think it is too much to worry about. He's got a number of broken bones and concussion. They've bandaged him up and they're taking good care of him. He just needs to rest for a couple of days."

Thorax was wiping his wet hands absent-mindedly on his apron.

"But why was he beaten up? How did it happen?"

"I don't exactly know. There were three of them. I got there just in the nick of time, I think. It didn't look as though they were going to stop. It was a violent attack."

"Oh my god."

"Can I ask...what is your relationship with the man?"

"We're friends, I suppose. We've been doing some work together."

"And do you know why he might have been attacked in this way?"

Thorax shook his head. Shock was written across his face.

Standing nodded.

"Well, anyway. I just thought I'd let you know," he said.

He walked back to his car, leaving Thorax with the news.

The barbarian stood in his doorway, a huge mountain of a man, fiddling with his hands and worrying himself sick.

John Thomas wasn't very experienced at dealing with witches. He had done some research however and thanks to the wonder of Google, he now knew something about them.

His initial preconceptions about these malevolent ladies of darkness turned out to be largely misguided. This was mostly down to the fact his expertise on the subject had been gleaned during his formative years, with *Grimm's Fairy Tales* and *The Wizard of Oz* forming the bulk of his source material.

He had believed, for example, that witches often had green faces and black pointy hats; that they were known for their facial warts; that they rode around on broomsticks; that they tended to have black cats; that they used cauldrons; and that they were fans of Black Sabbath. While none of these features were excluded from a witch's personal armoury, none were mandatory to afford a woman qualified witch status (QWS).

A witch, Thomas discovered, was defined not so much by how she appeared but by what she did and what she believed in.

If a woman was interested in casting spells and weaving magic, then she was probably a witch.

If she enjoyed bending nature to her will, she was probably a witch.

If she made sport by playing chicken with the Spanish Inquisition, she was, more likely than not, a witch.

If she routinely got dunked by a baying mob, she most probably had a certain witchiness about her.

Being burned at the stake would also mark her out as having definite QWS, as would a moral compass pointing somewhere on the scale between "amoral" and "completely bloody evil".

And if she danced naked under the sky, worshipped at the altar of a goat or did the horizontal dance of love with Satan himself, then the chances were, she was a witch.

Either that, or she was auditioning for *Britain's Got Talent*.

John Thomas's research had taken him down some very dark and disturbing avenues. It was necessary, though, to understand what he was letting himself in for before he visited the three witches. And despite the horror of what he read, the information was invaluable. He now knew what witches *liked* and in knowing this, he was able to arm himself with the means to achieve his ends.

Witches liked chaos.

They liked cooking children.

They liked a good porking by the devil and his minions.

And they loved Garibaldi biscuits.

The inception of chaos was a little outside of The Fixer's capabilities. Likewise, to involve himself in the procurement of children for culinary purposes was likely to lead to serious charges. It was also a difficult task to arrange a porking by the devil and his minions (though he might facilitate this, he thought, by the booking of a hotel room with a big bed and enough room to draw a half-decent pentagram).

But Garibaldi biscuits were well within his sphere of influence. And so it was, with a super-sized bumper pack of Garibaldis in hand, he fought his way through the horticultural disaster that was *Dun Roamin*'s front garden.

As many wayward adventurers had discovered before him, there was no door-knocker and no doorbell at *Dun Roamin*. Like many before him, John Thomas had to endure an uncomfortable few moments of wondering whether or not anyone had heard, after he had given a muffled announcement of himself by pushing in the letterbox and releasing it again.

When the barked reply came, suddenly, from the other side of the door, his skin began to crawl.

"We're closed for business!" It said. It had all the soothing resonance of a rusty bike.

"Um...I just wondered if I might have a word," John Thomas called, his face pressed to the door. He quietly hoped that they would refuse to see him.

"We said we're closed!" Came another voice, slightly less attractive than the first.

Thomas stood, deliberating. He looked down at the biscuits and decided it had to be worth a go.

"I've got some Garibaldis," he suggested.

There was a long silence, then the sound of muffled voices in heated discussion. Thomas waited, nervously. The chattering stopped, finally.

"Alright, it's open," said a third voice. "Come in."

The scene that greeted him on walking through the door shocked him.

Within a mere second of being in the bungalow, he felt unclean. The three witches were gathered around a silent cauldron. It was cold and still, its fire having gone out. They were ugly beyond description, their crinkled, grey faces pushed out into the damp, musty air around them, like devilish chicks awaiting their next feed. Thomas saw their empty, weeping eye sockets and the image, horrific and terrifying, buried itself in his soul like an arrow. He saw that their clothes were filthy, tattered rags, and that crawling lice moved slowly through their greasy, matted hair. The room smelled of damp and rotting meat.

John Thomas stared in silence.

"Who is it?" Said the nearest witch. "Who is there?"

"Tell us your name," said the second.

"And pass us a Garibaldi," said the third.

Thomas opened the packet of biscuits and stepped forwards. He didn't want to touch the women. They looked riddled with disease.

"My name is John Thomas," he said, in a level tone.

As he got nearer, he saw the cauldron was filled with a thick, grey sludge. Something was sticking out of it, that looked like the back of a head.

The witches sniggered. Thomas ignored them.

"And what do you want of us, *John Thomas*?" Said the furthest witch.

"Yes, what do you want of us?" Repeated another.

"I am here on God's work," Thomas said. "I believe that you can tell me how to get hold of the bachelor's plough."

The witches all began to croon, hideously. They swayed like drunken snakes, their eyeless sockets staring out at nothing.

"The plough," gurned one.

"The plough," repeated another.

"Give us a Garibaldi," added the third.

"I'll give you a Garibaldi if you help me," said John Thomas.

"Give us a Garibaldi anyway," said the first witch.

"No."

"Yes."

"No."

"Oh, go on."

"No. I need answers. If you give me the answer I am looking for, you can have *the entire packet* of Garibaldis. And it is a super-sized bumper pack."

"How many is that?" Asked the witch in the middle.

John Thomas looked at the packet and made a quick calculation.

"I don't know. About thirty?" He ventured.

The witches chattered and chirped and grinned like broken gargoyles.

One of them finally spoke.

"There is something else that we want," she creaked like an old door. "Get us that and *then* we will tell you how to get the plough."

"What is it?" Thomas asked.

Between the three of them, the witches explained what they wanted and how John Thomas could achieve it for them. They looked terrifying, malevolent, as they wove their plan, leaning over the cauldron with mad sightless eyes. John Thomas was mesmerised by their empty, chomping mouths and their crooked old bodies. Their heads nodded and shook like trees in the wind.

When they finally finished, John Thomas felt a weight like cold lead in the pit of his stomach. But he knew there was no other way.

He dropped the packet of Garibaldis into the cauldron and watched, fascinated and disgusted, as the packet sank a small way into the grey pulp. The witches all thrust their hands into the slop and grabbed the packet. They pulled the biscuits out and Thomas saw that they were all holding the packet, caked in grey slime, fighting each other for ownership.

"I'll be back with what you want," he said, stoically. "And when I do, I want answers."

He left them to it.

He had never been happier to get out of a place in his entire life.

It was like an emotionally charged scene from a hospital drama.

Thorax burst through the main doors of the Royal Boomtown Hospital and past a group of shocked-looking nurses. With barely-controlled panic, he banged through a pair of double doors, his face pinched with worry, and marched purposefully down the corridor. Were this an emotionally charged scene from a hospital drama, the camera would have been low, its angle looking up at him from a crazy angle. It would have kept up with his pace, keeping close to his determined bulk as he pushed through doors and marched down corridors.

There was no camera following the crazed barbarian. A length of flapping toilet paper protruded from the back of his trousers, however, and followed him faithfully along. He had pinched a loaf immediately prior to leaving his house and the toilet roll had become classically entangled with his woollen undergarments. Had he known about it, he would have been sublimely humiliated. Fortunately, he was blissfully unaware of the glances and sniggers that had been directed at him for the past hour on account of it.

He found Zeus's ward and ran in, his face etched with concern.

His Tony Blackburn hair-do remained poignantly still as he gazed down at the bed. A tear welled up in his eye. Zeus looked so small, framed by the crisp white hospital trolley. He looked tiny. Then Thorax realised he was looking at a midget with a hernia and that Zeus was in the next bed along.

Zeus stared up at him with bruised, puffy eyes. His face was cut and swollen, painted in a rainbow of greens and yellows and browns. His puny white shoulders, sticking out from under the bedclothes, looked bruised and sore. Thorax gave a concerned smile.

"I've brought you some grapes," he said. He stepped forward and placed the brown paper bag on the bed next to the ancient god. "And a puzzle book."

He laid the puzzle book next to the bag of grapes. Zeus nodded gratefully and winced as he tried to manage a smile. His mouth was lacerated.

"So how are you?" Asked Thorax. "What happened?"

With words that were clumsy and laboured, Zeus explained what had happened at the *Bird in Hand*. He told Thorax about the debt he was in and how .Father Christmas had been on his back for some weeks now. He explained how this was the reason he found out about the bachelor's plough in the first place.

Thorax ran a hand through his well-sculptured hair.

"I wish I had been there," he lamented. "I might have helped."

Zeus shook his head.

"It's my problem," he said. "My debt. I can handle those guys. When I've got the plough, everything will be okay."

Thorax looked him in the eye.

"I'll get the plough," he said.

Zeus nodded. He manoeuvred a battered arm out from under the bedclothes and helped himself to a grape. He chewed slowly and every movement of his mouth provoked a frenetically played concerto of agony. He picked out another grape. He wasn't sure if it was a real word, or just one that my mum made up, but the grapes were moreish.

"So what did that copper take you in for?"

"Oh, you know. He thought I was an illegal immigrant."

"Oh. And were you?"

"No. Never have been."

Zeus agonised his way through another grape.

"Look, I've been thinking," he mumbled. "Before you go wading in with Medusa, risking a compacted-mineral based end, it might be an idea to go and see an old friend of the Minotaur. Polyphemus."

"Polyphemus?"

"Yes. He's a Cyclops. He and the Minotaur go back a long way. You never know – he might be able to help. If we can avoid confronting the Gorgon, then I think we should. That woman unnerves me."

Thorax raised an eyebrow.

"Are you talking about...you know...*the* Cyclops?"

Zeus nodded.

"I think I read about him once," Thorax mused. "A huge one-eyed creature, fifty feet high. He lived in a cave and was the embodiment of pure aggression. He would seal the cave up with a boulder so huge that no ordinary man could budge it. He ate sheep, whole – and men too, if he got the opportunity."

"That's him," admitted Zeus, casually. "Though he has mellowed a bit, over the years."

"And what's the ocular situation now?"

"Still just the one."

"Will he be able to help us get the plough?"

Zeus tried to shrug, which translated as an almost imperceptible quiver of the shoulder.

"It's got to be worth a go."

"Is he local? Or am I expected to travel to Ancient Greece to have this conversation?"

"No, no. He's local. He lives on Church Rise. What do you think?"

Thorax nodded. He looked a bit like Tony Blackburn on steroids, in the act of giving an affirmative gesture.

"It's got to be worth a go, I suppose."

They talked for a while longer. At one point Zeus tried to play a practical joke on Thorax, trying to make him believe that his concussion was worse than it was, by repeatedly calling Thorax "Dorothy" and asking where he had hidden his family jewels.

Thorax saw straight through it and told him to stop behaving so childishly.

In retaliation, Zeus asked Thorax if he knew that he had a length of toilet roll sticking out from the back of his trousers. He knew full well that the barbarian would see this as another attempt at a practical joke and sure enough, Thorax made a point of *not* checking.

By such means, Zeus ensured that the toilet roll remained firmly *in situ* for at least another hour.

"*Can you take the rabbit out? No. Over there. Just put it over there. Next to the potatoes. No...the potatoes. That's fine. What? Yes, I did. He wasn't there though. I don't know, I think he went for a haircut. In the biscuit tin. Yes. I am, yes. Bloody flies...is it just Me or do they seem to be everywhere at the moment? No, just behind the...yes, that's it. Is that what I think it is? It is. It's a pair of underpants. He's been leaving his underpants on the fridge again...*"

John Thomas listened in, awkwardly.

The phone had been ringing for ages and when he picked it up he could hear God in the background, talking to whoever was with Him. It seemed that God had dialled John Thomas by accident and didn't realise that He was broadcasting.

It felt intrusive listening in, but it so happened that he did need to speak to the Good Lord.

"Hello?" He spoke into the phone, uncomfortably.

"*Why does he do that? It just doesn't make any sense. Eh? No, his underpants. Always his underpants. I know! That's what I keep thinking. But it doesn't seem to bother him. I'd be ashamed to leave My divine undergarments anywhere public, let alone...hang on...who's bought a new fridge magnet? Is that Bon Jovi...?*"

"HELLO!" Thomas shouted into the phone.

"*Who's been to see Bon Jovi? That's official merchandise that is. It's quite nice, though. Goes well next to the London bus. Oh bugger. I've dropped My toast. Did I just see Uriel? He's been popping in here all morning. In and out like a whore's drawers. I think he's lost something. Oh, really? How do you lose a harp? They're huge...*"

"HEEELLLLOOOOOO!!!!"

Realising that they couldn't hear him, Thomas put the phone down. It was the polite thing to do. It then occurred to him that on a landline, the connection is only severed when the person *who made the call in the first place* puts down the phone. The last thing John wanted was for his mum to pick up the phone and find herself listening into a heavenly dialogue.

Hoping that it worked differently when the call was from Heaven, he picked up the phone and put it to his ear.

"*...thirty-two stone. And I thought – how are we ever going to get her up here...*"

"HELLO! GOD!! CAN YOU HEAR ME? IT'S JOHN THOMAS. YOU'VE RUNG ME BY ACCIDENT!!!"

"*...but for the life of Me, I couldn't understand why anyone would want to keep a spider as a pet. I know. But...*did *he? I never knew that. He always seemed so reserved...*"

Desperately, Thomas jammed his fingers down on the cradle, repeatedly.

"*...launched it from a tomato sauce bottle, like some kind of ballistic missile...*"

It occurred to Thomas that a high-pitched noise might hit the required frequency to be heard. He put his mouth to the mouthpiece of his phone and gave a piercing whistle.

He put the phone to his ear and listened. It had gone silent on the other end. The silence was broken by God's voice, sounding baffled.

"*What the hell was that?*"

Thomas whistled again.

"*There it goes again. What is it?*"

There was another voice, separate to the Good Lord's.

"*I think it came from over here...*"

Thomas heard the voices getting closer. He whistled again.

"*What* is *that?*" Asked God, in wonder.

The other voice was very close now.

"*It seems to be...hang on...look! The phone is off the* hook."

Suddenly, it was God's voice on the phone, sounding anxious.

"Hello? Hello? Is anyone there?"

"God, it's John. John Thomas."

"John Thomas," God sounded relieved. "How long have you been there?"

"Only for a minute or two. I've been trying to get Your attention. You rang me by accident, I think."

"Thank *Me* it's you. I phoned into a radio phone-in yesterday. I thought the line was still open. Oh My good *Me*! Can you imagine if the whole nation had just heard..."

"What did You phone into a radio phone-in about?"

"They had a piece on dogs fouling in public places."

"Oh, right. Did you tell them who You were?"

"No! I remained anonymous. I don't think the Good Lord should have an opinion on things like that. Not officially."

"No. Anyway, God. I did need to talk to You."

"Fire away."

"Well, I've been to see the witches and they said they will tell me how to get the plough on one condition."

"Oh?"

Thomas suddenly found himself questioning God's omniscience.

"Er...thinking about it, You must already know what it is, O Lord."

God blustered.

"Oh...yes, yes. Of course. But I want to hear it from your own mouth."

"Oh. Okay. Well, apparently, they share this eye. It is a crystal orb, about the size of a cricket ball. It sounds a bit like a paperweight, to be honest. Anyway, Zeus stole the eye from them and without it, they can't see. They say he took it to a

216

local pawnbroker. They have asked me to get it back for them. But when I went into the place, the owner said he was still having it priced and until then, it wouldn't be for sale. It sounds like it might have quite a value."

"Hmm. You're going to have to break in and steal it."

John Thomas took the phone away from his ear and looked at it in disbelief.

"But God – good and Holy Father of all creation – I thought that You have specified, quite adamantly, *Thou Shalt Not Steal*."

There was a pause.

"Have I?" He is omniscient, omnipotent, and omnipresent. But God is unable to lie very convincingly.

"Yes. You wrote it on tablets of stone. For Moses. And the Israelites."

"Look. How about, *do as I say, not as I write on ancient tablets of stone?*"

"But my infallible Lord. It is a divine statute. It has helped to structure Judeo-Christian Western civilisation for centuries."

"Hmm. Yes. Alright. Well, I can sort that out. I'll do that in a minute. But you, John Thomas, you have got to *break into that place* and get the eye. I am relying on you. Get the eye and get Me the plough. You *must* get Me that plough, John Thomas."

John Thomas listened to his name, spoken with vehemence by the Lord. His euphemistic name had always detrimentally impacted on his self-image. But right now, he wasn't just sporting the name of a dangly todger. He was sporting the name of a dangly todger in the most precarious circumstances.

His bus driver training had never prepared him for all of this.

*

217

It wasn't audible to anybody below forty thousand feet but had anyone been up that high, they might have heard a banging noise coming from the heavens.

It was a sharp rhythmic sound, the sound of dense metal against stone. Every few moments there was a pause at which point there would be a whisper of satisfaction, or an angry expletive.

This went on for some three or four hours, at the end of which time, a small hatch opened in the sky. Something was dropped through the hatch and it plummeted to earth at speed.

John Thomas had just made himself a cup of tea when he heard the massive thud in his garden. His first thought was that a commercial flight had dumped its raw sewage directly overhead and that it had frozen on descent, to land in his garden, a solid block of waste. He had heard of this happening and it was just the sort of thing that would happen to him.

When he went out to investigate, though, he was surprised to see a tablet of stone embedded in the grass at an angle. It was about the size of an old LP cover, and a good few inches thick.

Inscribed on the stone tablet were some words, chiselled out in an untidy, ancient script.

~~Ammen~~ Amendment to the ~~You~~ Thou Shalt Not Steal ~~law~~ commandement :
Thou Shalt Not Steal unless ~~the~~ it be on the Lord's ~~his~~ business, in which case it is acseptable in the eyes of God.

The Fixer felt vindicated.

Thorax the Barbarian expected Polyphemus to live in a cave or, at the very least, some capacious barn conversion.

When he got to the Cyclops's lair on Church Rise, he was disappointed to find it was a small semi-detached house. Of the two houses, joined together as one, the Cyclops' abode was the more run-down of the pair, with old paintwork and dirty windows, but it was generally in good condition. Thorax pondered the dimensions of the homestead. For a creature purported to be around fifty feet in height and with an aggressive streak the size of the English Channel, the house was likely to prove a little cramped.

As he made his way up the garden path, Thorax tried to see inside the house but the dirty windows were backed by yellowing net curtains and he could see nothing. Nonetheless, he could not shake the uncanny feeling that some huge watchful eye, the size of a bicycle wheel, was staring out at him from behind that net curtain.

He had expected to find was a vast, immovable boulder blocking the front door. Instead, the most arresting obstacle to confront him was a sign on the door which read: *No Cold Callers Please.* Apart from a few very small rocks adding depth to the small flower bed just under the front window, there was not a boulder to be seen.

Bracing himself for a violent confrontation, Thorax the Barbarian pressed the doorbell. An electronic rendition of *Für Elise* burst into life, somewhere inside the house.

A booming voice called out, somewhere from within.

"Hang on a minute! I'm on the bog!"

The words offended Thorax's delicate sensibilities and for his own peace of mind, he tried to forget what he had heard. He stood at the door, waiting patiently. After a few minutes he heard the flushing of a toilet and then, a moment later, a shadow appeared on the other side of the frosted glass door.

The door opened wide and there stood Polyphemus.

The Cyclops.

It was undoubtedly him. A single eye blinked out from his forehead. His face was unshaven and rugged with centuries of aggression. The scars of countless fights and battles adorned his skin like jewellery. He had a big "P" embroidered on his pullover. It was definitely Polyphemus. And yet...

He was he was a lot *smaller* than Thorax had imagined.

Thorax looked down at the legendary monster. Standing at somewhere between four and five feet in height, he had a quality about him that could almost have been defined as cute. As he stood there, from inside the house, the succulent smell of roasted lamb wafted out. It seemed to hang around the pint-sized Cyclops like a coat rack.

"Can I 'elp you?" Asked Polyphemus. For a small man, he had a big voice.

"Yes, I hope so," Thorax flashed his most winning customer service smile. "I understand that you are old friends with Roger, the Minotaur."

" *Was,*" corrected the Cyclops. " *Was* good friends."

"Oh. Have you fallen out?"

"Yeah,"Polyphemus sniffed. He looked at Thorax and gave him a conspiratorial wink. "'Ere. Fancy a lamb chop?"

Thorax nodded enthusiastically. A lamb chop was *exactly* what he fancied. He hoped that the Cyclops had some appropriate sauce to go with it, such as a subtle mint sauce or a barbecue relish.

*

They sat in Polyphemus's living room, munching on their lamb chops.

The room was basic, with an old television, a couple of armchairs and a faded drinks cabinet. There was no carpet, which was a good thing, considering that Polyphemus dripped fat from his chop all over the floor. It made Thorax quite anxious to watch.

The Cyclops had a plate piled with chops and picked at them as though they were peanuts in a bowl. To the relief of his civic sensibilities, Thorax didn't detect the smallest amount of aggression in the creature. What he did uncover was a severe case of agoraphobia.

His suspicions were aroused by the way the windows were allowed to silt over and the fact Polyphemus had everything delivered to him rather than going out for it. When he asked the Cyclops about it, Polyphemus admitted that he had not set foot outside of the house for twelve years. His reason, in true agoraphobic tradition, was that the sky was too big for him to cope with. Thorax made a mental note to drop some support leaflets off next time he was passing by. He had seen such leaflets at the doctors' surgery. Agoraphobia is a debilitating condition, but it is curable.

"Do you mind me asking what happened with you and Roger?" He asked, tearing off a mouthful of chop.

"It was stoopid really," Polyphemus replied, his mouth stuffed full of meat. "It was over a plough."

"Ahhh."

"He's got this fing about ploughs, ya see. 'E loves them. They're like a mad passion...an obsession."

"Yes, I know."

"Well, we was great mates, me and Roger. This was before I was...ya know...'ouse bound. We used to go fishing and that. Well, one day I borrowed a plough off 'im. It was just some rusty old fing, nuffink special, like. I borrowed it to plough a furrow in me garden, to plant some peas."

"That seems like a lot of hassle just to plant some peas," said Thorax. "When I plant my peas, I tend to use a small trowel. It makes the job quick and easy and helps you to space them accurately and then, with a generous but sensible portion of general purpose compost accompanying each seed, the peas stand an excellent chance of healthy growth."

"Yeah. But ya know what it's like. If you've got access to a plough, you're gonna use it, ain't ya? So anyways, I ploughs me garden, like, but there's this big rock in the middle of the garden what I didn't see. It bent the plough's blade, like."

"Oh. And that upset Roger?"

"Upset 'im? You'd 'ave fought I'd massacred 'is entire family. Well, actually, I did. I et 'em all. A long time ago, it was. And 'e wasn't 'alf as upset then, as when I bent 'is plough."

"So what happened next?"

"'E frew a right wobbly and frettened me and gored me a bit with 'is 'orns. And 'e ain't never spoken to me since."

"Blimey. He really has got it bad, hasn't he? This thing with the ploughs."

"You ain't never seen nuffink like it, I'm tellin' ya."

"Well, the thing is...do you mind if I have another chop? They're absolutely delicious."

"Please, be my guest."

Thorax took another chop and began to know it with gastric intimacy.

"The thing is, Roger has got a plough that I want. And I don't know how to get it from him. He won't even talk about selling it to me. How do you suggest I go about getting it?"

The Cyclops shook his head, with certainty.

"You won't get it, mate. He'll be 'olding on to that plough like an elephant 'olds on to a sticky bun. Or an 'ouse spider 'olds on to an arachnophobe's mental sanguinity."

"But...there must be a way."

"Well, the only way I can fink of, is if you 'ad a plough that 'e wanted even more. Like, if you 'ad a really special plough. Then you could bargin with 'im. Swap the one 'e wants, for the one you want, like."

Thorax nodded. It was a nice idea. But the bachelor's plough was forged in Thor's own furnace. It would be a tough call to find a plough more unique than that.

"I've been told that if I show him Medusa," he said, slowly, wiping some dribbled fat from his chin. "Then she'll turn him to stone and then I can just take the plough."

Polyphemus laughed, loudly. He tore his chop apart with his bare hands, then shoved a piece of it into his mouth.

"That would work!" He laughed. "If you can get Medusa to go wiv you, then yep – the plough's yours! She ain't no noddin' donkey though."

Thorax nodded sullenly. He ate the rest of his chop in silence.

As he was leaving, he found himself having to ask the Cyclops about his diminutive size.

"How come you are so small?" He asked the question as inoffensively as he could. His Tony Blackburn hair-do shimmered in the sunlight. "I thought you were a giant."

Polyphemus nodded, sadly.

"Shrinkage with age," he replied, without emotion. "You've seen how old people get smaller, as they get older. They kind of shrink in their skin. Well, I'm somewhere between three and four thousand years old. I've shrunk considerably."

"And you are still shrinking?"

"Yeah. I've worked it out. Anuver two-fousand-four-'undred years and I'll be microscopic."

"Bummer."

"Yeah. I won't be 'alf the Cyclops I was."

"Oh well. Worse things happen at sea."

They shook hands, warmly. They had enjoyed each other's company and Thorax had been strongly affected by

Polyphemus' lamb-chop-based hospitality, which had been entirely unexpected.

Under the cover of night, John Thomas shinned his way up a drainpipe, which led directly on to the roof of the pawnbroker's shop.

It was just after two o'clock in the morning. It was a cold, still night.

The shop had a flat roof with skylights, and with the help of a screwdriver and precision laser cutting technology that he found in the cupboard under the stairs at home, he removed one of the skylights. He shuffled the coiled length of rope from his shoulder and dropped it through the skylight, securing one end to the roof. With a quick glance around him to check that there was nobody in the vicinity, he slid through the skylight and down the rope into the shop.

It was dark inside. He drew a small torch from his pocket and cast a thin beam of light around the shop. All he had to do was find the eye and he could get the hell out. This sort of thing really wasn't in his comfort zone. He felt positively intrusive.

He crept around the shop, alert for anything that might look like a paperweight.

Almost immediately he found one on a shelf next to some books. It was a snow-globe, with a tiny Swiss village inside. If you shook it, fake snow fell over the village in a microcosmic blizzard. He felt almost certain this wasn't the eye. The eye was thousands of years old and was created in the home of the gods, at Mount Olympus. This paperweight had a sticker on the bottom, saying "Made in Taiwan".

He didn't have a plan.

All he could do was explore the shop and continue looking until he chanced upon the eye. The place was a treasure trove of junk. He picked his way through the catalogue of miscellany, the ornaments, the trinkets, the jewellery and the countless personal effects. So many of these objects had sentimental value to someone. In here, they were almost worthless.

He was rattling his way through an old golf bag, wondering if the owner of the shop might have hidden it there, when he heard a noise from above. Anxiously, he flicked off his torch. There, above him, framed by the skylight, was a shadow. The silhouette of a man. Against the stars, he seemed to have an overly developed cranium. Thomas crept over to an old sideboard, his heart pounding. He crouched down next to it, trying his best to disappear into the shadows.

A second rope was dropped through the skylight and Thomas saw the man descend with beetling speed, into the shop. A torch flicked into life and Thomas watched silently as the beam began to pick out the various objects around the shop. He saw it pause at each object before moving on to the next. To John Thomas' growing discomfort he saw that the torch beam was moving nearer and nearer to where he was crouching. An embarrassing moment was becoming inevitable and by the time the torchlight got to him, he was resigned to it.

In the full light of the torch, crouched uncomfortably next to the sideboard, he gave an embarrassed wave. The torch jumped with the shock of discovering him.

"Who are you?" Crooned a voice. It was thin, well-spoken, laced with authority.

"Ah, hello." Thomas smiled and strained himself to his feet. He brushed himself down. The torchlight was trained on him. He stood there in his tight black clothes, camouflaged for the job in hand

"So. You too are here in the act of burglary." Beetled the voice.

Thomas nodded.

"Yes, kind of." He admitted. "But I am looking for something specific. I'm looking for a paperweight."

"I see. I am here for a garden gnome. Have you seen a garden gnome at all?"

"No, I'm afraid I haven't." Thomas sounded genuinely apologetic.

"Hmm. Well, I need to find it. Have you got a torch?"

"Yes."

"Well, don't let me stop you from you endeavours. I'm going to start looking for the gnome. If I see a paperweight, I will let you know. And if you see a garden gnome..."

"Yes, of course. I'll let you know."

Thomas flicked his torch back on and the two men began to root around the shop in silence, both intent on their own search.

After forty minutes, they were still searching. While neither of them had found what they were looking for, John Thomas did find a kettle and some coffee making facilities. He realised he was ready for a break.

He called over to the other man, in one of those shouty whisper things that is a living, breathing vocal paradox, asking if he wanted to join him for a coffee break. It would be a kind of burglar's elevenses. The man admitted that he was starting to flag a bit and he was, in fact, gasping for a brew.

Five minutes later, they were sitting on the floor besides the counter, each with a steaming mug of coffee in hand.

John Thomas was surprised to discover, in the first few minutes of casual conversation, that the man was none other than the fictional godfather of Victorian crime, Professor Moriarty.

"What – *the* Professor Moriarty?" He asked. "As in the arch-enemy of Hercules Poirot?"

Moriarty took a sip of his coffee.

"Hercules Poirot?" He sounded irritated. "No. If I had an arch-enemy, it would have to be that Sherlock "I-can-tell-you-your-precise-movements-for-the-past-two-weeks-from-a-simple-scuff-on-your-shoe" Holmes."

"Ah yes! That's it! The arch-enemy of Sherlock Holmes!"

In the halo from Moriarty's torchlight, Thomas saw a thin, determined-looking man. Though he was sitting down, his legs pulled up to his chest, he was obviously very tall. He had a pinched face, with eyes that were malevolent and calculating. The top of his head was hairless, though he had a rim of dark hair. It was what John Thomas always referred to as a wide parting. The most striking characteristic was his cranium, which seemed overly developed. Freakishly so. He looked deformed.

"What are you doing here?" Thomas asked., conversationally. He had never met a fictional character before. "I thought you died at the Reichenbach falls, back in Tudor times?"

"A common misconception," Moriarty conceded. "Although you're well out on the date. It was eighteen-ninety-one, to be precise. No. It was all an elaborate hoax, devised by Sherlock and I. He wanted out. I wanted out. The fame had become too much for both of us. Previous to that infernal Watson blabbing on about everything we did like some kind of over-excited schoolgirl, we had both been quite happy moving in relative obscurity, doing our respective jobs on either side of the criminal spectrum. He was relatively successful. And so was I. It was a good balance."

"So you..."

"So we agreed to stage a fight at the Reichenbach falls and make it look as if we had both gone over. More than anything, Holmes wanted to get away from Watson."

"But he came back."

"Yes. He discussed it with me first, though. He missed the limelight. More ego than sense, that man. I didn't like it when he came back. He said that he had escaped from the falls. The lie was getting messy, I felt. But you must give a man his freedom, I always believe."

"Blimey."

"Yes." Moriarty sounded reflective. "So anyway, I moved to Boomtown and I've been here ever since. I'm still the greatest criminal mind in existence, though. There is still a web of crime and iniquity for which I am the central hub. My reach is long and on the chessboard of crime's great game, I still control all the pieces."

"Crikey."

"Yes. Whenever you see a crime - in the street, in the newspapers, on the TV - you can pretty much rest assured that ol' Moriarty is at the root of it."

"It's hard to believe!"

"I am a phenomenon."

"You're telling me!" John Thomas took a respectful gulp of coffee. "So what do you actually do?"

"What do you mean?"

"Well. What do you *do*? I mean, if you're the hub of all this criminal activity - where do you actually fit into it all? Practically? Take that armed robbery on the King's Road last week. At the Off-Licence. Did you have anything to do with that?"

"Of course."

"So...what did you *do*?"

"I was in the background."

"In what way?"

Moriarty scratched his nose and sipped his coffee, quickly.

"Well, I was sort of...I kind of over-saw it."

"What - you planned it?"

"Not exactly. I was more...sort of...in the background. Like, if you imagine that armed robbery to have been a strand on a big web...well, I was the hub of that web."

"Did you know the robbers?"

"No. But they had ol' Moriarty behind them."

"So you didn't plan it, and you don't know the robbers. Forgive me, Professor, but it seems to me that you didn't really have anything to do with it at all."

"That's how I want it to look. That is why it's impossible to trace any crime back to me. Sherlock only ever came *close* to establishing a real, provable connection. But if you took me out of the equation, there would be no crime at all."

"How come?"

"I am the criminal mastermind. Any crime you see out there...ol' Moriarty has a hand in it. I'm a one-man crime wave. I cause the crime. I give it the go-ahead."

"But that armed robbery – you didn't know them. How could you have given it the go-ahead."

"They knew ol' Moriarty was behind it."

"Maybe they don't even know who you are?"

"Don't know Moriarty? Without me they would be nothing. Of course they know me."

"But I still don't see...it just seems that the reason no crime can be traced back to you is because you don't actually have anything to do with the crimes."

"Such is the intangible nature of my web."

John Thomas gulped down some more coffee. Either there was something so subtle about Professor Moriarty's operation that it would take a genius to understand it; or Moriarty was completely deluded and his vast criminal empire was all in his mind. Thomas had read Sherlock Holmes and it was something he had wondered about many times. For a web of criminal intrigue, it all seemed pretty flimsy.

"What are you a professor of?" He asked, taking a sip of his coffee. This was something else he had always wondered.

"Social trends," replied Moriarty, casually.

"A Professor in social trends?"

"Yes. You know. Why people do the jobs they do. Why people live where they do. What makes people move around. Family structures. Social economics. That sort of thing."

"Isn't that a bit of a wishy-washy subject?"

Professor Moriarty looked unfazed.

"No, it is very important. It is useful for such things as town and social planning. And it can inform government policy, too, if your area of expertise is of relevance."

"And what's your area of expertise?"

"Pets."

"Pets?"

"Yes. You know. Why people keep pets. What sort of people keep pets. What a pet brings to a person's life, their family, their community. How the acquisition of pets changes in correlation to social and economic changes. For example, more people buy reptiles during an economic boom, than in a recession. Did you know that? And rabbits tend to be purchased by families with young children and are only really part of the family *while* those children are young."

"Oh, right. I always imagined you to be a professor of something different. Mathematics, or science, or something."

"Social trends is a *social* science."

"Yes, I suppose so."

There was a pause, as they sipped their coffee, comfortable in each other's company. After a while, Moriarty spoke.

"And what about you. What do you do?"

"I'm a bus driver."

"Oh! Is it rewarding work?"

"It's a vocation," said Thomas, sagely. "You become a bus driver because you get the calling. It certainly isn't for the money! No. We bus drivers, we do it because it's what we *are*. It's *who* we are. It's in our blood."

"But the money must be adequate?"

231

"No, not really. To be honest, if we did it for the money...well. The nation's bus lanes would be empty, that's all I can say about it."

Moriarty looked troubled at the notion.

"That's an eerie thought," he said.

"Yes. It is apocalyptic."

They continued to converse for some time. Thomas learned that Professor Moriarty was at the shop to find a garden gnome with a valuable gem inside of it. After being stolen from a museum, the gem had been hidden in the gnome, which was then supposed to be delivered straight to Moriarty's home. Unfortunately, a mix up in the delivery consignment led to the gnome being delivered to a garden centre. From there it was sold to a woman who purchased it as a birthday present for her husband. She then had an affair with a crumpet taster, and this led to the break-up of the marriage. The husband wanted rid of the gnome, due to its painful sentimental value. And this was how it ended up at the pawnbrokers.

It was, like John Thomas's paper weight, proving a bugger to find.

They were just about to continue with their respective searches when they heard a noise coming from the roof. They flicked off their torches and watched as a third rope was dropped through the skylight. A dark figure slid down the rope and flicked on a torch.

"It's like Clapham Junction in here tonight," whispered Moriarty.

It didn't take long for the newest arrival to shine his light in the direction of the two figures sitting on the floor before the counter. The torchlight flicked from one to the other of the empty mugs before reaching the two men. In the halo of his torchlight, it could be seen that like them, this man was dressed all in black.

"Here on matters of burglary?" Asked Moriarty.

Seeing that the two men were clearly burglars themselves, the newest arrival relaxed.

"Yes," he said. "I'm after a mug. It's an original *World's Strongest Man* mug, from nineteen seventy-nine. There aren't many in existence and I know there is one here. I've got the other *World's Strongest Man* mugs from seventy-eight through to eighty-five. I *must* have this one for my collection."

"I'm after a garden gnome," said Moriarty.

"I'm after a paperweight," said Thomas.

They all shook hands, joking that they needed to invent some kind of secret burglar handshake. With the pleasantries behind them, they all continued the search, determined not only to find their own items but to help each other find their spoils. Teamwork won out. Just half an hour later, they all had their prizes. The sense of celebration was electric. John Thomas put the kettle on and made everyone a well-earned cup of coffee.

As they were sitting in front of the counter, talking about the job they had done, Professor Moriarty held up the garden gnome and shone his torch on it.

The gnome was pushing a small wheelbarrow and his eyes were full of life and mischief.

"It's a shame to have to break it," said the professor. "It's quite a nice gnome. He would have looked good in my garden."

And everyone had to agree with that. It was a very attractive gnome indeed. It would have looked good in *anyone's* garden. The wheelbarrow set it off nicely.

"A garden gnome, a paperweight and a *World's Strongest Man* mug from 1979," the pawnbroker explained. "As far as I can tell they are the only things missing."

Terence Standing made a few notes in his pad. It was a curious case. He had been called to the pawnbroker's shop near the Barrelway Shopping Precinct just after nine. Someone had broken in during the night and left evidence of their visit in the form of three used mugs, left on the floor by the counter. The obvious supposition was that three people had broken in. The strange thing was they had taken very little and what they had taken was seemingly random.

Standing poked around the shop. It wasn't obvious how they had entered and he wondered if anyone else had a key to the place. The proprietor insisted that he was the only one with a key. There were skylights, which afforded a fairly standard means of entry for some burglars – but the skylights looked undisturbed. In Standing's experience, if burglars came in through a skylight they left it open when they left. They didn't risk staying around to fix it back on. The only reason they might do so was avoid anybody noticing that they had been in. Yet this had clearly not been the case in this instance, as was demonstrated by the used coffee mugs by the counter.

"Was there anything special about the three objects?" Standing asked. "Anything at all?"

The owner screwed his face up.

"The World's Strongest Man mug is quite rare," he said. "But it doesn't have much value. The garden gnome is worthless, really. It would add a splash of personality to any garden – it had a really nice wheelbarrow, that set it off a treat – but that is as far as it goes. The paperweight...well, I am waiting for a value back on that."

"You think it might have some value?"

"Yes. It seemed to be made from some very rare, very dense crystal. It has a weird sort of property, too. When you look through it, it gives the illusion that you are seeing into the next world."

"What – like the future? Flying cars and self-warming toilet seats, that sort of thing?"

"No. The world of the dead."

"Oh. Right. Interesting." He made a note of it. "Who brought this in?"

The owner described the man who had pawned the paperweight. PC Standing stopped writing in his notebook, about halfway through the description.

"Did you happen to see what he was driving?" He asked.

"Yes, it was some garish orange car. A butt-ugly thing, it was. It had a square steering wheel."

Standing folded his notebook and returned it to his pocket. Lately there had been too many coincidences and he didn't like it. He didn't like it at all. It felt as though a symphony of circumstance was building up all around him, into a dramatic, final crescendo. Something significant was happening but as long as he was in the dark, there was bugger all he could do about it.

Stupidly, John Thomas allowed himself to be outmanoeuvred.

While he stood near to the cauldron, getting the information he required from the witches, they were already preparing their next move.

Two of the old hags engaged him cunningly in conversation. He told them that he had the eye and that he would give it to them once he knew how to get the plough. He then listened carefully as they outlined what he must do. He marvelled at their description of Medusa, the Gorgon, and how she could be used to bring down the Minotaur. He took on board their advice not to look her in the eye, for doing so would turn him into stone. It sounded dangerous but it was a clear route of action and he appreciated that.

As Thomas was talking to the two witches, the third was making her way around the room to the front door. By the time he had been given all that he needed, she was in position.

"We've told you all you want," said one of the witches. "Now give us the eye."

He handed it over without a second thought.

It was only when he turned to go that he realised what they had done.

The third witch stood in front of the door, blocking his way. She stared sightlessly into the room, her evil face full of hungry anticipation.

Behind him, her sisters began to cackle.

He turned and saw them moving towards him. The eyeless one was feeling her way around the cauldron. The one that had the eye moved with confidence, slinking towards Thomas, the crystal orb trained on her prey. They were both smiling horribly.

His heart was pounding as he backed away from the cauldron, towards the door. It was a classic pincer movement, a move even more classic than the Heimlich Formation.

"You *are* going to let me go?" Thomas asked, fighting the tremble in his voice.

"That was never part of the bargain," wheezed the witch with the eye. She took small, inelegant steps towards him. She walked like a beetle.

"We never said we'd let you *go*," said the second witch.

"You can stay for dinner," came the scraping voice of the witch by the door.

Desperately, Thomas moved away from the door. They were moving him into a corner. Both witches had moved away from the cauldron and were stumbling across the room towards him.

"You do know I am here on God's work," Thomas said, desperately.

"God!" Said the witch with the eye.

"God!" Said the second.

"God!" Said the one by the door.

The witch with the eye stumbled towards him, watching him carefully, her face a map of laughing hatred.

"God is nothing to us," she said, venomously.

"And He'll find another to do his work," said the witch by the door.

He reached the corner of the room and could go no further. The witches stumbled and crowed towards him, their arms outstretched. They were chomping their mouths, licking their lips.

"We'll need to get the cauldron on," said the second witch. "You're going to take some cooking!"

The thought of being eaten by these hideous creatures made John Thomas's stomach turn. They were bad enough on the outside. He dreaded to think what they were like on

237

the inside. He certainly didn't want to take that final ride to find out.

The witch with the eye was right on top of him now. Her outstretched fingers were just inches from his face. He ducked, sidestepped under her arm and leapt to the back of the room.

She spun to face him and continued to stagger towards him. The other witch felt what was happening and did the same. He watched them coming, their mouths working, their eyeless faces mooning at him as they approached. There was a window next to the front door and he thought about jumping straight through it.

The idea was sound enough but his imagination kicked into overdrive and played out some possible consequences. One was that the window was made from reinforced glass and he would bounce off, to land back in the room, unconscious. He'd be boiling in the cauldron by the time he awoke. Another possible consequence was that he would lacerate himself on the broken glass as he smashed through, hitting an artery and causing his own untimely demise. He decided that a dramatic leap through the window was probably not a good policy.

As the witches got closer, he grappled desperately for an escape plan.

When inspiration hit him, he cursed the perversity of his Muse.

He pushed the idea away and begged for another. The same idea came again. He begged the source of his inspiration – *no, please, anything but that* – but the idea would not abate. Nothing further occurred to him and to his horror, he found that he was left with no choice. God's work, he was beginning to discover, was less than glamorous. Verily, the path to righteousness was strewn with thorns.

The witches were nearly upon him. He could smell their reeking flesh, their putrid breath. He could feel the rank humidity of their bodies. They were moaning hungrily, chattering in brittle, involuntary squeaks. He waited until they were upon him, to give him the best possible chance, then dived between them and ran to the front door. The third witch stood before the front door waiting for him. Her face was crinkled, leathery and pinched with hate.

What his Muse had told him was this:

John Thomas, you are blessed with a manly charm surpassing that of most men. Women swoon as you pass them by. They dream about you in their beds. When they make love to their husbands and their boyfriends, it is you that they are thinking of. You drive women insane, with your natural sexual magnetism.[7] Now. These three women are, you can almost guarantee, somewhat out of practise in the ways of love. They cannot have been touched by a man, they cannot have felt a man's loving kiss, for...well, forever. And yet beneath it all, they are still women, John Thomas. They are still women, with a woman's passion and a woman's needs. You must work your manly charm on the witch at the door, to facilitate your escape. John Thomas, you must subdue her with a kiss. And if necessary, you must be prepared to cop a feel as well.

For a few seconds, Thomas stared at the witch before him.

---

[7] John Thomas was a great fan of British author, Alan Titchmarsh, and the Titchmarsh canon. His internal perception of himself was construed from Titchmarsh's novels and he was unaware of any schism between self perception and reality. A schism there was, however. A big schism. A schism so pronounced that it could legitimately be used as the very definition of the word "schism". It was like the mother of all schisms. The *granddaddy* of all schisms. It was a schism on steroids. A schism with an overly-doting mother and a consequent ego of gargantuan proportions, knowing only itself as the ultmate truth. It was a schism with monster-truck wheels added to its chassis. *BigSchism.* A schism with delusions of grandeur and a self-conceit that knew no bounds. A schism with a flashy car. A schism in platform shoes. A schism with a self-created double-barrelled name: *Schism Turner-Smithe.* It really was one hell of a schism.

She was all that stood between imprisonment and escape.

He looked at her foul, wrinkled face - the bristling hair that grew from her chin, the eyeless sockets, the congealed grease in her wrinkles, the putrid gummy mouth, the crawling lice in her matted hair - and he wondered if being eaten was necessarily such a bad way to go. But when he thought of that final journey through a witch's intestines, he knew he had to get out. Whatever the cost.

He stepped forward. Her empty eye sockets grew wide with surprise as he slid an arm around her waist and pulled her to him. Her body was limp and bony beneath his touch. She gurned uncontrollably and he could smell her breath, like an un-flushed toilet. Stealing himself he leaned in and kissed her leathery lips, trying to ignore the chin hair that scratched against his face. She gave a moan that was as sensual as a collapsing chair and she munched his face, as she tried to kiss him back. She sucked lightly on his tongue, drawing it in between her slimy gums. The inside of her mouth was like a birdcage and he felt something wriggle against his tongue. It felt like a maggot. She pressed herself against him and he felt her grinding her clammy body against his own.

The kiss lasted mere seconds. For John Thomas it felt like a lifetime. The witch swooned into his arms and he seized the moment. Holding her in his arms he turned before letting go of her. She fell to the floor next to him in an ungainly heap.

Thomas grabbed the door and yanked it open. He ran out into the open air, gasping for sweet, sweet breath. He ran and ran and didn't stop running until he got home, some thirty minutes later.

After one of the most traumatic episodes of his entire life, John Thomas sank to his knees and prayed. He clasped his hands together, his eyes tightly shut.

"Dear God," he prayed. "Give me a call when You get this message. Thanks. Yours sincerely, John Thomas. Amen."

The family had been browsing around the scrap yard for a few of hours and they kept coming back to the old bus.

As always when they visited, Roger had greeted them warmly then told them to browse for as long as they wanted. Every now and then he would pop over helpfully, to see if there was anything they needed.

Today, however, he was a little preoccupied.

There was a strange tension building in the air, all around, that he didn't understand. For reasons that he couldn't articulate, he felt that he was central to it. This morning he had picked up a telephone message from his old friend, Polyphemus. They had fallen out long ago and Roger didn't have any time for him. Polyphemus was a plough wrecker. But the message had come out of the blue. *I just wanted to see 'ow you are. Say 'ello, like*, the Cyclops had said. *I misses our times togever. So what's new? You still into your ploughs an' all that?*

It disturbed Roger. A call, completely out of the blue. And asking about his ploughs. Why was everyone so interested in his ploughs at the moment?

He wandered over to the family. They were standing at the back of the old double-decker bus, chatting happily about its rear wheel. All of the tyres were flat and broken, except for this one. The wheel was scuffed and caked with old dirt and diesel soot, but the tyre still had some air left in it.

"Nice piece, isn't it?" Mused Roger. He smiled at the family, then gave the bus an admiring look.

They all nodded, enthusiastically. The young boy ran his hands over the metal flank.

"It's just like a *dream*," he said, with childish innocence.

"It's the nicest bus in the *world!*" Exclaimed the little girl.

The mother shone down at her children proudly and found her gaze drawn back to the broken old bus. She smiled at it with wistful dreaming.

Ever practical, the father looked the Minotaur in the eye.

"We quite like this rear wheel," he said. "How much would you want for it?"

Roger thought for a few moments.

"You could have it for twenty quid," he said, reasonably.

The father looked over at his wife. She smiled.

"It would go nice in the hallway," she suggested.

"Yes it would!" The children chorused. "Oh *please* can we have it, daddy? *Please!*"

He laughed. Happily, he tousled his children's hair, ever the indulgent father.

"Well...I suppose it would be a nice thing to have," he said. He flashed Roger a beaming smile. "We'll take it!" He said.

"Yay!" Exclaimed the children.

The man's wife leaned over and kissed him, happily.

"Thank you darling," she said. "I am so lucky to have a husband so wonderful."

It took half an hour to remove the wheel. Roger used the magnetic crane to lift the rear end of the bus and then used a spanner and a wrench to remove the nuts from the wheel. He slid the wheel from the axle and brought it to the ground with a strained exhalation of air. He rolled it over to the family and they clapped their hands in glee. The father handed over the money.

"Thank you so much," he said. He was beaming.

The family all thanked Roger fondly

"Come again soon!" Insisted Roger.

"Oh we will!" They said.

They left the scrap yard, the father rolling the wheel in front of them. Roger watched, happy to see such contented customers. But as they disappeared out of sight his mind slid anxiously back to the tension that was hanging over him like a dark cloud. Something was happening. Something was *going* to happen. He only wished he knew what it was.

"It was horrible."

John Thomas had just finished telling God what happened when he took the eye back to the witches. God had been unusually sympathetic, encouraging Thomas through the most difficult parts of his narrative.

"Well, at least it's done now," He said, with divine benevolence. "You have done well, John Thomas."

"Thank You, O Lord."

"So. Medusa, eh? The Gorgon." God sounded omnisciently serious. "She's a bit of a monster, that one. You are going to have to be careful."

"I agree. I know You work in mysterious ways Your wonders to perform, O Lord, but why did You ever create a monster so hideous and so dangerous?" John Thomas asked.

"I didn't create her." God said, emphatically.

"But I thought You created everything in the universe?"

"Well yes, I did. Kind of. It's a bit more theologically complex than that, though. I don't fully understand it Myself, to be honest."

"Oh. So how am I supposed to get her in front of the Minotaur? I'm not using my manly charm again."

"I wouldn't expect you to. You're not Woody Allen - as much as you may think otherwise. Your manly charms won't work on everyone. Fortunately for you, that witch was blind."

"What is that supposed to mean...?"

"What you must do is *talk* to the Gorgon. Try to bargain with her. Find out what she wants and see if you can't exchange favours."

"But how am I supposed to talk to her without being turned to stone?"

The Good Lord chuckled.

"I've already thought of that," He said. "Have you got military night vision apparatus, with infra-red capability?"

"I think my mum has."

"Good. Well the way I see it, if you wear that you should be okay. Think about it. If you see Medusa in infra-red, you won't be looking into her eyes, you will merely be seeing her heat signature."

John Thomas shook his head in admiration. He wanted to give the Lord a round of applause.

"Lord, You really are omniscient and wise!" He said.

"Did you ever doubt it?" Asked the Good Lord. The hint of a divine smile was audible down the phone.

When they both hung up, after a series of uncomfortable farewells, the bachelor's plough seemed closer and almost within reach.

It was one of the most salubrious hotels in Boomtown.

Just a few minutes' walk from the town centre, The New Diamond Suite boasted a wealthy clientele and a five-star rating. It was known for its luxurious interior and its fine cuisine. It was less well-known for the fact Boomtown's most ruthless gangster operated out of the top floor. The fact was, he owned the place.

Zeus pulled up outside the hotel in his Allegro. There wasn't even any bounce in the rear-end now; the back of the car simply scraped along the ground in a constant shower of sparks.

There was a semi-circular car port at the front of the hotel, where taxis would drop residents off and wealthy customers would leave their cars, handing the keys to the concierge for parking. Zeus slotted the Allegro in between a Rolls Royce and a Mercedes limousine and climbed out, nervously. He knew how mad this was. He was visiting the lion's den; putting his head into the lion's mouth; extending his hand to the lion's paw; inserting a suppository into the lion's arse. The lion-based metaphors were endless. They didn't make him feel any better, either. He found himself wishing he had chosen a more comfortable image – such as a butterfly. He knew, however, that the act of putting a suppository up a butterfly's arse was a physical impossibility.

The fact was, he hadn't slept for days. Since coming out of hospital Zeus had been constantly on his guard, waiting for the car to pull up alongside him or the heavy hand to fall upon his shoulder from behind. He still owed Father Christmas a lot of money – he knew that – and the beating he had received at Claus's hands would not stand as payment for his debt. Claus would come after him and it could happen at any time.

The nights were the worst.

Lying in his bed, he found himself listening for any sound that would tell him Santa was about to drop down the chimney. The smallest tap on the roof or the gentlest breeze down the chimney would send him into paroxysms of anxiety. He no longer felt safe in his own home. The gangster had been in Zeus's bedsit once and there was nothing to stop him entering again.

It was while walking the streets of Pestlewick in the early hours of the morning, after hauling himself out of bed in a state of acute anxiety, that Zeus had contrived a solution. The idea presented itself to him in a flash and while not an ideal solution, it was workable. In it, he saw an end to his troubles. He was here now to present his solution to the gangland boss himself.

He bumbled though the revolving door and into the hotel lobby.

It was an expansive space, accentuated by a large chandelier hanging from the high ceiling. Leather sofas were scattered around, furnishing a polished marble floor. Zeus felt a little out of place, surrounded by the oozing confidence of tailored suits and high street fashion. The sense of wealth was palpable, and the very air smelled of expensive scent and designer perfume. In his beige trousers and maroon jumper, he knew that he all the contextual relevance of an elephant in a fish-tank. But he wasn't here to make a fashion statement.

Feigning confidence, he walked up to one of the reception desks. The manicured receptionist gazed at him, with a hesitating smile.

"Can I help you, sir?" She asked. Her dark hair was pulled back tightly. Her red lips were perfect, framed by a face that was smooth and without blemish.

"I'm here to speak with the owner, please." He said, with as much authority as he could muster.

"I'm sorry, the owner isn't based here. Besides, you would need an appointment to see him."

Zeus stroked his beard.

"He *is* based here," he corrected her. "He occupies the top floor, as well you know. I think that if you tell him Zeus from the *Bird in Hand* is here to see him, he will be more than happy to see me."

She looked slightly uncomfortable and hugely disinterested, as she picked up the phone and turned away from Zeus to hold a private conversation. A few moments later she turned back to face him, placing the phone back in its cradle. She gazed at him politely and said nothing.

"Well?" Asked Zeus.

A door swung open on the other side of the lobby and two large men came bursting out. They strode across the lobby towards Zeus. They were impeccably dressed, in dark, tailored suits. He immediately recognised one of them as Reggie Watts. The other one was unknown to him, but his face was hard and brutal and Zeus could see that he was well-acquainted with physical violence.

They came and stood on either side of the ancient god. Reggie Watts looked down at him with humourless eyes.

"You're healing up nicely," he said. Zeus gave him a wry smile.

"I want to see *the man*," he said. It seemed like the right terminology to use, but he was very much in unfamiliar territory here.

"He wants to see you too," said Watts. "Come with us."

They didn't lay a hand on Zeus. They didn't need to. Knowing what would happen if you didn't concur was persuasion enough. They walked back across the lobby to the door through which they had come in.

Zeus followed closely behind.

Santa Claus's office dripped with luxury. The walls were papered in rich patterned velvet and a cream coloured shag-pile carpet adorned the floor, flush with every wall. Expensive leather chairs were dotted around and a large oak desk stood in the middle of the room, giving it an air of formal decadence. Large, framed pictures hung from the walls, the most impressive of which being a black and white panorama of the Chicago skyline. A few suited men were positioned around the room, and the air was thick with cigar smoke.

The gangland boss was sitting at his desk. In one hand he was holding the phone to his ear. In the other hand he held a fat Cuban cigar.

Zeus was ushered in and he stood waiting, while Father Christmas finished his call.

"I'm not understanding you," Claus said, stabbing the air with his cigar. "You say you are a criminal mastermind? The hub of crime? Sorry...what was your name again? Moriarty. Professor Moriarty. Okay. So you want me to come and work for you?"

Claus took a large puff of his cigar. He looked simultaneously irritated and amused.

"And how would that work, exactly? Hang on...okay...so...I need to think of it like a huge web. A web of crime. Okay. And my operation would be one strand of that web. And you would be at the centre of the web, with all criminal activities spanning out from you. I see."

He put the phone on his shoulder and looked over at Reggie Watts and the other men with an expression of disbelief.

"So...sorry...hang on a minute. I'm trying to understand what you are offering here. Where would you fit into all of this? I'll be running my operation, as usual. But I'll be working for you. How would that work? Right. So I just need to see you as being the centre of this great web. Would you fund my operation in any way? No. Okay. So, would you plan any of our undertakings? No. Right. But you would be the criminal mastermind facilitating all that we do? I see.

"It would what, sorry? It would give me great kudos to work for you. Because you are such a criminal mastermind. Well, that is impressive, I must say. Do you mind me asking, Professor - what are you actually a professor *in*? Social what? Social trends. Oh, right. A specialism in pets? Right. I see.

"Fuck off."

Claus placed the phone back on its cradle casually. He was shaking his head.

"That was the weirdest conversation I have had in a long time," he mused, taking a long puff of his cigar. He glanced over and saw Zeus.

His bewildered expression suddenly became focused. His eyes narrowed and he looked the ancient god up and down. He wore the expression of an entomologist examining a particularly fine specimen and Zeus thought that he looked impressed.

"Well, well, well." Said Claus. He drew on his cigar and blew out languorously, watching Zeus through the smoke. "To what do I owe this unexpected pleasure?"

Zeus looked askance of the two men on either side of him. They nodded assent and he stepped forwards nervously, approaching Claus across the desk.

"Look, I know I still owe you money," he stammered. Claus tilted his head, graciously.

"That's a good start," he said.

"Yes, well, I pay my debts." Zeus stood up straight and looked Claus in the eye. "And I have a proposition for you."

"I'm listening."

"Well, you've probably worked out by now that I am having trouble getting the money together. It's not for want of trying. I just don't have access to the sort of funds I need. But

I want to pay you back. And I think I may have come up with a way."

"Go on," Claus blew out more smoke.

Zeus took a deep breath.

"Well, I'm a lorry driver, right? I do all sorts of deliveries and pick-ups. Some of them are nothing really – nothing of any real value, anyway – but often I'll have a consignment that's worth something. You see? Like a lorry load of whiskey, or computers, or perfume, or something."

Claus was nodding, slowly. His eyes were heavy-lidded and watchful. Zeus continued.

"So I was thinking, if I gave you the tip off next time I had a valuable consignment, we could work together to stage an ambush. We'll find somewhere a little bit out of the way, so that there are no witnesses. We'll meet there at a certain time and bam! You take the goods and I claim that I was robbed by persons unknown. It would be an easy job for you and would cover my debt."

Father Christmas stared at him across the desk. Zeus did not allow his gaze to drop. After a while, Claus took another puff of his cigar and tapped a finger thoughtfully on the desk.

"When do you think the next big consignment will be?" He asked.

"It all depends. But I get at least one good one a week."

Claus nodded slowly. He continued to stare at the ancient god.

"Do you think you're up to it?" He asked, holding his cigar before him like a truncheon of righteousness.

Zeus nodded vehemently.

"I owe you," he said. "And this is the only way I can think of, to make that right."

For a few minutes Claus said nothing. He sat back, gazing across his desk, meditating through the smoke from his cigar. Finally, he balanced the cigar on the side of his ashtray and leaned forwards. He was smiling, a pink gash slicing through his bushy white beard.

"You've got yourself a deal," he said.

Zeus took a deep breath. For better or for worse, he had just become an affiliate of Boomtown's brutal gangster community.

Were she to have put an advert in the *Times'* lonely-hearts section, it might have run something like this:

Mature woman seeks resilient man for fun and companionship. Must have GSOH and be comfortable with snakes. A natural empathy with stone is desirable. Looks unimportant - a non-judgemental personality a must. Would prefer solvent gentleman with own car.

Medusa, however, never *did* put an advert in the *Times'* lonely-hearts section. The search for love was not really something she was interested in and unless it was George Clooney - whom she did, admittedly, have something of a soft spot for - any man that tried to lay claim to her maiden's jewel would be given short shrift. More likely than not, he would be given the immediate status of quarry-fodder. George Clooney, just to qualify this point, would be treated to a level of Gorgonic intimacy beyond his wildest dreams and would experience what it is to be on the receiving end of a long and intimate snake job.

She had lived in Beverley Road for many years and her garden was strewn with the life-sized statues of living beings that had come under her petrifying stare. There were hedgehogs and badgers, foxes and birds. Most dramatic, however, were the human beings that adorned her lawn, like ornate garden ornaments. There were several postmen, a milkman, and a window-cleaner, two fleeing burglars, a Jehovah's Witness, a tree surgeon, a council surveyor and a schoolboy. Each and every one had made the mistake of meeting the Gorgon's hideous stare.

No one really got a good look at Medusa – not for posterity, anyway – but if they had, they would have observed a frumpy, squat creature, with a floral dress and open-toed sandals. She never wore make-up, there was no point, and her face was haggard and plain. Her arms and hands were pudgy, leaving her knuckles as a series of indents. Her skeleton was hidden under a podgy layer of flab. Upon her head, she had no hair as such. Instead, a hundred snakes writhed and slithered, moving over each other and undulating constantly with hypnotic momentum.

Apart from her hairdo, it was her eyes that really captured her petrifying character. Bright green, they twinkled with the unearthly fire that burned deep inside.

When Thorax the Barbarian sneaked up and knocked on Medusa's front door, the Gorgon was in the kitchen, making a stew. No sooner had he knocked, than the barbarian ran back down the garden path and hid behind the wall at the end of the garden.

A few moments later, Medusa opened the door. The green flame in her eyes was already beginning to flicker. It was not often she got a visitor at the door but when she did, the result was invariably the same. As it happened, she was ready for a new addition to her collection of garden statues and was hoping that her visitor would have adequate dimensions to block up the unsightly hole in her garden fence.

Glaring out, she was surprised to find no one there. At first she assumed it was local children playing "Knock down Ginger" (unbeknown to them, they were dicing, literally, with death) but when she turned to go back inside, she caught sight of the small package on the doorstep. Little did she know that this small package stood as a profound testament to the ingenuity of one Billy the Dwarf.

As it was, she didn't know what to make of it.

Once, a few years back, some local children had knocked on her door and ran away. They had left a package on her doorstep then, too.

On that occasion, the package had been the faecal signature of some large dog, wrapped in newspaper. The children had set fire to the newspaper before scarpering and when Medusa came out and found the burning object on her doorstep, quite naturally, she stamped out the fire. This led to her getting dog excrement all over her sandals and part way up her leg. She found it to be a most unpleasant experience.

She feared for weeks that she might have contracted toxocariasis. The smell seemed to linger up her nose for many days and furthermore, in having to get to the kitchen to clean herself up, she trod dog business all through the house. It was all very traumatic.

Now as she looked down at the package on her doorstep, she remembered this difficult memory and not for the first time, she wished that the culprits would one day come back to her door so that she could give them her special stare. The statues of two young boys, one on either side of her front door, would be a grand addition to her home.

The package that was currently sitting on her doorstep, however, was not on fire. It also lacked any obvious faecal properties. Were she to sum up its general appearance, far from making any reference to faecal waste, she would probably frame her description as a rabbit with mirrors attached to it.

Which is exactly what it was.

Billy the Dwarf's idea for testing his theory – that if you were to look at Medusa through a mirror, her petrifying powers would be ineffective – was to try it with a rabbit first.

He and Thorax had spent some considerable time devising a contraption that would enable this test to take place and they had alighted on a metal brace that would fit around a rabbit's torso. A series of mirrors placed at various angles

255

around the rabbit would ensure that anything viewed by the rabbit would be done so through the reflective medium. By leaving the mirror-clad rabbit in Medusa's vicinity, and ensuring its encounter with the Gorgon monster, they would soon know whether or not the theory was correct. Quite simply, the rabbit would turn to stone if the theory was misguided.

The theory turned out to be misguided.

Within seconds of Medusa answering her front door, the rabbit had frozen into a notably stonier version of its former self. Her very brief glimpse of the rabbit, before it caught sight of her in the mirror, showed it to be a curious little bunny with a twitchy nose. The eye contact soon put paid to that. No sooner had she registered what it actually was that had been left on her doorstep, than she found herself admiring a rabbit-artisan's version of Michelangelo's *David*. Unlike the original, however, this David was shrouded in a metal frame and a dozen strategically-placed mirrors. Also unlike the original, this David was more coy about displaying its genitals to all and sundry, preferring to keep them modestly hidden against its invisible underbelly.

Further contrasts with the original sculpture included the fact this statue was actually called "Starsky"; and that it was a rabbit.

The Gorgon stared down at the stone rabbit, wondering how it had come to be there and why it was so unusually attired. She didn't notice the Tony Blackburn hair-do rise up slowly, from behind the wall at the end of her garden. Thorax peered over like a barbaric Chad and saw the statuesque result of the experiment. He had bought Starsky earlier that morning, from a local pet shop. Starsky had hopped around excitedly, clearly believing this to be the start of a wonderful new life. Thorax felt bad for having raised the little fellow's spirits.

At the same time, he thanked his lucky stars that they tested out Billy's theory first.

*

For the second time that day, there was a knock at Medusa's front door. She was in the conservatory, drinking an afternoon cup of tea and browsing through her latest copy of *Woman's Own*. She liked to read about High Street fashion and the latest hairstyles, even if it didn't apply to her. She had always wished that her cranial snakes would be a bit more docile, so that she could have them styled into a bob or even a beehive. But it would never happen. They were feral little bastards.

Surprised at having a second caller, she pulled herself out of the chair and strolled to the front door. She had put this morning's curious delivery straight in the dustbin. She could have made room for it somewhere on her lawn but in the process of petrifaction, the mirrored frame had become fused to the rabbit and the whole thing looked unwieldy. She had enough rabbits, anyway.

When she opened the door, she was half expecting to find another mirrored animal. For some reason her mind chucked up the notion that this time it might be a garden worm in the mirrored frame. The thought delighted her and she was suddenly aware of the fact she had never turned a worm to stone. They didn't have eyes, she supposed, and so were unable to look at her. In that moment she realised that after all these years, she could finally have a pet. She had always wanted a pet. Something to love and cherish; some company for her, through the happy times and the sad. She resolved then and there to go out into the garden and find a worm before the day was out. She would give it a nice home – probably an old ice-cream tub, filled with garden soil.

She would call it Percy.

257

A huge man stood on her doorstep. He wore grey trousers and a blue cagoule. His hairstyle was fashioned into a nineteen-seventies style – reminiscent of Tony Blackburn. He stood stock-still and Medusa saw that he was squeezing his eyes tightly shut.

She waited in silence, examining this huge mountain of a man curiously. She wanted him to open his eyes. He would block up the hole in her fence nicely.

After a while, he spoke. He had begun to look distinctly uncomfortable with the lack of dialogue.

"Are you there?" He asked.

Medusa waited, in quiet amusement. He was stupid enough to open his eyes to find out, she was sure of it.

"Hello?" He said.

She would need the pallet truck to move him around the back, she thought. He would be heavy.

"Is anybody there?" Thorax asked, his eyes still screwed tight.

Gingerly, he extended his arm, waving it around like a blind man in the snow. Suddenly, a number of the slithering monstrosities on top of the Gorgon's head made contact with his fingers. He cried out and pulled back his hand as though he had touched a hot pan.

The snakes hissed.

"You *are* there," he insisted.

"Why don't you open your eyes and see?" Medusa prompted, her voice silky and seductive.

"I'd rather not. No offence, but I know what happens when people look at you. I saw what you did to Starsky."

"Starsky?"

"Yes."

She reached up to soothe the hissing, spitting snakes, stroking them gently with porcelain fingers.

"Well. It seems you have the advantage. You seem to know *me*. I guess you are here for a reason. What do you want?" She continued to stroke the snakes.

"I need your help," Thorax said, simply. He was keeping his eyes so tightly shut that it caused him to pull a ridiculous face, his mouth hanging gormlessly open.

"I'm not in the habit of helping people," Medusa said.

"But this is important. I am working for Zeus."

"That old lech!"

"Sorry?"

Medusa laughed derisively.

"Back in his day, he couldn't keep it in his trousers, that one. My god! It had a life of its own! It made the snakes on *my* head look positively tame!"

Thorax flushed red. Medusa went on.

"He would knob anything. Gods, mortals. He even tried it on with me once. I said, *eh, eh, what kind of woman do you think I am? I'm not letting that thing near me. I don't know where it's been.* The thing was, I *did* know where it had been. That was the trouble!"

"Well, he's asked me to help him with something."

"Hang on a minute. Is he still thinking he can get in my drawers? Has he sent you here to gain access to my virtue?"

"No, no. Nothing like that."

"What then?"

"We need someone turned to stone. We thought you might be able to help."

"What – I'm some kind of rent-a-petrifaction service now, am I?"

"No. We just...we need your help."

"I don't owe Zeus anything," she said, indifferently. "And I certainly don't owe you anything. Why would I want to help *you*?"

259

Thorax, who was useless at putting arguments together, crumbled. He stood helplessly, eyes screwed shut, and shrugged.

Medusa watched him with thoughtful, quiet interest. There was no doubt about it. He would do wonders for hiding the hole in that fence.

There were a few tricks that she had employed in the past, for adventurers like this, who were resolved not to look at her. It was all down to psychology. All she had to do was distract him with something mundane.

"I *could* help, I suppose," she said.

"Really?" Thorax's eyebrows lifted. His mouth remained gormless and open.

"Yes. I suppose it couldn't hurt. Mind you, I could do with some help right now. I've got something in my eye. Can you have a look?"

Thorax began to open his eyes, ready to lean forwards to assist, when he realised what she was doing. He squeezed them shut once more.

"You're not going to catch me out like that," he said, annoyed. "Are you going to help me, or not?"

She stroked her snakes and thought for a while.

"What do you think about this mole on my face?" She asked, her voice dripping with concern. "Do you think I should get it looked at by a doctor?"

Thorax nearly fell for it again. He stopped himself just at the last moment from opening his eyes.

"Look. I know what you're doing. It's not going to work. What will it take for you to help us?"

"It's not really the sort of thing I do," said the Gorgon. "I mean, if I were to turn someone to stone every time I was ask...OHMYGOD! WHAT *IS* THAT? LOOK OUT! IT'S COMING TOWARDS YOU!"

Thorax sighed. This was going nowhere. He realised that he was going to need to move on to Plan B.

260

Keeping his eyes tightly closed, he gave a formal nod of his head.

"Thank you for your time," he said, curtly.

He turned on his heel and felt his way back down the garden path. A few minutes later, after colliding with several lamp posts and falling flat on his face, due to an old bike that was left on the pavement, he remembered to open his eyes.

Zeus sat at a table in the old Salvation Army cafe on Grocer's Lane, going through the delivery manifests for the coming week. He sometimes liked to drop into the cafe for a cup of tea and a toasted tea cake. No matter which table he chose to sit at, it was always wonky. Today was no exception.

Every time he leaned on the table it moved dramatically, causing tea to slop over the side of the mug and all over the table. It was bad enough that the small metal teapot they gave him always dribbled more tea from the lid than actually came out of the spout. Nonetheless, he liked the place. It was homely.

He hovered his pen over the manifest, thoughtfully

It told him where his pick-ups and deliveries were and outlined the nature of the consignments. Most of them were routine, but one stood out as a perfect opportunity to stage the heist and get Father Christmas off his back. A large consignment of handheld games consoles was to be picked up from a warehouse in Bracknell and taken to an industrial estate near Bournemouth. There was a choice of routes that Zeus could take – but an obvious one took him straight through the middle of the New Forest. Here there were ample of areas where the "ambush" could happen at a leisurely pace, without any danger of being witnessed.

Zeus did an estimated calculation on the back of the manifest and figured that the consignment would be worth somewhere in the region of £300,000. Even if Claus was able to shift it out at a fraction of its retail value, he would make some serious money and it would easily pay off Zeus's debt.

He stabbed the manifest with his pen, a gesture intended to do nothing more than confirm to himself that he had just made an important decision. He hadn't noticed the telephone ringing by the till and was surprised when the cashier brought it over to him.

"It's for you," she said. She wasn't accustomed to taking calls for other people, a fact she made very clear through her tone.

Zeus thanked her and looked at the phone with a frown. He waited for the woman to walk away before putting it to his ear.

"Hello?" He said.

"Hello. Zeus?" He didn't recognise the voice on the other end.

"Yes?"

"It's God."

"Who?"

"God."

"Which god?"

"*The* God. The Divine Creator of the universe."

"What..Jehovah?"

"Yes."

Zeus gave a tired laugh and rubbed his face slowly.

"You're not still going on about that monotheistic nonsense, are You?"

"It's not nonsense."

"By the very fact You are talking to me now, it is nonsense. You're *not* the one true god. I'm a god. There are dozens of us out there. Hundreds. When will You ever get off Your ego trip and start sharing the love?"

"I am the one true God. Get over it."

Zeus shook his head in quiet despair.

"*Don't shake your head at me, Zeus.*"

He flung his head around nervously. He had forgotten that Jehovah was omniscient. It was an impressive party trick.

"What do You want, God?"

"I want you to give up on the plough."

"What?"

263

"You heard Me. The plough. I want you to give up on it."

"But why? Do You know what that plough can do for me? I am practically on the bread line. I drive a lorry for a living, for crying out loud. This is not the rightful existence of a god. You can understand that, surely?"

"The plough is not your property."

"It's not Yours, either."

"Yes it is." God sounded petulant.

"Well, okay. Let's imagine for a minute – just a minute – that I gave up on the plough. What is it worth? What would You give me?"

God thought about it. He hadn't expected such a direct question.

"A badge?" He suggested.

"No deal."

"Give up on the plough, Zeus. Or else."

Zeus hung up the phone and handed it back to the woman. He picked up his manifest and left the cafe. As soon as he was outside the heavens opened. Pouring rain hammered down upon his head. He couldn't help noticing that it was only raining on him. Outside of a small radius, the road was perfectly dry. He looked up at the sky, seeing the small dark cloud directly above him. He looked beyond it, into the heavens above.

"Tosser," he muttered.

High up in the sky, two clouds swished back together as the glorious telescope and the wondrous ear-trumpet were sharply retracted. God had heard Zeus's last comment. He found it most hurtful.

He did have to chuckle about the rain though.

John Thomas didn't usually feel particularly glamorous. The job description of God's Fixer on Earth promised great things but in practise, the work was mundane and often undesirable. Fetching a mug from a church was mundane. French kissing a hideous old witch was undesirable. These two activities pretty much summed up the two ends of the job's spectrum.

Today was an exception.

Having sneaked the military edition night-vision infra-red goggles from his mum's bedside cabinet (she kept the goggles hidden next to her secret stash of *Mills and Boon* books) John Thomas was now ready to use them.

He stood on the pavement at the end of the Gorgon's front garden, surveying her little kingdom and feeling the weight of the goggles in his hand. They were a serious piece of equipment. Made from moulded plastic, they represented a full headset. They boasted a visual range of five-hundred metres and could display a vast range of localised environmental heat signatures. There was a lot of technology in these goggles and for this reason, they were considerably, reassuringly, heavy.

Thomas looked at the garden. There were a lot of statues. He should have guessed this would be the case. There were animals, birds...people. To the layman they would look ornamental. Thomas knew different. They were dark relics in the Gorgon's wake, as she moved through the oceans of time.

Now it was time to put God's inspirational idea to the test, to go in there and to kick some Gorgonic hide.

He placed the goggles on his head, sliding them into place and suppressing a self-satisfied smile. This was cool. The goggles amounted to a huge contraption on his head, sticking out at the front by several inches, with a number of different sized lenses positioned over the whole. Thomas flicked a switch on the side of the mask and began to fiddle with the lenses. The house and garden became a surreal mass of different colours. Oranges, reds, yellows and greens. He was in business.

Confidently, he walked up the garden and knocked on the door. Inside he heard a voice. It sounded irritated. The words of an ancient myth drifted out – *you have got to be pulling my chain! Who is it this time?*

Soon afterwards, the door opened and there she was, standing in the doorway.

Medusa.

The Gorgon.

Through the infra-red detection circuits, she was a mass of glowing light, comprised mainly of red and yellow. She looked quite plump. Thomas could see the snakes on her head, moving with ghastly undulation. They seemed to move over each other, every now and then stabbing their heads forward, as if biting the air around them. He could hear their slithering hiss and it made his skin crawl. He suddenly realised that he might be the first man in history to stand face to face with the Gorgon and still be empowered to tell the tale.

"What in the sweet name...?" Medusa's voice trailed off.

"Ah, hello madam." John Thomas flashed what he hoped was a winning smile. "My name is John Thomas."

"What have you got on your head?"

"It's a military edition infra-red night-vision apparatus," he said.

"But it's the middle of the day."

"Yes, I know. Regardless of that, it allows me to see things not as they are, but through the medium of infra-red light waves. I can see things by their heat signature, as opposed to their physical reality."

"Oh, right."

266

"The idea is that you won't be able to turn me to stone."

Medusa nodded. It was a new one her, she had to admit, but it did seem to be working. And yet...

"Okay." She sighed, wearily. She was getting fed-up with people coming to her door and avoiding her petrifying stare. At this rate she would never get that garden fence filled. "I suppose I ought to ask what you are doing here?"

"I'm working for God," he said casually. "And we need your help."

"I've already had one god asking for my help today," she said, dismissively.

"Ah yes, but this is the One *True* God. The Father of all creation."

John Thomas heled his badge out for her to see. *John Thomas, Fixer.*

"I'm not really interested in helping any god," she said. She took a closer look at the strange contraption on the man's head. Unless she was mistaken, it was definitely starting to...

"We'll make it worth your while." John Thomas said, quickly. He was ready to bargain. Facing down the Gorgon was giving him a new confidence.

"Unless you can get me George Clooney, naked and ready-smothered in olive oil," Medusa said, "then you're probably barking up the wrong tree."

There was no doubt about it now. The contraption on the man's head was definitely turning to stone. It wasn't instantaneous. But it was definitely happening.

"How about a badge?" John Thomas suggested, and a further thought occurred to him. "We could probably get you a badge with George Clooney on it."

The Gorgon looked at him like he was something that had just crawled out of a drain. A rat, perhaps. Or an autonomous dump with perambulative capabilities.

267

The goggles were definitely petrifying and it was happening quickly now. A couple more minutes, she thought, and she'd be through the goggles and into the man's eyes. She just had to keep him talking.

"Well I suppose that *would* have something to recommend it," she admitted.

Thomas was about to pursue the matter further when he was suddenly aware how uncomfortable the goggles were becoming on his head. They felt heavier. Their flexibility had diminished, too. Furthermore, Medusa's heat signature was fading fast before his eyes and the equipment's visuals were becoming increasingly obscured.

Something was wrong.

He put a hand to his head. His fingers touched solid stone. There was a cracking noise coming from his head. The goggles were petrifying. It hadn't worked. God's idea *hadn't worked.* The infra-red goggles had only served to delay the inevitable. They were turning to stone under Medusa's fearful gaze...and he was next.

Panic welled up inside of him and he let out strangled cry. Quickly he turned away from the door and lurched crazily down the garden path, the weight of the solid stone headset bearing down on his head.

He didn't stop until he was out through the gate and safely on the pavement outside.

*

PC Standing was just climbing out of his Panda car when he saw the man come lunging through the garden gate. He recognised him immediately as the suspected single cell fundamentalist terrorist that had been praying in the middle of road down by the Minotaur Scrap Yard that time.

He had been called to the address by a resident, who claimed to have seen a sinister-looking man making his way up next-door neighbour's garden path. According to the neighbour, the man was wearing *one of those see-in-the-dark headset thingies, like the one in Silence of the Lambs.* Her worry was that he had a politician's daughter locked in the cellar beneath his house and was planning to use her skin for the purposes of misguided feminine adornment.

The man fiddled with the stone mask he was wearing and finally managed to prise it off. He found himself face-to-face with the policeman. He looked flushed and uncomfortable. He also looked strangely relieved.

"Why were you wearing a rock on your head?" Standing asked.

John Thomas looked at the night-vision goggles in his hand. It was true to say that they were now little more than a lump of featureless rock.

He gave an innocent shrug.

"Are you *sure* you are not one of them single cell fundamentalist terrorists?" Asked PC Standing

"No, really. I haven't got the stomach for it."

PC Standing nodded. There was more to this than met the eye, of that he was certain. He let John Thomas continue on his way before making his own way up the garden path to Medusa's house. He knocked on the door.

He just wanted to make sure everything was alright.

From inside the house a woman's voice called out.

"Hello?" She called. "I can't come to the door. I'm in the bath."

Standing put his face next to the door and called through.

"It's just the police, madam," he said airily. "I had a report that there was a suspicious character in the vicinity and I just wanted to check that everything was okay."

"I didn't see anyone," she called back. "And I've been out in the garden for most of the afternoon."

PC Standing left, satisfied that all was in order. The neighbour's call had probably just been a bit of neighbourly hysteria.

Inside, from behind a curtain, Medusa watched the policeman leave. She was happy to turn most people to stone – but a representative of the law was dangerous territory. If a policeman went missing, no avenue would be left unexplored to find him. The police would want to question everyone and before she knew it, she would be discovered for the Gorgon she was.

She knew where such a discovery would lead.

She would end up in a laboratory somewhere, being poked and prodded in the name of science. The indignity of it – *the humiliation* – didn't bear thinking about.

Besides this, she didn't like people seeing her naked.

Furthermore, she was scared of needles.

"Okay – back her up!"

Thorax leaned out of the passenger window, overseeing the careful positioning of the horsebox as Zeus reversed it into place.

This was Plan B.

When Thorax the Barbarian had gone to Zeus to ask him for his help, he thought that the ancient god seemed a little subdued. Distracted. Something was on his mind and though Thorax suggested that a problem shared was a problem halved, Zeus denied anything was wrong and refused to countenance further discussion on the subject.

He had listened to Thorax's account of his visit to Medusa and the unfortunate petrifaction of Starsky, with only vague interest. When Thorax outlined Plan B and asked Zeus if they could use the Allegro, Zeus had agreed without a thought. The Allegro already had a tow-hitch, from Zeus's caravanning days. Thorax knew where they could get a horsebox. There was one that always sat in a field just near Bluebell Woods and it seemed that no one ever used it. Thorax felt confident that nobody would miss it for a couple of hours.

The final piece of the puzzle was some cheese. Thorax always had a block of mild Cheddar in his fridge and they dropped into his place on the way, so that Thorax could pick up this vital ingredient.

The plan was a simple one.

They would back the horsebox up to Medusa's garden gate and lower the rear door. A piece of cheese would be laid at the far end of the horsebox, as bait. Thorax would sneak up the garden path, knock on Medusa's door then run for it. Medusa would come out, see the cheese and take the bait. As soon as she was in the horsebox, Thorax would slam the door closed and they would drive her straight to the scrap yard. Once there, they would get Roger to open the door of the horsebox - perhaps telling him that there were some old ploughs inside that he might want to take a look at. Roger would open the door, make eye contact with Medusa, turn to stone...and the bachelor's plough would be theirs for the taking.

It couldn't fail.

"Woah-woah-woah!" Hollered Thorax. The horsebox was in the perfect position, just a few feet in front of the gate. It gave him just enough room to lower the rear door.

Thorax told Zeus to leave the engine running, then climbed out of the car.

He walked to the rear of the horsebox, lowered the door and placed the lump of cheese at the far end. This meant that Medusa would have to go all the way in, to get the cheese. There was not much difference between catching a Gorgon and catching a mouse. In a way, catching a Gorgon was easier, since they couldn't scuttle under the skirting boards if they got spooked.

With barbaric agility, Thorax crept up the garden path and knocked on the door. Without a moment's hesitation, he ran back down the path and hid himself alongside the horsebox.

He crouched quietly and listened.

The front door opened.

He heard the occasional hiss of a cranial snake coming from the house.

A few moments later, wary footsteps began to approach down the garden path. He tensed himself up. If she peered around the side of the box, he would close his eyes and make a blind run for it, shouting to Zeus to *go-go-go*, as he ran past. If this happened, it meant that the operation was a failure, and it would be every man for himself.

He listened as the footsteps got closer, approaching the horsebox cautiously.

The Gorgon stopped at the garden gate. The barbarian knew that she was looking into the horsebox.

She would have seen the cheese.

Now was the moment. Either she would take the bait and enter the horsebox to get the cheese; or she would suspect something was amiss, at which point anything could happen.

To Thorax's delight he heard her footsteps move up the ramp as she made her way into the horsebox. The box shifted slightly under her weight. Thorax waited until she was at the front of the trailer, her focus fully absorbed by the cheese. Then, in a single barbaric stride, he pounced to the back and slammed the door shut. He slid the four bolts home, locking her in securely.

There was an enraged cry from within and Medusa's footsteps pounded across the horsebox. Her full weight slammed against the rear door. It held fast. She screamed again, a cry of pure rage and anger. She began to throw herself around the inside of the horsebox, flinging her body against all four walls in a whirlwind of rage. Thorax smiled and climbed back into the passenger seat of the Allegro.

Zeus looked at him quizzically and he smiled.

"We've bagged ourselves a Gorgon!" He said. In a moment of spontaneity, they did a high five, banging their hands together in the middle of the car.

It was an embarrassing moment.

Zeus had no idea why he made such a gesture. It felt at odds with his dignity, but he felt that Thorax expected it of him. Thorax on the other hand, believed that Zeus saw it as a natural means of expression and felt he would hurt the ancient god's feelings if he didn't go along with it.

Neither of them ever mentioned the incident again.

PC Standing was trying to ignore the fact that the owner of the Minotaur Scrap Yard had a bull's head. It seemed rude to ask about it, especially as the man himself hadn't alluded to it in any way. The village police constable didn't want to stare but it was difficult not to, when the very thing that you were addressing by way of conversation, was the thing you weren't supposed to be staring at.

The huge, broad head, with its massive, pointed horns, was impossible to ignore.

Terence Standing was at the scrap yard because the proprietor had recently installed a Thames Valley Police panic button. The panic button gave the junk yard a direct line to the police station. By pressing the button, Roger could notify the local constabulary that something was wrong and he would be assured of a police presence within minutes. It was one of the many ways that PC Standing was trying to strengthen community relations – though right now, he was feeling the strain.

He had just arrested Death, harvester of souls, for the third time in as many weeks, for drunk and disorderly behaviour. The Reaper had been threatening the manager of QuikMart, because he wouldn't sell him any more alcohol. When Standing got there, Cyril had the man backed into the corner of the shop and was holding his lethal scythe just inches away from the man's face.

It was a dangerous situation and Standing hadn't even opened up a dialogue. He had coshed Death around the back of the head with his truncheon (the sound of cracking bone was sobering) and handcuffed him immediately, without even needing to pull out the pepper spray. Unfortunately, this did not subdue the Angel of Death, who simply became increasingly unreasonable, shouting obscenities at the arresting officer and the shop manager. PC Standing had dragged him out and amazingly enough, within seconds of being squeezed into the back seat, he was slumped over, a mass of deathly robe and cowl, snoring fitfully. With his arrestee sleeping in the back of his car, PC Standing had decided to drop into the scrap yard, since he was passing, to introduce himself.

Whenever a panic button was installed, it was routine for Standing to pay the establishment a visit. This was largely to check that they knew how to work the button, but also to reassure the customer that they were safe. It was also a good opportunity to find out why they had installed the button in the first place. Often people would install a panic button because of an existing threat. Prevention was better than cure, Standing always believed, and if he could ascertain the nature of an existing threat, he could try to nip it in the bud before things got ugly. A bird in the bush is a problem halved, as his mum used to say.

The proprietor of the scrap yard, it seemed, wasn't in fear of a tangible threat. He had installed the panic button because he had a *feeling*; no more. For a little while he had been feeling that something was wrong, that something was building in the air around him. He had no idea what the nature of this *thing* was. He just felt certain it was there. And he felt, somehow, that he was at the centre of it.

His fearsome horns akimbo, he was self-deprecating when he told PC Standing this. He knew how stupid it sounded. PC Standing, though, was more than sympathetic. He had been sensing the same thing. He knew exactly what the strange-looking man was talking about and the fact was, he wished that he could install a panic button at his police station. The idea was ridiculous, however. It would be like God praying to himself for a miracle.

"Nice bus," Standing said, admiringly. The double-decker was at an angle now that its rear wheel had been

275

removed. It looked more heroic, somehow. It was a bus you could do battle in.

"Thanks," Roger smiled, gruffly. "You're welcome to it, if you want it. Good for spares or repair."

PC Standing winced. He hated to look a gift horse in the mouth but there was nowhere he could keep the bus. He would have loved it, too. He would have cherished it.

Someone, somewhere, was beyond lucky. That bus was going to make someone very happy.

He was just about to leave, when the lurid orange Austin Allegro squeaked into the scrap yard. It was pulling a horsebox. Standing recognised the occupants immediately. The old man was driving and as soon as he caught sight of the policeman, Standing saw him mouth the words: *Oh no, it's the fuzz*. Inside the car, both men tried to look casual and Standing could see that they were pretending not to have noticed him. The Allegro squeaked to a halt a few yards away.

"Do you know these men?" Standing asked the Minotaur.

Roger growled.

"I know them alright. I have told both of them that I don't want them here."

"Oh? How come?"

"They kept asking me about a plough. I haven't got any ploughs. But they won't take no for an answer, these two. They're an absolute pain."

Zeus and Thorax climbed out of the car and gave Standing and the Minotaur a little wave, in unison. They began to walk over, bobbing and nodding with ingratiating familiarity.

The Minotaur looked away, making a concerted effort to control his temper.

"What brings you here, gentlemen?" Standing took a few steps towards them.

"We just wanted a word with the proprietor," said Zeus.

276

"He doesn't want a word with you." Standing stared at them, humourlessly. "I understand he has banned you both from the yard. Therefore, you are trespassing. Now, I suggest you return to your car and make yourselves scarce."

"But..."

"*Now.*"

A sudden banging from PC Standing's Fiat Panda caused all four men to turn around sharply. The Grim Reaper stared out at them from the back seat, his dark hood pressed against the window. He saw that they were looking and quickly got himself into a kneeling position on the seat. He rucked his robes up over his backside and pulled a moonie out of the window. The four men were treated to a bony mass of pelvic girdle and a small glimpse of coccyx.

Standing cursed.

"Damn it. He was supposed to be asleep." He ran to the car to bring some decency back into the situation. As he ran, he called back to the two visitors. "Go back to your car and leave *now*. If I see you here again, I will arrest you."

Thorax and Zeus looked at the Minotaur, hoping to make a final plea. The bull-headed monstrosity continued to look away, concertedly. As they walked back to their car, dejected and forlorn, they heard a scuffle coming from the Fiat Panda behind them. It culminated in the sound of something being sprayed, followed by a loud and strangled cry. Death's choking voice rang out in agony.

They slumped back into the Allegro in disbelief.

Plan B had failed.

They all sat in Medusa's living room, drinking tea from little cups with dainty saucers. Zeus and Thorax sat with their eyes tightly closed and both had their mouths open in that gormless expression which often comes with shutting one's eyes tightly.

Medusa sat primly, her snakes writhing over each other in a serpentine cacophony of sibilant hisses.

The Gorgon sipped her tea and looked at her two visitors in amusement.

Following the failure of Plan B they had driven back to Beverley Road and reversed the horsebox once more into position, at the end of the Gorgon's front garden. It wasn't her fault that they had failed, and it was only the right thing to do, to get her safely back home. It was a relief to them both that Medusa had, by this time, calmed down in the back. She had stopped banging around, even before they reached the scrap yard.

Her silence was disconcerting, but it gave them hope that she would now at least be reasonable.

Thorax had knocked on the side of the horsebox and told Medusa that they were back outside her house. He apologised for tricking her into becoming their captive but insisted that it was of great importance and that, eventually, she would be well-rewarded.

Medusa didn't say a word.

"I'm going to open the door and let you out," Thorax said, uneasily. "Will you promise to behave yourself?"

Silence.

"Look," Thorax the Barbarian scrabbled around for the right words. "I'm sorry. We're *both* sorry. If there had been any other way, we would not have bothered you. I promise."

From inside, they heard a small scuffle.

"Medusa. Can I call you Medusa? It's not as if I didn't give you the chance to help out willingly. I did *ask* you if you would help. But you kept trying to turn me into stone. I don't want to fall out with you. Neither of us do. You're our favourite Gorgon."

There was a further little scuffle from inside.

"Really?" Came a quiet voice.

"You'd better believe it! We were just saying, on the way back here. Of all the Gorgons out there, you stand head, snakes and shoulders above the rest. You're a Gorgon apart."

"You're just saying that." She sounded downcast.

"No. Really. If I had to choose any Gorgon to be my Gorgon, I would choose you. Without hesitation."

"What's so special about me?"

"You just...well...you have that spark! You are the sort of Gorgon you could take home to meet your mum. You're the sort of Gorgon that would fill any room with sunshine. You're like...well, you like cheese, don't you?"

"Yes."

"Well, you're like a slice of exquisite *Gorgon*zola on a cheeseboard of supermarket mild cheddar."

Medusa laughed modestly.

"You're a Gorgon beyond all Gorgons, Medusa. I hope you believe that. And I'm sorry we tricked you."

Inside the trailer, he heard the hissing of snakes.

"Would you both like to come in for a cup of tea?" She asked, finally.

Thorax allowed himself a smile.

"Would you be offended if we kept our eyes closed?"

"No, not at all."

"See what I mean! A Gorgon in a million! Yes. We would *love* to come in for a cup of tea."

*

279

They shared some small talk while Medusa prepared the tea. As one would expect, most of the conversation revolved around the life and times of Oliver Hardy.

They eventually got on to the subject of the plough.

Thorax explained the importance of the plough and how it would change Zeus's fortunes and, with any luck, re-establish his divinity. He told her about the Minotaur's jealous attitude when it came to his ploughs and how they had planned to use Medusa to turn him to stone, in order that they could take the plough without impingement.

Medusa listened carefully, sipping her tea thoughtfully at various points.

When Thorax had finished, she put her cup back in the saucer with a gentle clink. Thoughtfully, she placed it on the coffee table.

"You know, you don't need to be so drastic," she said. "You're right. Turning Roger to stone would certainly do the job. You could walk away with the plough and it would be a job well-done. But what would happen to all the scrap metal in and around the village? Where would it go? Who would process it?"

Zeus and Thorax looked at each other, through tightly closed eyes. Their mouths gaped. Zeus' beard quivered, while Thorax's chin palpitated.

"I hadn't thought of that," said Zeus.

"Me neither," admitted Thorax.

"There is another way," Medusa continued. "A way to get the plough, while allowing Roger to live. All you need to do is send him to sleep."

Zeus and the barbarian were nodding.

"A tranquiliser dart," said Zeus.

"I was thinking more along the lines of a mermaid," smiled Medusa.

The two men looked at her, each devoid of gorm.

"Eh?"

"Eh?"

"A mermaid. A siren." Medusa retrieved her tea and took a sip. "A tranquiliser dart is risky. You could miss. And even if you didn't miss, Roger might have time to call the police or ring an alarm. But a mermaid! Did you know that if you hear a siren's song, you lose all sense of time and place? They are hypnotic. Hear the song of a mermaid and you will fall into the deepest slumber. If Roger was to fall under the spell of a mermaid, he wouldn't know what had hit him."

Thorax stared over at her, as much as anyone can stare with their eyes screwed shut.

"Where the hell are we going to get hold of a mermaid?" He asked.

Medusa smiled. She poured herself another cup of tea and looked over at her visitors with a pleased expression.

"Now that," she said. "Is just where I can be of help."

"I've just seen Zeus and that barbarian come out of Medusa's house," said God, with divine consternation. "And they were looking extremely pleased with themselves."

John Thomas cursed inwardly.

He wondered if it was intentional that the Good Lord always phoned when he was watching something good on the telly. In the lounge he could hear the bumbling voice of Columbo, questioning a suspect.

"What were they wearing on their heads?" He asked,

"Nothing." Didst sayeth the Lord.

"So how come they didn't turn to stone?"

"It looked like they just had their eyes shut."

Thomas cursed inwardly again. Why hadn't *he* thought of that?

"I watched them drive her to the scrap yard in a horsebox," said God. "They were there for a few minutes. Then they took her home again. I don't know what they're up to, John. But I don't like it. I don't like it at all."

"Did she not turn Roger to stone?" Thomas asked.

"No. That was the strange thing. They didn't even let her out when they got there. Mind you, that policeman was there. You know – the one who thinks you are a single cell fundamentalist terrorist."

"Hmm. Maybe we got lucky then. The presence of the police must have thwarted them from releasing the Gorgon."

"Yes, that's what I am thinking. And if that's the case, John Thomas..." The Good Lord's voice became grave. *"Do you know how close we just came to losing the plough?"* Zeus was within a gnat's testicle of getting hold of it."

John Thomas managed to split his attention. He kept half of his focus on God, at the end of the phone. The other half of his focus was in the sitting room, watching *Columbo*.

"I am running out of ideas, God," he said. He heard Columbo pause, deliberately, and he knew what was coming next. Sure enough, it came.

Just one more thing...

"Look, don't worry about it for now," said the Good Lord. "I've got a plan. In the meantime, just try and keep tabs on Zeus and that barbarian. Keep an eye on what they are doing. *Don't let them get that plough.*"

"But what is Your divine plan, O Lord?" Thomas asked.

"Well, I've been thinking. And I have decided that it's high time I paid a visit to the Minotaur Myself. It's time he had a visit from the Supreme Lord of all creation. It might help him to reconsider his position. I think that with a little Divine persuasion, he'll part with the plough."

"You mean – You are going to visit us, here on Earth."

"Yes."

"The last time You did that, a woman took a photograph of You in Your swimming trunks."

"It won't happen again. And certainly not at this time of year."

"God, can I ask You something?"

"Yes, I suppose so."

"It's about Jesus."

"Okay."

"Well, You know he is called Jesus H. Christ?"

"Yes."

"What does the H stand for?"

"Horatio."

"Okay. Thanks. I've often wondered. Let me know how You get on with Roger."

"Will do. And make sure you keep tabs on those two. We're close, now, John Thomas. But so are they. They could still pip us to the post."

"Yes, O Lord. I will keep them under close surveillance."

"Good man. Right. Bye."

"Bye..."

"Bye....."

"Bye......"

It was just past two o'clock in the afternoon when the old Scania lorry pulled off the main road and on to a small by-lane.

It snaked slowly down the old road, brushing the overhanging trees on either side as it lurched along. After a few minutes, it slowed almost to a stop, before turning into a small, rarely used parking area. This was the rendezvous Zeus had agreed with Santa. It was ideal. It was hidden enough so that no one would see the heist but close enough to the major arterial road for Claus and his men to make a quick get-away.

The plan was crude, but simple.

When Zeus pulled into the parking area, Father Christmas was already there, along with Richie "Thumbscrews" Hooper and "The Hat", Reggie Watts. A battered old lorry, a Ford, stood idling in the mud. The driver sat, ready, at the wheel. There was no trailer. That was, after all, what Zeus was here to provide.

The black Mercedes sat idle, alongside the lorry. Both of its front doors were open.

Claus and his men were standing in front of the cab, talking, when Zeus swung his rig into the lot, with professional aplomb.

Santa Claus beamed as the ancient god climbed down from the cab. Without a moment's pause, the festive personification strode over to him, outstretched his arms and clasped him in a boisterous hug.

"I knew you wouldn't let me down!" He boomed. It warmed Zeus to feel accepted.

"Right," Zeus smiled, as Claus pulled himself away to have a good look at his new favourite. "Where do you want it?"

Claus spoke briefly with the driver of the Ford and co-ordinated the switch.

Zeus positioned the trailer and unhitched it, leaving it for Claus's man to attach it to his lorry. Within ten minutes, the switch was complete.

The driver revved the engine, signifying his readiness to be on his way. Reggie Watts jumped up in the cab next to him and pulled the door shut. The lorry pulled away and within no time at all, it was gone.

Santa Claus had just acquired £300,000 of desirable merchandise.

Zeus stood facing the bearded gangster. He had crossed a threshold. He was now a criminal.

He felt dirty.

He felt *liberated.*

Right now, his conscience pricked him. But soon he would have the bachelor's plough. Once that happened, he would be above the moral landscape of ordinary men.

"You did good," said Claus. He was still beaming.

"Thanks," Zeus replied. He smiled sheepishly. He wasn't very good with compliments.

Claus was still smiling at him, warmly, when he intoned Thumbscrews Hooper's name. He spoke quietly, almost under his breath.

It sounded like he was giving some kind of command.

Hooper stepped forward and Zeus saw, to his consternation, that Hooper's face was a mask of focused aggression. Without a word, the hard-faced gangster swung his fist, landing a heavy punch on the ancient god's nose.

Zeus staggered back and fell to the ground.

"What the...?"

He looked up in time to see Hooper descending on him, a mass of fists and elbows.

For the second time in a week, Zeus took a pasting.

Hooper did a thorough job. He split Zeus's face just above his eye, broke his nose in two places and pummelled the ancient god's head with a violence unbridled.

Zeus couldn't believe it, even as it happened to him. It was the ultimate betrayal. He had given Claus a great thing – he had compromised his own moral integrity to do so – and this was how the Christmas patriarch repaid him.

He grovelled in the mud, wishing he could express his anger with a little more dignity, as Hooper showered blows and kicks all over his tender frame.

In a few minutes, it was over.

Zeus lay in the dirt, throbbing and moaning with the pain. He couldn't believe he had been so trusting.

Blood and snot ran down his face and soaked his beard.

Claus came and crouched next to him.

"Sorry about that," he said. He sounded genuinely regretful. "But we had to make it look as if you were ambushed. Like we agreed."

Zeus moaned. Claus slipped something into the breast pocket of his woolly cardigan.

"You've done a great job today," Claus continued. His voice dripped with sincerity. "You know, if you wanted to come and work for me, I could find work for you on the firm."

Zeus thought about it for nearly a whole second and then shook his head.

He had found his experiences of Claus's firm so far to be unsettling, stressful, frightening and incredibly painful. He hadn't really discovered any positives.

"There's good money to be made," Claus went on. "You could make some serious cash. I mean, I've even got girls working for me - working girls, you know what I mean - who earn more in a week than most people earn in a year.

Think about it, Zeus. If you change your mind, you come and see me."

Zeus tried to thank him, but it came out as a moan.

When Richie Hooper bent over him to squeeze his arm, apologising for what he'd done, Zeus involuntarily curled himself up into the foetal position and whimpered.

"Sorry, buddy," Hooper squeezed his arm anyway. His voice was tender.

The ancient god lay there as the two gangsters got into the black Mercedes and drove away. From their perspective, at least, it had been a successful mission. And if nothing else, Zeus could comfort himself with the knowledge that he was no longer in debt to the vicious gangster. If anything, Claus was indebted to *him* - and Zeus felt that if he ever needed anything of the firm, Claus would be pleased to help. It was a happy turn-around in his fortunes.

After a while, he sat up slowly and blinked in the afternoon sun. The compacted dirt of the carpark was cold and hard beneath him. He remembered the object Father Christmas had put into the breast pocket of his cardigan and he reached inside.

What he found there made him smile.

£5000, in fifty-pound notes.

There was something to be said for this criminal malarkey, and no mistake.

Nonetheless, it did bloody hurt.

A small hatch opened, high up in the sky, about the size of a standard loft hatch. After a small amount of scuffling, a rope ladder was dropped through. There was some grunting and a pair of sandaled feet appeared from the hatch. They waggled about until they found the rope ladder, then began to descend with obvious uncertainty.

A pair of white skinny legs followed.

Then the hem of a white robe.

A sacred backside worked its way through carefully, and after a few more rungs, the Good Lord was out, and making His earthly descent.

He was not prepared for how cold it would be. At an earthly height of forty-odd thousand feet it was absolutely bloody freezing. It was windy, too, and within moments of emerging from Heaven, He found Himself being battered around by a blustering gale. The rope ladder suddenly felt incredibly flimsy as He found Himself being flung all over the sky. It twisted and flapped in the open air and it was all the Good Lord could do to hold on.

Hanging on desperately to the rope ladder, He looked down. The rope ladder disappeared into the far distance. Far below, the land looked like a tiny patchwork quilt. It was a long way down and even in His omniscience, He had no idea how long it would take to make the descent. It would be a hard enough climb on a still day but with this wind, it was nigh impossible. Still, it was imperative that He made the trek. It was of the utmost theological importance.

After half an hour, He felt that He had made hardly any progress at all. He looked up and saw the hatch through which He had come. The small opening, through which one could attain the glories of Heaven.

The wind got worse the lower He descended and on a couple of occasions, the ladder was blown almost horizontal. He found himself hanging on for dear life, which seemed a paradoxical state of being for One so eternal and omnipotent. Nonetheless that was how it felt.

He didn't even want to consider what would happen to Him if He fell off the ladder. The Good Lord wasn't exactly flesh and blood, but He had mass. He was omnipresent, after all (though His mother used to make excuses for him, saying He was just big-boned). His mass didn't bear thinking about, but He felt certain that were He to stand on a set of bathroom scales, the dial would travel through a number of revolutions.

If He were to lose His grip and fall from the ladder, it seemed certain He would plummet like a stone.

He was cursing His own innovation in deciding to make this trip. Blown around like a disembodied leaf, He only wished He'd scheduled more clement weather. A sudden gust blasted him like a pebble-dasher and He was wrenched violently sideways.

The ladder began to spin wildly, and He wished that there was a higher authority than Himself, to whom He could pray. Unfortunately, the buck stopped with Him and He knew that He was going to have to deal with this one by Himself.

It was nothing short of horror that gripped His eternal soul, when He saw the 747 jumbo jet hurtling towards Him in the distance. He was swinging helplessly in the gale, wondering if the wind might just blow itself out, when He caught sight of it.

At first, it was just a dull glint in the distance. All too quickly, it grew in size and by the time He realised what it was, it was too late to do anything about it. It was difficult to judge perspective up here, but He felt certain that He was directly in its flight path.

It was approaching at speed.

For the first time in His existence, God froze. His mind wrestled with the situation, wondering whether it would be best to start climbing up or to start climbing down, in an effort to get out of the jumbo's path. Climbing down would be easier and He could probably put more distance between himself and the jet. However, if the jet caught the ladder, He would most likely be flung across the sky like a stone from a catapult. If He went up, and the jet caught the rope ladder, then He would stand a chance at least. The problem was, He wasn't sure if He could climb up far enough in the short time available to Him.

It was all academic.

He spent so much time debating the matter with Himself that the jumbo jet was upon Him before He could perform any avoidance manoeuvre. By the grace of Him, the jet was a wingspan away from the rope ladder and it passed without impact. The noise was terrific, though, and God felt his body freeze in instinctive fear as the roaring jet engines filled the sky around Him. The slipstream was immense too, and the good Lord found Himself being whisked through the air behind the plane, as a thousand winds battered His face. There was nothing He could do but hold on to the rope ladder and wait for the violent tempest to pass. It was one of the most traumatic episodes of His existence.

Just as the jumbo passed, a split second before the noise assaulted Him and the ladder was whisked into the plane's slipstream, God made the briefest eye contact with one of the pilots. The pilot stared out of the cockpit window at Him, a look of sheer disbelief on his face. The pilot would later tell his wife what he saw.

It was a man, he would say, *hanging on a rope ladder in mid-air. He looked somewhere between the depiction of God, by Michelangelo and Richard Attenborough.*

For the Good Lord, the jumbo jet was the hump buster that broke the camel's distinguishing feature.

"Sod this for a game of soldiers," He muttered to himself as He began to scale back up the rope ladder.

Divinely, He concluded that given the inclement weather, it would probably be prudent to send an angel on his behalf. Angels had wings and it was always much easier for them to make the inter-dimensional journey.

Besides this, they glowed. This gave them a holy authority that God could never quite achieve without wearing a wig.

When he ruled over the gods at Mount Olympus, Zeus never, *ever* experienced the humiliation of being professionally reprimanded. Now, as he stood before the Managing Director of *Bristow's Haulage*, he felt like a chastised schoolboy.

John Bristow was a formidable man with a temper to match. He was one of those people that leave school at the first opportunity and then carve their way up the career ladder through natural ability and force of personality alone. He had built *Bristow's Haulage* up from nothing, his first vehicle being a battered old Luton van. Now, twenty-five years later, he boasted a fleet of vehicles, with more than twenty full-time drivers and a full complement of office staff. His was a thriving concern. He liked to see himself as a beer-bellied Richard Branson.

Right now, he was a tornado of rage.

"What the hell were you thinking?" He screamed, his face crimson. Zeus was relieved that there was a table between them.

"I didn't mean to get hijacked," he said, weakly.

"God DAMN it. Do you know what you were carrying? Do you know how much that consignment was worth?"

Zeus was tempted to take a stab at it, to see how close his estimate was. He decided to play ignorant, however.

"No."

"*Three hundred and twenty thousand pounds,*" spittle flew out of Bristow's mouth. "This is going to put my insurance through the roof! Not to mention the company's reputation!"

Zeus ignored his pounding heart. It seemed that life, these days, was one eternal conflict.

"I'm sorry," he said. "But they really went for me. Look at the state of me. I didn't stand a chance."

Bristow leaned over the desk, his dark brow like thunder.

"I expect my drivers to take a bullet for me," he hissed.

"But there weren't any bullets."

"You should have found one."

"But it wouldn't have achieved anything. They were going to take the trailer whatever. I didn't need to take a bullet. They beat me black and blue."

"You should have taken a bullet," Bristow sulked.

Zeus remained quiet. He felt that they had turned into a cul-de-sac with this particular argument.

"I didn't want to be hijacked," he said, after a while. "I was just in the wrong place at the wrong time."

"So you can be in the wrong place at the wrong time when it comes to getting your trailer snatched. But when it comes to taking a bullet...well, then you seem to be very much in the *right* place."

"But I told you..." He gave up. "What happens now?"

Bristow looked at Zeus as if he had just crawled out of a drain.

"I get myself a new driver." He said, flatly.

"What?"

"You heard me. You're sacked. If you can't take a bullet for me, I don't want you on my team."

"But..."

"Get out. You're fired."

*

Bloodied, bruised and now out of a job, Zeus sat at the bar in the *Bird in Hand*. It was very rare for him to pay an afternoon visit, but today warranted it. He was on his third whiskey. Usually he would plump for a gin and slim-line tonic, but today he needed something stronger. The alcohol was starting to take effect. His head felt fuzzy and gratefully he could feel the troubles of the past few days beginning to melt away.

It wasn't that he loved his job as a lorry driver. It paid the bills, no more. Even then, the money hardly stretched. In fact, right now, he didn't even need the job. The money that Claus had stuffed in the breast pocket of his cardigan was the equivalent of about half a year's wages. He had plenty to get him through.

What annoyed him was the fact he had no divine authority.

He was a god but he was living like any mortal, having to bow and scrape to the whims of whichever boss he happened to be working for. Back when he was a god – when he was *really* a god – John Bristow would not have *dared* speak to him in the way he did. He would have got a thunderbolt right up his jacksie. But now Zeus had to toe the line; and that offended him.

He was confident that he and Thorax would get the bachelor's plough; but until the plough spilled forth some of its golden fruit, he would have to work.

He was on his fifth whiskey when the words of Father Christmas came back to him.

If you wanted to come and work for me, I could find work for you on the firm.

The problem was, he didn't like the idea of working for Father Christmas. It was risky work, and the job security was flimsy to say the least.

You could make some serious cash. I mean, I've even got girls working for me – working girls, you know what I mean – who earn more in a week than most people earn in a year.

The words rang around Zeus's head.

295

Working girls who earn more in a week than most people earn in a year.

It was then, right then, that Zeus had his idea.

In that very moment, he decided he would go on the game.

Talking to Medusa had been an education.

Thorax had no idea that there was a mermaid farm on the outskirts of Pestlewick, down by Swan Tail Lock. Medusa said it was a small affair, with around just twenty mermaids.

Until now, Thorax had never even realised that such farms existed.

Medusa had explained it beautifully. There are two types of siren, she had told them. Saltwater sirens are found out at sea and are the traditional kind – largely associated with old mariner's legends. These creatures are natural grazers, with no fixed abode or territorial instincts. They are free-roaming and will go anywhere that the current takes them. They like to inhabit rocky outlets and can be found generally where there is an abundance of oysters and other shellfish.

Saltwater mermaids are not farmed as a rule. Instead, they are harvested by sea-going trawlers and factory ships. There are several treatment stations around the UK's coastline – most prominently in Cornwall and on the coasts of Scotland – where such hauls are brought in for filleting. One specialist treatment station in Norfolk actually has a large facility for smoking the mermaids, which is particularly popular for the Chinese and Scandinavian markets. Most stations will salt the mermaids or preserve them in ice.

The other type of siren is the freshwater siren. These are found in rivers and lakes all over the world (though they thrive particularly well in the northern hemisphere). The nature of these mermaids is to return to the place of their birth for spawning, very much like salmon. Because of this, they are much easier to farm. In some regions, locals aware of a mermaid spawning ground will often adapt the area to create a specialised containment facility, wherein the mermaids can be nurtured, bred and slaughtered routinely. Such a facility existed on the Thames down by Swan Tail Lock, and this was where Medusa directed Thorax to, for the accomplishment of his quest.

*

Thorax chose to find his mermaid at night.

He had always held romantic ideas about night-fishing and rather liked the sense of solitude and the oneness with nature that it promised. There were practical reasons too. Medusa had informed him that mermaids are more docile at night and so he would find it easier to catch the siren and get her to the scrap yard. Furthermore, he had no plan for transporting the mermaid, other than to drag her along the ground. To make such a journey in daylight would have drawn unnecessary attention to himself, he felt.

It was a frosty, cloudless night when the barbarian made his way along the Thames towpath, whistling happily to himself. With a fishing rod over his shoulder, a bucket of live bait, a large net and a pair of industrial ear-protectors, he was ready to catch himself some mermaid.

As he got to where the Gorgon had told him the farm was, he conscientiously placed the ear protectors over his head. If he heard the song of a mermaid, he would be good for nothing.

The mermaid farm didn't have much in the way of a delineated boundary.

A sizeable stretch of river was squared off with red floats, which denoted the summit of a wall below the surface. Here, the mermaids were kept.

It seemed an adequate space for twenty mermaids, but Thorax doubted that they got much mental stimulation. He wondered if, like a bored tiger in a cage, the mermaids chewed their own limbs and paced up and down throughout the day, making swinging motions with their heads. Right now, he couldn't see anything that hinted at any sirens in the water, but he supposed that at night they were likely to keep themselves beneath the surface. He didn't know for sure, but he imagined them to have underwater dens, or some such place, where they would sleep and go for privacy.

He set his fishing rig up at the side of the river, sitting on the frosty bank. Ensuring that his net was close to hand, he threaded a hook on to the fishing line and picked out a juicy worm from the bucket. He punctured the worm with the hook, checked that his float was well secured and cast off.

The bait landed in the middle of the river with a gentle plop.

All he had to do now was watch and wait.

The night-float bobbed sedately, a gentle glow on the dark velvet surface of the water. Thorax sat hunched over, feeling the cold ground beneath his barbaric posterior.

Time passed.

An owl hooted.

A bat flew overhead.

A hedgehog bumbled by, lost in its own little world.

An orphan sailed overhead on a hang-glider, looking for a chimney to clean. Any chimney.

And then it happened.

The float disappeared. The gentle glow blinked out like a light going off. And Thorax knew he had a bite.

He never claimed to be much of a fisherman, but he had seen *Jaws* and he understood the principle of letting out the slack and then winding it back in. His Tony Blackburn hairdo glinting in the starlight, he battled vigorously, bringing his catch in and then letting it swim off again in its own flight of panic. With a barbarian's judgement he repeatedly let out the line, giving his quarry the opportunity to swim away, endlessly tiring itself out, before winding it back in again in readiness for the next round.

It was an epic struggle.

More than forty minutes passed and Thorax was feeling the strain as the thing on the end of his line continued to fight and struggle. For a moment he wondered if he had done the classic thing and hooked his line on to an old tyre or a supermarket trolley. He reassured himself that even if this was the case, then it would be a tyre or a supermarket trolley worth landing since it must have swum the equivalent of several miles during the course of the struggle. Any supermarket trolley or tyre with the presence of mind – and the muscle development – to swim so determinedly, was worth meeting.

Finally, the creature gave up the fight.

It struggled no more.

As Thorax reeled in his line, he saw it, emerging from the gloomy depths, a beautiful golden-haired woman, with the lower body of a fish. Her hair was soaked, plastered across her face, but as he pulled her up to the surface he could see how extraordinarily beautiful she was.

He couldn't imagine filleting such a specimen.

Her blue eyes were heavy. They gazed up at him, through the surface of the water, sad and resigned. Thorax dipped his net into the river and caught her up in it. He dragged her rudely on to the bank.

Silent with wonder, he crouched over her, gently twisting the hook from her cheek. He could see her mouth working, softly, deliciously and he knew that she was singing. For a moment he was tempted to take off the ear-protectors to have a listen – just a quick listen – but he knew that it would be fatal to do so.

It was what she wanted.

Medusa had warned him just how seductive, how manipulative these creatures could be.

"Right my girl," he said, trying to sound as fatherly as he could. It seemed like a good idea to try to establish a relationship of trust, since he was abducting her against her will. "You're coming with me."

He grasped her tail at its thinnest point and hoisted it over his shoulder. As he began to walk back along the towpath, with long, purposeful strides, the mermaid's head banged along on the ground behind him and her naked arms dragged helplessly behind her.

*

Like a questing archetype, Thorax the Barbarian marched towards the Minotaur Scrap Yard, holding on tightly to the tail of the siren.

What Medusa hadn't banked on was the biology of the mermaid.

A mermaid is as much fish as human being. She needs an equal amount of air and water to be able to survive. He couldn't have known that by dragging her along the path, away from the river, Thorax was slowly drowning the hapless creature.

With his ear-protectors on, he didn't hear her calling for help, begging him to take her back to the river. He was unaware of her laboured, gasping breaths.

Of course, he knew that she thrashed and struggled behind him. But he assumed that this was the natural manifestation of her feminine rage. He thought it was nothing more than a quasi-aquatic temper tantrum.

By the time he emerged from the towpath, onto the silent streets around Pestlewick, he was pleased that she had calmed down. In her subdued state, she was much easier to drag along.

It was only when he reached the scrapyard, and her delicate head had been banging uncontrollably against the pavement for more than fifteen minutes, that he realised she was dead.

In his ignorance, Thorax the Barbarian had committed mermacide.

"I still don't see why Gabriel can't do it," sulked Raphael as he squeezed himself through the Heavenly hatch.

God wasn't prepared to argue.

He didn't need to justify Himself; He was the Supreme Being. It was true that Gabriel was very good at this sort of work and he had proved himself a very able messenger on more than one occasion. But – and petty though it seemed – He felt that Raphael needed to learn some self-discipline.

The recent habit that he had developed of leaving underpants on the fridge had driven the Good Lord to distraction and however many times God brought him up on it, the angel carried on regardless. It was senseless behaviour and God simply couldn't understand it. He hoped that a bit of honest work would make Raphael think about his behaviour.

Muttering under his breath, Raphael dropped through the hatch to find himself forty-odd thousand feet above the Earth.

It was cold and it was windy but he didn't mind. He was used to this sort of altitude and had sensibly worn thermal undergarments for the occasion. He couldn't wait to get back, so that he could leave them on the fridge.

He began to flap his wings with practised grace and, like a pigeon on the wing, circled his way down through the night sky, to the quiet earth below.

*

Roger the Minotaur finished locking up the yard.

It had been a long day, made all the worse by the creeping sense of anxiety that continued to dog his every thought.

He checked the ploughs, hidden away under a corrugated metal awning at the back of the yard, before trudging lethargically back to his portacabin.

It was a cold, dark evening. There wasn't a cloud in the sky.

A billion stars twinkled magically across the velvet canopy.

With every breath, Roger watched as thick steam filled the air before his face. It was only six o'clock, but it felt later. He was ready for bed. As was his custom, he would cook himself something on his little camping stove and then settle down for the night on the floor of the cabin. Sometimes he would listen to the radio. Tonight, he intended to just roll out his little camp bed and hit the sack early.

It was as he was walking through the door of the portacabin that it happened.

At first there was music. A beautiful tinkling sound, like the gentle ringing of a hundred silver bells.

Roger felt as though he knew the music from somewhere; as though he heard it once in his dreams. It made him think of fields of golden corn and swaying barley. It filled the air like a symphony of joy and caressed his soul with gentle fingers. Then, almost without him noticing its arrival, an ethereal glow appeared from nowhere and washed the yard in its gentle radiance. Roger felt himself bathed in warmth and wonder.

He turned and looked up at the sky.

There, some twenty feet above the ground, was a beautiful winged creature. It was looking down on him, its face sensitive and kind. Roger watched in wonder, as it beat its wings gently against the cold night air. It emanated a gentle soothing glow and in this, Roger saw that it was wearing elegant white robes that hung down past its feet. Above its head there was a halo of pure white light. The music ebbed and flowed with every beat of its wings.

"What the bloody hell is that?" Roger muttered to himself.

He was a Minotaur of the world, but this was a new one on him. He didn't like the look of it one little bit. It looked hostile.

He moved back, slowly, into the portacabin, not taking his eyes from the winged creature for a second. It continued to smile down at him, full of heavenly benevolence. Slowly, carefully, Roger reached inside the cabin.

His fingers found the shotgun that he kept by the door and he wrapped them around it, firmly. It was already loaded, for emergencies. He continued to stare up at the aerial visitor, taking care that his expression gave nothing away. He didn't really appreciate that with the face of a bull, he only really had one expression anyway and that was one of plain incomprehension.

In a single practised move he drew out the shotgun and brought it up to his shoulder. The angel didn't even register what was happening before Roger aimed the twin barrels and pulled the trigger. It was a well-aimed shot and the angel exploded in a puff of white feathers, before dropping into the yard like a heavy stone. Roger was surprised that it didn't let out a cry or a moan, but the ethereal light dissipated almost immediately and the music stopped mid-tinkle.

The creature landed in an ungainly heap just a few yards away. Its knees were bent and its robes rucked up, revealing knee-length thermal underwear beneath. Its eyes were closed and as far as Roger could tell, it wasn't breathing.

The halo of pure white light rolled slowly across the yard like an old hubcap. Its momentum was curbed by a pile of old engine blocks, where it spun around on its own axis until finally coming to a complete stop. There it remained, flat on the ground.

Roger prodded the curious visitor with his toe. It didn't respond.

305

"I don't know what you are," he said. "But you are not welcome in my yard."

He gave it a final shove with his toe, before walking back into the portacabin and closing the door.

Whatever it was, he would clear it up in the morning.

Everything Zeus knew about prostitution he had learned from watching *Pretty Woman,* with Julia Roberts. With this film as his yardstick, he ventured out on to the night streets of Pestlewick to find out how much money he could make by selling his body.

It was new territory for him. With his slightly squat frame and his flowing white beard, he wondered if he would win any trade at all. However, he reasoned that people do have different tastes and he might be exactly the kind of experience the punters had been waiting for.

He gave himself the best possible chance by wearing some revealing clothes, which he hoped showed his body to its best advantage. He didn't have much of a wardrobe, but felt that a pair of skin-tight denims would show his buns off to their maximum effect and would create the illusion of longer legs. Worn with his cardigan undone almost to the bottom, the outfit as a whole would be teasingly provocative, leaving an appropriate amount to the imagination.

He didn't know where the red-light district was, in Pestlewick - if there was one at all - but the lower end of Grocer's Lane seemed a good place to start. As much as anything, it was only around the corner from where he lived and so it would be easy to get to and from work. There was good passing traffic too, which he assumed was essential to a successful patch.

Thus it was he found himself on the pavement at the lower end of Grocer's Lane, soliciting his bodily charms.

He wasn't sure exactly what you did, when soliciting.

He felt that he needed to indicate to passing drivers that he was for sale and so for the first ten cars or so, he stuck out his thumb. He quickly realised, however, that he looked like a hitchhiker, so he soon dropped this particular approach.

Instead he worked on looking casual, walking up and down the kerbside, tartly, holding his head slightly titled, with sultry disinterest. Whenever a car slowed to take a look at him, he put a hand on his hips and wiggled his backside in a way that he felt was provocative and teasing.

One or two cars sounded their horns at him, but he wasn't sure if it was out of admiration or if they were making fun of him. He didn't mind. It was the oldest profession in the world and he had nothing to be ashamed of.

He had been there for more than an hour, chewing gum and walking the kerb suggestively. During that time there had been one embarrassing moment when PC Standing had driven past. He had turned his car around and pulled up alongside Zeus to ask what he was doing there. Hoping that his clothing and general manner hadn't given him away, Zeus told Standing that he was waiting for a bus. Standing suggested he did so at the bus stop, a few hundred yards up the road, at which point Zeus thanked him but said that he would try his chances where he was. Other than that small episode, there had been nothing of any significance.

And then the sports car pulled up.

It was a Lotus Esprit. *Just like in Pretty Woman*, Zeus found himself thinking.

It pulled up alongside the kerb, just a few feet away from where Zeus was plying his trade. He looked over at it, wondering if it had pulled up to take a closer look at him, or whether the driver was merely stopping to read a map or take a call. In his head, Zeus could hear Kit De Luca – Julia Roberts' friend in the film – telling him that it was his for the taking.

You look hot, his mind's De Luca told him. *Go get it, girl!*

He pulled himself together and swaggered over to the car, chewing his gum with a careless attitude.

Work it! Work it! His internal De Luca called out from behind.

Spurred on by his friend's encouragement, he injected a bit more wiggle into his walk as he approached the car. He swayed his hips with sexual suggestion.

The car's passenger window slid down.

An attractive woman sat in the driver's seat. She was dressed in a black suit and her skirt rode up enough to show that she was wearing stockings underneath. Her hair was pulled back tightly, framing the glasses that made her look sexy yet sophisticated. The make-up she wore was elegant and expensive. The car smelled of exotic perfume.

Zeus guessed she was a businesswoman and thought that it was very possible she made her money by acquiring sinking businesses and selling off their assets. Just like Richard Gere in the film.

"Can you tell me how to get to The New Diamond Suite Hotel?" Asked the woman. She was holding a map and Zeus saw that it was upside-down.

He remembered the film.

"I'll do more than tell you," he said. He opened the passenger door without invitation and climbed in. "I'll show you."

They drove off and Zeus found himself thinking how much like *Pretty Woman* this actually was. The similarities were uncanny and he was amazed by how accurately the makers of the film had portrayed prostitution.

*

He made no secret about his profession as they drove to the New Diamond Suite Hotel.

In his skin-tight denims and his undone cardigan, it was difficult to deny. He acted the part to perfection, even putting his feet up on the dashboard at one point to paint his toenails. To do this he had to remove his steel toe-capped boots and his thick grey socks, but he wasn't embarrassed.

It was the oldest professional in the world.

He had nothing to be ashamed of.

When they got to the hotel, there was an awkward moment. The short drive had revealed there to be a definite chemistry between them, but the woman was not looking for a prostitute. She merely wanted to find the hotel.

The goodbye was protracted as they shared some small talk, both reluctant to break the chemistry. Finally, she gave Zeus some loose change from the car's ashtray, so that he could get a bus home. He smiled and thanked her, a suggestive twinkle in his eye. The thought of going back to School Road to tout for business once more, depressed him. This would have been a perfect job.

"Goodbye," he said. He walked to the bus-stop with an easy wiggle.

A few moments later, the woman came over. She was smiling. It was an embarrassed smile, but very warm.

"How much do you charge per hour?" She asked.

Zeus drew himself up to his full height. He was still shorter than she was.

It seemed he was in business.

"Two pounds eighty-five," he said.

"How much for a night?"

"A whole night?"

She nodded. Zeus made a quick calculation in his head.

"Twenty-eight pounds fifty." He said.

"Twenty-eight pounds fifty," She repeated.

She nodded, decisively.

"Come with me," she said. She looped her arm affectionately through his and led him into the Hotel.

In the night sky above, a glorious telescope retracted into the heavens. Silver clouds, painted by the cold moon, swung back into place.

God had watched the entire scene as it was played out below. He too had seen *Pretty Woman* and like Zeus, He found the similarities to be startling.

What He saw interested him greatly - but in spite of His godly thoughts, He dared not even hope.

*

Zeus couldn't believe his luck. He knew prostitution was going to be good - but he had no idea that it would be quite this luxurious.

The woman had the penthouse suite and once in the room, she ordered Champagne and strawberries. She seemed awkward at first, hardly sure why she had even brought him here. But Zeus was a professional. He did all he could to break down any barriers, to make her feel comfortable and uninhibited.

When he asked her what condom she would like him to use - he hunched at her feet, displaying an array of different colours and flavours, in a fan formation - she seemed uncomfortable even talking about it. He realised that he was going too fast for her and that he would need to go back to basics.

He needed to get her relaxed.

He needed to *turn her on.*

She was sitting on a leather chair, in front of the desk. Seductively, Zeus walked over to her, swinging his hips. With a suggestive flourish, he undid the final button on his cardigan. The cardigan swung open and he let it drop to the floor behind him.

He stood next to her, his legs pressing against hers. His skin-tight denims showed the shape of his legs and he imagined that his buttocks would be perfectly defined. Teasingly, he lifted one leg over hers, so that he was straddling her. He lowered himself down, slowly, so that he was mounted suggestively on her legs.

Tentatively, he ran his hands over her face, her shoulders, her neck. She shuddered under the tender touch of his fingertips. With careful precision, he moved his hands down, over her collar-bone, down further towards her breasts.

I'm bloody good at this, he thought. *Just like Julia Roberts.*

His hands moved over her breasts and he teased them slowly, rhythmically, through the thin material of her blouse. She sighed as he worked her, worked on her. Every now and then he leaned forward, allowing his ancient beard to tickle her face. He slid it over her like a tea-towel.

"I want you," she breathed. "I want you now."

Zeus gazed at her. His face was a picture of dirty innocence

"Just a minute," he said. "I just need to go to the bathroom."

He slid off the woman and wiggled his way seductively across the room. Closing the bathroom door behind him, he began to floss his teeth. Rampant sexual animal or not, it was night-time and if he was going to bed, he was damn well going to floss his teeth.

The door opened and she stood there looking in. With the floss stuck between his teeth, Zeus wondered if he had allowed the moment to slip away.

"What are you doing?" She asked.

"I'm flossing my teeth," Zeus replied.

She stood, smiling at him.

"What?" He asked, defensively.

She continued to smile.

"What?" He asked again.

"You're not like most whores," she said. "And more than that - you surprise me. Not many people do that, these days."

He shrugged. Surely personal hygiene wasn't an unusual thing, he thought.

"Finish flossing your teeth," she said, running a gentle finger under his chin. "And then I want you to come and make love to me."

When he returned to the bedroom, she was ready for him. Lying on the bed, in just her stockings, she looked flushed with excitement and ready for Zeus to take her as his lover.

Zeus unbuttoned his shirt and slipped it from his saggy body. His skin looked pale and white in the dim light. He peeled off his trousers - which turned out to be something of a challenge, given the tightness of the legs. He managed to remain standing as he hopped around the floor for two minutes, wrestling his way out of his denim confinement.

But when he finally removed them, she looked all the more excited, all the more ready for him.

He crawled on to the bed and slinked towards her, his beard trailing over the covers like cobweb handkerchief. He realised that she hadn't even commented on his novelty elephant trunk thong. He hoped that it was arousing her sufficiently, but he realised that she was probably past the point of trivial stimulation.

The ancient god of the Greeks slithered his way up the bed with the sensuality of a cheese and onion crisp on a water slide and began to earn his twenty-eight pounds fifty.

Roger was confused.

On the morning following his unearthly visitation, he had come out to clear up the remains of the nocturnal visitor. Diligently, he left the portacabin equipped with a pair of rubber gloves and some bin bags.

But when he got outside the creature was nowhere to be seen.

It hadn't been a dream, that much he was sure of. You just had to look around the place. There were feathers everywhere. But of the body, there was no sign. It seemed unlikely that the thing had got up and walked away. It looked completely mutilated when it was lying on the ground. He was certain that it was dead.

He sauntered over to the pile of engines to see if the creature's glowing hat was still there. It was. It lay on the dusty ground, a brightly glowing circle with a hole in the middle. It looked sacred and elegant, like an ethereal doughnut.

He picked it up, deemed it worthless and threw it in a nearby skip.

He was musing the fate of the strange creature – and what the hell it had been doing at his yard in the first place – when a huge figure strolled through the gates of the yard. From the Tony Blackburn hair style, he recognised the man immediately. It was that Thorax character. This morning, he looked full of purpose. He was wearing a pair of industrial ear defenders on his head.

Roger was about to confront him but saw that he was coming straight for him. In his hand he held a box of some sorts. As he got nearer, Roger saw that it was a tape recorder.

The huge, hulking parody of one of the nineteen seventies' most popular disc-jockeys stopped before Roger. Roger snarled at him, his bullish nostrils flaring with rage.

"I told you, you are not welcome here," he growled. The hulking barbarian didn't seem to hear him. He stared at him, his face triumphant.

"*Get out of my yard!*" Roared the Minotaur.

Thorax smiled, smugly, and lifted the tape recorder so that it was in front of the Minotaur's broad head. He clicked the PLAY button and watched for the consequences.

What he saw was the Minotaur's eyes begin to roll in its head as it bent its massive horns to the floor in an angry gesture of aggression.

It began to scrape its foot threateningly in the dirt.

This was not how it was supposed to be. The Minotaur was supposed to look instantly weary and then slump to the ground in a fitful slumber. The tape recorder was, after all, the recording of a mermaid's song. On realising that he was unlikely to get a mermaid to the scrap yard alive, that previous evening, Thorax had gone back to the farm with a tape recorder. He had sat by the river with his ear protectors on, thrown the entire bucket of live bait into the water and then waited for the emergence of some sirens. As soon as they appeared, their heads rising above the water with aquatic agility, he pressed RECORD. He could see their mouths working, could see them singing their magical song.

He felt certain he had outwitted Fate on this one. He would take the tape recorder to the scrap yard, play it back to the Minotaur and claim Bob as his uncle. It would be just the same as having a mermaid there, only there was no need for discomfort or a lingering death on the mermaid's part.

But it wasn't quite working out like that.

The Minotaur was not succumbing to the mermaids' spell.

He looked mad.

Really mad.

Thorax fiddled with the volume dial. It was already on full. He examined the tape inside, to be sure that the reels

315

were going round, and that the thing was working. It would be just his luck for the batteries to run out at this crucial moment. But the tape was playing. Everything was as it should be.

He glanced at the Minotaur with an expression of uncertainty. The Minotaur was scraping the ground so hard that he was carving a deep trough in the dirt. His head was down low, his horns level with Thorax's torso.

The horns were pin-sharp and they glistened in the morning sun.

Tentatively, Thorax lifted one of the protectors from his ears. He was surprised by what he heard.

Admittedly, the version of *Knees Up Mother Brown* coming from the tape recorder did have an atmosphere to it. It was as though the old East End classic had been arranged and performed by Enya.

But, it was *Knees Up Mother Brown* nonetheless.

It was not what Thorax expected mermaids to sing. It was clearly not one of Roger's favourite songs. Or perhaps it was. Maybe this was the problem. Perhaps he preferred a more traditional rendition.

This was all academic, however. The sirens' song was not working. It wasn't affecting Roger and it wasn't affecting Thorax. Quite obviously, the hypnotic power of the sirens' song did not translate to tape.

It meant that Thorax was royally buggered.

With an apologetic smile, he stopped the tape recorder and removed his headphones.

"Anyway," he said, conversationally. "I must be off."

"Arghhhhh.....what the hell are you *doing* here?" Roger growled.

"I don't know," Thorax answered.

It was the most pathetic response imaginable.

"I've got a panic button now," Roger thrust his head into Thorax's face. "It links me directly with the police station. I push the button and they'll be here in minutes."

"Oh?"

"Yes. *Oh*. If I see you here again, then that button will be pressed. You are trespassing."

"I didn't mean to. It was an accident."

This was the second most pathetic response imaginable.

Roger glared at the trespasser.

"And by the way – did you send that *thing* here last night?"

"What thing?"

"That thing. With the wings and the hat."

"I don't know what you mean."

Roger continued to glare at him.

"I don't know what kind of new secret weapon it is that you have in your arsenal, but if I see it here again, it's going straight in the crusher. I should have done it last night, when I had the chance. Now GET OUT."

Thorax heaved a disappointed sigh. He had truly believed that he would be walking out with the bachelor's plough. This was turning into an impossible quest. He thought of the portable crepe retail outlet that he hoped to buy with the money Zeus had promised him.

It was beginning to seem like an unattainable dream.

Zeus was in the bath, listening to Prince on his personal stereo.

He was feeling good.

After a night of impassioned love making, he felt that he had earned his money. The woman seemed happy – she especially liked his trick with the Champagne cork – and more than this, they had a definite chemistry. If this was prostitution, Zeus wished he had done it years ago.

The bath reminded Zeus of the hot-tub on Olympus. Carved from white marble, that too had been a large, circular tub. The bath in the penthouse suite had a jacuzzi facility, and the Olympus hot-tub had boasted the same, every time the flatulent Apollo had joined the party.

He luxuriated in the silky bubble bath, his eyes closed as he sang along tunelessly to Prince's *Kiss.* He was lost in this intimate performance when the woman came in. She was fully dressed, ready for the day's business. She stood in the doorway, smiling down at Zeus for a minute or two. Eventually he realised she was there.

He smiled up at her, sheepishly.

"Don't worry, I'll be out as soon as I have finished my bath."

She sat on the edge of the bath.

"No, no. Take your time," she said. "Look. I'm here for a few days. I was wondering. How much would you charge for, say, three days?"

"Three days? Day and night?"

"Day and night."

"Well..." Zeus thought about it. He calculated his rate. "Eighty-five pounds fifty," he said, finally.

"Sixty pounds."

"Seventy," he said.

"Done."

Zeus let out a delighted scream and disappeared under the water. He thrashed about for a few moments.

When he finally emerged, the woman was smiling.

"I've left you some money on the bed," she said. "You'll need to get yourself a decent suit. I need you to accompany me to a business dinner tonight. It's a very important meeting. You'll be my date."

"Wow."

They remained smiling at each other for some time.

After a while, Zeus spoke.

"Look, I don't know if I told you." He gazed at her, with a serious expression. "I'll do anything. But kissing on the lips is out. That's too...personal."

She nodded, warmly.

"That's fine. This is a purely business arrangement. As long as we both understand that."

They continued to gaze at each other over the bubbles, their eyes sparkling with passion.

*

God hardly dared to hope. His glorious telescope and His wondrous ear trumpet were trained on the New Diamond Suite Hotel and He had watched the scene unfold with growing excitement.

This was too much to hope for.

Before His very eyes, Zeus was falling in love. And if Zeus fell in love and a relationship blossomed...

He would be a bachelor no more.

Thorax sat with Billy the Dwarf in the *Boar's Head Tavern*. Like Tony Blackburn after a weekend of intense partying, he looked tired and despondent. Even his hair-do had lost its usual lustre and a critic might say that it was more reminiscent of Bill Haley than Tony Blackburn.

The two of them supped from their tankards.

"I don't know where to go from here," Thorax said. He took a gulp of his ale. He had just finished telling Billy about his failure to subdue the Minotaur with the tape recording.

Billy the Dwarf supped his mead. It frothed over the rim of his tankard like a log flume in a soap powder factory.

"Definitely problematic," he agreed. He tore open his packet of pork scratchings and pushed the open bag into the centre of the table. It was an unspoken offer for Thorax to dive in at will.

"I just don't know what to do. I've visited the Cyclops' lair. I've confronted the Gorgon Medusa. And I've braved the sirens. The quest is beginning to feel endless."

"Well, as I see it, you've got two choices," Billy crunched on a pork scratching.

"Oh?"

"Oui." Billy the Dwarf had never said "oui" in this life. This is just the author trying to show some sophistication, by demonstrating a subtle grasp of the French language. He could also have Billy the Dwarf ask for a kilogramme of apples, but he will leave this for another time.

"You can either meet the problem head on, and fight the Minotaur – or you can just give up."

Thorax plucked a pork scratching delicately from the packet and placed it into his mouth.

He shook his head.

"There must be another way," he said. "A third way. Fighting the Minotaur would be fine and dandy if I felt his ownership of the plough was unjust. But it isn't. He bought it in good faith. I can't just go wading in and pick a fight. It's wrong. It's morally repugnant."

"Then you just give up. You've done well to come this far, Thorax. Don't feel bad about knocking it on the head."

The door of the tavern swung open and the dark, cowled figure of Death staggered in. Hardly able to stand, he weaved his way across the *Boar's Head* to the bar.

Thorax banged his fist on the table. The table groaned.

"But if I give up, I'll be letting Zeus down. I'll be letting *myself* down. I don't know if I told you this, but if I get Zeus this plough, he'll give me enough money to start my own portable crepe retail outlet. You know how much that means to me, Billy. And I've come so far..."

"Then fight the Minotaur."

"There has to be another way."

Billy supped his mead and crunched on another pork scratching. He then dunked a pork scratching in his mead and chomped on it. Finally he performed a delicate operation, in which he held a pork scratching just above the table and carefully poured a few drops of mead on to it. The mead soaked in, sensuously. The dwarf popped the saturated scratching into his mouth.

Thorax watched the entire charade with dull fascination.

At the bar, the Grim Reaper was leaning across the fallen tree trunk, his vast empty hood thrust in the face of the barman.

"Gishadrrrrink." His voice was the tuneless grating of a stone slab. "GISHADRRRRRRINK!"

A few customers in the tavern looked around to see what the commotion was. Thorax and Billy hardly even noticed.

Billy stopped chomping halfway through the saturated scratching.

"Hang on a minute," he said. His eyes had glazed over. A bit like a bun.

"What?"

"I'm just thinking aloud here...but there may be another way."

"What is it?"

Billy the Dwarf was staring into space. He gazed uncertainty at the source of his inspiration.

"Well...and I'm just throwing ideas out here...you are pretty certain that a mermaid in the flesh would sink him, yes?"

"Yes."

"Okay. But getting a mermaid to the scrap yard without prior asphyxiation is not possible. Right?"

"Right."

"But what if the mermaid *was already dead.*"

Thorax stared at his friend.

"Then she wouldn't be able to sing very loudly." He suggested.

"Ah, yes. But what if she had *passed over?* To the other side."

"Nope. You've lost me."

Billy the Dwarf was now getting into his stride. Admittedly, this amounted to fairly minimal perambulation.

"Mermaids die like anyone else," he said, excitedly. "And when they die, they must surely travel to the underworld. So what I'm thinking is, why don't you go to the underworld and bring back a mermaid that has already passed over. A dead mermaid. But not dead like the one you killed. More...sort of...alive. You know – a shade. Shove her in front of the Minotaur and..."

"Lay claim to the uncontested will of my Uncle Bob."

"Exactly."

At the bar, Cyril was becoming increasingly aggressive. His voice reverberated around the tavern like a broken dream. "YOUUUUUU....GIVE ME A J-RINK! NOWWWW! I DEMAND TO BE *SHHHERVED*... *GIMME-A-JRRRINK*!"

Thorax reached for a pork scratching. His face had the expression of a cardboard box.

"Let me just get this straight. What you're saying is...go to the underworld and bring back the shade of a siren."

"Yes!"

"Let me put that another way. What you're saying is, go to the underworld and bring back the shade of a siren."

"Yes!"

"That seems a tad far-fetched."

"Not at all. You're a barbarian, remember? If anyone can do it, you can."

Thorax supped some ale. He reached a conclusion.

"You're off your vertically challenged rocker. Even if it was a sound plan - *if* it was - how the hell do you get to the underworld? I can't imagine it's as simple as taking the right junction off the motorway and then turning left at the next roundabout."

"You have to cross the River Styx."

"Oh, as simple as that?"

Billy was smiling broadly. His smile cut through his beard like a chainsaw through a tree.

"Surprisingly so," he said. "The Styx actually crosses the Thames, just north of Pestlewick."

"Eh? Where?"

The Grim Reaper was leaning back on the bar, waving his scythe around with uncoordinated panache.

"Why...don't nobody...givssssh me a JRRRRRINK in this place?" He demanded. "I'll cut you ALL TO RIBBONSHHH! I'm not meshing wiv ya. ANY OF YA! Someone give me a JRRRRRINK!"

323

"Just behind the railway station," said Billy, excitedly. "There is a length of the Thames - only twenty yards or so - where it intersects with the Styx. I've seen the Ferryman take souls across. He nearly got hit by the Caversham Cruiser, the last time I saw him. And then I thought he was going to capsize in its wake. But to be fair, I think it was going too fast."

"Are you pulling my barbarian's sporran?"

"No, I am serious. If you go there you'll find a bell. Ring the bell to summon the Ferryman and he'll take you across. He generally charges an obolus[8], but I reckon he'll do it for a tenner."

Thorax stared at his friend, with a sparkle in his eye. It sounded like a plan. He would go to the underworld and bring back a dead mermaid. She wouldn't die, as she would already be dead.

And then, a simple trip to the scrap yard with the hybrid shade...

Sometimes, Billy was an inspiration.

The rightful Blackburn usurped the evil Haley and took its place once more upon his cranium.

Throughout their conversation, neither of them noticed the man on the next table.

He was wearing a trilby hat and a false moustache. His face was concealed from sight, by the newspaper that he was holding up. Two eye holes were cut into the newspaper and he stared through intently throughout the entirety of their conversation. Behind the newspaper, John Thomas was smiling.

For once he would be ahead of the game.

"Right...I'll take you ALL on!" Screamed Death. He leaned forward, trying to maintain his balance and stay upright. He swung his scythe around loosely, hacking at the air. Slices

---

[8] Ancient large silver coin, traditionally associated with payment for Charon the Ferryman's services.

of freshly cut air drifted to the hard flagstone floor. "CAAAM ON! WHO'S MAN ENOUGH? EH? EH?"

For the first time, Thorax and Billy noticed the scene unfolding behind them. They turned and watched with casual interest as four burly men rose from a table in the far corner and approached the bar.

Heavily tattooed, dressed in leathers and badly battle-scarred, the men were part of the furniture, in the *Boar's Head*. They were a core element of a local biker chapter and the Boar's Head was the one place they could come to unwind. While they could put up with many things going on around them – bar brawls, arguments, knife attacks and even karaoke on some Saturdays – an obnoxious drunk at the bar shouting threats across the tavern was more than they could stomach. The fact this particularly obnoxious drunk was wearing a dark hooded robe and waving a scythe about meant nothing to them. Trouble was trouble, whatever its guise.

They moved to the bar and stood next to the drunk.

"Is this bloke giving you trouble?" They asked Valerie, the barman.

Valerie nodded. He looked unsettled by the Reaper's behaviour. He was not prepared to budge on his decision to refuse the guy any more alcohol though. This drunk had clearly had enough.

Cyril staggered round aggressively, to face the bikers. His hood had folded back a little, with all his swaying. A glimmer of pale skull peeped out.

"*Ish thish bloke givin you tchrouble,*" he mimicked, swaying backwards and forwards uncontrollably. "*Yyyyaaaa.* Whatchoooo gonna do 'bout it, PUSSY BOYS?"

Were he not the very incarnation of death – and were it not down to him and only him as to whether extinction befell an individual's mortal coil – his goading insult would have been tantamount to suicide. As it was, he merely suffered the worst hiding of his life.

Thorax and Billy winced as the Reaper was hurled across the tavern. His balance was such that he fell immediately, sprawling across the floor like a pile of rags.

"Yaaaa PUSSIES!" He repeated, turning round to face the bikers from his disadvantaged position on the flagstone floor.

They walked over, with an attitude of casual violence, to finish the job.

Between the four of them they owned a respectable armoury of martial aids and seemingly from out of nowhere, they produced a consignment of weaponry comprehensive enough to equip a small army. Knuckle-dusters, a heavy bike chain, a knife, a cricket bat and a crisp packet suddenly appeared as props in the arena of conflict. For good measures, one of them grabbed a bottle from the bar and smashed it across the back of a chair, to give him a newly improvised weapon.

Billy and Thorax looked at each other with a mirrored expression. It said, simply: *This is going to hurt.*

The beating lasted for ten minutes. During this time, Death was kicked, punched, chain-whipped, stabbed, bottled, crisp-packeted and beaten senseless with the cricket bat.

On one or two occasions, he actually used the word "oof", which would have been clichéd had it not been uttered with such sincerity.

He also endured the rather more creative assault of having one of the tavern tables lifted by all four bikers and rammed repeatedly against his head. The cracking of his skull was terrific, as were the cracking of his ribs. And his arms. Not to mention his legs and his pelvis. He finally stopped hurling insults just as his attackers were coming to the end of their assault. They were amazed that he had the courage or the stupidity to carry on hurling abuse throughout his ordeal.

By the end, he was curled up in the foetal position, waiting for the barrage of pain to end.

Having taught the drunkard a lesson, the bikers dragged him to the front door and threw him out. He hit the pavement outside with a resounding crack and remained unmoving, a slumped and beaten figure on the ground.

As far as Zeus was concerned, the dinner was a great success and he felt certain that he had done his client proud. He played the part well. The perfect companion, a model date.

Throughout the meal he had impressed her business clients with his wit and charm, winning them over with his light and airy attitude. When he wrestled unsuccessfully with his *escargot*, sending a whole snail flying across the restaurant, it merely served to break the ice. And when he yelled out GET DOWN HE'S GOT A GUN, every time someone popped a Champagne cork, it caused ripples of humour across the establishment (or so he thought), for each of the eight times that he did it.

He was certain that his keen humour was well-received.

At one stage during their meal, the conversation became quite tense, as Zeus's client and her clients tried to negotiate some rocky issues. Tempers were flaring and it seemed they were at a stalemate in the proceedings. Zeus, though, came to the rescue, making a turban out of a napkin and performing his impression of an Indian waiter. Once again, he felt that his efforts were well-received, even though the clients in question were of Bangladeshi descent. He took their silence as appreciation of his wit and delivery, though he was a little concerned that they may have found his Indian accent to be a little too Welsh-sounding.

At the end of the meal, he and his client went back to the hotel.

She was in a funny mood. Nothing he could say could bring her out of her reverie. The meeting had been hard for her. She had ethical issues with the whole deal.

Zeus was no businessman, but the talk of exchanging cocaine for illegal arms did strike him as being ethically flawed. He was sure he heard something about black market editions of *Trivial Pursuit* in there as well.

Whatever was bothering her, it had wriggled into his client's head like a brain worm. The ancient god tried to cheer her up by putting two pencils up his nose and calling himself Vlad the Nasal Vampire. But even that didn't work.

In the end, she told him she needed some time alone and she left the room.

*

A few hours passed and Zeus decided to go and find her.

When he reached the lobby, he heard piano music, doleful and beautifully played, drifting out from the hotel bar. He peered into the lounge, out of curiosity, and saw his client at the piano, lost in her own world. The staff had cleared the place up and the tables were stacked with chairs. A handful of workers now stood around, quietly, watching her play.

Zeus walked in. He wore nothing more than a dressing gown, and his pale legs stuck out vividly from beneath the hem. As he walked, the suggestion of his novelty elephant trunk thong could be seen pressed against the material.

He moved to the piano and stood next to her. She stopped playing and looked at him.

"That's beautiful," he said.

Their eyes met and he saw that hers were brimming with tears.

"Thank you guys," she said, turning to her small audience. "You can leave now."

They trailed out, obediently, closing the door behind them.

Zeus and his client were alone.

329

She stood up and, playing the part of the aggressive lover, pulled him to her by the lapels of his dressing gown. They stood, gazing into each other's eyes. Without warning, she kissed him, hard, passionately.

Zeus didn't think.

He returned the kiss.

He wanted this as much as she did. Yes, it was personal. *But they had something.* The air between them was electric. They stood and kissed, their hands moving over each other. Their passion grew in its intensity and they were fixed to the spot, tasting each other, exploring each other.

She pushed Zeus back, on to the piano.

Bursting with sensual need she ripped open his dressing gown. Her hand trailed over his novelty elephant trunk thong, before ripping it off violently. Zeus let out a small squeak.

His buttocks were resting on the piano keys and as she moved against him, moved on to him, the piano began to tinkle discordantly.

By the time she had slipped him inside of her, and she was riding him, he had begun to pick out a simple tune.

Finally, as they made love, there on the piano, Zeus managed to play Chopsticks with his arse.

High in the sky, the Good Lord, God, Father of All Creation, couldn't believe His luck.

He had witnessed everything. And He knew how Zeus felt about kissing.

No kissing on the lips - that's too personal.

But it had happened.

It had got personal.

Zeus was involved. Emotionally involved.

He was no longer a bachelor and that was all God needed to know. The rich pickings of the bachelor's plough were closed to Zeus, now.

The Good Lord's divinity was safe.

He grabbed a can of sparkling nectar from the fridge and sat down contentedly to watch *Murder She Wrote*. For the first time in a long time, His mind felt at peace.

Thorax the Barbarian managed to appropriate a bulky warehouse cage from the back of a lorry. It wasn't ideal but it would suit his purposes for the time being. The cage had a hinged door and trolley wheels. It was well-suited to bringing back a mermaid from the underworld.

He pushed the cage down Morewood Hill, over the roundabout and on to the Wessex Road. As he neared the railway station, he found a small footbridge that took him over the railway and down to the river.

He immediately saw that one small stretch of the Thames was thick with mist. It lasted for around twenty yards and Thorax knew that this must be where the River Thames interchanged with The Styx.

He pulled the cage through the mud of the riverbank until he found what he was looking for. There, next to the towpath, was a rotten old post with a large brass bell hanging from it. The bell was grimy and dented. A felt-tipped mallet rested on top of the post. Freezing air seemed to roll out of the thick mist. Suddenly aware of how cold it was, Thorax picked up the mallet and struck the bell. It gave a mournful chime, which resonated for a long time, even after he had replaced the mallet.

For a few minutes, nothing happened and then, finally, he heard a gentle splashing sound coming from deep in the mist.

He watched and waited.

A shadow emerged from the mist, some small distance from the bank. A wooden boat, with a dark figure standing on the prow, pushing the vessel along with a large, crooked pole. Thorax tried to see the features of the Ferryman, but the mist obscured him.

The air grew colder as the Ferryman drew nearer.

Through the swirling mist, Thorax saw the boat suddenly begin to list and rock. A loud splash announced the Ferryman's pole falling into the water.

"Oh *fudge*," came the muttered voice.

The boat tilted as the spectral figure leaned over the side in an attempt to retrieve the pole. Even through the thick mist, Thorax could see that it was drifting away from the boat.

He watched, vaguely uncomfortable to witness the collapsing dignity of the Ferryman, as he used a hand desperately to paddle the boat in the direction of the drifting pole. He finally managed to retrieve it but not before the boat had turned about, so that it was facing back the other way. Thorax stood patiently, trying to pretend he wasn't bearing witness to the Ferryman's plight, as the Ferryman performed a tricky manoeuvre to get the boat back around the right way.

The entire scene was accompanied by a cacophony of grunts and curses as the Ferryman battled with his ill-fortune.

Finally, he brought the ferry into the shore.

Thorax saw the Ferryman's face, skeletal and deranged. He wore a thick black robe and his ancient head was a tapestry of rotting flesh and exposed bone. His lips were gone and his mouth was pulled back permanently into a manic grin.

His hands were nothing more than ragged flesh hanging from brittle bone.

He held out a skeletal hand.

Thorax gave him an apologetic look.

"Um, I know you would prefer an obulus," he said. "But I don't have one. Come to think of it, I don't even know what one is. Will you accept a tenner?"

"Silver," wheezed the Ferryman in a guttural whisper. He remained motionless, his hand outstretched.

Thorax dug into his pockets and pulled out some loose change. He held it out for the Ferryman to see.

"Anything in there work for you?" He asked.

The Ferryman hovered a long bony finger over the barbarian's pocket shrapnel. Finally, he alighted on a twenty pence piece and picked it up, delicately, between a finger and thumb.

He slipped the coin into a large pocket at the front of his robe, and beckoned Thorax onboard, slowly.

Once more, Thorax gave him an apologetic look. He gestured towards the large cage that he had brought with him.

"I need to bring that along," he said.

The Ferryman looked at it. While he was largely devoid of expression, Thorax knew that it was a look of exasperation.

"Well where's that supposed to go?" The Ferryman asked. His voice was a watery grave.

"I don't know. Will it not fit in the boat with us?"

"I think it would be pushing it, to be honest."

"It does need to come with me."

"I wish you'd told me. I'd have brought the trailer."

"I'm sorry. I didn't realise."

Reluctantly, the Ferryman agreed to have a go at getting the cage onboard. He rucked up his robe and stepped out of the boat.

"Right," he said. "How do you want to do this?"

Thorax looked at the cage and then took an appraising glance at the boat.

"How are we going to get it in?" He asked. "Longways, or sideways?"

The Ferryman scratched his bony chin.

"I was thinking we're best trying to stand it up," he said.

"Okay."

"If we stand it up at the front, I'll balance it out at the back. You'll need to sit in the middle."

"Yeah, okay. Will it fit?"

"I think we should be able to wedge it in between the seats."

Thorax bent down to pick up one side of the cage. The Ferryman did the same. They lifted it together.

"Okay," said the Ferryman. "As she goes. Easy...easy. To you...to you..."

"To me...to me..."

"Steady..." The Ferryman's voice could command the dead. He had also done removals before.

It became clear to Thorax that they didn't have the angle right. It needed to be rectified.

"Woah, hang on. Drop it your side a bit. That's it. No...spin her round...that's it...just a bit more...that's it."

They eased the cage towards the boat, both wading into the river up to their knees.

"Gently...*gently*...nice and easy..." Said the Ferryman. He watched carefully to check that they got the base of the cage over the lip of the boat.

Thorax examined the angle.

"Right, we need to..." He tilted the cage by way of demonstration. "Bring her round, *bring her round*..."

"Nicely does it," said the Ferryman.

They brought the cage over the lip of the boat and levelled it up.

"Okay, bring her down," said Thorax. "Slowly...sloooowly...that's it...ease her in there."

They brought the cage down to rest, finally. It stood precariously at the front of the boat. For a few moments they admired their handy work.

"Right, let's get going," said the Ferryman.

Trying to salvage some dignity he rucked up his robe once more and stepped back on to the boat. It listed dramatically, with the unbalanced weight of the cage and the Ferryman had to stretch out his arms to assert some balance.

Thorax stepped into the middle of the boat and sat down, keeping a wary eye on the cage.

Resuming his usual dark silence, the Ferryman picked up his pole and pushed off, guiding his unusual cargo eerily and silently into the creeping mist.

*

He was glad to unburden himself of the cargo.

The barbarian was frankly too big for the boat. His vast weight made it sit precariously low in the water and on a couple of occasions sploshes of river water seeped over the side, into the boat.

The supermarket cage compounded the issue. Because of the fact it was upright, any list of the boat was amplified as the cage followed the natural force of gravity. The Ferryman found himself not only controlling the direction of the boat, as he guided it across the river, but also had to use his entire weight to keep the boat steady.

Every slight tilt of the boat was met with an exaggerated shuffle by the Ferryman, as he desperately compensated for the movement.

He had just dropped Thorax and his trolley on to the shore of the underworld when he heard the bell ring again, from the far shore.

It was turning into a busy day.

Dutifully, he turned the boat around and guided it slowly through the cold mist, across the Styx, towards the summons. Through the mist he saw a new customer standing on the shore, a slightly built, nervous-looking man. He shifted from foot to foot as the Ferryman emerged from the obscurity of the mist. As he got closer to the shore, he saw that the man was wearing a badge. It read, simply: **John Thomas. Fixer.**

The Ferryman pretended not to notice the supermarket trolley on the bank next to the man. It would be a damn sight easier than that cage to get on board - but nonetheless, any extraneous materials were a pain. More than this, he considered them an affront to his dignity and to the dignity of his position. The journey across the Styx was, after all, a journey through the metaphysical boundary that exists between the material world and the world beyond. It was no place for worldly materials to cross.

The Ferryman's job was to take lost souls over to the underworld; he was not a budget cross channel ferry service.

A few months previously he had very uncomfortably agreed to take a bright red Henry Hoover across the Styx, along with its recently departed owner. It looked so wrong, all red and smiley, with its shiny black hat, against the sombre backdrop of the creaking ferry, so gothic, dank and mildewed.

He badly felt that such cargoes were devaluing his image and his reputation.

The Raleigh racing bike that he had agreed to take over last year was the same. It made him feel like a cheap package holiday representative.

And then there was the easel, accompanied by a cardboard box full of painting paraphernalia. And the acoustic guitar. And the fishing rod. And the picnic basket.

The problem was, he just couldn't say no.

If he ever had a job interview and they asked him that ridiculously obvious question - what would you say is you biggest weakness - he would probably say it was his inability to say no.

That, and a fear of public speaking.

And spiders. He didn't like spiders at all.

It was a strange and unfamiliar land.

Thorax stood on the shore of the underworld and looked at the dismal landscape before him. The sky was a deep red colour, tinged with long wisps of black cloud. It was an unfriendly sky that coloured the vast land in a dim red glow. The entire place was immersed in crimson twilight. There was something apocalyptic about it. Every now and then lightening flickered threateningly behind the red sky.

In the far distance, Thorax saw rolling mountains. They went back forever, an endless mountain landscape. They looked ominous, silhouetted against the brooding sky. Before the mountains, the land was completely flat.

He gazed around silently at the vista of this world beyond.

On one side there were dark, rolling forests. The trees reached up to the sky, towering, dark and still. The forests were vast, foreboding. No light seemed to penetrate the thick forest canopy. All was black within. Across from the forests a bleak industrial metropolis spilled thick smoke into the dismal atmosphere. Dark churning mills threw out metal echoes of clanging oppression while a million chimneys spewed forth flame and soot into the sky above. Dull yellow windows flickered in the mills and somehow this made them look even darker. Thorax wondered who worked in those mills and what they produced. He shivered at the idea of such soulless industry.

As he looked across the eternal landscape, he marvelled at the variety of different environments, each as bleak as the next.

There were rolling plains, dusty and featureless. They looked cold and vast, like gaping nocturnal deserts.

There were colourless fields of grass, and grey swaying corn, devoid of nutrition.

There were huge lakes, silently mirroring the dark red sky.

There were rivers that flowed like thick sludge through the lifeless land; cold, black scars across the barren landscape.

Sprinkled around like funereal confetti, sleeping towns and villages looked broken and derelict, barely illuminated by a few broken streetlamps. From where he stood, Thorax could almost smell the dank odour of crumbling stone and rotten wood. Wastelands of empty nothingness punctuated a twilight world characterised by nothing but dead weeds and rusted metal.

High above, fiery dragons crossed the sky, while across the land, a billion souls milled around like zombies, going nowhere, looking for nothing.

Thorax surveyed it all. He tried to remember if he'd left the empty bottles out for the milkman. He thought he had, but he wasn't sure.

As he gazed, he wondered where he was going to find his siren. The place was huge. It spanned eternity. He could spend forever here, looking for what he sought.

To his right, on the bank of the Styx, there was a small wooden hut. It wasn't much larger than an outside toilet, what the Australians would call a "dunny".

An improvised wooden plaque nailed to the door, was inscribed with a single word: **Ferryman**. It put Thorax in mind of the railway workers' huts that one sees along railways lines. It was obvious that the hut gave the Ferryman some simple shelter between jobs, a place for him to keep out of the rain.

Thorax decided to take a look inside. Curiosity killed the cat but there are no historical accounts of it ever having taken out a barbarian.

He pushed open the door and peered in with mild interest. It was dark and smelled like an old shed. An extinguished paraffin lamp hung on the wall above a modest wooden table. A small cooking stove, a saucepan and some tea-making facilities sat on the table and next to it, stood a simple wooden chair. Just to the right, pinned to the wall, was a *Topless Glamour Model* wall calendar from 1986. Next to that was an up-to-date calendar, promoting Massey Ferguson tractors.

Thorax saw that the Ferryman had scrawled delicately under one of the dates: *Mum's birthday.*

It was the collection of large grey canvas bags, piled in the corner of the hut that caught his attention. Venturing into the hut, he knelt down next to the bags. They were each tied with thick, frayed string. Curiously, he undid one of the bags and pulled it open. It was filled with large silver coins.

Thorax picked one out and held it up before his face. He knew what it was immediately. *An obulus.* These bags, bulging with silver were where the Ferryman kept payment from his customers. The barbarian stood up, thoughtfully. *An obulus is a rare thing,* he thought. *And such a quantity...*

Something that Polyphemus had said came back to him. It swirled through the air like a drugged-up mirage.

He could hear the Cyclops' voice and in his mind's eye, he could see him saying the words. Curiously enough, the brain being what it is in terms of a creative organ, the Cyclops delivered the words while tap dancing on an empty stage, wearing a top hat and twirling a cane.

His *words*, however, were a guiding light.

Now that he was here, Thorax wondered if it was really a siren that he needed after all.

He re-emerged from the hut back into the dim, heavy atmosphere of the underworld. He scanned the horizon, wondering how best to proceed, wondering how to get where he needed in this strange, unearthly place. It seemed impossible to know.

And then a taxi came along.

Thorax saw it kicking up dust as it lurched across the uneven ground. So vast was the horizon that it took more than ten minutes to reach him. When it did he was delighted to see that it was a battered old London Taxi. Its sign was lit and the driver, while admittedly a skeleton, looked cheerful. He was smiling broadly, though it might be argued that, the skeletal visage being what it is, he didn't have much choice.

Although he was the only person around and the taxi was heading straight for him, Thorax felt it was only proper to wave it down. It pulled up next to him and the driver lowered the window.

"Where to, guv?" He asked. Thorax saw that he was wearing a chequered shirt and a green woolly jumper. He liked him immediately. He told the driver where he needed to go, and the driver smiled.

"Jump in," he said, his manner friendly and welcoming.

"I have a bit of cargo," Thorax apologised.

"No worries, guv'nor!" The driver said. It was an attitude in stark contrast to the Ferryman's, Thorax thought.

He leaned forward good naturedly and flicked a switch.

The orange *Taxi* light went out.

PC Standing listened to the owner of the scrap yard sympathetically, as he related his concerns. Roger had accidentally pushed the panic button. It was more a Freudian slip than an accident. He was unsettled to the point of being genuinely worried and the presence of a policeman in the yard massively reassured him.

"You're saying he's been back?" Standing asked, his voice revealing his impatience with the man to whom he alluded. "Thorax the Barbarian."

"Yes. But it's not just him, officer. There are other things. Like this creature that arrived over the yard the other night."

"Creature?"

"Yes."

"What kind of creature?"

"Oh, it was horrible. It was all glowy and white. It had these giant wings – like a huge insect it was. A moth. And it wore this bright hat, all lit up. Like some kind of cosmic piles cushion."

"What did it want?"

"I don't know. I shot it. But that's the funny thing. In the morning, when I came out to clear it up, it was gone."

"Could it have been a pigeon?"

"No, I don't think it was a pigeon. It was too big."

"And you don't know what it was?"

"No. But like everything these days...I reckon it was after a plough. Everyone seems to want a plough nowadays. Why won't these people just leave me alone?"

Standing sighed, in sympathy. He had watched the emotional journey of this poor man-bull and it really had been a rollercoaster.

He was just about to reassure the owner of the scrapyard that he was always but a few minutes away and that the panic button would summon him at any time, when a man sauntered into the yard pushing a supermarket trolley.

Standing recognised him immediately, as the man who prayed in the street; the man that liked to wear a rock on his head. He still suspected that he was a single cell fundamentalist terrorist. What was obviously the illegal possession of a supermarket trolley did nothing to dissuade him from his suspicions.

As the man approached, he looked unnervingly confident. He pushed the trolley over the uneven ground, towards PC Standing and the Minotaur.

Neither could have known that in the trolley, hidden under the grey blanket, was an undead mermaid from the underworld.

*

John Thomas had arrived in the underworld shortly after Thorax and, like the barbarian, had managed to hail a cab within minutes of being there.

The cab had taken him directly to the Ocean of Despair, where, he was informed, shoals of mermaids resided.

Taking a leaf out of Thorax's book, when the wily barbarian had kidnapped the Gorgon Medusa, Thomas had used a piece of cheese as bait.

Leaving the piece of cheese in the supermarket trolley, and the trolley on the shore, he waited patiently until a mermaid crawled out of the ocean and dragged herself inelegantly over to the trolley.

No sooner was she leaning into it, to grab the cheese, than John Thomas was upon her with the blanket.

With the foresight of a dyslexic rabbi, he was wearing his industrial ear protectors, ensuring that he was safe from her

343

mermaidenly wiles. He bundled her up in the blanket, securing her tightly with a knot, and bundled her, body and song, into the trolley.

Soon after that, he was back in the Ferryman's boat once more, heading back across the Styx with his cargo *in situ.*

*

Standing and Roger saw that he was wearing industrial ear protectors.

TAKE THOSE OFF, mouthed Standing. He knew that the man was unable to hear him. He prayed to God that the ear-protectors weren't some kind of explosive suicide device. He knew how these single cell fundamentalist terrorists worked.

The man continued to walk towards them, his face impassive and confident.

He stopped just in front of them

THOSE THINGS, Standing mouthed, once more. TAKE THEM OFF.

The man ignored him. He saw the policeman's command. But he ignored it.

"I don't like this," Roger muttered. "I don't like this at all."

I'LL ASK YOU ONE MORE TIME. TAKE THOSE THINGS OFF.

"What's he got in the blanket?" Roger asked, taking a step back. Everything he had been feeling in recent weeks was amplifying now into one huge noise. Whatever it was that he had been worried about...it was here. Now. He could feel it in his horns.

TAKE THEM EAR MUFFS OFF!

John Thomas unknotted the blanket in one quick, elegant move. It fell open and there, sitting up in the middle of the supermarket trolley, the blanket around her midriff, was a siren.

PC Standing stared at her. She was a beautiful creature. Her long dark hair fell over her shoulders in sensual tresses. Her brown eyes stared out, wide and lovely, and her long eyelashes batted her cheeks with seductive flirtation. Her shoulders were elegantly sculptured, her white arms like well carved alabaster.

She was poetry in the flesh.

"Look at the jugs on it!" Whispered Roger, leaning forward to get a better view.

The siren began to sing.

Standing was surprised by the choice of song as it began to flow, hypnotically, from the siren's mouth.

He would never have had her down as a Chas and Dave fan. As she gently sang the words to *Ain't No Pleasin' You*, he found himself thinking that if Enya had ever collaborated with Barry Manilow to produce a cover version of this song, then this was pretty much how it would have sounded. It washed over him gently, like the lapping waves of a warm ocean. He watched her, mesmerised, as she sung, gently weaving her beautiful magic before him. She was beautiful...

...the sound...

...was beautiful...

Next to him, he was vaguely aware of Roger slumping to the ground in a heap.

He understood what had happened. It made you sleepy, this music. It lulled you, in a wonderful, sensual way. He was feeling sleepy himself. Roger had given into ecstasy and succumbed to the ultimate dream invitation.

Terence Standing felt himself rocking, swaying, as he watched the siren and listened to her song. Every lyric that fell from her moist lips dropped into his soul like a crystal raindrop. His head became heavier and heavier as the glistening drops filled his mind. You could die listening to music like this. You could die. And you'd still be happy.

Such a perfect woman.

Such a beautiful voice.

Such...such...

PC Standing slumped to the floor next to the Minotaur.

From his position next to the supermarket trolley, John Thomas stared down at the crumpled bodies, hardly able to believe that he had succeeded.

He looked up at the heavens and began to smile.

Back in the underworld, Thorax had given up on the abduction of a dead mermaid. The ferryman's hut had inspired him onto greater things.

The whole mermaid thing was a good idea, in principle. It was workable. But he saw problems with it.

Getting the mermaid into the cage would be difficult. It would have been easier had he brought along some cheese, but that hadn't occurred to him back in the mortal realm. Apart from this, he didn't even have a fishing rod with which to catch the hybrid freak with an admittedly-seductive voice. To capture her, he would need to dive into the water and wrestle her into submission which, while wearing industrial ear protectors, was bound to be a challenge.

Then there was the issue of getting her back to the underworld, once he had accomplished his quest and gained possession of the bachelor's plough.

Having used the mermaid to subdue the Minotaur he would need to remove the plough to a place of storage, before wheeling the mermaid all the way back to the Styx and then going through the whole charade of getting the cage back on the Ferryman's boat for her return. Not to mention unloading the cage and ensuring her deposit back in her underworld domain, once he reached the other side.

It was all a lot of hassle.

The discovery of the Ferryman's stash of silver coins – his *obulii* – gave Thorax a much better idea. It stemmed from something that Polyphemus had said.

Whenever his mind played back Polyphemus's words, the Cyclops was on that stage, tap dancing while wearing a top hat and twirling a cane.

But the message was uncorrupted:

The only way I can fink of, is if you 'ad a plough that 'e wanted even more. Like, if you 'ad a really special plough. Then you could bargin with 'im. Swap the one 'e wants, for the one you want, like.

If Thorax could find a plough even more special than the bachelor's plough, a *unique* plough – the *ultimate* plough – then he might have something that he could trade with the Minotaur. It would be a much fairer way to lay hold of the bachelor's plough. Everyone would be a winner.

When the taxi driver picked him up from the shores of the Styx, Thorax asked if there was a blacksmith in the underworld – a gifted blacksmith who could forge something magnificent from the very fires of hell. The taxi driver had suggested Wayland the smith. Wayland had a workshop on the outskirts of the industrial heartland.

"He is kinda like your *blacksmith's* blacksmith," the taxi driver had chirped, happily. "He can make whatever you need."

Thorax thought the name was familiar. He knew that Wayland was his man. Thanks to vast amounts of re-appropriated obulii, Wayland would have as much silver as he needed to fashion the ultimate plough.

A plough forged from the currency of passed-over souls.

The Plough of Death.

And it was but a taxi drive away.

*

Wayland's smithy was a small stone building on a dark and dreary cobbled street. There were other buildings around it, houses, shops, an old inn. Everything looked lifeless and dreary.

The souls of the dead walked the street, hopeless and forlorn. Some of them sauntered into the old inn, while others

348

stared listlessly into the dreary shop windows. As they shuffled past each other they all seemed unaware of each other's presence. One of the lost souls walked into a bakery and came out eating an iced bun.

When the taxi dropped Thorax outside the smithy, Thorax could hear the roaring furnace inside. The heavy clanging of metal provided a harsh soundtrack to the dismal street.

The smithy's stable door was partially open and the bright orange glow of a flickering flame cast changing shadows into the gloomy street. The tinny sound of a radio seemed to be audible and Thorax thought he recognised the familiar sound of *Steve Wright in the Afternoon.* He grabbed the cargo of canvas bags from the taxi and dropped them in front of the smithy door.

With a sharp knock, he ventured in.

Wayland the smith was bent over his anvil, hammering out a vast horseshoe. It was the size of a wagon wheel. He was a broad man, with a deeply lined face and hands like anvils. His straight dark hair came down to his shoulders, but he was bald in the middle. He wore a leather jerkin and his exposed arms were massive and mapped with burns and scars.

Wayland looked up at his visitor. He had a pleasant, enquiring expression. The smithy was dark, lit only by the fire of his forge. The tools of his trade hung from the walls, cast in gloomy shadow.

"Hello," he said airily.

"Ah, hello," Thorax smiled as he took another step inside the smithy. "Are you Wayland?"

"Yes I am," said Wayland. He rested his hammer at the side of the anvil. The vast horseshoe cooled from white, to red, to a beautiful sunset orange.

"What are you making there?" Asked Thorax.

"A big horseshoe," Wayland informed him.

"That must be one hell of a horse," Thorax ventured.

"Yes, I agree. I haven't got a customer for it yet. I was a bit bored so I thought I'd make it in case someone ever did come in, wanting a particularly large horse re-shod."

"Oh, I see. So - do you have a bit of spare time, only I..."

"*Do I?* I've got more spare time than I know what to do with. I'm bored out of my tree. Look at this."

Wayland reached behind him and pulled forward a trolley. It was stacked with small metal objects. On closer inspection, Thorax saw that they were tiny buildings forged from metal. The detail was intricate and quite marvellous. For some reason, Thorax felt that he recognised the little models.

"Recognise them?" Asked Wayland.

"I feel like I do..."

"They're exact replicas of the entire *Lilliput Lane* collection," Wayland explained. "I get so bored, that I just embark on random projects. This was my last one. I finished it yesterday, when I put the finishing touches to the Farmer's Cottage. I mean, look at it. What a complete waste of time."

"Well, I don't know. I think they're rather nice."

"Yes, well. Thank you. I suppose they are, in their own way. But come on. It's a bit of a come down. I am *the blacksmith's blacksmith*. I've made weapons for the gods. I've fashioned impenetrable armour for knights of myth and legend. I forged the very keys that open the doors to the hidden world of fantasy and the imagination. I even made a new carburettor for God's Austin Maxi, back in the seventies, when the old one eroded."

"Hmm."

"For a blacksmith of my credentials, fashioning the *Lilliput Lane* collection in metal is really quite banal. Before that I made some wind-chimes for my close friends and family. And before that, I went through a stage of making novelty belt buckles. I am frustrated, friend. Bored and frustrated."

"Hence the gigantic horseshoe."

"Hence the gigantic horseshoe. I hope to make an even bigger one next time."

"I can see that it might become an obsession."

"Yes. That does concern me."

"Well, I may have a commission for you. I don't know if you'd be interested?"

"Try me."

Thorax explained his vision for the Plough of Death. As he outlined his ideas – referring to the raw materials heaped right outside the door – Wayland's eyes grew wider and wider. The smith could almost be seen to salivate as he leaned over his anvil, lapping up every word that fell from his visitor's mouth.

When Thorax had finished explaining it, Wayland looked intense and excited.

"Can you help?" Asked Thorax.

"Does the Pope look at porn on the internet when no one is watching?" Wayland replied, happily. "Go and bring those bags in. I'll get the furnace primed."

Just as Thorax was turning to get the coins of death, Wayland stopped him.

"While I remember," he said. "There is a documentary on tonight, about Tony Blackburn."

Thorax wasn't quite sure how to answer such a random statement.

"So what?" He asked.

"Well. I thought you might be interested..."

"Why would I be?"

"I just thought it might be the kind of thing you'd be into. You know. Tony Blackburn and all that."

"No, not really." Thorax looked perplexed. "And anyway. Does he?"

"Does he what?"

"The Pope. Does he look at porn on the internet when no one is watching?"

"Well, you have to wonder, don't you? Anyway. Go and get me those coins. You shall have your plough, wayward traveller. You shall have your plough, as forged in the fires of old Wayland himself!"

*

When Thorax entered the scrap yard, lugging the bright, silver plough behind him, he was surprised to find that somebody was already there.

He was even more surprised to see that the person was wearing industrial ear defenders and stood in the middle of the yard with an undead mermaid in a supermarket trolley. The bodies of Roger the Minotaur and PC Standing were slumped at his feet in an ungainly heap.

Thorax was amazed that somebody else had thought of the same thing. He had believed his dead mermaid solution to be unique and highly imaginative. But it seemed that others had thought of it too. It saddened Thorax in a place deep down in his soul – a place that yearned for the purity of experience that comes with true creativity.

Will I never have an original idea? He lamented.

It occurred to him immediately that the other person must also be there for the bachelor's plough. What else would require the negotiating leverage of an undead mermaid? It was only the plough, it seemed, that required such levels of innovation for its procurement. And so in this final moment of his quest, the moment of his expected triumph, Thorax found himself with one last obstacle to overcome.

He had competition.

And the competition was armed and dangerous, his chosen weapon: *mermaid.*

352

From where he stood, Thorax could hear the gentle, caressing tones of the siren as she swayed around in the supermarket trolley with her mesmerising beauty. He thought he could hear the odd phrase as it drifted over to him on the breeze. *More rabbit than Sainsbury's...time you got it off your chest...was I to know you'd bend my ear 'ole too...you're becoming a pest...rabbit...rabbit...*

Her voice was quiet, the words obscured, but even now, Thorax could feel his eyes beginning to close, could feel the gentle tug of sweet oblivion on his soul.

He felt the weight of the plough, where he had hoisted it over his shoulder, and it began to push down on him. Standing there, gazing at the scene before him, he found himself swaying in time with the mermaid's song. Sublime relaxation washed over him and he thought how comfortable the muddy ground looked, and how much he wanted to lay on it, ready to sink down into the sweet arms of sleep.

The plough didn't matter, after all.

Nothing mattered.

Zeus didn't matter.

The portable crepe retail outlet didn't matter.

Nothing mattered.

A voice in Thorax's head spoke out indignantly.

What do you mean *the portable crepe retail outlet doesn't matter?*

Whatever it was that had been falling to sleep inside of Thorax suddenly woke up with a start.

He still had his own ear defenders around his neck. Quickly, he pulled them up and fitted them over his ears. He couldn't believe he had nearly fallen for his own ploy and lost any chance he had of acquiring the means to realise his dream of a portable crepe retail outlet.

He blinked himself into wakefulness, amazed at the soporific power of the (admittedly large breasted) hybrid freak.

353

Resolutely, he re-established his grip on the Plough of Death and walked over to the man and his mermaid.

The man looked around at Thorax with a start. He had been smiling, but his smile faded quickly.

Thorax dropped the Plough of Death and stood, face to face with his nemesis.

From an outsider's point of view, the two nemesii would have looked like they meant business, standing in the middle of this scrap wasteland, facing each other with ear defenders on their heads. Thorax looked down at the slumped bodies on the floor, then over at the singing mermaid. He couldn't hear what she was singing, but he was able to discern some of the words by the movement of her lips. It looked like she was singing *My Old Man's a Dustman*.

Clearly realising the peril he was in, John Thomas pulled a handkerchief from his pocket and threw it at Thorax.

It was ineffectual as a weapon. All it did was land on Thorax's shoulder. Thorax leaned forward with a barbarian's purpose and ripped the ear defenders from John Thomas's head. He saw the man's face turn pale as his fate dawned on him. A look of panic washed across his face, to be replaced, gradually, by one of contented tranquillity. Thorax watched as the man's eyes began to grow heavy and he swayed, slowly, on the spot. It took several minutes for John Thomas to succumb to the seduction of the mermaid's song. When he did he hit the ground like a children's entertainer with his hand up a toy emu's backside.

With the obstacle removed, Thorax lifted Roger from the ground.

He was a large beast at the best of times. As a dead weight, he weighed a tonne. The veins stood out in Thorax's neck as he carried the Minotaur over to the old double-decker bus. He wrenched open the doors, boarded the bus with his huge cargo, and closed the doors behind him. He dragged Roger up the stairs (he had to tilt Roger's head so that his horns didn't get wedged) and only then, when he felt he was safe from the mermaid's song, did he dare to take off his ear defenders.

The mermaid's song, as he had hoped, was inaudible. He glanced out of the window and saw that she continued to sing soulfully over her sleeping audience.

With everything in place, Thorax gently shook the Minotaur awake. He positioned him in such a way that when he did eventually wake up, he was looking out of the window. So it was, the first thing the Minotaur saw, on waking up – bright, silver and vibrating with its own internal energy – was the Plough of Death.

Thorax watched as the Minotaur's eyes grew wide and he pressed his huge, hairy broad face against the window. He was trembling, awe-struck, unable to take his eyes from this most unusual of ploughs.

At which point, Thorax began to bargain.

God

"I saw what happened," said God.

John Thomas rubbed his head. Not only was he feeling a little bruised and lethargic after the whole mermaid episode but God had interrupted him while he was watching the *Antiques Roadshow.*

Frankly, he was getting fed up with it.

They were just about to value an Edwardian chamber pot when the phone rang and thanks to God, John Thomas would never get to find out how much it was worth.

"What *did* happen?" Asked Thomas. From the moment the ear defenders had been torn from his head, he didn't have a clue. All he knew was that when he woke up, he was in the passenger seat of PC Standing's Panda car, with the village constable asleep at the wheel next to him. They were parked in the Pestlewick Railway Station car park, a place known as a quiet spot for illicit lovers to get intimate. A dogging spot, if you will. This worried John Thomas deeply.

And when he woke up PC Standing, the constable was no less concerned.

Neither of them voiced their anxieties, however, hoping that the dark and unwholesome thought would eventually go away.

"Well," said God. "After the barbarian took your ear defenders from your head you took a dive. Must have been that mermaid, I reckon. The barbarian, he drags the Minotaur on to that double-decker bus of his. And he must have made a deal with him. Because when they came out, they were both wearing ear defenders and they were both smiling. They looked like old friends. The barbarian had that plough he had brought with him. I think he must have got it from the underworld. He gives that plough to the Minotaur and the Minotaur comes back and swaps it for the bachelor's plough."

"He gave the barbarian the bachelor's plough?"

"Yes."

"You mean..."

"Yes." The good Lord sighed. "Zeus now has the bachelor's plough. The Minotaur swapped it willingly for the new one."

"Oh no."

"So anyway. After that, the barbarian says he'll come back for his plough later. He pushes the mermaid back down to the Thames, where it intersects with the Styx. He tips her out of the trolley, throws the trolley into the river..."

"Not another abandoned supermarket trolley in a river. Tell me You're not serious. There will be no room for the water if this goes on."

"It is the way of the world. He throws the trolley in the river, rings the bell and then legs it, leaving it for the Ferryman to take her back across. Then he comes back, puts you and that policeman in the police car, pushes the car to the station and leaves you in the car park. The last thing I saw, he was on his way back to get the plough. It's over, John Thomas. It's over."

"We've failed."

"Well, yes and no."

"What - so we've failed and we haven't failed?"

"Well...yes and no."

"So...we've failed and we haven't failed and we've failed and we haven't failed?"

"Let's just say we've been lucky. The theological status quo is safe for another day."

"How come?"

"Zeus has got involved with a woman."

"And what - she wants him to sell the plough because it's too dangerous? My mum made me sell my bike once, because..."

"No, no. Think about it, John Thomas. The *bachelor's* plough. The magical properties of the bachelor's plough are only effective *if you are a bachelor.* Zeus is no longer a bachelor."

"Oh! So..."

"So he can plough all he likes with the bloody thing. He ain't gonna get no gold!"

"But that's...that's brilliant!"

Thomas could tell that God was smiling on the other end of the phone.

"Now," said God, becoming serious. "I need to ask you something. I seem to have misplaced an angel. The archangel Raphael. You haven't seen him have you?"

"What does he look like?"

"Beautiful curls. A sensitive face. A soothing internal glow. A halo of bright white radiance. Luxurious white robes. Large white wings, made from feathers of a pure and ethereal hue. Tends to come with a beauteous music that fills the air whenever he is around."

"I don't think...oh hang on..."

"You've seen him?"

"No. No. My mistake. I'm thinking of Arnie, the greengrocer."

"Oh. Oh well. Keep your eyes open. I'm sure he'll turn up. He's not very good at reading maps. I think he might have got lost."

God could not have known the fate of his hapless angel. It was beyond the imagination even of the most unimaginative of storytellers.[9] Well. Actually, that's not true. He *could* have known. By rights He *should* have known. But in fairness He had been quite preoccupied of late.

"Okay. While we're asking questions, I wonder if I might ask You one, O Lord."

---

[9] See The second part of the Pestlewick Trilogy - "Fallen Angel".

"Yes, I think I could plumb My sacred benevolence to furnish an answer. Fire away."

"Well, you know when they put Jesus on the cross..."

"Y-essss..."

"And he was there for ages, suffering and in agony..."

"Y-esssss..."

"And he kept asking You to help him, to relieve him from his suffering..."

"Y-essssss..."

"And he asked why You had forsaken him..."

"Y-esssssssss..."

"Well – why *did* You forsake him? Why didn't You just rescue him from his anguished plight?"

God fell silent. He remembered looking down on Jesus on that terrible day, through His telescope, seeing His son's suffering. He remembered the words of His son, as He leaned out of Heaven with His ear-trumpet held aloft. *Father, why hast thou forsaken me?*

But most of all, He remembered descending from Heaven and clambering down the rope ladder, with a claw hammer clenched between His teeth. He had been resolved to rescue His son, to yank out the nails that bound him to his dreadful agony. It had been a windy day then, as well.

Too windy.

Finally, God spoke, His voice thoughtful and enigmatic.

"I move in mysterious ways My wonders to perform, John Thomas," He said. "That's all you need to know."

Zeus awoke to find the woman, his client, zipping her bag shut. It was early in the morning and she was fully dressed. She looked as if she was just about to leave. Had he not awoken, he would have missed her.

He sat up in bed. His hair was dishevelled. His grizzled white beard stuck out to the side at a forty-five degree angle.

"What time is it?" He smiled at her, raking a hand through his hair. Last night they had made love like whippets in a sandstorm.

She smiled back at him, politely.

"Just after seven," she said. She scanned the room to check that she'd packed everything.

"Where are you going?" Zeus asked her. Something was wrong. He could feel it.

"I'm leaving. Going back home."

"What?"

"I was only here for a few days. You knew that."

"But...what about us? Where do...*we*...go from here?"

The woman stared at him as if he was a stubborn log that had just re-emerged from the lavatory u-bend, having given the previous impression it had been fully flushed away.

"We don't go anywhere from here," she said, curtly.

"What about *us?*"

"There *is* no *us.*"

"What?" His head began to spin. "But...we've got something. We've had a great few days. There's...we've...we're not going to throw it all away!"

"Get real, sweetheart. I'll pay you for your time. Seventy pounds, I think we agreed."

She pulled out her purse and peeled out some notes. She held them out.

"Here. Take seventy-five."

Zeus didn't move. She dropped the money on the bed in front of him.

"I don't want your money!" He pulled the bedclothes aside and jumped out of the bed. He stood on the floor, naked as a baby (with a congenital problem causing it to be impossibly white of skin, with saggy areas and too many wrinkles to describe).

"Don't be stupid. You've earned it."

"Earned it? *Earned* it?" Zeus was screaming now. "What we've had these past days...that's not been about money. It's been...I let you kiss me *on the lips*, for crying out loud."

"Oh, come on! Wake up and smell the coffee! I don't know what you think we've *had*, exactly. But I've just been using you for sex. You're a whore. Just a whore."

Zeus staggered back, as if he had received a physical blow.

"How can you *say* that?" He cried. "I can't believe you've been leading me on! The chemistry. You can't deny it's been there!"

"Look," she said. "I've enjoyed the sex. But please don't read anything more into it. You've been an object to me. A toy. Nothing more. You have kept me occupied while I've been in the area. You're just a whore."

"But..."

"*You're just a whore.*"

Zeus stared at her in disbelief. His eyes were blurred with tears.

"Isn't there a chance? Don't you think that one day, even if not now, even if not tomorrow..."

The woman shook her head. She seemed to find the whole scene distasteful.

361

"Let me be frank with you," she said. "I could never, *ever* get serious with a man that can play Chopsticks with his buttocks."

She picked up her bag and walked to the door. She gave Zeus one final look.

"It's been fun," she said. "Thanks for everything."

And she was gone.

The clouds slid back into place, high up in the sky.

With His glorious telescope and His wondrous ear-trumpet, God had just seen the entire scene as it played out in the penthouse suite of the New Diamond Suite Hotel. He had to use a periscope mechanism to actually see inside the building, but what He saw disturbed Him mightily.

Zeus had the plough. *And* he was a bachelor once more.

From here on in, God would be on tenterhooks, watching anxiously for any sign that the ancient god might be getting ideas above his station. If he merely used the plough for riches, that would be fine. But God knew what that could lead to. He knew that wealth leads to power and power, if used correctly - and combined with just a sliver of immortality - can lead to divinity.

If Zeus gained divinity he would go on a smatting spree. Then he would be unstoppable.

From now on, God would have to keep tabs on the Grecian god and hope that his ambition didn't get out of hand. For the Divine Lord of All Creation things would be very different now. It was all going wrong.

It wouldn't have been audible to anybody lower than forty thousand feet, but had anyone been up that high - for example, they might have been in a hot-air balloon, trying to break a world record, or simply unable to find the vehicle's "down" button - they may have been aware of a magnificently omnipotent voice echoing from the heavens. And with a keen ear, it is possible they might have made out the sacred words of this divine voice.

And lo! The Good Lord didst pray.

"Me,

"Who art in Heav'n,

"Hallowed be My name.

"My kingdom come,

"My will be done,

"On Earth as it is in Heav'n (and elsewhere 'cross the vast cosmos that I didst create).

"Give Me this day a good, sumptuous loaf of bread (a country loaf with a good crust wouldst be preferable),

"And forgive Me My trespasses (which I don't make, for I am perfect and beyond reproach),

"As I forgive those what trespass against Me (sometimes),

"And lead Me not into temptation,

"But deliver Me from evil (should it dare show it's face in Myne realm).

"For Myne is the kingdom,

"The power and the glory,

"For ever and ever,

"Amen."

Sitting at the bar, in the *Bird in Hand*, Zeus downed his fourth gin and slim-line tonic.

Still the tears would not abate. Every time he thought of her, of the times they had shared, of the special moments they had created, he found himself wanting her, *needing* her.

She had come into his life and turned it upside down. And then she had left him without so much as a goodbye. Well, perhaps she had afforded him a goodbye. But it didn't account for much. He was heartbroken.

Dave the barman knew Zeus. He knew when one of his customers was hurting. He didn't ask him what was wrong. Sometimes as a barman, you know when to talk and when to pour. This was definitely an occasion to pour.

He replenished Zeus's glass every time it was emptied and left the broken man to his thoughts.

Whenever Zeus let out a loud sob and put his head in the crook of his arm, face down on the bar, Dave acted as though he hadn't even noticed. It was a delicate act to pull off, but he played it to perfection. Dave was an expert in emotional facilitation. He knew how to facilitate grief, just as he knew how to facilitate happiness, celebration, violence, philosophical speculation, industrial carpet cleaning and drink-fuelled procreation.

By his sixth gin and slim-line tonic, Zeus was proclaiming his undying love for the woman. By his tenth, he was stating that he couldn't go on.

When Thorax entered the bar, some hours later, the dark cape of evening was pressing against the windows.

Dave had lost count of the number of gin and slim-line tonics his customer had knocked back. Thorax the Barbarian saw his friend, jaded, lost, sitting at the bar and talking to himself, letting the tears roll down his face unhindered.

He walked over tentatively and pulled up a bar stool next to the ancient god.

"What can I get you?" Asked Dave, glad to see that someone had arrived who could tend to the broken old man.

"I'll have an ale, please," said Thorax. "And whatever he's having. Oh - and do you have any tankards? I prefer my ale from a tankard."

Dave nodded obligingly and bustled off to fix the drinks.

Thorax put a hand on Zeus's arm.

"What wrong, old friend?" He asked, gently.

Zeus looked round at him, slowly. His eyes were red with tears. He blinked, gazing at the barbarian through a haze of grief.

"A woman," he sniffed. "A woman."

Thorax nodded, with feigned understanding. It was feigned because he didn't have the first idea what Zeus was talking about.

"*Chessez la femme*, eh?" He prompted.

"No," Zeus sniffed, despondently. "I don't know where the supermarket is. I don't even care. She's broken my heart, Thorax. She took me for a ride and she broke my heart. I'm just a whore to her. A *whore.*"

Thorax looked down at the bar, awkwardly. He was glad when the drinks came.

"I've got the plough," he announced, taking a long gulp from his tankard.

Zeus looked at him. He blinked thrice. Thrice. His face became focused.

"The plough," he murmured. "I'd almost forgotten...you've *got* the plough? You've really got it?"

Thorax nodded.

"It's hidden away in my garden shed," he said. "It's safe. It's yours, Zeus. The bachelor's plough is yours."

A weak smile played over Zeus's lips.

"I knew you could do it," he said, quietly. "Didn't I *tell* you? I *knew* you could do it? You are a barbarian, Thorax. A barbarian down to your toes!"

Thorax took another long swig of ale. He wiped his mouth with his sleeve.

"Thanks," he conceded. "It wasn't easy. But yes. I did it. *We* did it."

Zeus nodded, slowly.

"Well done, Thorax the Barbarian," he said. "Well done!"

He sipped his gin and slim-line tonic.

And there at the bar, as happiness and grief danced a slow waltz across his heart, he allowed the tears to spill freely down his cheeks.

The Final Soliloquy

The lights went down and a single spotlight trained itself on Zeus, sitting at the bar.

In the pale white beam streaming down on him, motes of dust could be seen to dance and eddy. It was a busy evening in the *Bird in Hand*. But Zeus was entirely alone.

He put down his gin and slimline tonic and turned around on the bar stool to face the spotlight. His face was etched with pain, engraved with tribulation. Here was a man that had been on a journey and now, after trials unspeakable, he was at his journey's end.

He folded his hands and gazed out into the blackness of the watching theatre.

He coughed, loudly.

And then began.

"And so it is," he said. "My book is open on its final chapter. O'er seas of mighty tempests have I travelled to reach my journey's end...and here I find it, in grief, 'pon the cushion of a faded bar stool.

"Much have I seen and much have I known, as I have walked the recent streets of life, seeking nothing but the dignity and respect for which I hunger. And riches too, would I have, were they available to me 'pon the roadside bare.

"Standing 'pon the shoulders of others have I reached the giddy heights to which I so aspired. Standing on the shoulders of others, have I discovered the platform by which I may attain the goal that heretofore was so far out of reach. And now I have my prize.

"And yet. And yet...

"Loathe is my heart to drink the liquor of joy, *for my heart 'tis dead and black*. 'Tis hardened, as stone. Love, I have known. And love, from me, hath been ripped asunder, like a pair of pants from a wholesome hunk. Love, I have known...but I know love no more.

"I know love, no more."[10]

The house lights went back up and Zeus turned back to the bar. The atmosphere was clearer somehow and in a funny kind of way, the ancient god felt unburdened.

He caught Dave's eye.

"Are you still serving food?" He asked.

Dave nodded.

"I'll have a steak and kidney pie, with mash, please," said the ancient god. He glanced at Thorax. "Fancy a steak and kidney pie and mash?"

"Actually, that sounds pretty tempting," said Thorax.

"Two steak and kidney pies and mashes," said Zeus to the barman.

Dave flung his tea towel over his shoulder and disappeared out the back to start work on the two meals.

At the bar, Thorax the Barbarian and Zeus, father of the Olympian gods, sat quietly, musing over their imminent pie and mash with gastric anticipation.

They both liked mashed potato and were both very fond of pies.

The peas that came as standard with Dave's pie and mash were not a vital constituent of the meal. Both men could take the peas or leave them.

This was not to do the peas a disservice, however. They would both eat the peas – they just wouldn't be overly upset were the meal served *without* peas.

The End

---

[10] If this does not win a Booker prize, then there is no justice.

No rabbits were hurt during the making of this book.
Except for Starsky. Starsky really copped it. He copped it big.

A humble plea

For the love of all that is holy – for Thorax, God, Zeus, John
Thomas and even the Stygian Witches – *please leave a review
about this book*. People read reviews. It is the world we are in.
If you make it a *good* review, I will consider buying you a pie.

I won't beg you to help me out with this, but just for the
record, I am on my knees pleading.

As well as leaving a review, please tell everyone you know to
read it. Even if you don't like it. And *especially* if they
WON'T like it. That will teach them. Ignorant bastards.

About the Author

Stephen J Brookes lives in a village on the outskirts of Cambridge, in a house that was built on an ancient Indian burial ground and is consequently infested with poltergeists.

It is a sad fact that while he wants to be taken seriously, he remains a figure of fun. People laugh at him as he walks by, as if he were some kind of Victorian freak. It perturbs him, but as he is quick to point out: *He is not an elephant.*

As well as writing books that nobody reads, Stephen plays music that nobody hears and bakes cakes that nobody tastes. Perhaps worst of all, rumour has it that when he is not writing books, playing music or baking cakes, he kills pigeons in lurid, ritualised killing sprees. In today's strangely politicised law enforcement landscape, funds are rarely channelled into investigating acts of pigeocide, which is why he continues to elude justice.

However, when his chilling crimes are finally discovered, police will find a drawer full of beaks in Brookes's garden shed, which he keeps as trophies.

It is quite chilling.

Be sure to avoid the other books in the Trilogy:

Fallen Angel (Coming soon)
Messiah (Coming a bit after the first one)
Revelation (This bastard isn't even finished yet)

And be sure to avoid connecting with the author:

www.stephenjbrookes.com

Twitter @theSJBauthor

e. thestephenjbrookes@gmail.com

About the cover design...

I'd like to extend a huge and heartfelt thank you to the amazingly talented Alex Gallego, who designed the cover for this book.

Despite his fixation with domestic sink plungers, he sees straight to the heart and soul of a project and brings it to life through images. An amazing guy!

You can connect with Alex through his web site:

www.alexgallego.com

Printed in Great Britain
by Amazon

67302914R00222